I0671242

INTO THE DECAY

BOOK ONE of the GODS OF DESTRUCTION SERIES

Justin K. Arthur

No part of this work may be reproduced or transmitted in any form or by any means, electronic or mechanical, including photocopying and recording, or by any information storage or retrieval system without the proper written permission of the copyright owner unless such copying is expressly permitted by federal copyright law. Permission must be obtained from the author. Address requests for permission to make copies of material to Justin K. Arthur, 56 Chesterfield Lakes Road, Chesterfield, MO, or to the email address kingjotun@gmail.com.

ISBN: 0997704608
ISBN-13: 978-0997704600

First published 2015 by Thurston Howl Publications

Copyright © 2016 Justin K. Arthur

Revived Edition 2016. All rights reserved.

Mailing Address:
56 Chesterfield Lakes Road
Chesterfield, MO 63005

kingjotun@gmail.com

Cover design by Krystal O'Brien

For Lacey, Jonny, Krystal, my family, and everyone else who helped me along the way.

And before She dove into the earth She turned to the first follower.
"I will remain in my sleep until the eve of the world's life," She said.
"I will awaken only then by the offerings of both a royal family and their enemy.
When I do, all souls below the earth shall rise to the surface and none after shall continue on-- all will wait for me where I will reappear."
-From the Teachings of the Goddess.

Justin K. Arthur

PROLOGUE

It dashed out of the building, emerging into the sight of dozens of onlookers. It glanced around rapidly as it heard the footsteps descending the stairwell quickly after it. It took off as fast as it could, heedless of the people unfortunate enough to be in its way. The bystanders dodged to the side, screaming in fright as the creature's claws came within inches of them. The sharp weapons glimmered in the moonlight as it rushed past. The only things that frightened the innocent bystanders more were the things embedded into the sockets of the its visage. They were two black holes, devoid of anything save for nine red circles nested inside each other like the lining of a pit, one ring in each slightly bigger than the others. People covered their eyes in fear when they saw the creature approach, but many were not fast enough and found themselves drawn into the dark, red-ringed wells.

It darted down the streets as loud horns called throughout the cyclopean city. Alongside these calls came the thudding of countless feet; those of the commoners taking cover around it, and those of the guards rapidly approaching. It frantically continued running down the tight streets as it looked for any possible refuge. It found nothing but a blockade of guards waiting for it, and it heard another group of guards approaching behind it. The creature watched as the guards in the blockade readied their crossbows. Its black eyes rapidly searched for anything it could possibly reach before the bolts flew at it. It jumped upward, narrowly avoiding the crossbow fire as it sailed toward a wall. It landed and quickly embedded a claw in the wall to keep from falling. The guards called out in surprise and a louder voice urged them all to reload rapidly as the creature grabbed onto the nearest window ledge.

It pulled itself up onto the ledge and locked eyes with a woman. The woman did not even have a chance to scream before she became drawn into its bottomless sockets. Her breathing grew more and more rapid before she finally collapsed onto the floor. "Don't just stand there!" roared the voice from before. "Stop that demon!" More soldiers with crossbows poured onto the street, armed to the teeth. Most raised crossbows at the demon but the ones directly below it held pikes into the air to skewer it once it was felled.

The demon truly started to panic before it slammed its claw into the window, easily shattering the glass and sending it flying everywhere. It pulled itself through the window, the broken glass not even cutting its skin, mere moments before another volley of iron bolts sank within the spot where it had just been. It carefully sidestepped the unconscious woman and looked about for a door in the dimly lit room. It made to rush toward the door but a little boy and an older girl blocked its way. The sparse lighting of the tenement kept the demon hidden in shadows; they could only see the red circles in its two black eyes, and like their mother they too fell within.

The demon's panic grew as it heard the guards burst through the main door to the building. It crashed through the room's door and ascended the staircase as fast as it could while the guards climbed up after it. Several humans still moved about the stairwell in an attempt to reach their own rooms but got knocked aside as the demon rushed past them. It had to get to the top. It had to, before the guards caught up with it. Maybe on the roof it could escape and hide.

It finally emerged onto the roof of the building, blanketed in the darkness. The lights held by the guards on the streets below could not illuminate the demon as it looked around, gauging the distance of the other buildings surrounding the one it stood upon. They were just far enough away that it could not safely jump.to them Down on the street a guard managed to see its outlined form and called out, alerting the rest. They wasted no time and all aimed upward toward the demon, even if it was too far away for most of their bolts to hit.

Trapped! It turned around and saw the guards emerge out onto the roof. It glanced between them all but none of the guards fell into the demon's wells, refusing to lock eyes with it. It backed away as more guards came in, pikes pointed at their target. The demon felt its back touch the cold railing of the rooftop and stopped. A sudden jab from a pike made the demon leap up onto it in shock, its clawed feet barely keeping a grip on the rail as the guards closed in. It now had no choice, though it had never done this before. It had to, even if it barely knew how to use them.

The guards watched in amazement as two constructs of energy shot out of the demon's back. They mirrored each other perfectly. Each one was a thick, translucent flat pane, like red stained glass, both curving and extending to an upturned point. Each one was as long as the demon was tall. Along the bottom jutted out several extensions like the main piece, curving and ending in sharp tips and looking almost like a flattened, skeletal bird wing. The edges themselves looked sharp enough to cut flesh with ease and the constructs let out a humming noise. The guards recovered from the marvel of the sight and charged forward, hungry for the demon's blood. The demon let itself fall backward and plummeted toward the ground. It hurriedly flapped its wings but only succeeded in steering itself directly into one of the viaducts cutting across the street, causing its wings to shatter and disintegrate as it hit the ground. Dazed, but still conscious, it leaped onto its feet and held out its claws menacingly as guards rushed forward with pikes at the ready.

The demon dodged the first pike and sliced at it, severing the metal head and leaving the guard with just a splintered stick, then more pikes came from every direction as guards approached from both sides of the viaduct. The demon frantically ducked and weaved through the stabs, destroying every pike it could while it desperately looked for the slightest reprieve from its inevitable fate. It continued its search in vain as it spied more guards now readying their crossbows. Then it stumbled.

A single pike embedded itself in the demon's shoulder, and the guard pulled back his pike in triumph as the demon let out a high-pitched scream in pain. It collapsed onto the ground, holding the wound as it began what the guards could have sworn were the sobs of a human child. The soldiers around it fell silent as it curled up into a little ball. The one who had called out the orders earlier stepped forward with a club in his hands. He simply shook his head before bringing the club down on the demon.

The demon slowly felt itself come to, its vision blurry, and it moaned in pain as it tried to stifle its sniffling. Its eyesight quickly came back and it realized it was trapped. Its hands were bound together tightly by heavy steel chains, as were its feet. It struggled to break the bonds but could not muster the energy to do so; not after everything it had endured that night. It looked around further and saw that the chains on its feet were connected to a massive metal ball by a few feet of thick metal chain. It finally noticed where it was and felt its hopes crumble; it was on the walkway of the wall. Just past the battlements was a fate worse than anything the guards could concoct, and they knew that.

"Bring forth the demon!" called the same voice as before. Six people carried the demon forward; one man on each limb and two especially large men carrying the metal ball behind them. The demon's pulse quickened and its sobs came back in full force as it was moved closer and closer to its horrible fate. It looked at each face nearby, crying as it searched for the slightest bit of sympathy from any of them, but it found nothing but cold facades dominated by contempt. All the while it was forced closer to the edge of the city, with nothing but the steep drop downward just past the walls visible amidst the fog.

The demon arrived before the man who had knocked it out near the viaduct. He was tall and muscular, with short brown hair, and he had the ghostly-white skin almost all the residents of the city had. "It is truly an experience to stand so close to such pure evil," the captain of the guard sneered. The demon let its head fall to the ground as it continued to sob, hearing the distaste in the man's tone. Its shoulder still hurt greatly, even if the wound was no longer bleeding. The captain made no effort to look it in the eye as he continued his speech. "...even now it puts on a final facade in an attempt to gain pity from us. But it is of no matter; you are just as foul as the rest of your kind we have found in our city, and you shall suffer the same end. Such is the fate of all mockeries of the Goddess.

"Demon," he said, "For your crimes against the city of Tantallos and its Goddess-fearing people as a whole, you shall endure a punishment far worse than anything we could inflict upon you. By the order of King Vikenti the Fierce you shall be thrown over the wall while bound in these chains, thereupon to be left for dead. You shall join the countless others of your kind for defiling our city with your murderous acts. Should you ever enter our city again, be it on your feet or on your wings, you shall be tortured until death claims you. Do you have anything to say before your sentence is carried out?"

The demon stopped its crying for a moment, tears still flowing. "Please," it begged with the voice of a little boy. "Please don't... Please." It managed before it resumed crying.

"Your attempts at gaining my pity are pathetic." Said the captain of the guard. "Now be gone; and may the Goddess have mercy on your soul, supposing you have one." The two men carrying the metal ball dropped it onto the lowest part of one of the battlements and started pushing it closer to the ledge. The ball slowly rolled forward, its incredible weight threatening to crack the stone beneath it. The humans let go of the demon and it frantically jerked its legs back to try and keep the ball from rolling toward the ledge, but t was all to no avail. Within a few seconds the ball reached the edge of the wall. The stone finally cracked and fell away. With nothing holding it back the ball rolled off the wall, the short chain dragging the demon off the walkway with it. It screamed in fright as it plummeted off the side of the wall, soon obscured by the sea of fog floating around the city. It descended into the Decay.

CHAPTER 1

I created your world out of a dream, so it is into dreams that I retreat. My words can be found within.
-From the Teachings of the Goddess.

Daina slowly tiptoed down the cold stone hallway, chilled almost to the bone in her simple nightgown and bare feet. She carried a torch in her hands, holding it low in an attempt to hide its light. She could hear it in a nearby hall of the ossuary, its claws clicking against the stone floor as it calmly searched for her. She shuddered at the thought of its hideous features, with its matted fur, its oversized tusks and the horrible sight of its gouged-out right eye... and its mouth, easily large enough to snap her up in one bite.

She stumbled slightly, letting out a yelp as she nearly fell over. She heard the mire beast growl, then its steps speed up, and she took off as fast as she could, dashing down the corridors while the mire beast easily kept up with her. She was fast, faster than any person she had ever raced against, but she was nothing in comparison. She could run all day long, but her chaser could run well into the night. And no matter how fast she ran, it could run faster. She turned a corner tightly, barely keeping herself from crashing into a wall of overly neat stacked bones topped with skulls. Again she let out a slight yell as she nearly collided with another equally macabre stack against the side. She paid the skeletal remains no mind as she pushed herself further down the hallway filled with bones; each stack was neatly organized, as if the bones were simply bottles of alcohol placed on cellar shelves.

The mire beast's pursuit grew louder and louder as it romped through the tunnel-- bones were sent skittering everywhere as it obliterated the stacks in the mad rush toward its prey. Countless bones were cracked carelessly underneath its scarred and padded feet. It let out a roar as it found itself getting caught on tightening corners.

Daina risked a glance over her shoulder. The mire beast was still chasing after her but it was no longer gaining. The deeper she descended into the ossuary, the smaller the tunnel became. She still made herself run as fast as she possibly could. Although there was a great distance between them now, she didn't seem to be moving away from the approaching monster fast *enough. It roared again, displaying its glimmering white teeth accustomed to tearing apart flesh with ease, though humans were too small a prey to put the saber-like fangs to good use. They were simply swallowed whole in its cavernous jaws.*

The tunnel grew smaller and smaller and soon Daina started getting caught as well. She forced herself to go further in, even as the mire beast continued to slow down. The bones along the tunnel seemed to purposefully stick themselves up to jab her in the side, hindering her progress, but even as the hallway kept her from moving, the mire beast continued to close in on her. Soon it was but a few feet away, and then just inches behind her. It let out a triumphant roar and opened its jaws wide to grab her.

Then she found herself falling. She landed in a pit, her fall broken by a massive pile of bones, thankful none had pierced her body. She let out a shriek as she saw things moving in the pit. Were they white snakes? No, they were arms; arms and hands bound together by tendons that had defied the passage of time. They reached out from all corners of the pit and grabbed her, holding her steady and freezing the screams in her mouth. She could not get herself to look away as something then rose in front of her: a half-rotted corpse, bloated from its own decay in the humid pit and festering with an abundance maggots, only one of its eyes still intact. "I'm coming for your blood, Daina," it said in a raspy voice. "And after I've taken your blood I shall make you wish you had never been born."

Daina woke up, shooting upright and panting heavily. She slowly calmed herself as she looked around; she was still in her bed, wearing her nightgown. To the side was her dresser, littered with her various knickknacks and mementos. She grabbed the small stuffed felt toy she kept hidden under her pillow and held onto it. It had been a week since that dream, a week she had been so thankful for in her nineteen years of dreaming. No one she had spoken to knew what to make of her dream; why would she be running through the catacombs? Why would a mire beast be pursuing her? And why would a rotting corpse long for her blood? No one could say; it was just one of the nightmares that plagued her the most. Recurring nightmares were nothing new to her.

Every citizen of Tantallos spent most of their sleeping time writhing in agony from their nightmares. Not a single Tantallosian could say otherwise; you could not live in the city and avoid enduring countless numbers of them. From the dirtiest whore to the daughter of the king, every person within the city's walls saw a never-ending barrage of horrible images in their sleep. Mothers and fathers dreamed of their children rotting into nothingness before their eyes, while babies saw their parents die even as they were held by them. No one wondered if other cities dealt with such a fate. No one knew of other cities to begin with. All they knew and all they needed to know could be found within the thick walls that surrounded their old, cloud-scraping city. Deprived of space, their buildings extended into the sky as high as ten stories in places. However, no matter how high a tenement or tower was built, there was still nothing to see.

There was nothing outside of Tantallos but the Decay. The Decay was agonizing death and slow destruction. It was everything not surrounded by stone walls placed upon a hill. No one knew what made the Decay so corrupt; the only thing that mattered about the Decay was that it was corrupt to begin with. Every Tantallosian child had been taught stories of people falling off the walls and arriving back at the rusted main gates with limbs and facial features completely gone. Oftentimes their hair would be falling out and their flesh would be coated in moss and slime, and those were the ones who came back at all. No one ever mounted search parties for those unfortunate enough to fall off the walls for fear they too would succumb to the Decay.

One does not enter the Decay willingly, for one cannot survive in the Decay. Nothing good can. The only things able to live in the great expanse that is the Decay are monsters equal in corruption and filth as the mire they live in; giant creatures with misbegotten features and twisted, crooked limbs capable of ripping apart steel. The tainted soil of the Decay prevents all plant growth except for one species of vine-- the cud plant. No one knows that much about the cud plants, whether they are actually immune or if they simply grow faster than the Decay can rot them away. Both possibilities have long been debated.

However, the most feared creatures are the ones that retained their shapes within the Decay. Somewhere out among the myriad of monsters are demons, the last surviving remnants of the terror that foolish Summoners had caused throughout the city. The macabre magicians had worked in secret, harvesting flesh and bone from their neighbors in order to pull demons from their own world, into Tantallos. In their decades of activity they brought forth several of these fiends to harvest them for a variety of intentions or to use them as labor, but every attempt to control one failed drastically. No human could compete with the strength, speed and prowess of a demon, and if it was an arch demon, the Goddess have mercy on the hopeless fool who was stupid enough to call it forth.

But those days were long past; no Summoner still lived in Tantallos and the city had been enjoying something close to prosperity ever since Vikenti the Fierce came to power almost twenty years ago. When a section of the wall of Tantallos crumbled he had been the one soldier to stand his ground.

Although countless monsters and mire beasts poured into the city, he fought off or killed each and every one that came with a massive two-handed sword said to be heavier than most people, dubbed the Back Breaker. Not a single civilian had fallen victim to the jaws of a creature from the Decay, not so long as he stood guard over the hole.

Such death-defying deeds did not go unrewarded and the king had adopted the orphan warrior as his own heir. The aged king's health had already been failing and he had fathered no children of his own with his deceased queen, so it was only a few months before Vikenti and his pregnant wife; though this was unbeknownst to all, took their spots on the throne. No one in Tantallos spoke up in objection to the hero of their city becoming their new king.

And so began what the Tantallosians called an age of prosperity, though many found themselves unable to remember the proper meaning of the word. Although few buildings were built, fewer collapsed from age and damage. Even better, the walls remained in excellent condition and not once in his reign would they collapse again. The only problem was the eternal issue of food; the last famine had been over a decade ago but it had more than taken its toll. The only thing preventing another was the smaller amount of mouths to feed, but many feared even that would not be enough in the end.

Was there another period of prosperity to match Vikenti's, or were there instances of famine that could be studied for lessons in case another was coming? No Tantallosian could say. Inside the walls or not, memories rotted away like living things in the Decay. No one could remember a time when the Decay had not constantly been there around them, surrounding their island of life like a series of waves preparing to completely overwhelm them. Even the oldest citizens could only tell what their grandparents had told them, and any of them would be too caught up in their own dementia to relay a story of even the slightest coherence.

As such, Tantallosians keep to the moment and focus on little before or after that time, and this moment was a special one; a call for celebration throughout the cyclopean city. After all, it was not every day a symbol for prosperity and kindness turned nineteen.

Daina returned the felt toy to under her pillow; she was too old for such things, but she had slept with it since she was an infant. She slowly pulled herself out of bed and roughly fixed it up, even if the servant would readjust every bit anyway. She moved to her dresser and clothed herself in the modest garb typical and expected of any Tantallosian no matter what social status; non-revealing grays and similar shades of colorlessness with only the flesh of her hands and feet exposed. Given how cold every day in Tantallos was, there were few who dressed in less. She brushed her golden wavy hair and let it flow freely around her ghostly white neck, looking at herself in the mirror; her hair was getting a bit long. She would need it cut soon before it became too much of a hassle for her to maintain.

She pulled on one of her older, more beaten-up pairs of sandals, though any normal Tantallosian would still have died for them, and made her way out of the bedroom. She emerged into a bare but well-lit hallway and was quickly approached by some nearby servants. "Good morning to you Princess Daina," a servant said happily while bowing. "A very happy birthday to you. Do you require anything of us, milady?"

"I appreciate your enthusiasm, but I require nothing today," said Daina smiling back. "The people of this castle have given me enough with their diligence despite the world we live in."

The servants all nodded and thanked Daina before resuming their previous duties. Daina recalled what she had been planning to do and made her way to the staircase at the end of the hall. She then glanced back behind her and realized that one of the wall guards had again accidentally left the door to the walkway open; the captain of the guard would definitely not be happy.

She let out a sigh before rushing over to the door and shutting it tightly; no need for all the soldiers to be punished for just one absent-minded guard. That done, she turned back toward the staircase and quickly ran up to it. She stepped onto the cold stone steps and carefully walked down the spiral, stopping at the last floor and stepping down. It was the barracks and armory, and just down the hall was the staircase to the dungeon. Hallways connected the armory to the rest of the ground floor, which included the extensive kitchen and main hall. The dungeon below was the only underground structure save for the catacombs elsewhere in the city. She went straight ahead, dodging and avoiding soldiers while they also struggled to move out of her way. She traveled briskly down the hallway and moved to the front of the storehouse. Rather than disturb the quietly dozing guard she instead sneaked inside the storehouse.

Most of the guards would be doing their rounds on the walls or moving out to police the city, so the majority of supplies were missing from the storeroom. Daina looked around the big room and eventually spotted one man in the back inspecting pieces of armor left behind, carefully examining each one before sorting it. She approached this tall, muscular man quietly, watching as he adjusted his red helmet. Although he said that he frequently painted it red, many expected that it was just another of the countless pieces of Tantallosian military armor that was rusting away. Few things were not in this day and age.

"Good morning, Captain of the guard," said Daina, giving a slight curtsy out of respect. "You said to come and visit you first thing in the morning, correct?"

"I didn't hear you come in, princess," said the captain. "May I be but one of many to wish you happy birthday before I give you your present, though I must admit that I'm perplexed as to why in Tantallos you would want such a thing, even if it's so small. Not a single soul within these walls would ever attempt to harm you; every person in this kingdom adores you."

"People tell me that, and it makes me think that there are more than a fair share of crazed citizens who adore me too much," said Daina. "And it's not like I'm using my father's *Back Breaker*, nor am I going to be seeking out giant killer monsters to slay with it. I doubt I could even pull part of that huge blade off the ground to begin with."

"I still think your fears are unfounded, but I did promise you this," said the Captain as he moved over to a nearby box. "Just be careful not to cut yourself with it. This is no crude wooden stick boys jab at each other's sides." He reached into the box and fumbled about for a few moments before closing his fingers on his target, pulling his hand out of the box, holding a small object covered up in a surprisingly clean rag. He carefully handed the object to the princess, who quickly unwrapped it and found herself holding a dagger like she had never seen before. The blade was bright, shiny, and brown; it looked fairly sharp despite a slight layer of dust. The handle was made of the same material. In many ways it was like her in its slender and light shape, perfect for quick stabs and strikes. It was largely devoid of intricate markings and designs. This was not just an ornament doomed to gather dust alongside her other knickknacks; this was designed for combat.

"That dagger is made of bronze, rather than the iron weapons most of the guards use," said the captain. "I have no idea how old it is, but needless to say no Tantallosian blacksmith has made one of those recently. Though it should be fine besides a need for a little sharpening."

"I love it," said Daina, smiling. She bowed to the Captain. "I cannot thank you enough for this, even if it may not seem like a great gift to some. It will be quite a contrast from the upcoming barrage of dresses and jewelry that will make up most of my birthday presents."

"Pardon me for assuming, but I thought that you enjoyed those sorts of things, princess?" Said the Captain.

"Don't get me wrong; I do enjoy those sorts of things," said Daina. "I'd have gone insane long ago if I didn't, with all the events I must attend in them. But even the most elegant gown won't stop a desperate mugger from trying to knock me down and take advantage of me... a dagger might."

"I will never understand your worries about that sort of thing," said the Captain, "but what's more important is that you enjoyed the gift. I'm glad to have been of service."

"I thank you again," said Daina. She turned to leave but then stopped. "I hate to bother you once more, but I must ask; is the training room open at this hour?"

They heard the sharp sound of his iron-toed boots hitting the stone floor before they saw him. They all turned to bow in reverence before moving out of the way as he progressed down the hallway. He was a colossal man, over six feet tall, and dressed in gray garb that almost looked like he was wearing sheets of stone. His hair flowed gray and was kept cropped close to his head to keep from emphasizing where it had receded. His short beard still retained a few flecks of gold from his youth. In his right hand was a wooden cane with a steel tip, sharpened to a point in case a need for it arose.

On his head sat a steel crown, as devoid of glamor and extravagance as most things in Tantallos. It looked like the battlements of the wall around his city, save for the uprising piece in the front and center. This piece was adorned with a diamond surrounded by a band of gold leaf. The dot inside the circle was the symbol of Tantallos, purity protected by a strong barrier. King Vikenti continued walking down the hall until he came to his destination. Checking inside to find it empty, he sighed and shook his head before turning around and going back to the staircase.

He descended the stairs, stepped off on the armory level and walked down the hall, guards bowing and saluting him after getting out of his way. "At ease," he said to all of them before continuing down. He listened carefully, eventually picking up noises coming from the training room. The King ambled down toward the room, fighting the aches and pains he had gained throughout his battles before ascending to the throne, from the lowly street thugs to the massive mire beasts. He finally arrived at the door and peeked through a crack in it before sneaking in as silently as a man of his age and size could. He watched in interest as the girl ran about in front of one of the straw dummies. She strafed back and forth rapidly as if it was a real opponent and that it held a metal sword instead of a wooden one. She moved with an agility and nimbleness that Vikenti knew she had definitely not inherited from her father, and he continued gazing at her as she jumped back, aimed at the dummy and hurled the dagger clutched in her fingertips. It flew ahead of her, barely grazing the dummy's shoulder before colliding with the wall and falling to the floor.

"Damn it," she said under her breath. She panted very little; she was not even close to being out of breath. She quickly retrieved the dagger. "That is the third time in a row."

"So that's what his present for you was," said Vikeni as he stepped toward Daina. "Don't be so hard on yourself; you'll get better once you have more than a morning to practice with it. It's not one of the toy daggers you somehow talked me into letting you play with."

Daina turned to Vikenti. "Morning, daddy," she said. She placed the dagger under her belt before walking forward and giving her father a quick hug. "Sorry that I'm covered in sweat. I've been practicing with this since I received it."

"I figured as such when you did not show up to breakfast some time ago," said Vikenti. "I had figured you had either not been woken up or you had gone down to this floor for your gift. The other nobles have been asking what happened to you."

It dawned on Daina. "Oh, Goddess!" she moaned, smacking herself on the forehead. "Forgive me for taking Your name in vain, Lady of Dreams." She looked up at Vikenti. She was tall for a Tantallosian woman, but still shorter than her father. "I had completely forgotten about it. I'm sorry, daddy."

"No harm done," said Vikenti, smiling. "It gave me an opportunity to be rid of their ploys for attention, if anything. Don't worry; they'll still get a chance to curry favor with me later. I'm sure you will get plenty of the same tonight as well. But in the meantime, how is the dagger?" He gestured toward the blade Daina held.

"Decide for yourself," said Daina. She pulled it carefully out from under her belt by the handle, bringing it up and adjusting her grip so she was holding the blade before offering it to Vikenti. He took it, examining closely.

"It's a good blade," he said, handing the dagger back to Daina. "I thought for sure the Captain would try giving you some pitiful excuse for a butter knife, but I guess he knew better than to try."

"I'm glad it was something like this and not a larger blade," said Daina. "If I'm performing so horribly with this thing I shudder to think what would happen if I used a broadsword or battle-axe. Couldn't you just see me charging into battle with one of those?" She smirked at the thought.

"You've always been so much like your mother, Goddess rest her soul," said Vikenti. "She was not the best fighter, either. Give yourself time to get used to your dagger, its weight and its unique qualities. You'll be throwing it expertly sooner than you think. And until then, you can simply stab whatever enemies you may have."

"That will need some work as well," said Daina, pointing to the dummy's chest. Only a few tufts of straw were coming out of its sack body. "I can't leave much of an impact."

"Strength is not all that determines a fight, honey," said Vikenti. Immediately after he said this he found a part of his mind trying to remember the origin of that nickname given to children and loved ones; he came up with nothing at all. "You should see the way you move. You're just as athletic and fast as your mother was, if not more so. The slow-moving foe trying to cleave you with a battle-axe might find it difficult if you're able to run circles around him. You'd have a more difficult time finding a Tantallosian willing to do such a thing to you."

"There has to be at least one person who wants to do something like that, daddy," she said.

"Not while I'm your father," said Vikenti. "No one in this city will ever harm you. Now come on upstairs; the chef said he is preparing something especially tasty for lunch. I can only imagine what is coming our way for dinner."

CHAPTER 2

Do not turn your back on those who seem beneath you; for although they may not all be beautiful, strong or wise, such qualities are not what makes an angel.
-From the Teachings of the Goddess.

And tasty the lunch was-- by Tantallos standards, at least. The progressing years had made proper cultivation and animal husbandry an increasingly difficult process; there was only so much space inside the completely walled-off city. Thanks to the vacant housing left behind by the famines, Tantallosian workers had been scurrying about the streets to make the most of it. Families had moved from the buildings bordering the farms into these vacant structures, allowing the ones next to the crops to be torn down. Each bit of rubble was taken away and used in some other building project, from forming mortar and cement to making decorative additions to the side of a house. Crop rotation was carried out effectively and efficiently to ensure the soil remained usable; attempts at proper cultivation with soil from the Decay had proven disastrous.

All this Daina knew but ignored as she stared at the pieces before her. She looked at the board and evaluated every possible move before moving a piece diagonally to be in range of the king.

"Check," she said. "Daddy, you're trapped."

Vikenti grinned and then moved one of his own pieces straight ahead, taking out the imposing piece. "I shall rule for many years to come, Daina," he said dramatically. "I shall not fall in battle so easily, not to my own daughter!"

Daina grinned as well and moved a piece in an L-shape, again within range of the king. "That looks like check-mate, daddy," she said. "But don't worry. Under my reign Tantallos shall reach a new age of enlightenment and prosperity."

Vikenti sighed. "The Decay must be rotting my mind," he said, "or perhaps you have truly surpassed me."

"You can tell the noblemen you let me win for my birthday," said Daina, grinning.

Vikenti smiled back and started putting the pieces back on the board. He picked it up with both hands and the piece Daina had used to win fell off. She grabbed it and examined it for a moment; she recognized the fully-armored man, but not the strange creature he rode. It was a valiant creature with a long face and four powerful legs that ended in hooves.

"Every time I look at the knight I can't help but wonder what animal he's riding," said Daina.

"Some gallant creature from centuries ago," said Vikenti. Daina put the piece back on the board. "My grandfather used to tell me stories about them, yet I cannot remember what he called them. But apparently they were very useful creatures and many such knights rode them into combat."

"Certainly an odd animal," said Daina. "I can't imagine something that big that wasn't a predator of some sort. What possible food source could it feed on? Is its long neck and head for reaching fruit?"

"I could not even guess what it was like, my dear daughter," said Vikenti. "What a pity."

Daina left her father to return to his duties and retreated back to her room. She changed into less restrictive clothing, put on a pair of more comfortable fur-lined shoes as opposed to her sandals, and tied her hair up to keep it out of the way. Last but not least, she ensured her dagger was sheathed, hidden away under her clothes.

Daina left her room, turned right, went down the hall to the guard door, passed through and shut it behind her. She then took a breath and started jogging down the battlements, waving at occasional guards as she passed them and getting a salute in return. Very few guards patrolled the walls; there was little to watch out for besides potential structural damage and civilians were not allowed onto the walls except in rare cases such as fixing any breaks. This gave Daina plenty of time and space when she ran for hours, nothing but her thoughts accompanying her and her favorite birthday gift now hidden away. That thing was not going to be leaving her any time in the near future.

Daina never bothered with looking out into the Decay; during the day little to nothing moved beneath the dark, overcast skies. Mire beasts and other such predators favored the night. The city, however, was always an incredibly interesting spectacle. The cyclopean collection of buildings was like a living being, constantly moving, changing and altering itself; all hopefully for the better. Every now and then a building collapsed, but nothing was ever put to waste and soon something else replaced it. What was erected in its place could be anything, from another apartment or store, even perhaps a greenhouse, though glass was an uncommon resource.

Daina wondered if such thoughts were just the ideas of a naive girl who had spent little time in the dirtier parts of the city; she had not even seen them besides what she saw on her runs. The wall of Tantallos went on for miles and even Daina would be hard-pressed to perform an entire lap within a day. The wall stood on its own away from most buildings and it was a royal decree that nothing be built next to it for the builder's sake should a collapse happen. The only structure built in such a way was the castle, which directly connected to it at two points. However, the castle still stood dozens of feet above the Decay and was sturdily built upon a rock face. Even while other sections crumbled the castle held true.

Daina continued her long jog, not even beginning to feel winded. She gave another polite *hello* to a nearby guard as she passed him, still maintaining her pace. She then looked at some of the houses of the court's nobles as she ran by; all of them were satisfactory at their bureaucratic jobs, most of them were favored by the public, and almost none of them were liked by her. As she passed she thought about every young nobleman who had attempted to secure her affections, though they spent most of their time at the various brothels throughout the city.

She shuddered at the thought of marrying one of those noblemen and thanked her father for not forcing her to do it. How could any young woman be expected to marry such a man, so experienced that it was a genuine concern whether or not parts of him had been rotted away by some harlot's diseases? She could never lower herself to marry one of them, no matter how many questions her disinterest in the subject raised. She would much rather marry a man old enough to be her father than one of those whores. If those men were also poor women they would have the same label.

She pushed these thoughts to the side, just before reaching the spot she had planned to stop at before turning around. It was nothing more than a small alleyway that got reasonably close to the wall. It was angled so she could stare far down it. Although it was fairly dirty as far as alleys go, it did not feature any raw waste or other disgusting items. The trash consisted mostly of worthless, broken objects that could easily be cleaned up and tossed into the Decay if someone spent an hour or two loading it into wheelbarrows. Only one or two back doors even connected to the alley, though, so nobody bothered with the effort. One of the buildings had a massive faded orange stain about a story above the ground from a painting incident. No one had ever tried to clean it up.

She had been stopping at this point and looking down that alleyway for the past eleven years. Every time she had checked she had seen nothing at all of note. She turned around and jogged back along the wall toward the castle, not let down by this disappointment. She had been doing it so long it had just become a ritual, and she had a lot more time to waste before the favorite part of her day arrived.

Even as the sun fell, Daina's day grew ever brighter. The torches throughout the castle were set up and the chandeliers in the main room were lowered, so that the could be candles replaced and lit. She arrived back at her room from various activities she had engaged in after the wall run to find a servant setting out a fancy but not uncomfortable dress for her. It was of simple, minimalistic design but still stood out thanks to its lavender color, providing a stark contrast to the commonly dull and colorless ensemble most Tantallosians wore. The dress went down to just above her feet and also covered her small bosom, the sort of modesty she enjoyed having.

And she did not forget to strap her dagger in its scabbard to her thigh. One could never be too safe, after all, even at a birthday feast in her honor. She slowly walked out of her room and to the staircase, expertly keeping her balance in her heels from years of practice. She ever so carefully walked down the stone steps, slightly leaning against the wall for support to keep from tumbling down, then proceeded to navigate through the twisting maze of the castle until she arrived at the main hall, the lit chandeliers hoisted up into the ceiling to illuminate the grand chamber. King Vikenti was not present at the throne, presumably still busy closely working with the servants to make the celebration as great as it could be.

However, she saw guests appearing at the large main doors and being serviced by the greeters and she sighed, forcing herself to walk down the hall and welcome them all personally to the event. She would much, much rather have a more private party with a very small list of guests, but entertaining the nobles with such events was an important detail.

She said hello to members of the clergy and dozens of nobles, from the older couples that ran their houses to the youngest children to the women whose dresses were as basic as hers, and to the many men who had competed for her hand at some point. The list was a lengthy one and hardly forgettable: Dimah, who had repeatedly labored for her attention but had then gone on to sleep with one of her servants the same night; Geni, whose commoner mistress had a way of showing up where she had not been invited no matter what; Pepik, who had actually tried to use his sexual experience to entice Daina to marry him; and Yefrem, who had made no attempts at such silly games and had immediately asked to take her to bed. Daina gave him credit for at least being honest about what he was really after.

Soon almost all of the party guests had made their way into the main hall from the courtyard and had found their seats at the long tables lined up throughout the hall. Each of the four lines consisted of five tables, stretching from the front wall to the beginning of the throne's steps. Perpendicular to these long tables was a single especially long table stationed directly in front of the throne for the royal family, the greatest of the nobles and the highest-ranked members of the Church of the Goddess. All of this was overseen by the mounted head of an especially large mire beast, the greatest of foes Vikenti had slain on the day the wall had collapsed.

Although all of the noblemen and noblewomen had shown up, several members of the lower classes had also been allowed to come to the party and share in the festivities. Most of them were guards and servants that normally worked in the castle, accompanied by their families and close friends. They were the ones who had been allowed off for the evening and invited to join the event by Daina herself. It was one of the only small rewards she could give to the loyal citizens who had looked after her all these years.

Daina herself sat at the main table just below the wooden, dead gaze of the stuffed mire beast head. One of the eyes had been destroyed by Vikenti's blade when it had passed into the creature's head, and the other one had been removed and presumably discarded. The taxidermist had instead replaced the eyes with two pieces of dark wood, but his expert stitching had made the head look almost exactly like it had when the beast was alive. Daina chuckled at how, as a child, she had kept thinking it would suddenly leap down and snap her up in one bite. She sat close to her father and several of the highest nobles in Tantallos. Fortunately, the children of these nobles were all too young to compete for her affections like the others did so fiercely. Even so, she found herself staring at some of the boys sitting around her, laughing with each other and making silly jokes. She wondered what sort of harlot would they choose to be their first, supposing they did not instead play around with some naive, unfortunate common girl. How long would it take for them to become like the others?

She caught herself thinking these awful things and worked to push them out of her mind, instead forcing up more positive memories. After all, this was a birthday party, a happy event, and she had better be merry. She looked down instead to Father Maxim, head of the Tantallosian Church of the Goddess. She had always trusted him implicitly; he and the other priests cared nothing for the sensations of the flesh.

The last guest finally arrived at the doors, accepting the offers of the courteous greeters before finding his seat among the many. Soon after he walked to his seat the hall doors were forced shut. Thunder began booming loudly outside and rain suddenly bombarded the aged roof of the castle. The ever-present clouds started pouring, completely dousing Tantallos in rain, soaking anything and everything exposed to it and making some of the stone surfaces slippery. Daina made a note of this; she would have to be careful on tomorrow's run. For now she had to calm the butterflies in her stomach and address all of her guests.

She got up and raised her gilded chalice of wine. "Every year I host this event and every year it seems more and more of you grace me with your presence," she began. "It flatters me to no end to see so many of you show up to celebrate with me, truly." She kept her volume high enough to reach everyone in the crowd and made eye contact with every corner of the room. She did not stumble over one word. "Several of you I have sadly not had the pleasure of meeting, and for those of you I have met I am still terribly sorry. You must believe me, it was an accident." This got a few laughs, bringing up some of the more comical memories involving her. She smiled as well, even if many of those memories were ones she would rather be forgotten.

She continued, still projecting with the same amount of power. "It is undoubtedly your admiration that makes me love this position the Goddess has placed me in, and I would only give it up if it would help you all and the rest of our fine city. Hopefully with your support, diligence and fortitude I can continue to aid our ancient, durable home. With that in mind, I dedicate this toast to each and every last one of you, all of you who make Tantallos the great city that it is. May its walls stand for centuries more." Glasses clinked, alcohol was consumed and Daina sat down to a round of applause.

"Very well done, princess," said Father Maxim. "Only a true member of royalty could deliver a speech so finely. Your speaking teacher must have taught you well." He smiled at the reference to himself.

"I couldn't have said it any better myself, Father," said Vikenti, looking down at his daughter. "Your mother would have been so proud to see you give such a speech. Not a doubt in my mind."

"I'm flattered," said Daina, holding her utensils but not eating. "Though I must admit that a lot of that was not as truthful as it should have been. I'm honestly not sure if I would want to help all of them, even if I could somehow make the difference. Too many of these people are undoubtedly cruel to their families or wasteful of their money while other people are struggling."

"It does not seem like you to make such accusations of your party guests," said Father Maxim. "It is part of my oath to not reveal which of them have come to my confessions, but of the many I see here who have, I have come across nothing of the sort. They admit to sins no greater than all too often being forced to leave their families alone for long periods of time for the sake of their jobs. These are generally kind people assembled before you, princess."

"Father Maxim," said Daina, "I appreciate your efforts but you can only do so much. Sadly, so many of the citizens in Tantallos have turned away from the Goddess and faith in Her church as a whole has been waning away. While many of these nobles will still claim to follow Her practices, they all too often do sinful acts while She sleeps. I pity their souls when they meet Her."

"Do not pity them, Daina," said Vikenti. "The Goddess gave us the right to refuse Her if we wished, even if it pains Her. Barring that, what you consider to be the main aspects of their personality may just be your generalizations based on the habits of the few you have seen. The one you dismiss as being a cruel wife-beater may actually be a gentle giant who would sooner die than do anything of the sort. The one you claim to be frivolous and wasteful in this economy may be using those funds to perform various charitable acts for the less fortunate around him. Even the smallest act of kindness is appreciated; if a Tantallosian won't help someone, then no one will. We're alone."

Daina let her head fall, feeling somewhat ashamed but still rather sure of her beliefs concerning those before her. She had seen too much from them to think otherwise by this point; she saw how the nobles treated their servants even as they only tried to help their masters. "I guess," she said. "Honestly, I don't think I am allowed out of this castle enough to truly understand the workings and thoughts of the citizens. I have a never-ending army of tutors, nobles and servants to give me secondhand knowledge concerning Tantallos, but that cannot possibly compare to what lies out there. My runs on the walls only give me the slightest glimpse into this titanic city. I'm always told that the civilians adore me and my philanthropic attempts, but I can't be certain of anything. Those lower in rank will say anything to maintain the approval of the heir to the throne. If I was a commoner I doubt I would be able to say less than complimentary words about my superiors and escape harm."

"Perhaps that was the case decades ago, but Tantallos is no longer the same city as in our history books," said Maxim. "The people of this city love you. They see you as the symbol of an approaching golden future, and not just because of the color of your hair. You may not see them as so valuable, but many a commoner would deeply long for just one of your qualities. You're beautiful and very generous, even if your heart is not truly in your charity. You are quite the problem solver when you're placed in a situation that calls for it."

"I'm weak," she said. "And I can be a clumsy oaf."

"To me it looks like your greatest problem would be your low self image and confidence," said Maxim. "You can claim you're weak as often as you want, but I think you just don't trust yourself enough to perform to your fullest physically. A person who did not know you particularly well may even go so far as to label some of what you say as false modesty, though I know better than to think that."

Daina thought about this, but still could not see herself performing great feats of strength or balance. All she saw was herself dropping a heavy object on her foot or falling off a platform. "Maybe so, but even the philanthropy I'm praised for having cannot do that much for Tantallos," she said. "I can organize a supply drive or set up a soup kitchen, and I do have some influence on the politics of this city, but most of my job is to just sit at my father's side, smile and look pretty while he does all the real work; that and being the fantasy of every little commoner girl throughout Tantallos. But even my father cannot help all the people in this city. How can I possibly make a difference with that in mind?"

"Any act of kindness, no matter how small or meaningless it may seem at the time, can make a difference so big it changes the fates of everyone," said Vikenti. "Take your very first trip into the city, for example. You were barely eight years old but you had your heart set out on exploring the city streets. You found yourself passing by several starving or ill people but you were not able to help, nor could you order any of the guards in your escort to provide them aid or respite. They had no food or medicine to give those people and all you carried was a small sack for yourself."

"I did not feel a need or desire to help those citizens," said Daina. "I did not know them at all. It's easy to say you want to help everyone, but when you get so close to these faceless strangers it becomes difficult to make that effort. At least it does for me... I can organize a food drive from the seclusion of the castle study and never once visit the storehouse it's taking place in."

"You say these things but I know at least some part of you thinks differently," said Vikenti. "I know exactly where you stopped that day before turning back for home. The guards frequently tell me about how you stop at that exact same spot when you're taking your runs on the wall, and I remember just how proud you were to have done a certain act of kindness when you came back and told me about your day."

"Yes," said Daina. Her gaze again fell toward her plate and she continued to simply stare at her food.

"You came across a blind boy that the guards couldn't get to move out of the road," said Vikenti. "He looked about your age, and whether it was difficult for you to help him or not, you still did so. You gave him the food you had on you and made sure he got all of it instead of some other person stealing it from him. The poor child was so weak he couldn't even talk."

"He was different, daddy," said Daina. And she clearly remembered the boy talking. He had been stumbling over his words as if unused to speaking them, but he had said *Thank you so much.*"

"He could not have been that different from the countless other people starving out in the streets," said Vikenti. "After all, you had never met him before. For all you knew he was a petty thief or some orphaned street urchin or perhaps something worse than that. You could not have known. And he probably did not look that much weaker than the other people starving on those streets."

"I'm not sure how to explain why I helped him, daddy," said Daina. "Just something-- I don't know how to describe it. Something about him made me want to help him even if the others did not make me feel the same way. And it's not like I'll ever see that boy again. I really don't know why I look down that alley every time... my little sack lunch could not have been enough to save him from starvation."

"But at the same time, it may very well have been what kept him from passing away on a cold night," said Vikenti. "And he, like the many others you've managed to help, will never forget that selfless act of kindness you did for them. It may seem like a small bit of needless charity to you, but it may be repaid to you fivefold in the future."

Daina sighed; once again her argument had been defeated. "If there even is a future," said Daina. "Tantallos is a hardy city and has survived countless troubles even while everything around it rots away, but how long until our time comes, how long until the Decay topples our thick walls and brings this city to its foundations?"

"We are all that remains in this world, so that day will never come," said Maxim. "The end of days won't come until the Goddess awakens. She remains sleeping under the surface of our world and we still find the strength to carry on so we shall continue to do so. Hopefully She does not come back in our lifetime, but if She does then you can rest assured we will never have to worry about the Decay again. She will bring the dream to an end and our nightmares will be over."

Daina breathed a sigh of relief when the conversation finally ended, even if it left her with a slight hollow feeling inside. Vikenti noticed this and thought it over; this was certainly no way for a young woman to act on her birthday. The topic of discussion should not be something so bleak, but rather something joyous and uplifting. "So, tell me Daina," said Vikenti, "what sort of gifts did the nobles bring you this year? How many dresses in relation to how many gifts you'll actually use?"

CHAPTER 3

I am the only true being of this world. Beware of any who claim to have been made by something else; that which is otherworldly is a demon, an abomination who only wishes ill will on you. Fear them.
-From the Teachings of the Goddess.

The feast continued as the storm never ceased its pounding against the stone walls. However, as time went on, the storm finally subsided while the party inside raged just as fiercely as when it had begun. Although most tables were finished with their meals, drinking competitions and other such games started up and kept them all entertained.

Daina watched all this from the seclusion of her table, thankful no one was forcing her to join in. Daina turned into quite a different creature when she became intoxicated; not so much meaner, but rather she was a bit too truthful concerning her feelings of other people. Many a suitor had been offended by this, though Daina would insist that the primary reason was her dislike for alcohol.

Soon every last nobleman and noblewoman had cleaned his or her plate while the slowest eater of the less wealthy finally finished consuming the bread he had used to hold his food. Dozens of servants scurried about the hall with damp rags in hand, using them to clean off the tables and scatter the crumbs to the floor. All of this was done while the more heavily inebriated attendants were helped out of the hall and allowed to stumble back home since the storm had finally ended. The castle dogs, a various collection of mutts with the occasional pure-bred among them, snaked through the crowds of humans to get at the larger pieces of food that the servants had left on the floor. Hidden away in dark corners or in the rafters, the mice watched and awaited their chance to feast upon what remained.

In moments the rowdier and less friendly guests found themselves looking for their homes in their drunken stupor. Daina breathed a sigh of relief; this now diminished group included most of her countless suitors. At the same time many of the more sober participants also left; this group consisted mostly of the lower class who had very busy schedules coming their way tomorrow. Even with so many gone, dozens still remained for what this group considered to be the best part of any event hosted by the king-- a story from the Captain of the guard.

He had served the crown and the city for a combined total of twenty-five years, longer than any person still on duty, and was said to be just as tenacious in combat as ever. In those decades he had assisted Vikenti in fighting back the mire beasts after the wall collapsed, stopped fiendish thieves from stealing the treasures of Tantallos, collected his wedding band from the Decay after he had accidentally dropped it and --of his greatest achievements-- had personally organized and executed the hunting down and removal of no less than five different demons. Each one of these demons was far fiercer than any warrior in Tantallos and none were even ten years old. Although most of his stories were heavily embellished and a fair amount may not have even happened, each one still made for a very entertaining sit.

But as entertaining as some were, there were still plenty that were all too real and familiar to the dozen-or-so people clustered around him in chairs, Daina and Vikenti among them. These sorts of stories were always more gruesome and chilling. As terrifying and intimidating as the monsters that roamed just outside the city walls could be, the most frightening creatures of all were the ones that lived on the inside. Not even the great fortifications could protect them from such fiends.

"Tonight I shall tell you a story I have not told in many a year," he began. The lights in the chandelier were beginning to die down, making it seem all the more unnerving in the great hall. "It is of a killer who had roamed our streets not too long ago. This killer was none other than the Red Light Murderer, the roamer of the streets and alleyways of Tantallos.

"But this was not something as weak as a human thug, no. This murderer was a powerful demon." The room grew ever more silent as images started appearing in the minds of everyone present, bestial creatures with disappearing and reappearing wings that seemed like sheets of red stained glass, glowing and pulsating with some sort of unholy power the Goddess could never have created, savage creatures not even a step above animals, with flesh that appeared cracked like dried ground, flesh so durable even shots from a crossbow would barely harm it.

"It would be almost eleven years ago that he started his horrible work," said the Captain. "When exactly this unholy blight descended upon our unsuspecting city cannot be said for sure, but after being called forth he left a mark that shall never be forgotten by the countless families he affected. For several dark and frightful months he prowled the streets of the poor and impoverished, striking in the darkness without pity or remorse. He cut, chopped and mutilated several women beyond recognition. In just one month he had managed to kill sixteen unsuspecting women of the night, and again I remind you all that happened but within one month; this beast continued his murder spree for two months more.

"He gorged on their flesh, effortlessly cleaning it off the bones and cracking them open to get at the marrow in the larger ones. Those of us who investigated the tenements of the victims by the insistence of neighbors found unfathomably horrible sights; mutilated bodies alongside the ones he had eaten, brothers, sisters and children foolish enough to get in the way of the killer as he feasted on their kin. Though even their corpses could not compare to what remained, or what didn't remain, of those he had chosen to feed upon."

Many people cringed as they heard this. "It is the shame of the Tantallos guardsmen that we were not able to catch him sooner," said the Captain. "He had killed thirty-eight harlots and their families before we were able to devise an appropriate trap to catch him. The smallest problem was choosing an observable location in his territory; the biggest was finding someone who was willing to risk her life to attract this fiend. In the end, she had performed her job well, almost too well, and she had been nearly killed by the demon before we were able to storm the tenement and face him in combat." A few gasps came from those sitting closest to the Captain.

"However, the dozen guards sent into the tenement to apprehend him proved too little and he easily incapacitated them before escaping to the streets. Every guard in the city was called to that neighborhood from their nearby stations; if it had not been for every single guard present that night we could not possibly have kept track of him in the confusion. The guards fought to maintain their pursuit after him and to keep the panicking citizens under control." He leaned forward slightly as he continued his tale.

"We attempted to form a perimeter to keep him trapped in the neighborhood, but he managed to get past us and enter some of the more middle-class areas. He ran about, nowhere to hide, horrifying each and every civilian unfortunate enough to meet him. He very nearly started a riot in this new neighborhood as guards everywhere struggled to keep him contained.

"Many of the more foolish guards charged into battle with the creature on their own, armed only with a crossbow or a pike. They were completely unprepared to compete with the animal's unfathomable strength and combat prowess. Its massive hands were able to slice through metal weapons as if made of paper and its wrists somehow managed to parry blows. He seemed to move along the guards, reacting unimaginably fast to disarm or knock out any fool who tried to hurt him." His audience edged themselves closer.

"As the chase continued the guards came at him in bigger and bigger groups. At least one guard had attempted to grab him by the hair, but the demon's scalp was completely covered in sharp, thin spines that pierced both gloves and flesh with ease. No single limb of this monster was not deadly in some way; even its feet had small hooked claws on them.

"Finally we managed to corner the creature before it could fly away and completely escape us," he continued. "It held up for a few moments more, dodging our strikes with its incredible reflexes. But it eventually made a mistake and a lucky strike managed to take it down, and all of this torment had been done by a very young demon indeed; it was child-like in form, a twisted mockery of the Goddess' greatest gift to us. The youngest one we had ever encountered.

"The demon woke up shortly thereafter to find itself heavily bound together and chained to a massive metal ball; we were not able to take any risks with the monster. Many guards called for its death right then and there, but we Tantallosians would be no better if we were to kill a fallen opponent. We are above the death penalty, even with monsters like demons, unless we are truly faced with no other choice. Even as the sniveling creature begged to be spared despite all of its crimes, we moved it onto the wall and pushed it out into the Decay, to suffer whatever fate the cruel world outside these walls had in store for it."

He looked around back and forth, cuing people to lean in further as he changed to a softer voice. "When the sun slowly rose that morning, not even four hours later, several of the guards including myself gazed down that wall and looked out into the Decay. We saw the metal ball and the chains, but not the demon they had been attached to. Although it has not let itself be seen since, it is said that the demon has thrived outside our walls, patrolling the Decay just out of our sight and killing mire beasts for food as we would poultry. It is also said that the demon desperately longs to taste the flesh of a young woman again and so finds itself unable to enjoy the meat of other animals because of this burning desire. Any woman or girl unfortunate enough to be outside of the city will be immediately set upon by it and brutally murdered. For demons have no pity, no mercy and no tears to shed for any life but their own."

The audience sat silent around him, the great hall seeming even colder than usual as the story sank into their bones. Many of them reflected upon these events from secondhand knowledge; a few even recalled their accidental encounters with the demon as it had been fleeing from the guards. One of them even managed to recall the demon making him faint and the horrifying nightmares that immediately followed.

But none of them could match the shock and horror felt by their princess, who caught herself shaking some from it. Daina had been eight when the demon had begun to feed upon the populace. While it had not reportedly killed anyone that young (by only a couple years), now she was in the general age group of the harlots it had targeted on those cold nights. The Red Light Murderer put her opinions of the nobles in a new perspective-- as horrible and immoral as she considered so many of them to be, she would much rather be forced to spend time with one of those whorish men than be left at the mercy of such a monster. All she had in a battle was her speed, and how could her speed possibly allow her to escape such a powerful predator, even if she could run for hours?

She had no doubt in her mind that the demon could keep up with her, pass her, or just start flying and grab her from the air like a hawk --she thought that was its name; she had only read about them in books-- would grab a mouse. Humans can kill, but a demon is built to kill and do nothing else. It would catch up to her and within a few moments tear her into unrecognizable pieces of meat and bone. Or maybe it would just break her legs so it could feed on her while she still lived, taking delight in her screams.

I will never trust such a monster, she thought to herself. *Never! Absolutely never, not so long as the Goddess sleeps beneath the earth. Even if I had no choice!* It's just like in all the fairy stories. The terrible monster proves itself great at putting on a friendly facade, pretending to be nice to the young child who comes across it. But they always have a much darker purpose just below the surface of their scaly, slimy or cracked skin. Even if she was a princess, no monster that has killed thirty-eight innocent women could possibly have greater intentions in mind for her. *Never forget that*, she told herself.

The storytelling night continued on. Some of the guests with younger children left, but many still remained. Despite the mood his opening story had set, the Captain of the guard followed it up with increasingly lighter and more humorous adventures and escapades throughout Tantallos.

He was in the middle of a tale about rescuing some girl's pet from a building's ledge when the hall doors suddenly slammed open, making everyone jump in their seats-- a few even let out yelps in surprise. Everyone in the room turned to see a limber, panting young man in light armor running up to Vikenti as he apologized to everyone he passed. He managed to keep his balance, despite how winded he looked. He knelt before Vikenti, thankful for the short opportunity to catch his breath.

"What is the matter?" asked Vikenti, displaying little emotion. A message runner could mean anything at this hour.

"I apologize for the intrusion, your majesty," the runner said in between breaths. "I hate to interrupt, but we have a situation down at the main gates that we're completely unprepared for. This event has never happened to us before as long as anyone can remember and we need your guidance as soon as possible."

"What might such a problem be?" asked Vikenti. "Are monsters or demons trying to get in through the main gates?"

"Not monsters or demons at all, your majesty," said the runner. "Quite the opposite. It is people. There are people at the main gates!"

A silence fell upon each and every person present, their looks of shock directed at the runner. People... from the Decay? To the best of their knowledge not one person had fallen into the Decay recently, let alone several. Barring that, no one had ever made their way back through the Decay unharmed. How could there possibly be people at the main gates?

"I hate to do this to you, diligent runner," said Vikenti, "and I know how tired you must be, but you must get back to the main gates post haste and get the guards to let them into the city at once!" The guard finished catching his breath and got back up upon the king's request, bowing and taking off back through the main doors as fast as he could.

The remaining guests immediately sprang into conversations as they too got up to head for the main gates while the Captain of the guard quickly dashed off to find and organize whatever soldiers still remained on duty. Who knew what powers these people might have if they could manage to survive the Decay! It was best to be safe. Vikenti got up from his seat and called every servant to him before ordering them to prepare for the new arrivals and told them to spread the word to any other servants they encountered. The hall needed to be fixed up to prepare the welcoming for these visitors.

All this left Daina standing to the side while everyone around her rushed about. She thought about it all in a state of childlike wonder; just what sort of people could these mysterious travelers be? One thing was certain: they could not be demons. Demons never bothered trying to approach the gates as crossbowmen were always on standby above. Even if they were demons they could easily attempt to fly over the walls just to be as easily spotted because of their glowing wings. And there was no animal she knew of that could so expertly fake the act of being a human in order to try and get inside the city walls.

So how did they manage to get here? How long had they been traveling? What had they been eating and drinking? The waters of the Decay are filthy and poisonous. How did they manage to keep the giant monsters and mire beasts at bay? Did they completely resist the effects of the Decay or were they being rotted away by it even as she thought it over? But most important of all her questions, where did they come from and were there more of them?

She turned toward her father and found him sending off the last few servants while making his way back to the throne as fast as he could despite his slowing agility brought on by age and battles. She rushed up to him quickly. "Daddy," she said, "I can't help but feel like a third wheel. May I go meet these travelers at the main gates, give them a formal welcome on your behalf before they're led to the castle?"

"That idea would be wise if this city did not hold so many people within its walls," said Vikenti. "And you can be certain that every single one of those people has heard about these travelers as well and will be trying to get as close to the main gates as possible. Even if you managed to make your way through the crowd to the gates you could still end up seriously injured, whether the crowd intended to do so or not. It would not be safe in the slightest."

She thought this over and agreed. "I still wish to at least observe these new travelers," she said. "Would you be fine with me watching them from a distance, perhaps on the walls? I'll never get so close as to be in harm's way. Please, daddy."

Vikenti thought this over for a few moments and then sighed. "Every protective instinct tells me to say '*no*' to your request," he said, Daina looking crestfallen at this, "but even if I did say so I'm certain you would still rush off and travel down the walls anyway, so yes." Daina's face lit up. "But stay to the walls and walk carefully. The rain will have made the walkways slippery and all of the guards will be at the main gates-- no one will be there to look out for you."

"Do not worry about me, daddy," she said. "I'll be fine. I have run along those walls almost every day of my life. Thank you so much for this chance." Vikenti nodded and watched Daina dash off toward the nearest staircase. She climbed it rapidly and sprinted through the hallways, finding herself out on the walls within moments. Vikenti turned back and continued issuing orders to servants, ordering the hall to be cleaned up and move aside the tables and benches quickly. Each speck of food was swept up and thrown out. Nothing was missed. Vikenti let Daina slip into the back of his mind; after all, it was just another run on the walls for her.

CHAPTER 4

All of you have powers similar to Mine, but some of you have skills that others don't. It is together that your powers become as great as Mine; support each other and keep each other safe.
-From the Teachings of the Goddess.

Daina barely remembered to shut the door to the walkway before darting down the stone wall. Although she made no noise outward besides her breathing, internally she sighed in relief that the walkways were off-limits to civilians at all times, lest they become just as packed as the streets she saw before her. She passed only a few guards as she made her way ever closer to the gates. It was incredibly grueling, even for her, but eventually she saw the large, rusted portcullis appear in front of her. Guards and workmen scrambled all over it, cleaning off as much rust as possible so the gate would be able to rise. Workmen even dangled on ropes from the walls above it to get at the corroded areas on top.

She looked away and stared in amazement at just how large a crowd had managed to form in such a small amount of time. Almost every last Tantallosian was present to see these travelers, as if they were the primary event of Tantallos' annual harvest festival. Dozens upon dozens of guards managed to make a barrier of pikes and shields around the main gate, keeping the excited mob away. Workmen continued to work rapidly to get the gate working, a group so thick Daina could not possibly see the travelers from her angle. Eventually they managed to get the portcullis clean enough for it to rise slowly and stubbornly into the air. Even Daina gasped in awe; no one had ever seen the portcullis in motion. The few people unfortunate enough to have to enter the Decay did so via a very small side door hidden away at the left of the main gate. It had been painted and decorated so thoroughly it looked almost exactly like the rest of the stone around it. The only other way into the Decay was to be lobbed over the wall, a method saved for garbage and demons. But an occasion such as these travelers needed to be celebrated with a grand entrance.

Daina slowed down and took one of the few paths extending directly out from the wall. It connected to a guard house, which had a small hatch built onto the roof. The guards normally inside were undoubtedly already down on the street. She charged to the edge of the roof and leaped off, sailing through the air until she landed nimbly on the roof of a building only a few feet away. She made a few more similar jumps and found herself on a rooftop not even thirty feet away from the street. As perfect a vantage point as she was bound to get.

She congratulated herself on not even stumbling once as she had run on the slippery walls; it would not have been the first time she had taken a fall on the walkway, injuring less her body and more her pride. She also pondered the complete lack of any measures taken to prevent more dangerous falls, such as a railway or something similar along the inside; nothing to shield a clumsy or unfortunate person from a possibly deadly fall to the ground. She filed that issue away in a corner of her mind to discuss with her father and the counsel of engineers and builders the next chance she had.

She pushed all thoughts to the side and looked down at the gate in fascination as the portcullis rose up six feet in the air. The few seconds seemed to last an eternity as the ancient device struggled to get even higher. What seemed like ages later it finally stopped at ten feet, more than enough to welcome in the travelers. The crowd grew silent as they saw shapes stirring in the fog before finally emerging from it. Six people appeared before the city of Tantallos, people unlike any the Tantallosians had ever seen. Three were covered head-to-toe in gray, plated armor. Not a single bit of their flesh could be seen through the thick suits of metal; even their faces were completely obscured by their full helmets. Each helmet had two joints to adjust parts of the helmet. One worked for the visor that covered the mouth and the other for the visor guarding and hiding their eyes. The armor looked so excessive and heavy Daina was surprised any of them were able to move.

The knights parted some to allow a fourth one to walk in front of them. He too was in full armor, but his suit was as red as blood save for his gray gauntlets. All four knights were colossal figures, but he stood the tallest at a staggering seven feet in height. He was undoubtedly the tallest person Daina-- no, anyone in Tantallos had ever seen. Daina stood five feet and seven inches and she was considered tall in her city. The red knight made gestures toward the other three and they immediately obeyed him, moving about alongside him to form a diamond shape with him at the point. Daina was not shocked at all that he was the leader.

Daina could not deny that these knights were fascinating, but she still managed to pull her attention away from them to look at the next character slowly emerging from the fog. This person could not have been any less like the knights. He appeared to be an older, graying, rather fat man in robes. From a distance they appeared to be similar to the gray robes worn by the priests of the Goddess, which Daina had always thought looked similar to nightgowns. Then she got a better look at the front of him. On his chest and ten-tasseled hat was the unmistakable symbol of the Church of the Goddess, a beam of light rising out of a cracked dolmen forming a shape similar to a hammer or maul. Daina was relieved by this; she could definitely trust this man. He was undoubtedly part of Her pious order, and they were all good people. But his clothing looked even more majestic than Father Maxim's with its slight gold trim around the tassels and edges of the robes and the golden outlines of the symbol. No Tantallosian priest wore something like that.

But it was the final person who took her and the entire city by surprise. Out of the fog stepped a man over six feet tall. Although he was dressed in simple, gray garb similar to what most Tantallosians wore, no one even noticed. He seemed to have a palpable air of accomplishment, an aura of worth that could almost be seen; this was a man above anything petty or worthless. This man was above most of the citizens.

His short-cut hair was surprisingly well-groomed for someone who had just been walking through the Decay for an unknown time and its golden color rivaled that of Daina's. Those who were close enough to look him in the eye found themselves staring at a bizarre color around his pupils; an emerald green. This man was so toned and well-built most people started thinking that he could wrestle an adult alpha mire beast and win without a fight.

He was a beautiful creature like no other, and already several of the younger women staring at him found themselves swooning. There was even a girl watching from the roof of a building who found herself fascinated by him. Something inside her clicked as she eyeballed every perfect, refined feature on his body, and she could tell with one look this man was nothing like the whorish nobles who had so often tried to appeal to her, or at least so she felt. He looked too great for such low actions; he had to be a king, or perhaps a lord, something great.

"Greetings, welcoming citizens of this island in the Decay!" called out the man. His voice was deep and powerful, the sort of voice that raises the morale of an entire army and wrecks the courage and confidence of their foes. It was the voice of a champion. "We come in the interest of peace! I am Prince Alkin, heir to the throne of the city of Tulroy!"

The crowd burst into chatter as people shared the news of this unfamiliar name. At least, unfamiliar to most. Elderly citizens being helped along by their children and grandchildren suddenly lit up their faces as they heard the name they had not heard in so long. "Tulroy!" many of them called out, an ancient memory surfacing in their half-gone, dementia-ridden brains. "Tulroy, the city built into the cliffs!" It was a name they had not heard since they were children but had always kept with them.

"You are all correct!" said Alkin, his eyes panning across the crowd to look at as many people as possible. He never once stumbled over his words or fidgeted with something on his person. "We are indeed from the city built into the cliffs. For so long we have existed some miles away from you, separated by a mountain range and the everlasting Decay, thinking that our city was the last one to remain alive. But, just a short time ago we had the good fortune to become aware of your presence, possibly the only other group of humans left in our world.

"Now, my good people, do you have a king, lord or person of authority who reigns over your extensive city? We wish to speak with this person as soon as possible and would appreciate whatever assistance you can offer us in getting to him. I'm afraid we have little to offer after our grueling journey through the Decay. Even my own sword has been lost in one of its sickening bogs."

Countless people called out that no payment was necessary and countless more issued the basic directions of following the main street up to the castle. The crowd slowly parted to make way for the six newcomers, Alkin and the older man walking in the center of the diamond formed by the four knights, the red one still leading the way.

Tantallosian guards attempted to keep the crowds at bay, but such actions were unnecessary with the four knights present. They continued to maintain this diamond shape despite the surging crowd. The moment the crowd got within reach of the knights the people immediately pushed away from them. The few unfortunate enough to find themselves in the way of the newcomers immediately scurried to the side, sensing a feeling of dread lying just behind the full helmets. Whatever was hidden away in those suits of armor was not something to be trifled with; not unless you were tired of living.

But none of this had any impact on Daina. They were just guards, hired hands performing their job by protecting this wonderful man. He could probably take care of himself, but nevertheless they gave him the space he deserved. He was a truly great man; she could tell just by looking at him. He would be far greater than any of the hedonistic nobles prowling about the city for women. But she could hardly meet him if she was still watching from this roof; she had to get back to the castle well before he arrived. She had to look her absolute best for him. She would have to be quick to beat him there to get ready.

She leaped from roof to roof, crossing back over to the guard house far faster than when she had come from the other direction. Once back on the walls she took off like a fired bolt from a crossbow for the castle, unable to stop her thoughts and eyes from constantly drifting back to the mysterious Prince Alkin as he ambled up the main street. The crowd cheered, clamored and followed him every step of the way; no one even noticed the girl dashing down the battlements at record speeds. He was a man Daina knew she wanted to spend time with. None of the other suitors who had attempted to court her had ever given her such a feeling as he did, even from this distance.

She continued running along, passing the prince and making excellent progress back to her home. She thought over in her mind what would be the most dignified way to greet him as the Tantallosian guards finally managed to force the crowd back and got them to disperse. The civilians retreated into the side streets but did not go far. Countless people watched him from their windows and many more watched from just inside the alleys and avenues connecting to the main street. Daina found herself craning her neck more and more to look as she increased her lead on the six visitors. She was definitely going to be able to beat them to the castle-- if she could catch her breath quickly enough she might even have time to change into one of her nicer dresses.

And then she felt her world flip over as an unfortunate misstep cost Daina her footing. She fell at an angle, landing on her arm and rolling to the inside. Her body rolled a foot too far and Daina tipped off the wall. An instant before she would have plummeted one of her hands found a grip on a misshapen stone. She quickly brought up her other hand to this grip, but the fall and the run had taken their toll on her. She was weakened and out of breath from her sprint; her attempts to recover her strength were not enough to pull herself back up like she could any other day. In moments her arms would give out and she would fall to the ground dozens of feet below. She risked a glance downward; below her was nothing to stop her fall. Nothing but cobblestone road and hard-packed dirt. She let out a scream.

Even from that distance four of the travelers had heard her. The knights turned and looked in that direction and saw the young woman struggling to pull herself up. The buildings between them and the wall were shorter as the Tantallosian vertical development had not come to them yet, so they remained only one or two stories tall with the occasional slanted roof among the flat ones. The other two newcomers looked as well and Alkin's eyes became as large as dinner plates. The six all exchanged glances before Alkin took off in the direction of the scream at top speed, a speed only Daina could have beaten. But he was still fast, and very sure-footed; he could stop and turn on a coin, aiding him immensely as he snaked his way through the network of houses. His five companions stood still and watched this scene unfold from a distance, not taking a single step toward the source of the scream.

Alkin finally cleared the network of houses and soon arrived right in front of the wall. He skittered to a halt up against it and looked up at Daina struggling to keep her grip. "I'm here to help, miss!" he called. "Just hold on for as long as you can! I'll be right back after I find something to catch you with!"

"Catch me with your arms!" she pleaded. Her fingers were slowly slipping off the rock; already some of her digits no longer had a grip. She could fall at any time.

"I don't trust myself enough to catch you!" he called back before taking off like a charging animal. He looked around frantically as he ran down the nearest street, eventually laying eyes on a small cart up on blocks. It was fully stocked with various clothing made from patches of torn cloth. The wheels lay at its side, taken off to keep the cart from rolling away while the merchant struggled to sell his questionable wares. Daina continued to hold on, even as more of her fingers lost the stone beneath them. Soon only a few fingers held onto the stone by their tips. Finally the last bit of misshapen rock disappeared from under her fingers and she fell, falling toward the ground and letting out a final scream.

A split second after she had lost her grip she landed with a thump in a wooden container full of clothing. She checked to make sure she was still in one piece, and outside of a slight headache she had been completely unharmed. She then realized she was in a cart and let out a yell in surprise when she saw the cart was not on the ground. The entire cart, clothing, princess and all, lay on Alkin's back. He showed no signs of exertion as he tried to keep it as steady as possible. Then it dawned on Daina; he had moved the cart to this spot fast enough to catch her as she fell.

Countless people left their houses and shops to stare at this sight in awe and wonder as Alkin let the cart slide off his back onto the ground and twisted his torso to crack it a couple times after he did so. He then turned to face Daina, not a bead of sweat visible on his head. She stared at him, overwhelmed by her emotions, which now included thankfulness and relief. He was even more handsome up close. "It is fortunate you were able to hold on for that long, miss," said Alkin, looking kindly at Daina. He offered a hand and carefully helped her out of the cart. "Not many women could hang there for as long as you did; I was worried I would not reach you in time. May I ask your name and where you live? You need to get home. That was quite a fall you took."

Daina finally got her emotions under control and got her mouth to move enough to create words. "I live at the castle," she said, her heart finally starting to slow down. "I am Princess Daina of Tantallos."

CHAPTER 5

I am the only true Being that watches over you. Those who follow a false being or act as if I do not exist shall be consumed by Me. Perhaps in their complete destruction something better may be created.
-From the Teachings of the Goddess.

"The Goddess truly gave us a gift when She dreamed of you, Alkin," said the fat priest. "Nothing less than genius. My dear Alkin, you are truly incredible."

"Perhaps in speed and might, Father Abdaas," said Alkin, "but I do what all people should strive to do, honestly. I personally would feel ashamed if I simply stood by and watched an innocent girl fall to an untimely death. It would not matter if this girl was royalty or a noblewoman, or even if she was a harlot, though Goddess knows she could certainly be both. It wouldn't even matter if the one falling was a man and not a woman."

"A person who knew you less would accuse you of false modesty, but I know better," said Abdaas. "Do not downplay yourself. There are people who would strive to do what you do but most of them never could, not without your speed and might. Rather than just grab her in your arms, you lifted up a fully stocked cart to catch her in. Not pushed or pulled, mind you; *lifted*. The people were stunned. And who does this random damsel in distress happen to be? None other than the marriageable daughter of the king of Tantallos. Our cities will be allies until the end of days for certain."

"Not a shred of that is thanks to you or your guards," said Alkin. "You all simply stood and watched as this innocent person feared for her life. I've seen your guards perform amazing feats and the red one is far greater than me in strength and speed. How could you all just stand and watch as she nearly fell to her death?"

"My athletic days are well behind me for the most part," said Abdaas. "She would have fallen long before I even arrived at the walls, let alone found something to catch her in. And never mind the guards; they are here solely to protect us and no one else. We're the diplomatic ones, so they consider us more important at all times."

"That's an explanation, but that's not an excuse," said Alkin, folding his arms. "Talk to them about the terms of their contracts so this doesn't occur again."

They then heard a loud slam from the side and turned to face the corner of the great hall. Abdaas was unimpressed, as was Alkin, but both of them had bigger concerns on their minds than the extravagance of a gathering hall. They looked and saw the king of Tantallos fussing with the position of his simple crown and the fringes of his basic robes as he rushed down the staircase and to his throne. He had just gotten back from checking on his daughter in her bedroom and looked very relieved to see her unharmed. He darted onto the throne and sat down, ignoring the griping and groaning his joints made as he looked at the two travelers and their four armored guards.

"It is my utmost pleasure to welcome you all to Tantallos," he called out, his face beaming, "especially the man who saved my daughter from her death. I am Vikenti the Fierce, King of Tantallos and slayer of beasts like the one above my throne." One of the gray knights made a slight scoffing noise and the red knight immediately stared daggers into the knight's helmet. The gray knight cowered and turned his focus solely onto Vikenti. "...I hope to make your time in this old city as comfortable as possible," said Vikenti. "Just say anything, ask for anything, whatever you want, and I shall see to it personally that you are granted it."

"We graciously appreciate your offer but do not ask for anything in return, your highness," said Alkin, bowing in respect before the king. He rose back up. "I am Prince Alkin of Tulroy, sole heir to the throne, and with me is Father Abdaas, head priest of the Tulroy Church of the Goddess. The other four may seem dangerous and threatening, but they are the bodyguards of Abdaas and me. I must admit I know little about them, but they have proven themselves as unparalleled warriors in our travels. They will cause you no harm."

"I was not too concerned," said Vikenti. "Not even a demon would try killing a king in his own hall, but I do appreciate the thought. If they are even half as powerful as you they would be terrifying opponents indeed. But I must ask. How did you and your subjects of Tulroy come to know of us? We have seen no signs of humanity outside of these walls for decades. The few structures that remain in the Decay are in ruins. The only creatures we know to live in the festering swamps are monsters and demons."

"Up until less than a week ago we too thought the same about our city," said Alkin. "Few to none travel to the top of the plateau Tulroy was built into, but recently one was sent up to investigate something for Abdaas. While there the skies were clear enough for him to just see past the mountain range and spy a large stone structure off in the distance. He informed my father of the sighting at once and went back up to the top with several scholars. They examined the sight from there and discussed what they believed it to be." The prince began. "There are many different sorts of buildings out in the

Decay; stone villages, crumbling towers, even the collapsing remains of churches. But its relation in space to the mountains disproved that notion; it was much bigger than it looked. They hypothesized that the structure was so large that it could support a human population, provided the walls were as effective at keeping out the Decay's effects as the walls of the plateau are for us.

"My father then organized a group to travel to the city. I am the greatest prince and warrior of Tulroy, so I volunteered to lead this group out into the Decay. Head priest Father Abdaas also decided to travel with me, and by his influence we obtained the help of the four you see behind us. Abdaas and I are charismatic enough to befriend this unknown nation of humans and the knights and I are strong enough to fend off whatever horrors might actually be calling the structure home."

"Your mere presence here proves you have the strength needed to take down most any monster in the Decay by yourself," said Vikenti. "No man I know of is strong enough to resist the Decay for as long as you have. I've known good men unfortunate enough to enter the Decay for but a few hours and they returned with mold growing on their rotting skin, yet you all appear to be completely unharmed."

"We are not that strong; no creature of the Goddess is," said Abdaas. "Rather, surviving the Decay is a matter of observing a creature not of the Goddess' creation that lives in it." He reached deep into his robes and those near him could hear a slight rustling and clinking noise, like pieces of metal knocking against each other, as his hand fumbled about in some inner pocket. Finally he found what he was looking for and pulled out his hand, revealing a glass vial filled with a yellowish liquid some scholars would call formaldehyde. Sitting on the bottom inside was a black, severed eye with a red tendril coming out the back. The eye had nine irises, each one separated by blackness. Even as they were, the rings enticed one to look deeper and deeper in. Abdaas put the eye away before anyone could do so.

"That was a demon eye!" said Vikenti. "What purpose does it serve?"

"If a creature of the Goddess carries a demon relic near them, the effects of the Decay are completely nullified," said Abdaas. "But it must be a first-class relic, like this eyeball. Alkin carries a small bone on his person and the other four have their own, I believe some quills. These relics all came from the same demon; Alkin had killed it single-handedly when it had attempted to enter the city."

"It was the hardest enemy I've ever fought, bar none," said Alkin. "Though I must admit I almost regret it, if the doctrine concerning demon souls is true, Father."

"Demons deserve the loss of their souls at the jaws of the Goddess," said Abdaas. "Perhaps their complete destruction will allow Her to make something much better out of their essence. It is the least that can be done for those abominations."

Vikenti stroked his beard as he heard this atypical dogma. "Truly fascinating," he said. "The head priest here in Tantallos, Father Maxim, suggests that demons have no souls to begin with as they were not made by the Goddess. I'm sure he would love the opportunity to discuss the differences between what you both teach."

"I'm afraid that will have to wait for the next time I am in your city," said Abdaas. "For now I am simply here to construct a solid alliance between your city and ours. Then perhaps we can discuss setting up a stream of emissaries so we can best share the knowledge our cities have. But only with your approval, of course, and not a moment sooner. We would hate to encroach."

"You would never," said Vikenti, "not after everything you've done. My advisers and I would certainly be honored to form an alliance with Tulroy and its people, but I would prefer to first visit your city so I can see it myself. My daughter and advisers could handle the few issues that would need to be addressed while I am gone. But all of that is a discussion for tomorrow; for tonight I insist you let me provide you with suitable accommodations for the night. Your trip through the Decay could not have been pleasant." Six servants sprung out of doors and stairwells and approached the travelers. The four servants targeting the knights worked slowly toward them, an anxiety building inside. Alkin nodded at his servant and let her lead him off to his room, and the four knights followed suit with their servants.

Abdaas, however, refused his servant and instead walked up to Vikenti as he got off his throne. "I do beg your pardon, your highness," he said, "but my lord the king requested something for me to ask the ruler, and he said it was best if not in Prince Alkin's presence. It closely concerns him, but I fear he would object if he learned of what I was about to suggest."

Vikenti looked slightly puzzled. "What do you mean?" he asked.

Abdaas thought about proper word choices for a moment. "My king asked, if the structure turned out to be inhabited and if the ruler had an unmarried daughter of the proper age, that our kingdoms should form the greatest bond of all. Prince Alkin is not married himself, and his majesty the king wished for him to be married to the daughter of this other king for his son's sake. To do so would also pull our kingdoms even closer together and cement a greater future for all. But if you would rather not I fully understand, and my king will as well. He understands the attachment a father has to his children. He has no wife, and from her absence do forgive me from assuming that is the same with you."

Vikenti took all this in and ran it through his mind a couple times. "Prince Alkin has proven himself to be a hero, yes, a hero whose actions were possibly even greater than those that placed me on the throne," he said. "But I still do not know him or his father and kingdom very well, and I certainly would not want to force my daughter into marriage, no matter how beneficial it would be. Arranged marriage has not been practiced in Tantallos since my father's childhood days, and such an act could destroy my Daina." He sighed. "I shall go to her and ask her myself concerning this. If she is willing to wed Prince Alkin, then I shall agree. If not, then I hope our cities can form a strong bond without a royal matrimony."

Abdaas smiled warmly and bowed slightly. "Thank you for your consideration, your highness," said Abdaas. "I shall explain the situation to Alkin as well, but I will make sure to remind him that nothing is yet set in stone. I hope to hear the news from you in the morning." With this, he turned back to his servant and approached her. The servant stepped up and Abdaas let her lead him to his guest quarters. Moments later he found himself in the same hallway as where the other guests would stay, and one more room belonging to the princess.

CHAPTER 6

*I dreamed of you both, man and woman, different but similar still. Enjoy
each other, adore each other and bear fruit. Nothing makes me happier than
to see your love.*
-From the Teachings of the Goddess.

Vikenti quietly walked down the hall, careful not to disturb the rooms of
his guests as he made his way to Daina's quarters. One of the knights left his
room and made his own way to Abdaas' room, moving as quietly as he could,
given the amount of armor he was wearing. Vikenti paid him no mind as he
stopped by Daina's room. He knocked and then entered, finding her sitting on
her bed. She toyed around with her sheathed dagger, tossing it back and forth
between her hands before looking up and noticing her father. She was
wearing one of the nightgowns she often wore to bed; this one was slightly
shorter and stopped about half a foot above her feet.

"It's been quite an exciting night for this kingdom, you especially," he
said, approaching his daughter. "You do you feel?"

"I feel fine, Daddy," she said. "Alkin caught me not a moment too soon;
I didn't even get a scratch. I can't believe he lifted up a whole cart full of
clothes just to catch me in it! Do you think I'll get a chance to talk to him
tomorrow?"

"I'm certain you will," he said. "I imagine he'll be here for some time.
Though, there's something I have to talk to you about. It concerns him." He
moved around Daina and sat down on the bed next to her.

"Is he married?" she blurted, afraid to hear the answer.

"Oh, no, not at all," Vikenti assured her. Daina felt a part of her relax.
"But the high priest of Tulroy, Father Abdaas, informed me that his father
was looking to arrange a marriage between him and the daughter of the other
city's king. You."

"What?" asked Daina. She felt the oddest of sensations come over her;
she did not know what to make of it. She had never felt it concerning a man.

"I cannot deny that such a partnership would be of massive benefit to
both our cities and would greatly unite us," said Vikenti. "But, I am still
going to give you a choice. If you were to marry him you would most likely
be taken back to Tulroy to rule at Alkin's side, until death do you part. I

cannot say how long it would be until you had a chance to come back and visit Tantallos, if you ever got such an opportunity. And in my age I don't know if I could endure a trip through the Decay to visit you."

The king looked at his daughter and saw a colliding mess of emotions in her eyes. "I would be delighted to marry him," she said. "I do admit that I do not know him very well, but there's something about him. I can't explain it; I've never really felt it before. I almost feel like he's above me, like I don't deserve him at all. I don't know how to say it. I just know he's good, unlike all those other noblemen. How did you feel when you met mother for the first time?"

"I felt much the same way that you do right now," said Vikenti, putting an arm around Daina's shoulders. "And even then I knew I was in love with her. The day I married her was the happiest day of my life."

They embraced each other. "Thank you, daddy," she said. "For everything. This has been the best day of my life. And don't worry; I'll find time to come and visit you."

They broke their hold and let go of each other. "It's good to know that you have no reservations about it," he said. "I'd recommend you make preparations for a trip tomorrow; pack up whatever keepsakes and mementos you wish to take with you. I do not know how long Alkin and the others plan to stay here in Tantallos, so I'll make sure a detail of armed guards and servants are ready at a moment's notice to accompany both of us to Tulroy. I'll make sure to be thorough, but do be warned. The Decay is not a place you want to stay in for any amount of time, especially since you've never been out in it before."

"I can agree," said Daina, pointing to her window. "That's the closest I've ever been to the Decay. But with Alkin, those four knights, the finest of Tantallos' guards and my father I won't have a thing to worry about. The monsters won't even dare touch me."

Vikenti got up from the bed, gently touched Daina's head and gave her a kiss on the forehead before he let go and walked to the door. "Good night, Daina," he said. "Rest up for tomorrow. I can't believe how fast you have grown up." He walked out and quietly shut the door behind him, leaving Daina to ponder what was to come.

Alkin left his room and silently shut the door behind him. Glancing down both ends of the hall, he made sure no one was around before heading to the door that led onto the wall walkway. Within moments he was walking along the edge of the wall, turning around before he wandered too far away from the castle. All too possible he would get lost, especially with such a cyclopean, sprawling city like Tantallos. The little he managed to see in the light of the moon alone intimidated him; he could not even fathom how massive it looked during the day. He then looked to the moon. What an incredible sight it was. Very little of Tulroy extended outside of the plateau; mostly just the vineyards embedded into the sides hundreds of feet above the Decay. The sky was almost always filled with clouds, covering up and hiding the lights in the sky no matter what time it was. Between the poor sunlight and infertile soil, it was always a constant struggle to grow plants. But Tantallos had skies clear enough to let the sun and moon shine down on the city, surely enough to support many different crops. The bountiful plant life he saw hanging in windows or in front of houses was a shock after growing up with nothing but tough vines frequently dotted with bird nests. The people of Tantallos must have a far greater diet than that of Tulroy's citizens.

Alkin stared at the landscape before him and felt a slight smile coming to his face. This island, this oasis... this lost garden, had managed to bring back a child-like sense of wonder he had not felt in such a long time. He jumped suddenly when he heard footsteps coming from nearby, his ears perking up on impulse. He turned around to see the girl, the princess, from earlier approaching him, shifting a sheathed bronze dagger in between her fingertips. She wore a very basic garb and cloth slippers but did not appear to be very cold; perhaps she was used to the chilly weather. She shoved the sheathed blade into a strap on her thigh before walking up to him.

"Oh, hello," she said, trying not to blush. Alkin could not remember how many times he had seen this happen. "I'm sorry. I didn't know you were here. Not that I wouldn't have come if I had known you were here. That is..." She cut herself off and seemed to stress herself out rethinking her words. "I just walk out on the walls when I can't sleep and need to think over things. Don't let me bother you."

"Not a chance, milady," said Alkin. He turned his body around so he was not craning his neck at her. He smiled warmly and relaxed his muscles, doing all he could to look casual and welcoming. "Father Abdaas had told me about these possible wedding plans. Effective almost immediately, he said."

Daina felt herself calm down as she saw Alkin behave so informally. "What do you think about them?" she asked.

"I honestly don't know," he said, looking away to the city. Daina felt something inside of her start to ache preemptively. "It is nothing against you, Daina; you're not to blame for my feelings in the slightest. You're a beautiful young woman and any man should strive to have your love. But, there are many other things that factor into this."

"What sort of things?" asked Daina, afraid to hear his answer. "I hate to pry, it's just, I don't know, I feel I ought to know. Do you have a love back home?" *There is no way he could not, right?* She thought to herself._*A man like him.*

"No," said Alkin, looking back at her. Daina felt a little relieved but kept it hidden. "I do not have someone back home. But this is one thing I am not sure about in the slightest, and it is one thing I cannot possibly make a mistake about. I'm uncertain about so much of it. For example, I'm five years your senior from what I've gathered. It may be very common in Tulroy, and I assume in Tantallos as well, for the man to be older than the woman, but I'm not comfortable at all with such a difference. No matter that my parents were similar to our ages when they were engaged to each other. Imagine if we were both, say, five years younger, how awkward it would make things for us."

"But I have a much bigger reason than just that, and I've been questioned about it so much. I have no experience with this sort of thing at all. Imagine; I, the mighty Alkin, have killed creatures blades do not harm and have performed other deeds people told me were impossible. But not once have I bedded a woman, even as the other noblemen around me played with their harems."

He turned his head away. "I have never met a woman who has captured my interest, made me feel a sense of longing, though many have certainly tried to make me feel this way. Don't feel jealous as they never made any progress with me, but Goddess knows every damsel I've had the pleasure of saving has tried to wed me, from a harlot I kept from being mugged to a noblewoman who nearly got carried off by some deformed-looking flying monster. These proposals have come from girls even younger than you to women so old they could be my mother." He sighed. "I'm sure you've heard enough of the women chasing after me. I apologize."

Daina worked up the nerve to move a bit closer to him. "Don't be afraid," she said. Alkin turned back around to look into her eyes. "You are not alone in your inexperience. I've never been with a man. I've had my share of admirers as well similar to you, but none of the nobles who have vied for my affection have appealed to me." She chose not to mention why they did not appeal to her. "It's almost as if I've been waiting for someone special, someone who helps me be my best, and you're definitely that person. I know you're too good for me, but I feel like..." She stopped. She could not think of the correct words to say; she simply hoped Alkin understood what she meant. In retrospect the lines came off as sappy to her, but what other reason could there be for why she had not settled for one of the Tantallos nobles all those years ago? Not all of them were so promiscuous like the ones she tended to obsessively torture herself over.

"Thank you," said Alkin, managing to smile again. "That does make me feel a lot better about all this. Perhaps we can get along together." Daina got closer to him, longing for him to do something no man had ever done to her. She closed her eyes as she came right up against him, but then opened her eyes when she felt a pressure around her body instead of on her face. She found herself in Alkin's warm grip, him embracing her gently.

He moved his head to the side of hers and spoke softly in her ear. "I'm not comfortable with kissing you, Daina. Not yet. Perhaps once I get to know you better, but for now I'd rather stay like this. It would be unfair to you for me to play with your emotions. I really hope I'm not breaking your heart right now. I'll gladly marry you and do what I can to make you happy, but please be patient with me."

"It's fine," said Daina, hiding the intense disappointment in her voice. They broke off their embrace and found themselves awkwardly looking away from each other before making their way back to the castle. They quickly slipped in one after the other and shut the door behind them. Once inside, they bid each other a good night and walked their separate ways. Alkin went back to his room and immediately fell into a deep sleep before he even got underneath the bedsheets; it had been a very long and very busy day.

CHAPTER 7

Everything was created by Me, thus so shall everything come back to Me.
When you find yourself before Me, can you honestly say you've lived the way
you should?
-From the Teachings of the Goddess.

Daina paced around her room. An hour had passed since she had walked back after her talk with Alkin and had attempted to sleep. However, even as she pulled herself into bed she could not possibly find slumber. She ended up tossing and turning endlessly, unable to keep her eyes shut. After her conversation with Alkin, she was far too excited to even fathom sleep. She was rather disappointed, yes, but still more excited than anything else. She eventually gave up even thinking about sleep and slipped on a pair of sandals. They were held fast to her feet by a series of straps and bands that went up almost to her knees; she always felt odd wearing them but they did not hinder her too much when she was running. Better than a sharp rock stuck in the ball of one's foot.

As she walked randomly about the castle, careful to keep quiet so as to not disturb any of the sleeping servants and guards, she found herself wondering what it was about Alkin that had her so infatuated with him. Was it just his unparalleled appearance, or was there something else to him? She usually went with her gut on these matters, but that resulted in nothing but a conflicted feeling brewing inside her. Even her stomach was busy mulling this over, unable to find a satisfactory answer. Whatever the answer turned out to be, at least she would not have to lose her virginity to a complete whore of a noble. That was one weight off her mind. Alkin would not lie to her, after all... or so she hoped. She did not know him very well, after all.

Some time later she finished her walk, ending up back in the hallway that led to her room. Yet even as she stood before her door she could not even consider sleep. She looked around and saw a sliver of light coming out from behind one of the doors. She thought hard about whose room that was; Abdaas' room, she supposed. Curiosity took hold of her and her feet started moving ahead, quickly taking her to the door. All of Tantallos would be asleep by this point, and priests of the Goddess usually went to bed earlier than the laypeople. So why was Abdaas not sleeping as well?

She slowly approached the door, careful to make as little noise as possible with her sandals still on. Every time her feet slightly clicked against the stone her heart leaped into her throat, but each time she did not get caught. She felt her side and confirmed that her dagger was still there; why she felt the need to feel it, she could not say. In moments she was right up against the edge of the door, slightly holding onto it by the handle to steady herself as she listened in on a hushed conversation. It was between Abdaas and at least one other person. If there were other people, they had not spoken up yet.

"...so be very careful. We don't want to botch this," said Abdaas.

"Calm down, Abdaas," growled a low and powerful voice. It was rough and gravelly, like one of the nobles who grew his own plants for smoking in pipes-- Daina had never seen the appeal. "Your plan is going as well as it possibly could, all things considered."

Daina peeked around the corner and saw the source of this voice; the red knight, the bottom part of his helmet down but his mouth still obscured. The three gray knights were also in the room, standing slightly behind the red knight as they all faced a seated Abdaas. "Our *Prince Perfect* already ensured a strong friendship between the two nations by saving that clumsy princess. It's to the point where he, you, and four royal enemies are inside their castle. We could walk right down that hall and go into her room."

"Yes, but that is no reason to not exercise caution at all times," said Abdaas. "We won't get another chance at this and you're all one request to remove your helmet away from being identified. You don't want your souls to be consumed by the Goddess, do you?" The knights nodded. "Now, collecting the bones should not be too hard as long as none of you attract too much attention while in the catacombs. Once you've collected them, I'll need you to collect the king's flesh and the princess' blood, but preferably..."

Daina, leaning in as she grew hooked on every word, accidentally put too much weight on the door, making it move slightly and causing it to creak. Abdaas jumped and the four knights immediately turned and faced the door. Daina's eyes locked with five other pairs, though she could only directly see one. "It's the princess!" said Abdaas, pointing at her while staring at the knights. "Seize her before she can alert the guards!"

Daina took off faster than a fired bolt before the knights could reach her. The knights quickly followed behind her as she made her way down the hall, hoping desperately to come across a servant who had not fallen asleep. She tried to keep herself under control but between her current peril and everything she had just heard she could not keep her thoughts straight.

They want to kill her, and her father, too? Why? Why do they want their blood and flesh or whatever body parts they were talking about? She had to get to her father and warn him before they leave with him and kill him. Why would these travelers do such a thing to him? And could Alkin be a part of this heinous plan as well?

No. That was one thought she simply could not comprehend. He could not be a part of such a conspiracy to commit regicide. He would never do such a thing; she knew this. She just knew it. He must not be aware of this horrible plan. There was no way he could agree to let something so terrible happen. He was a prince. He would stop it if he knew. He could easily stop them all.

She ran down the hall, which seemed so much longer than it ever had to her as the seconds seemed to last eons. She continued her dash for the main staircase, sacrificing her stamina to get every bit of speed she could, when one of the knights seemed to almost materialize in front of her. She could not possibly tell which one it was in the dim moonlight, but it was definitely not the red one. She let out a slight shriek between breaths and turned around, barely dodging the attempted grabs of the other knights as she darted past a glowering Abdaas who also reached for her. She forced herself to think as her situation grew more and more dire. She could beat her father in games of strategy. She had to have something, and quick; she could only run so long if she kept up this speed, and so long would not be long enough.

But they could only run for so long as well. And those massive full-body suits of armor had to weigh a lot, possibly even more than her, to say nothing of how they hindered their movement. That was how she would escape them. She continued dashing down the hall, saving energy by not looking at her chasers. She reached the door and yanked it open, not even waiting for it to fully swing out of the way before charging out onto the wall. She thanked herself for wearing her sandals, lest her feet be cut to ribbons by the sharper stones on the walkway. Such wounds could easily make her falter and endure a horrible fate following closely behind her.

A good, long run on the walls would do it. She had run on this wall so many times before, so often she knew every staircase connecting to it, every guard house, even every noble family's house that happened to be within throwing distance. She would rely on her endurance to last until they tired out, then she would get off the wall immediately and disappear into the labyrinth of houses, never to be seen by them again. She would find the home of a guard, or preferably a noble and hide with them until morning. They would not dare break into the house of a noble family and slaughter everyone inside just to get at her. Right?

She broke her focus from the track ahead to give the slightest of glances behind her. She saw them emerging out of the castle and she kept up her pace. She continued her frantic sprint down the walkway, still strong and keeping her breath. She smiled a little on the inside; she had to be safe now. She could only imagine how the heavily-armored knights were doing. She risked another glance over her shoulder. They were keeping up with her. Her eyes grew to the size of dinner plates and she forced her head forward again, telling herself that it was just her imagination. But it was not some delusion; they were not far behind her. How could this be possible? How could they possibly manage to do this? No one could manage to run as fast and as long as her with all that armor on. No one could. At least, no human could.

Out of the corner of her eye she saw one of the knights moving to the side of the wall before leaping off of it and onto a tall building nearby, slamming into the stones but not breaking through. The wall knight jumped from building to building, its unimaginable bounds allowing it to catch up with Daina as it left massive depressions and cracks in the structures it used as platforms. It somehow found grips on every surface it landed on and in moments it paced itself right alongside its prey. Daina stared in complete shock. And then she heard a slight hum as the three knights behind her sprouted wings. She could not tell, but one gray knights' wings looked gnarled and twisted, reaching away from its body and sprouting downward protrusions like the branches of a tree. The other gray knight generated wings that were basic and simple in design, especially in comparison to the other gray knight's; they were simply a series of straight lines with no curves or bends.

But the most impressive wings were the red knight's, which were absolutely colossal in comparison. They dwarfed the other relatively diminutive wings, each one a foot or so longer than the knight was tall. They were rough and jagged in shape, nothing but points and crude curves forced together into a shape similar to the other knights' wings. They struck Daina as if a child had broken a piece of red glass artwork and had poorly attempted to glue it back together. The wings looked so sharp a part of her wondered if they were capable of cutting flesh. These were wings of pure energy bound into a corporeal form, a sort of feat only one creature could possibly manage. A demon.

She sacrificed precious breath to let out a scream as loud as she could, all while the demons flew around her and cut off her escape. The jumping demon, which had not generated any wings and unbeknownst to Daina was incapable of doing so, leaped off a building and landed at Daina's side. She turned to face him and then found massive, towering gray figures to her front and sides. She backed up while she reached for the only possible lifesaver strapped to her thigh, but then backed into something cold and hard.

She turned around and slowly looked up at the gigantic red demon moments before he delivered a powerful backhand across her face. She fell to the ground, pain coursing through her whole body as she struggled to focus on anything. Her vision grew blurry and she could not even prop herself up while her head reeled from the powerful blow. It had been as hard as a rock;

the part of her that could focus was amazed her skull had not been obliterated from the impact. Not even so much as a broken tooth. This demon had great control over his power. The demon knelt down and carefully wrapped his cold, metallic fingers around her throat. He slowly lifted her up into the air, Daina unable to even attempt to resist as the other demons got closer to her. They moved in laxly; they knew she was helpless. She could do nothing but gag and gasp for breath as the red demon held her, the claws at the end of his plated digits coming dangerously close to cutting the skin of her neck. Her vision finally cleared enough for her to try to stare at her captor but she could see nothing through the grating of his visor.

"Amazing," he said. "I'd have thought that blow would have knocked you out like most humans. But that's unimportant. Your little spying on our conversation was really a blessing in disguise for us; you fail to hinder our plans in the slightest and we have you exactly where we want you. I think we could work with this, don't you three think?" He said the final sentence aggressively, turning his head to look at the three smaller gray demons. They quickly nodded in approval. Even if they disagreed they knew better than to say otherwise. "Don't just stand there. I can hardly collect her blood while I'm holding her up. Whichever one of you has the cleanest claws; Abdaas would have a tantrum if we tainted it."

The three demons moved in, all of them approaching from the side opposite the red demon to maintain their distance. Daina started shaking as one of the demons brought her hand out away from her body while a third demon readied a vial with a glass stopper. The stopper was connected with a metal hinge that worked in such a way as to keep the stopper in unless a part of the hinge was pushed. The fourth demon grabbed her other limbs to control what little energy she could muster to fight back. She could not possibly escape the vice-like grips of her captors, not without her skin getting pulled off from the friction. The demon with the vial raised one of its massive gauntlets and Daina caught a glimpse of its claws, barely noticeable against the rest of its full armor. However, one look was all it took to ensure that one always noticed and recognized them as demon claws. They connected with the digits of the gauntlets perfectly, even seeming to bend with the digits. They were about an inch wide and extended six inches outward, curving very slightly. They also looked to only be edged on the palm side, which was why the red demon had not lacerated her face when he had backhanded her.

The claw met the arm at the wrist, connecting cleanly into the skin. There were also four lines of plating that extended halfway down the forearm, shortest on the inside and longest on the outside and only a couple inches across each; the pieces located between the two on either side were halfway in length between the smallest and longest. These parts were ridged heavily, perfect for blocking a slicing sword. The main claw itself was several sizes too large for the human hand that would have best been fit onto the demon's arm, yet the demons seemed to be able to move their claws expertly, not like a cumbersome person.

The demon extended his index digit carefully; although it was articulate in its movements it was still clumsy in comparison to the dexterity of a human hand. It slowly and lightly brought the tip of the claw along Daina's arm, moving down some and tearing open the flesh with ease. She let out a groan in pain, her teeth bared tightly, as the demon squeezed her arm to force more blood out of her body and into the vial he held closely against her skin. Daina kept herself from jerking around wildly, but the armor-like plating that made up the claws still roughened her bare flesh, leaving it sore and red.

Fortunately she only had to endure this for a moment, and after a few painful seconds the vial was full. The gray demons collectively let go of Daina and backed away from her, the red demon still holding her tightly. The demon that had bled her latched the bottle shut and handed it to the red demon who released his grip on Daina and let her fall onto the ground. Daina sputtered for breath as the demon that had cut her unlatched the bottom part of his helmet and brought the claw that had cut her inside. She heard a sucking noise as the demon contemplated her flavor, followed by a moan of approval.

"Now that is a delicious human," said the demon. Its voice was nasally and bothersome to listen to. Daina wished she had the strength to cover her ears. "After what seems like eons of eating nothing but mire beasts and other half-rotten creatures, that's amazing. Not even the humans I've eaten were that good."

"You do look like a meal fit for a king, princess,"said the red demon. He chuckled loudly a few seconds after saying this. "Fit for a king. I make myself laugh sometimes." Daina began hearing a loud panting coming from both the red demon and the tasting demon. The other two demons backed away as they approached her.

They started unscrewing the bottom covers on their helmets, which fell down to reveal their jaws. The demon that had tasted her blood had a horrible set of grotesque fangs, seemingly random in their placement; Daina could not help but think of a dog's mouth as she stared at them. The red demon's teeth were almost strikingly human, but impossibly white, as if not a speck of food had ever graced them. That could not possibly be the case. Daina's screams were caught in her throat as she tried to figure out which set of jaws was about to tear into her.

"She's mine, Jurek," said the tasting demon. "I drew first blood on her. I earned her."

"And I'm the one who maimed her with one backhand," said Jurek. "Do yourself a favor; stay quiet and back away." As he said this he shifted his wings slightly upward, making himself look even bigger. The tasting demon did likewise. "You wouldn't dare try to steal my favorite prey right from my claws. She's right in the age group I like to eat, and if she was on the other end of the human class system she'd be in the same occupation as my victims. You preyed on children; such hunts prove nothing of what you've earned."

"How about this, then?" growled the one who had tasted her, holding up the claw he had licked. "You wouldn't dare to try taking the prey from one who has already tasted its blood. I feel the itch growing, and I won't be able to hold myself back. Take her from me and I'll kill and eat you instead."

"At least your vice isn't constantly working against you," growled Jurek. "My lust for human flesh is growing twice as fast as yours. I've barely been keeping it under control since the moment we arrived in my old city. The human scent is driving me crazy; so much fresh meat, so defenseless, and I can't grab any of it. Give me the human now or I'll go berserk, eat her and then eat you for standing in my way. And I'll still be hungry."

Daina took this moment to slowly try pulling herself along the stone between the bickering demons. She could not possibly get back up and run, but she might be able to pull herself down a nearby staircase. With any luck she'd roll and make enough noise to attract people, or break her head open and save her the pain of dying by the claws of a demon.

"Stop it, both of you," hissed the third demon with wings who had stood motionless and quiet until now. The wingless demon remained silent. "Jurek, you know these streets better than any of us, especially the ones in the worst sections of the city. You've spent more than enough time at this banquet. We came from different clusters of humans, all of which have succumbed to the Decay and rotted to nothing but stone buildings. You could easily find yourself a replacement snack in the slums."

"What was that from the weakling?" scoffed Jurek. "You think you deserve this, Wesan?" He looked down and saw what Daina had been doing; she had only managed to travel a few feet. He grabbed Daina by the foot and roughly pulled her back. He once again grabbed her around the neck and raised her up into the air. Daina did not even bother with struggling. After all, they would just catch her again and hurt her some more. "...Or maybe your worthless cousin." He looked to the wingless demon. "What about it, Tulsan? Able to form a single sentence to say if you deserve her or not?"

"You don't deserve it and we don't deserve it," said Wesan. "But he does. He's the one who extracted the blood from her perfectly, and if it hadn't been for him you'd be doing this all on your own. I doubt you could perform this task so expertly by yourself."

Jurek spent a few quick seconds contemplating this before scowling.

"Fine," he said. He threw Daina to the ground in the tasting demon's direction. The demon immediately grabbed her and threw her over his shoulder. Daina bumped against his wings, which were hard and burning to the touch. She struggled to keep herself from hitting them and searing her flesh. "Take her out into the Decay and do whatever you wish with her. You seem to enjoy your torture. Take as long as you need, too. We have all we need from her." He stopped and then thought of something else. "Make sure you're far away. A search through the Decay for our little princess will keep this city more than occupied while we collect the other ingredients."

"That is so kind of you, Jurek," said the demon. "You really are too generous. And I bet none of your backing down has to do with me being *dal Afxanos*."

"Being *dal Afxanos* in this landscape is like being *dal Richtos* in a desert," said Jurek. "Now get going or I might decide to follow you and eat you anyway."

The tasting demon growled as one of the other demons, Wesan, stifled a snicker. Daina wriggled some as she continued to try to keep herself from touching the wings. She almost felt relieved when the tasting demon pulled her off his shoulders and adjusted his grip so she was held in front of him, her arms pinned at her sides, still unable to reach her dagger. Daina was kept still for just a moment before the demon readjusted his arms. One arm wrapped around her wrists so tightly she feared her bones would crack; the other arm went around her neck, so tight the demon only had to flex to choke her. This done, the demon walked over to the edge of the wall.

He started to flap his wings. It only took a few flaps before Daina felt a wave of energy blast off them. The wings suddenly became brighter, a clear beacon against the dark night sky. The energy seemed to push downward, lifting the heavy demon and his prize off the walkway. Daina's fear became overwhelmed by her amazement as the demon moved away from the city. Then he took a slight dive and disappeared into the fog.

Over a hundred feet away the demon emerged from the fog, flying horizontally, holding Daina's torso in a similar position as well but letting her legs dangle. Daina finally managed to force a scream out of her mouth after all that happened, but it was far too late. She was already too far from the city for any of her subjects to hear her. The one scream she did manage was cut off when the demon's lock around her neck tightened.

"Silence, your highness," he hissed. "Your light hair alone is attracting the attention of many different sorts of monsters. You don't need to alert even more of them. Most of them would not be half as nice to you as I." Daina tried to respond despite the asphyxiating grip but only managed to produce a gurgling, gagging noise.

"I can only imagine what you tried to say there," he said, "but don't worry, little girl. I'll make sure to drag out your death so I can hear those lovely screams of yours all night long. Just that one was music to my ears, and I can't wait to hear the next several dozen. But that's all fun for later tonight. For now I just want to get you back to my lair in the Decay. The competition for a delicious human like you is fierce, and I'd rather not deal with some group of mire beasts." The flight into the Decay continued, every monster underneath them turning and facing them as they flew overhead. Daina still struggled in the demon's grip. She was going to die, she had come to terms with that. But the least she could do was deny this demon the satisfaction of his meal. She would rather fall down into the waiting jaws of a mire beast and satisfy that mindless creature instead.

It only required the right wriggle, the slightest of squirms that slipped her out of the cold, metallic grip of the demon and sent her plummeting into the sea of fog. Even though it was breathtakingly cold, she still felt sweat coming down her face. She tried to use it to make herself more slippery, but in the end, it was all for naught. Even as she struggled she felt her strength wane and finally die off. The demon had attempted to grip her in such a way so to not harm her unless he wished to do so, but his massive claws were too sharp and clumsy to not inflict pain on her. Her struggling further exacerbated this, tearing herself open on the claws and ripping her skin on the ridges that extended further up the forearm.

The demon worked hard to keep himself from throwing Daina to the ground. The smell of the blood from her wounds continuously crazed him, making him salivate even more madly. It took all of his self control to keep from tearing her to pieces right then and there to feast on her. Even as he fought against these desires some of Daina's blood dripped down into the sea of fog and started rousing a few of the more tenacious predators. Finally, Daina went lax in his grip, exhausted. All she could do was stare as they went further into the Decay, Tantallos getting smaller and smaller behind her as one of the mountains loomed large ahead. The speed at which they traveled amazed Daina; demon wings may be incredibly obvious sights in the night sky, but they were fast and surprisingly silent save for the slight humming. They made for a presence more felt than heard.

Of course. She saw how well the nature of the wings fit them with how quiet they were. It made them all the better at killing helpless humans in the city as they slept. She could imagine the other three demons right at this moment, making their way through the streets of Tantallos, looking for some poor harlot or other unsuspecting, unknown commoner, tricking them into coming to a secluded location and then brutally murdering them before eating them down to the bone. Then breaking the bone to get at the marrow, and then shaving the bone to make picks for their teeth...

She stopped herself there. It did not help her in the slightest, and she did not even want to think about what they planned to do to her father.

As her strength finally left her she felt nothing of substance grow in its place. Instead an intense sadness bubbled up to the surface. She was dead, doomed to be nothing more than a meal for a demon and then discarded like a human would do with chicken bones. Then this demon would rejoin the other three and do the same to her father, but not before collecting his flesh for some horrid purpose, all while being ordered about by that red colossus of a demon, Jurek, himself a pawn of Abdaas' will.

A part of her clicked as she thought this over. Red. A demon who knows his way around the poverty-ridden areas of Tantallos, relishes the consumption of girls similar to her in age and wears nothing but red. Red. The Red Light Murderer. She thought of nothing more than the irony of such a happening. It was almost poetic that the last demon thrown out of the city would return with the purpose of causing its downfall by the destruction of its leadership.

Daina gave up trying to escape the grip of the demon, a horrid creature but not the most dreadful she had ever met. Adrenaline still coursed through every vein of her body, but she remained calm as she consigned herself to her fate. She still had her dagger, after all; maybe it was good that she had been unable to get to it before being attacked. Perhaps she would get a chance to shove it down the throat of her killer before he tore off her hand with one bite.

CHAPTER 8

Size means nothing if it slows you down. The smallest hunter can easily dodge the strikes of the biggest.
-From the Tomes of the Huntmaster.

Countless creatures moved about in the fog below Daina and her captor. The Decay housed far more predators than just mire beasts. All sorts of vicious monsters roamed through the dead land under the cover of the moonless night, and every single one had been drawn to the glowing red beacon, visible even through the fog. One such monster walked a far distance ahead of the two, making its way through the soup-like fog, relying on its hearing and smell to sense predators and prey alike. Both worked expertly in this regard, but they were not necessary.

Only the most foolish of predators would even try attacking it. It was the apex predator of the Decay, a creature unmatched by anything roaming the landscape along with it. It could even hold its own against the demons, though more often than not it would rather the situation not come to that. And there was one demon it definitely did not want to encounter. The monster did not usually leave its lair during the night; it did not like night hunting at all, primarily because of the fog that robbed it of its sight and made it feel damp and moist. It disliked the activity, but it was better than pacing back and forth in its lair.

Ever since the four demons had passed by, including the one it feared above all else, it had been unable to fall asleep. It walked as lightly and as quickly as it could through the mud, the hooked claws on the inside of its feet clicking against the occasional stone or brick; the monster figured there had been a road through the Decay at some point, but it had never seen the path as such.

As the monster continued its walk back home, looking for a more open spot where it had plenty of room, it came across a few creatures it could identify in the sea of fog. However, it found nothing worth killing and taking back to its lair. Too gamey, too fat. Too covered in spines more bristly than its own, too dead and rotting away, something it could not stand trying to eat. Too close to the foul, scum-filled water that made shivers crawl up its spine. Sadly, these awful specimens seemed to be the best the nighttime world of the Decay could offer. What a productive night it had been so far, all because it could not fall asleep. Then the wind changed and a scent blew from behind the monster, a scent that made it stop and ponder the aroma. It was just a slight whiff but it was the sweetest of aromas it had ever inhaled during its life in this wasteland. It was the scent of blood, nothing new to that, but it was the blood of something truly remarkable. It saw other creatures nearby stirring at the smell; it was not the only thing being roused by the scent. It saw even more animals rise and look toward the source behind it.

The monster turned around and saw the slight red glimmer just piercing the sea of fog from above. Only one thought came to mind of what the glimmer was. It quickly moved over to a tall dead tree nearby and jumped up onto it, pulling itself up to the top within seconds and getting its head up high enough so it could see past a thin layer of fog. The monster's eyes cut through the night like it was day, allowing it to easily examine the creature flying toward it. The sight confirmed the creature's suspicions; the glimmer came from a demon. It was covered in plates of armor, but what caught the monster's attention was what the demon was holding. The demon held a female human, most likely an adult of similar age biologically to the monster. Nothing too spectacular about the demon's catch though human rarely got eaten out in the Decay.

Then the monster found its eyes drawn to the human's hair. Her wavy locks were a far brighter shade than most humans' hair, and they caught the little light present and illuminated her head, almost like a beacon. The monster's eyes widened as it took in this new development and turned to look at the oblivious demon as it soared overhead, making its way to the mountains. It descended from the tree and took off after them, looking around in the hopes of finding a more open area. It knew this demon; it had been its closest neighbor and it had tried too many times to take over the monster's territory. It was a tough opponent as well, the second strongest it had ever fought. But now was the moment where the monster ended the feud that had formed between them once and for all, and the moment where it claimed the greatest prize it had ever sought.

Even with her new nonchalant attitude, Daina could not help but gulp as the demon left the boggy valleys of the Decay. Now it soared over the mountains she had only seen from a distance. Although infinitely less wet than the flat lands below, the mountains were also blanketed in dead trees and other lifeless plants. She looked at the range, which extended almost completely around Tantallos in a circle save for a small pathway between two of them. Many cave entrances were littered throughout the mountain the demon flew over, and nasty-looking multitudes of rocks filled in the spaces between mountains from avalanches long past. No human could walk between them safely.

But all these hardships were of no concern to the demon. He easily soared over the dead mountains, a feeling of anticipation growing inside him as he got closer and closer to his home. In moments he had cleared the side of the mountain and another valley emerged before him. It was not unlike the Tantallos valley for the most part, but there were far more ruined stone buildings and even villages dotted throughout, and off in the distance Daina saw a massive plateau stretching from one side of the horizon to the other. A part of her could guess at what it was-- Tulroy. No matter, though; Tulroy or not, her life would end out in the Decay.

The demon flew lower to the ground, aiming for a slightly elevated part that managed to emerge out of the dense fog. It appeared to be an exceptionally dense cluster of trees that were unusually tall for the Decay; many of them reached twenty feet tall and almost none of them appeared to be broken or fallen. In the center lay a noticeably taller tree stretching around forty feet up in the air, with some of its limbs contorted to make a small chamber near the top of the tree. Soon she was hovering over the small forest, and a part of her ached as she turned to face the mountain and found herself unable to see even the slightest bit of Tantallos. The demon had won. There was nothing left to do but wait to die.

The demon got further and further downward, adjusting himself so he was descending vertically. As he looked at the dead trees below him they seemed to move, their limbs bending and shifting as if stretching after waking up. He grinned as he moved over to an especially thick patch of trees in front of the big tree. He let go of Daina and let her fall. Taken by surprise, Daina could not help but let out a shriek as she fell, but that shriek of terror turned into one of surprise as the dead branches she landed on worked to twist themselves around her limbs. They wrapped themselves tightly around her wrists and ankles, nothing holding the rest of her body up from the muddy forest floor below. The demon landed in front of her, his claws facing toward the ground as they seemed to almost glow with a dim green aura.

"Being *dal Afxanos* is worthless in this wretched place, they kept telling me," said the demon. "Said it's even more useless here than it is back home, and you don't even know what that means."

"I can take a guess," said Daina, thinking of the trees.

"I'm not here to teach you about my culture," said the demon. "I plan to have some fun with you before I let my trees use your remains as fertilizer."

Daina managed to break her eyes away from the demon and glanced around, endeavoring to turn her head and stare at the forest. The trees all moved slightly, and here and there Daina noticed slight green sprouts on trees that moments ago had looked dead; kept alive by the demon, no doubt, their soil fertilized by the leftover pieces of his victims. Even as she looked the trees moved around rapidly, reaching downward like gnarled hands and grabbing anything trying to enter the forest. Many of the trees held only the skeletal remains of old animals while others contained prey that weakly struggled, doomed to be on the demon's menu once he was finished with her.

The monster finally located a suitable area. It was relatively flat and dry, but that was not the most important part. What mattered above all else was that it was clear, around fifteen paces in diameter. It was glad to have found this space; it could not possibly catch up with the demon unless it took to the air. It started flying and broke through the soup-like fog, sighing in relief as it left that damp valley. It did have the advantage of speed; it was faster and more agile than most demons, including the feared one. It used what little altitude it could gain so quickly to dive down, further increasing its speed. It made its way over the mountain, wondering just how much time it had until it was too late to save the human.

The human's hair, that lovely bright shade similar to that of gold. Many things had faded from the monster's memory in times past, but throughout all of it the human's hair had never been forgotten. It had seen the same hair flowing in the breeze as the human had run down the walls of her city almost every day, always stopping at the same point before going onward or turning back for her home. Every time it had been hunting by the city at that hour it had found itself watching the human, always making sure to stay hidden so she did not see it. Only the Huntmaster knew what she would think, what she would do, if she knew who her stalker... no; observer was. She would become just as fixated on appearances, but in a different way.

The monster pushed its guilt concerning its watching to the side. Time was running out for the poor human. The demon would be foolish enough to drag out the torment of his victim, but he did not have good control over his own strength. It was all too likely he might cause too much damage and she would be unable to recover. It had seen the way he treated his prey. The monster had been in such a situation itself, caught in the forest trap when it was younger. It had managed to escape, but the human's captor was no ordinary foe. He was an arch demon, especially powerful and terrifying. He was far stronger physically and could easily defeat it in a fight. If it had not been for its own wits, it would have died then. It had spent years taking steps to avoid the arch demon, but now it had no choice if it wanted to save the human from certain death.

The monster descended and landed near the forest, careful to stay out of the range of the grasping and reaching trees. It needed to clear a path through to safely fight the arch demon, but it could not do that the easiest way without possibly killing the human. It looked around for a few moments and spotted an adult female mire beast, about average in size for her kind, gnashing her saber teeth wildly as the scent of the human drove her insane. It was easily three or four tons in weight, likely more. The mire beast slowly approached the forest, apparently aware of its trap, but unaware of what was about to happen to her instead.

"And now a few more streaks up your arms," said the demon. His mouth visor was down, showing off his fang-filled grin as the demon relished the activity. He lightly dragged some of his claws up Daina's arms, cutting just deep enough to draw blood. Daina kept her teeth bared, doing everything in her power to keep herself from screaming. She could not keep herself from crying, but she hoped to deny the sick monster at least some satisfaction. "You're trying so hard not to scream," said the demon. "It's so adorable, the little spoiled princess trying to be at least a little strong before her death. Try all you want, little girl. I know how to get my screams." He thought for a little bit. "How about we damage that pretty face of yours?"

The demon reached forward with both claws, eight blades touching the flesh by her cheek bones. He pressed in, digging the blades in a bit more than on her limbs. He then dragged the claws down the side of her face as slowly as possible, his grin growing even more as she let out a cry in pain. The cry continued as he brought his claws all the way to the bone of her jaw before pulling them out of her flesh. It had not pierced the flesh into her mouth, but it was more than enough to reduce her to a sobbing wreck. The pain was so intense Daina barely noticed the rubbing sensation as part of a claw picked up some of the blood on her cheeks. The claw went up away from her face and the blood-covered blade moved to the demon's mouth, where he then licked it. "Even better than on the walls," said the demon in sick pleasure. "You humans only get tastier as your stress grows. Judging the difference, I'd say you're as good as you're going to get. It's been fun, little princess, but they'll want to see me back at your home town eventually."

"Tantallos will discover your masquerade and they will kill you all," whimpered Daina, trying to make herself sound defiant despite everything. "I hope when the Goddess consumes your soul, that She chews it to bits." At least that was one comfort she would have while her soul went on to Paradise. Perhaps not an immediate retribution, but her afterlife was far better than what this monster would suffer.

The demon chuckled some as he heard this. "Ah, your Goddess makes me laugh," he said. "She is so much more brutal than the being I worship, yet you call us the monsters. But I don't want to talk religion; all this talk about consuming souls has made me hungry. Tell me, princess; which arm would you like me to tear off first?" The demon raised his claw, Daina's eyes unable to look away from the sharp blades. Suddenly there was a loud roar. Both of them looked away from each other, Daina to her left, the demon to his right. Something massive came hurtling toward the forest and within moments it crashed into the forest, shattering through the trees like they were twigs and coming to a stop around ten feet in front of Daina and the demon. It had easily traveled fifty feet.

Daina's eyes widened. It was a massive mire beast, knocked out cold from its journey through the forest. It moaned slightly in protest as the entire area fell silent. Daina heard nothing, but the demon could hear a pair of feet walking forward, the hooked claw on each clicking against the occasional stone. The visor of the demon's helmet obscured his vision, so he took it off in order to see unhindered. The creature underneath the helmet was just as ugly and terrifying as Daina had feared. Tan quills ending in brown tips covered most of its scalp, extending every which way like a child who had not combed his hair. His flesh was a similar brown, and if Daina had known what sunbathing was she would have thought it similar to that in terms of coloration. The skin was also patterned like dried, cracked ground and looked thick and rough to the touch. He turned his head to face the one who had interrupted his meal. As he turned his head Daina caught a glimpse of his eyes for a moment.

The stories she had heard so many times were true; they indeed were pure black with nine red rings of varying width nested inside each other, providing the illusion of descending into the centers like wells. Had her glimpse been longer she would have seen that the seventh deepest circle in each was especially thick. The eyes immediately started drawing her in, locking her gaze, but the demon finished turning his head and saved Daina from the horror that would have followed. "Is that who I think it is?" barked the demon. "If that is, I think I might just have to squeal in happiness!" He looked to Daina. "Don't you go anywhere, now. I just have one thing to deal with before I eat you alive."

The demon leaped off the treeline and sailed slowly down into the path created by the thrown mire beast. The demon thought nothing of this feat; he could easily hurl the same beast a greater distance. Once he was further in, he brought his wings up and flared them, making them grow brighter than normal in a frightening display of dominance. A similar glowing red appeared opposite the demon, illuminating the shape of the challenger. Branches and roots reached for it but their reach fell short. Daina did her best to ignore her pain as she tilted her head to stare at this new challenger. What she saw did not fill her with hope. Quite the opposite, in fact.

The monster was human in shape, the body covered in colorless but modest garb. It looked to be around a foot shorter than the demon, an inch or two below six feet. Red hair flowed down its head in sharp-looking shapes not unlike the quills of Daina's would-be killer, but they grew in a much thicker and well kept manner. Out of its back two elegant, smooth, seamless red wings came that glowed just as brightly as her captor's. They were beautiful wings, wavy and full of curves, similar to the stained-glass windows in the Church of the Goddess; particularly one of the ones depicting fire. It made the skeletal, bird-like appearance of the wings a work of art. A sizable, hooked claw extended from in between its big toes and the toes adjacent to them on each foot. On the ends of its arms were two claws, a much darker gray than those of its opponent, the ridged extensions going a similar distance up the forearm.

It was another demon, over a head shorter and young in the face, but just as vicious-looking.

"If it's not the runt with the cutest wings ever," said the tan-haired demon, smiling and relaxing some as he locked eyes with his opponent. "When I saw those wings years ago I thought you were an especially small female. Finally come by to let me tear you apart, have you?"

The young, well-maintained demon kept its combat stance, its eyes staring back at the tan demon with hatred. "Let the human go," he said, his voice light in pitch but still full of power. Each word sounded just as mighty as the creature that had thrown the mire beast should be. "Let her go or I will kill you."

"Now this is just adorable," said the tan demon. "But it's not enough to let you get away with interrupting my snack. To be fair, though, I should have done this the first time I came across you." His claws seemingly glowed green again and roots shot up around the young demon. The young demon's wings dissipated, barely avoiding being pierced by the roots as he stared around him, then roots came up from under his feet, wrapping around his ankles and wrists, root after root reinforcing their hold on him as they kept him right-side up. The tan demon approached, smiling, amused by the defiant look in the young demon's eyes.

"Come now," said the tan demon. "You may be a runt, but you're not this weak and stupid. You're a smart little kid, aren't you? You escaped my little trap once. I never got the chance to ask you how, but no matter. It seems a bit silly that you'd fall for it again. If I knew you were actually this weak and stupid I'd have gone to your little tower and killed you years ago."

"Thank you for coming this close to me," said the young demon. "If I had known you were this talkative and stupid I'd have burned down your little forest and killed you years ago."

64

Suddenly his claws glowed a dazzling white, setting the roots around him on fire as waves of heat came off the metallic gauntlets. The tan demon backed away as the young demon effortlessly ripped his claws free of his root bonds before freeing his feet in two slices. He fell to the ground, landing on his feet, letting his claws cool down as the woods around him burned. His clothes remained unharmed by the flames; so much time spent attached to his body had helped alter them some.

"Never would have guessed you were *dal Kafteros* all this time," said the tan demon. "No matter; you don't have the strength to back up your little piles of embers and I'm the one with the suit of armor. You should fly away now before I gut you like I'm going to gut her."

"And you should shut your mouth!" yelled the young demon, charging forward while emitting a roar that terrified Daina even more than anything the other demons had done. She quickly started working at freeing herself from the grip of the trees, her own blood making her limbs more slippery. The tan demon braced himself as the young demon closed the short distance between them. The tan demon brought his claws up and blocked the young demon's slices, the blades caught by the ridges of the claws.

The tan demon pushed the young one off, sending him stumbling back several feet. He then charged forward to deliver a stab but the younger demon rolled to the side, letting the tan one go past him. The young demon then jumped to his feet in a moment but he did not charge forward. He examined the armor blanketing the tan demon; plate metal, sturdy material, almost every weakness covered without sacrificing mobility. A crushing blow might dent the plates. No, that would not be enough to hinder the tan demon. Not significantly, anyway.

Then he saw the opening; a slight gap in between plates at the shoulder blades. A small space, but more than enough for him. Now he just had to exploit it, that and avoid getting lacerated. All these thoughts occurred in just a couple seconds to the young demon. The tan demon turned around and his claws glowed green. The young demon leaped up into the air fractions of a second before roots shot up of the area surrounding his spot, all stabbing inward. He temporarily regenerated his wings, soaring over the tan demon. He dissipated them and dropped to the spot by the tan demon before he finished turning around.

As the young demon's claws glowed white flames sprouted on them, covering the gauntlets and moving upward to blanket his arms up to the shoulder. He charged forward and struck out at the tan demon, avoiding his defending claws and slamming against the tan demon's breastplate with the back of a claw. The tan demon yelled in surprise, the bent metal pressing painfully against his chest. He parried the blows of the young demon rapidly, focusing solely on defense as he backed away from the onslaught. He risked a strike at the young demon's unarmored chest but his claws hit nothing but air as his target dodged to the side and grabbed his stabbing arm as it sailed past. Using his opponent's momentum, the young demon redirected the charge and sent the tan demon tumbling forward into a tree.

The young demon did not wait a moment before pointing his claws at his fallen enemy. A stream of fire flowed off them, engulfing the tan demon in wreathing flames. The tan one roared in pain as he forced himself up and charged at the younger demon. The young demon snuffed the flames and brought up his claws just in time to prevent the blow from taking off his head. The force of the swing still knocked him off his feet, sending him flying back. He landed on his back and bounced once before landing on all fours and immediately charging back at the tan demon afterward.

The tan demon's eyes widened as the young demon closed the distance, but not before the armored defender generated his gnarled wings and took to the air, evading his smaller enemy by a matter of seconds. The young demon stopped instantly and sharply with barely a loss in his motion before generating his own wings and taking off after the tan demon. They rose higher and higher, the decreasing air supply slowly killing the young demon's fire except at the claws themselves. The young demon was largely deprived of his powers, but they were hundreds of feet up in the air, and the tan demon was powerless as well.

The tan one dived forward, sacrificing precious altitude as he flew at the younger demon who dissipated his wings but regenerated them after only a split second, sending him just far enough down to avoid the tan demon's charge. He took off after the tan demon, who had only turned around just in time to lock claws with him once again.

As the airborne battle continued, Daina busied herself with freeing her limbs. She finally got one of her arms out of the grasp of a branch, the arm's wrist covered and dripping with her own blood. The branches surrounding her made no effort to grab it again; unlike most of the other trees the ones holding her had not been enchanted by the tan demon and only moved when he willed it. She contorted herself enough to reach into her gown and grab her dagger, pulling it out of the sheath and placing the blade in her hand outside. This done, she immediately set to work on freeing her other arm.

After a short time she had freed it too, allowing her to pull up her torso to get at her ankles; part of her waist was propped up by a select few branches. As she steadily cut away at the rough limbs she took the time to look around the dark forest. All sorts of eyes appeared in the darkness, approaching from every angle, their bodies not illuminated by the glowing wings above her. There was no moon in this area of the Decay, giving her little light besides the two pairs of wings and the one pair of glowing claws above her. The fighting demons did not stop any of the animals from approaching the forest, looking for a way in without triggering the trees. Although the ones holding her did not move, almost all of the others writhed like grappling, gnarled hands as more animals arrived. Any one of these giant monsters could easily knock down the trees still holding her in place, and then her fate would be sealed. Freeing her limbs would definitely not help her fight them off, not with her little butter knife she called a dagger. But she still might be able to run away from them. Perhaps she could get to the big tree; there might be a hollow part of it or some sort of crevice she could stash herself in.

Above her the two demons still fought bitterly, each one playing every trick they knew to land blows. The young demon seemed to almost float around the other, ducking and weaving through blows by the width of one of his quills. It would only take one blow from the tan demon to throw the young demon back down to the ground, one lucky swipe to shatter his wings like glass. But every time that blow came the young demon prevented it. He would disintegrate and regenerate his own wings, block the attempt, or deliver one of his own hits to knock the tan demon off. One successful dodge granted him a moment to look back down at the forest; with the tan demon no longer guarding his prey the other animals were moving in. Even if he had spent the time enchanting every tree there would not be enough to keep them from getting to her.

He immediately turned back to his opponent and dodged a charging strike from the tan demon, letting him go past before latching onto the spaces between plates of armor. The tan demon let out a roar of frustration as he tried to shake the young demon off. The tan demon's thoughts became overtaken by a rage against the indignity he was suffering; failing to kill this runt even at his greatest. He was going to tear the young demon's smooth skin off, knock out each humanoid tooth and then pluck his eyeballs out one by one before he would allow him to die. The young demon was not going to kill him-- The tan demon could not move as fast but he was still stronger, and almost entirely covered in the best armor this half-dead world could offer. It was even somewhat holding up against the claw strikes, though the young demon had not tried to pierce it but rather dent it. Likely his claws would tear through it but still get caught, leaving him open for a counterattack. He could not remember the name of the metal, but he was definitely going to thank Abdaas once he finally took down this undersized weakling. The young demon broke off from the tan demon's back, leaving a slightly bigger gap by the shoulder blades than before. The tan demon quickly turned around and charged again but the young demon avoided him by a claw's length. The young demon then dived downward, heading back to the forest. The tan demon swooped down after him, letting out a yell; how dare the red demon try to run away from him. He was going to die even slower now because of his cowardice.

Daina kept her focus off the battle and continued working away at the branches holding her ankles. Then came the final strike, weakening the branches just enough for her weight to send her breaking through the remaining ones until she landed roughly on the forest floor. The sticky mud had thankfully cushioned her fall, but she almost felt on fire from all of her wounds, especially at her wrists, ankles and face. She pulled herself up as fast as she could, but already she had gotten coated in the muck she landed in. It inflamed her wounds even more, and the cool mud did not chill her enough to deaden the pain. After everything she had suffered through it was a struggle for her to think straight.

But then another squeal cut through the night air and caught her attention; another one of her would-be predators had been snatched up by a killer tree. All this time she had heard the shrieks and whines of the foolish animals, but this one was closer than the previous ones. The cries came from all around the forest as creatures made their way in, filling up the enchanted trees as they went. While the trees worked very well to incapacitate prey, they could only hold one or two animals at a time and there were not enough trees for all the beasts. Once they got past the trees the animals would easily be able to catch her and eat her alive.

She hobbled her way over to the big tree, starting to feel dizzy from her wounds. She looked it over and saw a small opening at the bottom by the roots. She let herself collapse onto the ground and slowly wormed her way into the tree, grimacing as what little of her that had not already been coated in mud got its own layer. It took her some time and each second she kept expecting the jaws of a monster to drag her out, but she eventually got herself inside a hollow part of the tree. It was roomy enough inside for her to stand up, shiver and cringe at the filth she was covered in. She had never felt so miserable and wretched in her entire life. The situation had not changed. She was still dead. She would not live for another hour; it was just a question of what would kill her. Would it be one of the demons fighting over her, or maybe one of the animals getting ever closer to her hiding spot? Would an enchanted tree grab her too tightly and pierce her heart, or would the Decay itself rot her into nothingness? She pushed those thoughts to the side; whatever small favor extended her life a bit more was welcome at this point. Maybe she would die in one of the less painful ways.

The fight still raged outside, the young demon's claws starting to spawn more flames as he got closer to the ground. He quickly pulled up, less than an arm's length out of the reach of the grasping wooden limbs. Despite all the other noise he could still single out an indignant yell; the tan demon was about to dive down at him. He rolled to the side just moments before the tan demon would have struck him like a hawk would a mouse. The tan demon was traveling too fast and was not agile enough to pull up before he collided into his own forest. He broke through tree after tree, many monsters screaming as they fell down to the floor, still imprisoned in their wooden cages. The tan demon struggled to pull himself up but felt himself forced back to the ground by the young demon as he dived feet-first into his back. The young demon wasted no time and again stuck his claws into the chink in the back of the tan demon's armor. He brought his arms up, yelling as he tore off the plates of metal, exposing the tan demon's cracked and dry-looking shoulders. The tan demon glowed green and used roots beneath him to force himself up fast enough to knock the young demon off his back. The young demon recovered by the time the tan demon had turned around, who let out another roar and stabbed forward with a claw, the young demon dodging once again by a miniscule distance. The young demon grabbed the claw as it moved past him and hurled the tan demon to the side, smashing him into another tree. He did not waste a single moment and charged forward as the tan demon lay there dazed. He grabbed the tan demon by the quills and lifted up his head before slamming him into a large, unbroken bit of tree. He did this repeatedly, unharmed by the tan demon's sharp quills, reducing his foe's face to a pulpy mess.

The tan one struggled to keep his focus long enough to concentrate on the trees around him but failed with every blow to his face. Any little thing could buy him enough time to escape this unbelievable foe: a large branch, a gnarled root, a tiny twig that conveniently got in the young demon's eye. Anything. The battle was lost. The prey was the young demon's. His home was ravaged, torn apart and burning in some areas. If he had just one moment he could use it to escape, get back to Tantallos, get Jurek and the others to come back and tear this runty demon apart for him. Jurek could kill any other demon out there, no matter how many attacked him at once. This small fry would be nothing to him.

He felt another point of pressure on his back as he struggled to move; the young demon pressed a foot into the middle of his back to keep him on the ground. The foot helped hold him in place as the young demon reached for his right claw, grabbed it and brought it upwards. Then, with a quick but powerful jerk the young demon tore the limb off the tan demon's body. The tan demon let out a wail in pain as his opponent did the same thing to his other arm. His thoughts dimmed, but one still remained: he should have given him the human. The tan demon sputtered as blood came out of his mouth, slowly relaxing his body in death as the young demon let out a triumphant roar. The young demon stood there for a few seconds, panting heavily as he took in what he had finally done.

He finished catching his breath and moved off the carcass, walking a few paces before turning around and pointing his white-hot claws at the tan demon. The dead body was surrounded by dead branches and twigs, with the fallen trunk of a tree right by his face. There was no way he would not burn. Flames sprung up on the young demon's claws and again flowed off the tips of his digits like a river, engulfing the tan demon and everything nearby in their brilliant glory. Between this and the fires that already existed, the entire forest was set ablaze. The flames spread quickly, greedily swallowing the dried and dead branches as they made their way throughout the area. The few animals fortunate enough to have not been caught in the trees ran away in fear while their brethren were roasted alive. Only one creature in the forest was immune to the flames and their toxic fumes, and he was busy looking for his prize.

Daina put away her dagger; it would do her no more good. She leaned against the side of the tree, just wishing she could curl up into a little ball and wake up somewhere safe. Although she had not seen the finale of the battle, she had been listening and knew who had won. Even now she could hear the approaching flames all around her. It seemed she had two options, being burned alive or torn into bits and eaten by the smaller demon. Both seemed horrible, but being burned alive seemed much worse. She considered pulling her knife back out and using it to cut herself open again. Maybe bleeding to death like that would be quicker. It would not be suicide if she would die anyway, would it?

She moved to reach for her dagger when a black claw burst through the bark in front of her face. The digits bent inward and the tore the wall away from her, exposing her to the young demon. He stood there, panting, covered in the blood of his opponent. She pushed herself against the back of the tree to stay as far away from him as possible, the urge to scream building inside of her, and then she looked into his eyes. It only took one look, and then their gazes immediately locked together. She looked deeper and deeper into his eyes, unable to resist. Each of the nine circles gave the illusion of depth, enticing her to look further and further in. She found herself almost sinking into the centers, made up of the darkest blackness of all. Already it was too late, and she could do nothing to break away as she started to get lost in the dark pits filling his eye sockets.

She felt clammy all over, sweating intensely, and not just from the heat of the fire surrounding them. The noise around her slowly faded out while a high-pitched buzzing grew to replace it. Her vision started blurring, but she still could not break her eyes from his as he moved forward. She slumped more against the tree, her feet sliding forward until her legs finally gave out and she fell onto the ground, all while the demon reached out to her with a claw. Finally her vision blurred into nothingness and sound completely cut out as she fainted.

CHAPTER 9

The best way to hunt is to understand your prey. The best way to understand your prey is to grasp how they speak to each other.
-From the Tomes of the Huntmaster.

Some time later a new shape flew over the mountain, illuminated by a basic pair of wings attached to an armored demon. Wesan flew over the sea of fog as quietly as he could, pondering how little noise there seemed to be at this time of night. It took him almost no time to arrive at the edge of his destination, raised above the swampland surrounding it. He landed just outside of the dead zone and observed the remains of what had apparently happened just recently. The entire forest had been burned to the ground, resulting in a fine layer of ash that covered everything nearby. Several fallen trees were still burning while others had become nothing more than collapsing piles of embers. The smell of burnt flesh dominated everything else with dozens of scorched carcasses all over the place. He spent several minutes inspecting the charred remains of animals before he finally came across the body of the forest's protector. Parts of his armor at the shoulders were missing, along with both of his arms. The ruined metal pieces could be found nearby but the limbs were nowhere to be seen. Wesan shuddered at the thought of the creature that had done this.

This definitely explains why he didn't come back after taking her, thought Wesan. *I thought he was just taking his time with her; it's almost fortunate Jurek thought differently. Even more fortunate that whatever killed him isn't here anymore.* He shuddered again.

But what creature of the Decay could have killed him so brutally? Being *dal Afxanos* only made him stronger during the daytime, but even at night he was still far stronger than Wesan, and he had fought against this foe in a place that catered to his alignment. Even if the killer got past the barrage of branches and roots, he would still have to survive in close combat with a vicious foe. Between his claw skills and full suit of armor there should not be a creature capable of taking him down. Except for another of his kind with a favorable alignment, of course, and given the carnage around him there was only one logical choice; this killer was *dal Kafteros*.

He grew even more thankful the killer was gone and decided to take a further look around. Large sections of trees had been broken and splintered to bits, as if something had come crashing through them. He noticed two strips in particular that looked like this. But the oddest part was the large tree in the center; compared to the trees around it, it was relatively unharmed. But at the bottom there was a section of bark that had been ripped open, exposing a place inside. Several footprints that consisted of five toes and a dot led up to the tree, then away in a different direction, and then they disappeared.

Definitely a greater one of his kind, footprint and dot sizes suggesting that he either had small feet or was rather small as a whole, and he was definitely *dal Kafteros*. But as unfortunate this had turned out to be for Wesan's partner, how lucky it was for those who remained. He backed away from the tree, found a more cleared area and generated his wings. He took off into the night air, leaving the destroyed forest behind and still wondering what this mysterious killer looked like. Though it was no concern if he came across them; as tough as he could be, he still stood no chance against Jurek.

Daina was in a small, rocky chamber alongside many others her age. She was waiting there for her mother as she went off to do some business. She had her pet, Pistiaem, with her to keep her company; the others there didn't like her because she was so small. She sat to the side with Pisti while the others talked and played in the cave. The big man stood just outside the entrance, on the lookout for danger. He was tough, but mother was tougher. The other children paid her no mind as she pet Pisti with one of her claws. Pisti's fur was really short but just long enough to cover the evenly-spaced bone plates. Pisti sat on her haunches and panted as Daina continued petting her.

Then they felt a shaking. All the kids quieted down as the ground shook every few seconds, a loud stomping growing louder and louder with each shake. Pisti stood up and clenched her jaws together, looking toward the cave entrance. There was little outside besides the bright sky with the massive white arch cutting through it. Mother said it was a ring of rocks in the sky but Daina couldn't think of how that could be. Another shake brought her back to the problem at hand. Something huge was coming. She had seen many giant monsters but she had always been safe by her mother. She'd be safe here, too. The big man wasn't as strong as mother but he could still kill it.

"Mi Prosopsei," said the big man. Daina felt a chill go up her spine to see the big man taking the Huntmaster's name in vain. He looked back to the children. "Pimas! Kribe! Uzas al trogo!" She and all the children gasped but immediately took off for a deeper corner of the cave, Pisti running right at

her side. They hid back in its depths while the big man sprouted his wings and took to the air. They only heard a lot of yelling as he and the other big man nearby went to fight the monster.

The monster let out a loud, deep roar, and everyone in the cave shivered. It was coming to eat them all, slurp them up like a patch of ripe glik *berries. They heard the two men fighting it, attacking it with everything they had. But many of them, including Daina, knew that the trogo was too heavily armored for them to kill it on their own. Then they heard two final cries from the men as the trogo finished with them. Trogos didn't like adults; they only liked children whose claws were small and whose quills were short. It stomped over to the cave entrance and brought its head down, its black eyes staring in and looking at each one of the dozen children. Its long beak tried to reach in and grab one but failed to get far enough. The children sighed in relief; perhaps they were safe.*

The beak retreated and then broke through a wall of the cave, exposing the children. It was a colossal trogo, easily big enough to eat them all. Its massive body was supported by two large back legs and four smaller front legs, the two smallest equipped with basic thumbs. The entire body was covered in a thick hide that housed hundreds of tiny bones that helped deflect claw strikes. Its long beak featured many black stripes. These were actually metal reinforcements that grew alongside the beak. The trogo let out a roar of triumph and struck above the hole it had made with its beak, breaking away more of the ceiling and moving the rubble away with its front hands. The children screamed in fright, almost all of them crying. Daina kept herself calm and held Pisti close.

*"Pisti," she said quietly. "*Kribe ap ol trogo. Lega mita. Lega Maiah.*" If her mother could reach them in time, she would deal with the trogo. She always won. But the children would need all the time they could get. Daina swallowed her fears and dashed out of the cave right past the beak of the trogo, yelling and screaming at the beast as she ran. Pisti took off opposite her, but the other children remained frozen in fear. She yelled at them repeatedly to run but still they stood their ground, horrified by the colossal predator before them. She tried to lead the trogo a distance away but it made its move before she could.*

The world closed around her as the creature brought its beak down on her waist, and then she felt herself get thrown into the air by the jerking motion of its head. She caught a slight glimpse of light before the beak closed on her again and she tumbled downward, sliding into a wet, cramped hole. The moment the pressure was released on her body she stuck her claws into the wall. She climbed her way to the top, digging both hand claws and the smaller claws on her feet into the roof of the trogo's stomach. For the first time in her short life she could not see anything at all, and the very air she breathed was foul and burning. She felt herself weaken as she heard shrieking. Despite all her attempts to save them, the other children had doomed themselves by not fleeing.

It became a struggle to keep conscious, her body suspended above the noxious pool of acid below her, her hearing dominated by the cries and screams of the others as they begged for their mothers and fathers. Then she heard nothing but the beating of the trogo's hearts. She too began to beg her mother to arrive and save her before her grip faltered.

Daina's eyes shot open, breathing rapidly, body covered in sweat. The dream slowly faded into her memory, but she could not possibly forget it. It was far more vivid and horrifying than a week of her normal nightmares. As her heart calmed down some from the nightmare, she let herself breathe a sigh of relief. She was not dead, or at least she did not appear to be. She ached all over; she had imagined that in Paradise you would not feel such pain. So at least for now she assumed she was still alive. The horrible dream still haunted her but she forced it to the side so she could figure out where she was.

She was bundled up in ratty but rather clean blankets; she was wrapped up in enough layers to stay very warm. She was not in the clothes she had been wearing and just had on undergarments. This alarmed her, but it was better than still having those soaked and ruined clothes on. In the corner of her eye she could see some clothes similar to what she normally wore and the strap for her dagger's holster nearby. That was all fine, but where was she?

She struggled weakly in her blanket cocoon. Her arms and limbs ached with every inch, but she slowly managed to wiggle herself out. Whoever had wrapped her in the blankets had done so too tightly. She slowly forced herself onto her feet, grimacing at the sight of her scabs, but at least most of them would heal up. She felt her cheeks and tenderly prodded them before jerking her hands back. Those would definitely become scars. She looked around her chamber. It was a small room made entirely of stone, similar to a room in her castle but a lot colder and more depressing. A staircase opposite her led to... somewhere. All she could tell was that they went down. The stairs that went up simply went into the ceiling. They were covered in various bottles and jars, apparently used for storage. The only other thing of note in the room was a small window with no pane of glass separating it from the outside world, resulting in a cold wind blowing inside. Pain came with every slight movement as she made her way to the window. She gazed out, looking upon the overcast morning of her normal world instead of the bizarre, bright day of her nightmare.

Outside was the Decay. It was the Decay, but different from the sections she had seen before. It looked to be a distance south of the forest in which she had nearly died as she could see some smoke rising far away. To the east she saw the mountain she had been taken over, but she could not see past it to gaze upon Tantallos. The area around her was surprisingly dry, containing almost no bogs or bodies of water. She also saw an overgrown cobblestone path that appeared to go from the direction of the mountain to somewhere near the structure she was in.

She looked down at the ground, about two dozen feet below her. The structure was about five feet away from a moat of water that looked surprisingly clean, though Daina knew better than to try drinking it. As she looked back and forth, she figured that the structure was a stone tower of some sort; some nearby rubble suggested that it was once the bell tower of a church. The part that housed the bell must be long gone, thus the staircase to nowhere. There were a few other small stone buildings nearby but they were so dilapidated it was a miracle that they were still standing.

In a brighter time, this had once been a small farming community only notable for having a church while most others did not. The farmers in other nearby communities would come to this church whenever it was time for services. Now it was as dead as the former farmland that surrounded it. She started wondering about her terrifying nightmare. Not a single thing in it had been from her life; she had never known her mother, and she certainly did not have claws on her hands and feet. She had never even imagined such a dry landscape. And what was wrong with the sky? It did not have a cloud in it, and the bizarre, thick arch going throughout it! And what was everyone saying? She had never heard such a strange language with its basic articulations; each vowel only got one pronunciation and paired vowels were pronounced separately. Not one bit of it made sense.

To say nothing of the titanic monster that had eaten her and the other children. She shuddered as she thought of the gluttonous beast. No creature in the Decay was that horrid. She needed someone to talk to about this. And maybe she could find out why she was still alive. She made her way to the staircase, but before walking down she found herself looking at her left arm. She had four cuts in it near the shoulder, not deep but still aching. She could not recall the tan demon doing that to her. She looked further down her body and noticed another four cuts on the outside of her left thigh. Both sets had the same spacing and length. It was as if something had been carrying her and had accidentally cut her. They were cuts left by demon claws.

She was surprised by this, but not as scared as she would have thought. She had no complaints about being alive, but why had the demon with the red quills not eaten her? He had intruded on the tan demon's territory and brutally killed him specifically to obtain her; surely he would want to enjoy his meal afterward. It wasn't like she could put up a fight against him, after all. His eyes alone had made her collapse like a sack full of produce. He could not have asked for a more vulnerable target. Did he prefer his food to be alive, alive and screaming while he slowly ate it raw?

She trembled at the thought and nearly jumped when she heard something moving below her. Someone else was there with her, someone evil, someone monstrous... someone not trustworthy in the slightest. Somebody vicious who was going to try and eat her or do something else that was just as horrible and much more humiliating. She had never heard of it happening but there had to be a reason she was still alive. *No.* She pushed that terrible possibility to the side. She had to at least confront this creature. She could tell how people were in just a few minutes of talking to them. Maybe he would not be so horrid... as far as demons go, at least.

She returned to her pile of clothes and quickly put them on; she had been shivering horribly. She then went back to the staircase and slowly walked down it, leaning against the rough stone wall for support. Although all her wounds were sealed up, Daina had still lost a lot of blood on top of all the other things she had been put through last night. She could not help but feel a little light-headed. She had never fainted once in her life. Never. She was the one woman of high standing she knew who had not. No spell or spectacle, no vividly-described monster, no chilling haunted house at the annual festival had ever even made her feel weak.

All the same, something in that demon's eyes had defeated her in just one glance. She thought it may have been a culmination of everything else that night, but no, that could not be it. Something about his eyes did it. She tried to think back and figure out what it was in those red-ringed eyes that had knocked her out but no particular element came to mind. She could remember the eyes vividly; she could even remember that the fifth rings were slightly larger than the others, but the memory did not make her even feel dizzy. After a slow and careful process down the cold stone staircase she stepped onto the ground floor. Although it had undoubtedly been used for some other purpose originally, it was now a storage area of some sort. All kinds of supplies were neatly organized in it; dry wood, assorted jars of miscellany, blankets that ranged from clean linens to filthy rags, rusting tools of all walks of life and clothes of every kind. Male, female, child, adult; every sort and size was accounted for and the clothes ranged significantly in quality, although most were rather tattered. What little space remained was filled up with needless collections of knickknacks, the only exception being the foot-long passage between the main door and the staircase. Whoever lived here was a pack rat.

Daina continued moving on, eventually coming across her pair of sandals on top of a sack. They looked surprisingly clean to her and were largely devoid of mud. She took a moment to put them on, strapping them up tightly. At least now her feet would not be freezing on the cold stone floor. She finished making her way over to the entrance of the tower, moving away from the wall and managing to stand without any support. Her strength was quickly returning to her, but she still ached all over from her wounds. She got up to the threshold and noticed two hinges on one end of the entrance. The door attached to them must have rotted away long ago. She looked outside and saw a light only a couple dozen feet ahead. It was a small fire, with what looked to be a young man turned toward the flame so his back was facing her. He was sitting on a large, flat rock with his hands in his lap.

She looked down at his bare feet, touching the ground and facing outward. The feet were a little large, but each one only had five normal human toes. The skin of his legs looked hairless, smooth and pale, nothing like the broken flesh her captor had. She noticed the same normalcy on what she could see of his arms. Well, a man being hairless was not that common, but it was not unheard of. She found herself scratching her head at this sight. Who was this young man and what had happened to the terrifying red-quilled demon? Did this hermit show up right before the demon was able to tear her apart and had managed to convince him to give her up? He certainly could not have fought off the demon; she had seen that horrible creature in battle. The only possible way was through diplomacy, but demons were evil and uncaring creatures. Would it have agreed to relinquish her?

These were all questions he would undoubtedly be willing to answer. He could be trusted. She could tell it right away; this person was nothing like the two monsters that had fought over her. "Um," she began, "hello, sir." She took her first step out of the door and walked toward him. She slowly and carefully worked over each word she chose; she dare not offend the one person she could trust out here. "Was it you who saved me, after I fainted?"

"That was me," said the young man. His voice was light and surprisingly pleasant, though there was not a lot of emotion in it. The little she could discern was that of relief. "You recovered a lot faster than I expected you to. I was thinking you'd be up on the top floor for much longer; most people tend to be out for at least a whole day and it's barely morning. I expected you to come to in the evening, especially considering how fast you collapsed after... that."

"I'm fortunate that I took such little time, then," she said. "I just endured the most horrifying nightmare I've ever had in my entire life. But I'm fine now, sir. Thank you." She made a slight bow; even if the man could not see her it was a polite gesture to make. "And thank you for taking care of me all this time. When I fainted I thought for certain I was going to die horribly in my sleep. Every misshapen creature in the Decay was trying to eat me alive, and then the massive forest fire started up all around me, and worst of all this horrible, terrifying demon appeared right before--"

A sudden glimmering in the man's lap caught her eye, making her pause mid-sentence. Using the small amount of light available she looked closer and saw his arms. The ends of them did not connect to fleshy hands but instead large plates of a dark gray, almost black, metal, connverging at the wrist. Four ridged protrusions went up his forearms about halfway, the ones on the inside covering his veins and going out a slightly smaller distance than the others. Long, sharp claws extended about six inches from each finger, four inches on the thumbs, starting at the furthest-back knuckle and seeming to bend as his fingers moved. They were much larger than any human's hands she had ever seen. Of course, all this time she had been assuming he was a human.

She let out a shriek and backed away in horror as the demon stood up and slowly turned to face her. All her thoughts of her demon captor not being so horrible were immediately vanquished by the fear flowing through her body; she could barely even think straight. She noticed a band of white, clean cloth tied around his head that covered his eyes, though his vision did not seem to be hindered at all by it. His wings were not present and the claws on his feet were fully retracted, leaving only his eyes, claws and spiny hair as reminders of what he was. But that was more than enough for the horror she had seen flying and fighting above her to terrify Daina to her core.

"Oh, my loving Goddess!" she whimpered, unable to stop herself from trembling like mad as the demon slowly walked toward her. She backed away every time he took a step forward until she found herself up against the wall of the tower; she had moved away at an angle, which was why she had not gone back inside the building.

"Please, I beg of you, frightening and powerful demon, please stop! I am Princess Daina, daughter of King Vikenti the Fierce, ruler of the great city of Tantallos!" She started talking faster and faster as the demon neared her. "It is in your best of interests to not kill me! I have no doubt that my father has already discovered my absence and is undoubtedly sending out search parties into the Decay to look for me as we speak and they will assume I took shelter in one of the few remaining clusters of buildings in this Goddess-forsaken swamp so it would be best if you didn't kill me before they arrived and came across you!"

The demon paid her words no mind and continued to get closer to her. She looked around frantically but there was no possible way for her to hinder the approach of this unnatural monster. All she could do was stare at his indifferent face in nothing short of horror. Before she knew it the demon was within a few feet of her, and despite being only a few inches taller than her she seemed to almost shrink before his gaze. "Well, I guess I cannot stop such a mighty and terrifying creature such as yourself," she said rapidly as her mind went berserk. "You may be an unparalleled and mighty demon but you have to eat like all creatures and I guess it's good that the demon who captured me to begin with didn't get the pleasure of consuming me but please don't make me suffer as I have been through so much horror tonight already so please be quick and slice my jugular with those menacing, sharp, beautiful claws of yours!"

"*Mirke dal mi Prosopsei*, will you shut up!" roared the demon, his human mouth snarling in frustration. If he had the fingers for it he would have been rubbing his temples. Daina's mouth immediately snapped shut and she started to quiver even more in the presence of this irate monster. "That is so much better. If only more humans could figure out how to do such a thing. I've lived in your world for over a decade and I still don't understand how you can be so talkative when your own death appears to be at hand." The demon took a few breaths, letting himself vent a little bit more. Once he had calmed himself down he got down on a knee to be at eye level with Daina, who had been reduced to her haunches. "Tell me something, Princess Daina, daughter of King Vikenti the Fierce and all the intimidating status that comes with such a parent," he said. "Why do you think I went to the trouble of killing that very powerful and heavily armored arch kuvi so I could save you?"

Daina was still too scared to properly form an answer to the question. It took several seconds for her to force her mouth open so she could spit out a few words at the demon. "Um," she began, "you prefer your prey to be alive and screaming when you eat it? I don't know, I've never met a demon of any sort until last night so I don't know any of them at all. Maybe you get pleasure from inflicting severe pain on your victims? The other one seemed to and I thought you might share his interests to some extent. I really don't have any clue so please don't kill me for assuming such things about you just because you're a demon." She paused for a moment, freezing up as she saw a snarl grow on the demon's face for a short moment. "That is, if you do eat humans. Do you eat many humans?"

The demon's snarl faded a little, looking a bit more solemn. He seemed to be going over something in his head before he responded. "I've eaten dozens of humans," he said. Daina felt sweat break out all over her body as she looked at this murderer, not even three feet away from her, down at her eye level. She thought he would be trustworthy, but that was unlikely. She could not trust him. Not unless she wanted to end up like his victims. "Humans certainly taste better than the disgusting, half-rotten animals that call this mire home, and even dirt's better to eat than those wretched cud plants. So I won't harm you for thinking such things about me.

"But you're still wrong in every way. If I had wanted to eat you I would have cut your throat while you were still conscious, probably once I had returned to my home. A good kuvi isn't pointlessly cruel to fallen prey. And I'd like to note that there is little to no meat on your lanky body. You would be lucky to last one meal, no, one snack, for a male kuvi like me."

He paused for a moment. "And you don't seem too distraught at the moment to not notice that you aren't wearing the same clothes you were wearing before I saved your royal hide. Except for the sandals and your dagger's scabbard and strap your clothes had been completely ruined, and soaked through with blood. You should be fortunate I collect some of the alleged garbage that gets thrown over the walls of your city or you'd be wandering around without any dry clothes at all. I'm sure what I've grabbed for you isn't the normal fancy and elegant clothing you're used to but if you want your torn-up nightgown back I'll point you to the bog I discarded it in. I threw it away to remove your scent from this place."

Daina was too frightened to be embarrassed by the thought of something, or someone, sniffing her clothes. "Thank you for it all the same," she managed to say, before something horrible occurred to her. Her eyes widened and she looked the demon over.

"Stop with that look," he growled. "I don't need my *Ateni* to tell what you're thinking. And no, I did not take advantage of you while you were incapacitated. The very idea that some humans would do such a thing sickens me. I don't think there's a single kuvi who would willingly, so force those thoughts out of your head."

"Okay," she said. "Thank you for sparing me of that, even if it's not that great a comfort after everything I've endured. But I am not ungrateful, not at all."

"So you've calmed down enough to form complete sentences?" said the demon. He backed away and let Daina pull herself to her feet. She leaned a little against the wall. "I have an idea. We're going to start this entire conversation over. We have a lot to do together and I can't have you constantly trembling and whimpering because I'm so fearsome to you. You're Daina, daughter of King Vikenti the Fierce, princess of the great city of Tantallos. I'm Aleksei dal Kafteros, son of Aleksei dal Kafteros and Maiah dal Richtos, terror of the Decay."

"What was it you keep referring to yourself as?" asked Daina. "A kuvi? I guess that's what your kind chose to call themselves?"

"You guess correctly for once, princess," said Aleksei. "We are the kuvis, servants of the Huntmaster. Kuvi simply means 'hunter' in your tongue, but that's what we're best at. And I want you to keep something important in mind."

A massive snarl grew on his face. He reached forward, grabbed Daina by her shirt and pulled her forward to bring her closer to his enraged visage. "I hate being called a demon! Every time I hear it I want to tear the speaker's arms out of their sockets, so I think you can agree it's in your best interest to never direct it at me again. Ever. It's no concern of mine, since I can cauterize your arms after I pull them off like you pull a wing off a roast chicken." His snarl died down and he let go of Daina, who immediately moved back from him and crouched down.

She gulped, but did find herself feeling a bit guilty. Demon was not flattering in the slightest, and undoubtedly infuriating when one already has a name for his own kind. "I'm sorry," she said. "I never knew you de... I mean, beings referred to yourselves as kuvis or I would have done so. I'd rather call something or someone by the proper name. Don't think I'm just trying to protect myself."

"I don't think there's a single human who ever asked me," he said. "It's something I'm used to. "Can't say the same for those who did say it, though, but that's a story for another day. Get up. You can't be comfortable down here." Aleksei stood back up to his full height and Daina forced herself upward so she was back to slightly below his eye level. She returned to leaning against the wall as Aleksei folded his arms, the blades of his claws facing more-or-less downward.

Aleksei moved a few feet further away from Daina, allowing her to calm down a little more. "So, Ah-leck-seh-ee," said Daina, carefully sounding out the syllables of his name. The separate vowel pronunciation would require some getting used to. "Why did you save me?"

"There has to be a reason for me to save a helpless person?" growled Aleksei. "Perhaps I saved you because I didn't want to see some poor human get brutally killed by an evil fallen servant of the Huntmaster." Daina felt her heart speed up; hopefully he wasn't at arm-severing rage levels yet. "Oh, don't fret. I can't blame you for asking, and yes, I didn't just save you out of the goodness of my heart. I've been living in this wretched and wet land for most of my life, ever since I was a child. And I'm sure you've gathered by now that it isn't the nicest place to spend so much time, but now it seems that I have a human female more than capable of helping me get into Tantallos."

Daina felt herself calm down more as she took in all this lunacy. "I doubt even I could help you with that. Princess with you or not, Tantallosians view your kind as the most dangerous monsters in the entire world. I don't know one who doesn't. Unless you're able to change yourself completely into a human, more than just your foot claws, you aren't entering the city or at least staying in it more than a day."

"Undoubtedly the case for some normal kuvis with their broken skin and fang-filled mouths, but I'm an arch kuvi," he said. "Yes, I am a runt; something called Bloodfire Syndrome, I don't know for sure, but I'm still stronger than any human so add that to the list of things not to talk to me about. If anything, my smaller stature will help me blend in. Besides that, arch kuvis like myself are similar enough to humans in appearance that we can almost pass for them with a little covering up. We look weaker, but it helps the foe underestimate just how powerful we actually are. My quills grow in thick enough to look like spiky hair and one piece of cloth covers up my eyes."

"You've thought about this a lot," said Daina. "But humans don't have massive claws for hands."

"They don't?" asked Aleksei, faking a look of confusion. "Oh, I'm amazed, you're right. You don't have massive claws for hands. I guess it's fortunate that you brought that issue to light or I don't know what I would have done! Thank you for mentioning this minor detail!" He stepped forward. "As far as anyone who asks knows, these are just gauntlets I wear over my hands. My hands became ruined and rotten from prolonged exposure to the Decay and I don't want to make the innocent people around me retch from the sight of them."

"Anyone who asks me will be told that they are gauntlets," said Daina. "Gauntlets that just so happen to be much bigger than any human's hands are and have claws attached to each finger." She felt a little bit bolder as she continued to talk to him. She could trust this demon; no, *kuvi*, at least until his plan was finished and he was loose in Tantallos. But then she would be back in Tantallos as well. He was not stupid enough to try and hurt her once inside those walls.

"Demons shed layers of their claws so the claws can grow and repair themselves," said Aleksei. "These shed layers immediately degrade into fine piles of lesser metals and we usually eat them afterward to get nutrients back I doubt any human would know that. Besides you, that is. Perhaps I'm wearing the shells of kuvi claws." Daina nodded, and as her fear finished fading away she started to feel the cuts on her body throbbing again. Aleksei backed off as she gently touched her wounds.

"I'll tell the people who ask that those are what your claws are," she said, "but please don't ever use them to carry someone again. Your claws are painful, even if you try to be gentle."

Aleksei stepped forward until only a foot separated them, and then he raised a claw in front of her face. It was palm forward, the fingers relaxed slightly, the tips of the blades nearly touching the top of her head. "Prososium claws like these are not made to be comforting or soft, like human hands," he said. "Claws like these are not made to display affection or handle things that are delicate and small. The Huntmaster gave us these claws for one purpose and one purpose alone; killing. If those who discovered that firsthand were still alive they'd agree. Make sure to keep my claws in mind if you ever get any ideas about betraying me."

The claw was so close to Daina's face it was starting to get fuzzy and see-through. If Aleksei happened to trip or fall, or even relaxed his arm, it would smash her face in like an egg. "I'm not going to betray you, Aleksei," she said. "You're a dangerous creature, but I have to trust you to keep me alive. I don't betray those I trust; I barely know any to begin with. I just ask that you move a few paces away from me."

Aleksei nodded, lowering his claw slowly, and backed away while facing her. "It's good to know that we finally understand each other," he said. "Feel free to take whatever you want from my stores; I don't plan to ever come back here. I think I put your bronze dagger on top of one of the piles of clothes. I don't really have any food you'd want to eat but I can cook a slab of meat for you. I've also been boiling some water from the moat surrounding this place; about as clean as Decay water gets, but it still needs some more boiling to kill off the things living in it."

"Thank you," said Daina. She slowly made her way back into the tower, never once facing away from Aleksei until he returned to his spot by the fire.

CHAPTER 10

Never take your foe on just appearance. Soft fur may cover a resilient hide,
or a small set of teeth may take attention from deadly claws.
-From the Tomes of the Huntmaster.

Aleksei set up a spit and skewered a large piece of flesh. He held it over the fire, moving it as needed to cook it properly while he waited on Daina. It took some time but eventually Daina came back outside, dagger outside of her clothes at her side and several choice garments providing better coverage and protection for her. It would not do much against a swipe from a kuvi claw but it might help with other residents of the Decay.

It also helped cover up her wounds, though there was nothing she could do about her face.

"Welcome back," said Aleksei. He occupied his time by gnawing on a bone, getting at the last bits of meat his teeth had somehow missed. Daina found herself drawn to this, trying to see what kind of bone it was. What the bone was or what creature it came from, she could not say. She then noticed something interesting about his teeth.

"Thank you, Aleksei," she said. "Your teeth... how are they so white? I've never seen a mouth so bright. I take good care of my teeth and they aren't that white."

He stopped gnawing on the bone and tossed it to the side. "I wish I could tell you," he said. "I can't exactly care for my teeth with these claws; I'd lacerate my gums. But my mother's teeth were just as bright as my own. No matter what I eat they never get stained or chipped."

"All the better for you, I suppose," she said. She made her way over to where Aleksei was sitting and took a seat on a nearby rock facing the fire. "But I find it odd that some of you kuvis would have teeth like humans while others have mouths full of fangs like dogs." She saw the dead carcass of some animal she had never seen before nearby and the skewered piece of meat cooking over the fire.

"I never understood the anomaly either, but I just find myself fortunate that I have these teeth and not the fangs," he said. "I'd undoubtedly sever my own tongue with them. I've finished eating, and I think your breakfast should be finished cooking by now." His claws turned white-hot, burning away any meat stains or other dirty blotches before he reached forward and grabbed the end of the skewer. He pulled the skewer off the fire and ripped a piece of meat off the end. He offered the piece to Daina. "My hands are clean; don't worry."

Daina cautiously took the piece of meat and nearly dropped it from the heat. She tossed it back and forth between her hands a few times while blowing on it and it quickly cooled down enough for her to hold. She squeezed it a little and inspected the torn areas, all brown, no blood and little juice at all. "How long was this meat over the fire?" she asked.

"I can't give you exact figures, but I had it over the fire long enough to cook the meat all the way through," he said. "I can't imagine you'd ever want to eat your meat rare, or even have the stomach for it."

Daina stared at the piece of meat in her hands; it was far too dry and overly cooked for her. To her, eating something well-done was like chewing on gristle. "This meat is so overcooked a single bite would dry out my throat," she said. "Only a grandmother would eat meat like this. Are you going to assume that I'm so weak even my stomach cannot take something slightly less cooked? Are you going to chew my food for me next?" The thought was repulsive, but she paid it no mind. She just needed to make a point.

"Until such time that you prove yourself able to endure conditions I face every day, I will make such assumptions," he said. "It doesn't help that you fainted faster than most people unfortunate enough to lock eyes with me."

"Look, Aleksei," snapped Daina, "if you're going to keep treating me like I'm a helpless child or elderly woman I might as well walk back to Tantallos on my own. Trusting you and letting you baby me are not the same thing. Just give me a quill of your hair and I won't rot away. At least then I won't have to endure your constant attending to my every need. I have legions of sycophants willing to do such things in my home. I don't need a kuvi doing the same."

"So far the only thing you seem to not need my help for is talking," said Aleksei. "You're going to need to do more than that to change my mind, especially after all the whimpering when you saw me after waking up."

Daina groaned and threw the meat to the ground. "That's it," she said. "Tear me off a piece of that carcass, quill-head. I want something bloody."

Aleksei stared at Daina in intrigue, not sure how to react to the quill-head insult. Something familiar glimmered in his covered-up eyes. "You wasted a good cut of meat. I wouldn't eat it, but I'm sure it was still good. It might still be fine if you clean it off some."

"I know you can hear me and I know you can understand me," she said. "Tear off a piece of raw meat, quill-head. I want something juicy and dripping, not that cut you nothing short of burned for me."

"That's definitely one of the less common names I've been given," said Aleksei. "But hold on, *princess*, while I grab you some raw meat." He stood up and moved over to the carcass. He reached in with one hand, took hold and tore off a slab of raw flesh, as red as his quills and dripping with blood. He walked over to Daina and handed it to her. She grimaced at the sight and feel of the meat as the blood soaked through her gloves; she would need to get new ones from Aleksei's stores.

But that did not stop her from continuing with her plan. Even as she was repulsed by the meat she forced her head downward and her hands upward, the two eventually meeting at her parted lips. She sank her teeth into the piece of raw meat and slowly tore a piece off the slab, bringing her head back up as her eyes widened. She continued to fight back her revulsion as she chewed away, her face contorting in every possible manner as she kept down the urge to spit it out and vomit. After what seemed like an eternity she managed to choke it down and swallow each last bit. She shuddered afterward and felt more than a little sick.

"You have made your point, Daina," said Aleksei. "How about you let me take that meat from you and cook it some? You look about ready to throw up."

Daina nodded and let out a worrying belch. She felt a burning in the back of her throat. "Please do," she said. "Cooked but still bloody." She handed the meat back to Aleksei, who took the well-done meat off the skewer and replaced it with the raw meat. "But please stop treating me like a child, Aleksei. Yes, I like dresses and yes, I'm not good with a sword or a bow. But I do need a chance to do small things on my own. You're the one person I'd expect not to pamper me. I get enough of that every day of my life."

"Thank you for proving me wrong, princess," he said. "I would have been driven insane otherwise. I'll ease on my berating you, but when you're faced with something we know you cannot handle, don't tell me to stay away just because you want to prove your worth."

"I know my limits," said Daina. She put a hand over her stomach. "I'm not stupid, just proud." Immediately after these words left her mouth she shut it, shot up and ran over to the nearest building. She dashed behind it and Aleksei listened in to the noises she was making as her stomach told her what it thought of the raw meat. She soon wandered back, wiping off her mouth and looking even paler in the face. "Okay, perhaps some of both. May I please have that water?"

CHAPTER 11

The only foe more dangerous than a vicious monster is its mother.
-From the Tomes of the Huntmaster.

The early morning light revealed a fever of activity all across the city of Tantallos. Everyone was out and about, from the poorest child to the highest nobleman. In particular, one watchman was wandering a section of the wall, his head darting back and forth as he looked down each side repeatedly while walking. Decay, Tantallos, Decay, Tantallos. The view of the Decay alone was enough to terrify a person, even if the fog was starting to lighten with the morning. But he could not deny that the situation demanded it. Only an hour or so ago a maid had gone into Princess' Daina's room for a routine check, only to find the bed undisturbed; no one had slept there last night. Daina was known for making her own bed in an attempt to save the maids some time but she made it in a way different from her servants. The servants immediately checked with the guests but they all said that she was not there. The four knights were absent, but Abdaas had said they had left to examine the town.

A frantic search went throughout the castle, done as quietly as possible to not awaken the king. Ultimately, such attempts proved fruitless and they were forced to disturb Vikenti and inform him of the situation. His groggy attitude vanished immediately and he sent off servants to inform the guards and have all those available postpone their current tasks to look for his daughter, post haste. He even had servants spread word of a reward through the streets for the safe return of Daina to the castle. And among one of the many places being searched was the perimeter of the city. This guard was but one of many checking the walls in case she had fallen somewhere. He hoped she had not fallen into the Decay; by the time he could inform other guards and get a rope down for her to grab onto, she might have no arms to grab them with. She might even be dead. Already Vikenti was pulling out his gray hair from the situation.

He continued his search as he had for the past hour, hoping to see some glimpse of the princess, alive and well. He found nothing of the sort, but then something caught his eye; not on either side of the wall but on the walkway. He got down on one knee and inspected it closely; it was a bloodstain. The other guards using the wall as a shortcut or doing a perimeter search had not noticed it because of its small size. He found himself fixated on this stain as he stood up. How did it get there? The princess was often known for running along the walls, but that did not mean this was her blood. And why would she choose to run on the walls at so late an hour?

Then he heard a voice calling to him from several dozen feet below. He turned around and looked down at an older man. He was standing at the base of one of the wall's staircases, looking up at him nervously. "Thank you for hearing me, sir," said the man. "You're one of the guards looking for Princess Daina, correct? If not, can you direct me to one?"

"Do not worry; I am a guard," he said. "Do you have information concerning what happened to her? And does it relate to this bloodstain?"

"I'm afraid to say that the two are connected," said the man. "It's about something that happened just last night. I'll tell you, but I don't think you'll believe a word of it."

"I'll take any lead I can to find her," said the guard. "Meet me at the steps and we'll talk about it." He quickly moved to meet the man, almost jumping down the steps until he was on the same level. Once there he listened intently as the witness explained what he had seen, and what the guard heard terrified him to his soul.

It took Daina some time but she eventually cleaned the taste of vomit out of her mouth. In moments she was feeling healthy, and so ravenous that she quickly devoured the next piece of meat Aleksei prepared for her. He had cooked it exactly as she liked her meat. She and Aleksei went back into his home, she to change her gloves and he to unearth a metal canteen from his collection of human memorabilia. She filled it up with the remaining water and slung it by its chain strap over her shoulder. After all, she had no idea how long she would stay in the Decay with no drinkable water.

And after only a few more moments in the old village they finally set out for Tantallos, walking out of the small collection of buildings briskly. Aleksei glanced back at his old home, but just once. He would never return to it. The two walked at each other's sides, Aleksei going slow enough so the still-weakened Daina could keep up with him. He did not want to have to carry her.

"I guess you don't have to carry me," said Daina, "but if you did we would be able to get back to Tantallos much faster. I've seen you lift far greater weights, and I'm nothing but skin and bone. I wouldn't be hindering our speed and we would get there faster."

"We would get there faster but you would bleed to death halfway to the main gates," said Aleksei. "I do not trust myself enough with my claws to carry something as delicate as a human being with cutting it; not an insult of your capabilities, mind you. Humans are just softer creatures. Consider the markings I left on you when I flew you back to my home from the forest. Do you want more of those?"

Daina felt the cuts on her arm, but then a strange thought came to her. It was bizarre, but it continued to grow on her. "I cannot believe I'm asking this, Aleksei," she said, "but how did I taste?"

Aleksei furrowed his brow slightly and turned his head to look at her. "Come again?" he asked.

She had expected such a reaction. "How did I taste?" she asked again. "You undoubtedly got some of my blood on your claws while you were carrying me and I'm curious. After getting my blood on your claws, did you clean it off immediately or did you give it a taste? I can't help but wonder."

Aleksei paused for a moment, carefully thinking out what he was about to tell Daina. Even what he came up with made him feel weird to say. "Do not be worried by this, but you are delicious," he said. "There is no parallel for you. You're fit for a huntmaster and nothing short of that. Are you a particularly physical person?"

"Too much physical activity requires one to be particularly strong," said Daina. "I'm not built strong enough to lift great weights or wrestle, nor would I be allowed to do such things to begin with. But I was always fast on my feet, so I occupy my time with running. And just recently I've been training myself with the usage of daggers."

Daina smiled a little as she saw the awkward look on Aleksei's face. "And I'm not worried about your enjoying my taste. Too much is depending on me for you to kill me for a meal, or a snack, if I'm so small a prey in your eyes. It reminds me a bit too much of the tale of Agrafena the Jinx and her unfortunate lover; he always had to keep saving her from certain doom. I hope to not be like that with you, though."

"I cannot say I know that tale, but it would definitely be best if you didn't act like her," said Aleksei. "We have a long way to go and I cannot protect you from everything, especially if we encounter an arch kuvi like myself."

"Maybe one fast little human at your side will be enough to tip the balance in your favor," said Daina. "I'll gladly help whenever I can. It feels good to have someone I can trust, have a conversation with and such things. Not many trustworthy people back in Tantallos."

"That is a terrible statement about your city if you're willing to trust the murderous kuvi who openly admits to eating members of your race," said Aleksei.

"You may have eaten some of my kind, but you aren't going to eat me," said Daina.

"Perhaps not all of you," he said. "It is a tough decision, princess. I'd love to get back into Tantallos, but you are certainly tasty." He brought a claw to his chin as he pretended to ponder something. The corners of his mouth attempted to perk themselves up but did a poor job.

Daina chuckled. "I'll give you a stomach ache for sure, too much of a good thing," she said. Something then occurred to her. "This bizarre conversation reminds me of something else I've been meaning to ask you about."

"What could that possibly be?" he asked.

"It concerns last night," she said. "After I fell unconscious from looking into your eyes, I had an incredibly vivid dream; It seemed so real, but not a single part of the dream was my own. I was in this dry, rocky landscape. The skies were bright, not overcast like the skies of the Decay, and there was a massive bright ring or arch spread out across it."

Aleksei perked up some as he heard this. "Go on," he said. "I believe I know of what you speak."

"I was a kuvi, basically," she said. "I had your claws, your quills. I had some sort of pet similar in nature to a dog I called Pisti. I was speaking a language I didn't understand a word of. I was in a chamber with several other children and we were being looked after. I was waiting on my mother to return for me."

"And then the trogo arrived and swallowed you whole and alive?" asked Aleksei. Daina could not see them, but his eyes were as wide as dinner plates.

Daina stared at Aleksei in shock. "Yes," she said. "And it was the most horrible nightmare I've ever had. It felt like it was happening." Something occurred to her. "It did happen, didn't it? It happened to you!"

"You're correct," he said. "I was only five when that creature put me through the most painful experience I've ever endured. Adult trogos like that one do that sort of thing all the time; most predators in Proso do to juvenile creatures. They use their beaks to dig us out of our hiding spots and rely on their thick stomachs and throats to keep us from escaping their depths. I was lucky; my claws were developed enough for me to latch myself onto the roof of its stomach." He shuddered. "The other ones weren't as fortunate. I was trapped in that chamber for almost an hour with each breath burning me, the acids of its stomach but a few feet below me. This trogo had caught all those kuvis to feed to its own young. By the time it regurgitated its catch, I was so weak I could barely move. It didn't expect any of its catch to still be alive, but it was of no matter. One of its young would kill me shortly anyway."

Daina looked at Aleksei in horror. "Almost an hour in its stomach?" she asked. "And people wonder how you manage to endure the rotting effects of the Decay. But how did you escape from the jaws of this trogo's young?"

"My mother saved me," said Aleksei. "Pisti managed to reach her in time for her to catch up with the trogo. She saw me there, at the mercy of the beast's young, and attacked with a ferocity no other kuvi could possibly match. She tore the trogo and its young apart, then immediately took me far away to recover." He sighed. "She was the most powerful kuvi I've ever known. If it wasn't for what she taught me I would never have survived in this wilderness."

Daina took this all in. "She took down that monster all by herself?" she pondered. "Your mother must be a woman with no parallel." She looked down a little. "My mother died giving birth to me, but my father always told me she was a wonderful person."

A silence then fell on the two as they continued walking, unsure how and unwilling to keep the conversation going. They just continued studying the floor, alone with their thoughts. But it was not long before something crept up on both of them and smacked them across the face. Their noses wrinkled together as they looked around and took notice of the nasty, rattling things bordering the road and littering the entire landscape.

"*Mirke dal mi Prosopsei*," cursed Aleksei, slipping back into his home tongue for a moment. He quickly covered his mouth and nose, as did Daina. "I forgot how many bogs were on the path back to Tantallos. I so wish I could just carry you back." Daina nodded, but as she looked at her companion she saw something beyond simple revulsion. As they walked past the bogs bordering the roads or extending into collapsed sections he started shaking some, as if cold, and many times he moved around her to stay as far away from the foul-smelling pools of stagnant liquid as possible.

"Is something the matter, Aleksei?" she asked.

"Of course not, Daina," he answered hurriedly. "Nothing, nothing's wrong at all. I just don't like those bogs. You can tell why, I'm sure. I'd prefer to keep my distance from those things so make sure not to get in my way. That's very appreciated, thank you. Let's move on."

"All right, quill-head," said Daina. "No need to be so defensive about it."

Aleksei said nothing more, giving Daina time to ponder this development as they continued their walk. The bogs slowly decreased in number, eventually ending as they entered a section that might have once been a forest. Long-dead trees littered the landscape, the remains of their shells keeping them standing, and every now and then was a nasty-looking pool that could not have been more than a couple feet deep. Aleksei did not act so oddly concerning these when they were nearby. Daina mulled this over as well in her head.

Then another thought came back to her. "Aleksei," she said. "I'm sure I mentioned it earlier, but now that I'm so far away from your home I must ask, just in case something happens to you."

"Nothing will, if we avoid any of my kin, but what worries you?" he asked.

"Nothing worries me," she said, "but some people discovered that kuvi relics, such as your claws or your eyes, keep people from being rotted by the Decay. Could I have one of your quills or something in case we're separated?"

"I highly doubt we'll get separated, but it cannot hurt to make sure," he said. "Can't have you going back to your city missing an arm, after all, but... only if I get a lock of your hair in return."

"Why do you want a lock of my hair?" she asked.

"If we get separated, surely you would want to be reunited as quickly as possible," said Aleksei. "I can find you with it. Having a kuvi as a bodyguard has its advantages."

Daina shrugged, pulled out her dagger and carefully cut off a lock of her hair. At the same time, Aleksei winced as he quickly pulled a quill out of the back of his scalp. He accidentally snapped it in two while doing this but managed to hold onto one of the pieces. They made their swap and both pocketed their new gifts, Daina being careful not to pierce herself with Aleksei's quill.

"Tough enough to survive a monster's stomach and the Decay," said Daina. "I saw but a glimpse of where you came from. Is it mostly dominated by swamp as well and that was just a small area?"

"There are many areas dominated by swamp similar to your own," said Aleksei, "but the badlands like you saw are the most common, and almost all areas are much harsher than the Decay. The world of Proso is such a dangerous and inhospitable realm I cannot imagine a single place on its surface where a human could survive for a week. We kuvis are to Proso as you humans are to the world you live in. There are many creatures far greater than us in size roaming about. Some just eat plants and the like, but many like the trogo eat meat, and each creature is terribly great at catching its prey.

"Kuvis are unique creatures in comparison; we are among the few beings with no third eye on the back of our heads, we are among the smallest predators and we can only reproduce with a partner. I do not grasp the mechanics, but a single member of a species can keep it from going extinct. If we kuvis wiped out all the trogos but one, it could repopulate the species with duplicates of itself.And that's to say nothing of the landscapes that dominate Proso," he continued. "Many of the swamps have a constant downpour of undrinkable rain, while others are dominated by carnivorous plant pods that feed on blood. Other areas, like the Melted Shores of the west, are so hot from constant volcanic eruptions that there are rivers of lava flowing throughout. Only someone like myself could survive there as only a kuvi *dal Kafteros* is immune to the heat and fumes. Then there are jungles filled with predators of which are unparalleled with camouflage, and there are vast sandy deserts riddled with monsters that drag you into their pits to be slowly digested over a thousand years. Worst of all, there are immense stretches of impossibly deep ocean filled with sea creatures that are just waiting for you to fall in so they can snap you up in one bite while also drowning you." He shuddered. "Pray you're never unfortunate enough to be taken there. The safest area I can think of is Proso Center, but most kuvis don't enter its walls. It's mostly those on pilgrimage or those in the Huntmaster's Order, though I did study for a time there a couple months after... the trogo incident. Mother thought I should learn from the kuvis there."

Daina listened intently, fascinated by every last word. Even now she was imagining what these areas were like and the differing kuvis who adapted to each place, even if most of these areas she only knew by textbook descriptions. "Please don't stop," she begged. "Where did you live?"

"The area I lived in was hundreds of miles north of Proso Center, near the edge of the continent but thankfully far away from the ocean," said Aleksei. "Most people call it Mouth. It is actually a vast, unmoving creature extending countless miles in length. It is a monster with no face, but rather it's covered in pit-like mouths with lashing tongues that prey upon the parasites living in its flesh. It's said the Huntmaster lets it live solely to keep the Cold One contained in her chamber beneath it."

"The Huntmaster," said Daina. "You've mentioned him several times. Is the Huntmaster your god?"

Aleksei's face seemed to brighten as he heard this question. "He certainly is, princess," he said. "*Mi Prosopsei* is the guardian of our world, our greatest champion and the watchman of all kuvis. Wherever a kuvi may go, no matter what he has said or done, *Prosopsei* travels in his heart." Aleksei put a claw to his chest and then reached down into one of his pockets. He pulled out a small, obsidian circle that featured eight fang-like protrusions that all pointed inward. "My mother gave this to me during our time in Proso Center. I lost the chain to it long ago but I still keep the medallion." He put the icon back in his pocket.

"You've said a lot about your mother," said Daina. "I hate to pry, but what about your father? You haven't said much, or anything at all, concerning him."

"I never knew my father," he said. "He was murdered after my mother became pregnant with me. I always imagined him fighting fiercely, even in his last moments, but my mother avenged his death on his killers even as I was growing in her."

"I don't know what to say," said Daina. "I just wonder if my father would have done the same if my mother had been killed and had not just died."

"King Vikenti seems like a good man just looking for the best concerning his kingdom," said Aleksei. "If Vikenti has kuvis who murder his people merely tossed into the Decay, I cannot imagine he would kill such murderers, or at least not with the same sort of brutality a kuvi would show to such a villain. You humans love to beat yourselves up for what you believe to be terrible about your kind, but there are those who do much, much worse things."

"I suppose we are just guilty creatures," said Daina. "But even if you're a killer you don't strike me as a cruel or sadistic one. You seem merciful, at least as much as one can in this place. Are there other kuvis similar to you?"

"I'm the most merciful and forgiving kuvi you'll ever meet," he said. "Perhaps it's because I was dragged into this world as a particularly young child, before life could harden me and turn me into a stone-cold killer. All the other kuvis are much older than me and would have definitely eaten you before you could let out a single plea for your life."

"Then I'm especially glad it was you who came to rescue me from that kuvi last night," said Daina, smiling as she placed a hand on Aleksei's shoulder. He flinched for a moment, but then relaxed before trying to do something he had not attempted in so long. He forced the corners of his mouth up, showcasing his pearly-white teeth but in a nonthreatening, almost friendly, way. Daina noticed the change in his thin face immediately. "Quill-head, are you smiling?" she asked. "I don't think I've seen you do that once."

Aleksei quickly covered his mouth with a claw, unsure of what to make of his own expression. "Not at all, princess," he said. "I just have something stuck in my teeth."

CHAPTER 12

Although I have bestowed upon you great power, I cannot teach you to use it to its fullest. Don't be shocked or embarrassed if your power lies in an area that seems weak compared to others.
-From the Tomes of the Huntmaster.

Wesan flew back to Tantallos, keeping low to help avoid any unwanted eyes from the tall buildings looming above him. The city was still busy waking up, but it never hurt to be careful. He spotted a section of wall not occupied by a guard and landed on it, immediately dissipating his wings before someone saw them. But he was nowhere near the castle; he was at a location in a different area of town. Jurek had chosen it so they could carry out less savory tasks away from suspicion, at least in the eyes of Abdaas.

He made his way down the wall and through the winding streets, surprised by how active the people already awake were; but it was of no concern to him. Though every human who looked at him made him wonder; could they see past the visor? Could they see his quills, his fangs, his eyes? He pushed such thoughts to the side as he resumed his tracking of the scents of his partners until he arrived in front of an abandoned tenement. He moved in through the entrance, which was missing its door, and made his way up to the top floor. Tulsan was busy working on a small, flexible human bone, gnawing on it to get the last pieces off before breaking it open for the marrow. Wesan stared in disgust at what remained of Tulsan's victim; such a kill was so effortless it was almost insulting. Though it did make him wonder if a mother and father had also been killed last night.

He took the steps around the oblivious Tulsan, far too occupied with his lust for flesh to notice him. Wesan made his way into the other room of the apartment, coming across Jurek as he feasted on an older man with the remains of an older woman by him. He tore into the flesh greedily, blood dripping from his mouth but failing to tarnish the brilliant white of his teeth. Blood dripped down his chin but did not show up on his red armor. He saw Wesan approach and dropped his meal.

"Well, to speak of the Cold One," said Jurek. "We were wondering what had happened to you on your errand. I was, at least. That idiot Tulsan probably didn't even notice. There's not much left of this happy little family and no, you can't have what remains. These two are mine. They may have had another child staying over at a friend's or relative's house, though."

Wesan groaned. "I'd never live down the disgrace of such an easy kill," he said, glaring at the uncaring Tulsan before turning his head back to face Jurek. "And never mind how you can consume two adult humans and still long for more." He looked at Jurek intently, their pit-like eyes locking. "I went to his territory. He was brutally killed but not eaten. All evidence suggested it was an arch kuvi, definitely *dal Kafteros*. He seemed to be after the princess, as I couldn't find her body nor her remains."

"I think we both know what he did with our little girl," said Jurek, licking his chops. "This opportunist arch kuvi of yours decided he wanted to give her a try."

"You're certain it's a he?" said Wesan.

Jurek looked at Wesan oddly for a moment. "I'd say it's more likely than a she," said Jurek. "I've met a few kuvis in my time in this world. All the same, good for that arch kuvi, whoever he, or she, may be. Do you want me to find him and get him to help us? We don't need him at this point but you never know what might happen."

"Whether he joins us or not is of no concern," said Wesan. "We're so close to finishing this as it is. Speaking of which, have you spoken to Abdaas about the blood?"

"Not yet," said Jurek. "I considered dropping off the vial first, but that princess had to be so damn tasty. Got me in a blood-lust I just had to satisfy. Mom and dad here weren't the only humans I've eaten since last night." He reached over to a small table nearby and gently picked up the stoppered vial of blood. "But all that remains is for us to get the king's flesh and raid the city ossuary. The latter might be difficult without knowing our way around but we could kill the king at any time, though preferably at night."

"You make it sound so simple," said Wesan, the outermost ring in his eyes flaring as he said this. "I wouldn't trust Abdaas to even get us a map of the catacombs. He'll undoubtedly invent ways to overly complicate this matter. He's as senseless as his cruel Goddess."

"I will not argue about Abdaas, but I can't agree with you concerning the Goddess," said Jurek. "If a world was unfortunate enough to have me as its deity I too would consume those who kill my people." He got up from the floor slowly, as if he was struggling under the weight of his armor. "Abdaas has plenty of his own problems, but whatever gets us out of this world is fine by me." He adjusted the bottom visor of his helmet to fully cover his face again. "I think it's time we talked to the portly pious one." He turned to Tulsan. "Finish eating and fix your helmet, Tulsan! We're moving out!"

The three kuvis finished fixing their disguises and quickly made their way out of the tenement, Jurek's stride improving immensely the moment he touched the stone street outside the building. They made their way to the castle, everyone around them making sure to give them space; there were royal orders not to accost or bother the knights, and all three smelled of death.

The day continued to drag on for the two in the Decay, Aleksei and Daina forced to stop often so she could recuperate. As they walked through the dead husks of what existed before the Decay they passed by every shape and size of animal. All sorts of mangy, half-crazed creatures were rummaging and scurrying about, from scrawny rats missing most of their fur to giant predators lurking about just over the hills, their dark and scarred flesh helping them to blend in. There was even a mire beast dozing on a large rock, unafraid of anything else in the Decay, except one; not even the mire beasts dared get close to the apex predator of the Decay and his human companion.

Eventually they came across a felled monster lying nearby the road and a sizable predator that was busy feasting on it. One look at Aleksei sent it darting away from its kill, but not traveling far. Aleksei took note and quickly tore off two slabs of meat before rushing away with Daina, letting the hungry creature return to its banquet lest another greater animal show up to take it. They then stopped to make a fire. Rather than prepare a spit Aleksei positioned himself over the fire, adjusting the meat when necessary while the flames wrapped themselves around part of his arms and his torso.

"If you were anyone else I know I'd be screaming at you about what you're doing," said Daina. "To think, fire and its fumes don't affect you at all. It must be great to be a kuvi, so strong and tough."

"In an environment such as this and most places in Proso, we'd like ourselves no other way," said Aleksei. He checked on the slabs of meat and found that they were just about done. He backed away from the fire and gave one to Daina, who immediately started digging in. "But there are some ways that we find ourselves at a disadvantage in comparison to humans. There are almost no artists in kuvi culture, for example. You might find this hard to believe, but oversized claws you couldn't feel a hammer blow through do not help one perform the delicate movements required of painting and sculpting. And our claws make us constant fumblers, near impossible to work on small objects and the like. Even kuvis *dal Spazos* find it difficult at times, and they're the closest things our culture will have to artisans because of their manipulation of metal, and even in their circles, the only artist I can think of is Malek, head of a theatrical group. Mother never wanted to discuss him for some reason."

Daina swallowed her mouthful of food. "Artistic talent always finds its way to the surface despite any hindrances," said Daina. "And you're not dumber than a human; you're probably smarter. There must be something creative you're adept at."

"There are... some things, to be sure," said Aleksei. "Not so much myself, but kuvis can do things that don't require hands. In particular, there are many kuvis who enjoy oral storytelling, but... I can't continue, really. Most kuvis feel it's a waste of time if you're a skilled fighter."

"Nonsense," said Daina. "You can do both; you don't spend every moment fighting, after all. Tell me a story, quill-head." She hoped that he would agree to.

"Sorry, princess," said Aleksei. "But I'm not going to do something so... weak and mundane. Storytelling is for the elderly whose claws have gone dull, who just spend all day watching children while their mothers hunt and fathers work. I'm a young kuvi; I have no time for such a hobby. I need to be busying myself with more important labors."

"You can say that all you want, but I know you don't believe what you're saying," said Daina. "You're just trying to get me to stop talking, even though I don't mind if you like storytelling."

"I never said I liked storytelling," growled Aleksei. "And if you're aware that I'm trying to get you to stop, maybe you should actually take it as a sign that you should stop. Haven't we discussed my abilities concerning your limbs, dismemberment and cauterization?"

"You've made your point," said Daina, putting her hands up in surrender. She had finished eating her cut of meat. "But even if you don't like storytelling, perhaps you'd be open to hearing one from me? We seem to have nothing better to do on our trip, and perhaps you'll find the story useful. It's based on true events."

Aleksei sighed, but he calmed down. "Go ahead," he said.

"A long, long time ago," began Daina; she looked up and judged the position of the sun through the gaps in the clouds. "I'd say about fifteen hours ago, give or take a few, there was a lovely princess who lived in a majestic castle with her father. She loved her life, even if she hated and didn't trust most of the people she had to share it with. She devoutly followed the teachings of the Goddess and, unlike most children, she ate her vegetables without complaint." She smirked a little at the stupidity of that line. "Then, on a cold, dark night, a group of mysterious travelers entered her city. She met the group; four powerful and massive knights, a high-ranking priest of the Goddess and the dashing prince of the city of Tulroy, so handsome and charming she fell for him immediately. The two of them met and were set up to be married. Everyone was happy."

Aleksei found himself surprised by this revelation. "You're due to be married?" he asked. "It seems inevitable, but I'd... have thought you'd have been married before this point. You're rather scrawny but I imagine many humans find you appealing. But pardon my interrupting. Please, continue."

Daina looked annoyed by this comment. "The beautiful and not-that-scrawny princess decided to take a walk that night when she heard..." the horrors of the night came back to her in full force. "Oh, forget this whole idea! I'm no storyteller."

"Then just tell me what happened," said Aleksei, his voice calm.

"Well, I was on my way back to my room from a walk around the castle; I couldn't sleep with all the excitement. While in the hallway I overheard the other five travelers, not the prince from Tulroy; his name is Alkin if that detail matters to you. They mentioned something about collecting bones, and then they said that they also needed my father's flesh!" She held up her arm, shoved up a sleeve and pointed out the particular cut that had been given to her on the walls. She moved the sleeve back into place. "They also needed my blood for some reason, but they've already collected all they need of that. I need to get back to Tantallos to warn everyone of what those knights really are and if I'm not quick about it those cruel monsters are going to tear my father apart!"

Before she could stop herself a barrage of horrible images started flowing into her mind, each one more gruesome than the last. One showed a knight tearing off an arm, another of a knight ripping off a leg, and then a third of the red knight slicing off Vikenti's head in one slash, all while Abdaas watched in approval. She stopped herself and forced the images to the side. Those horrible things would not happen. She was getting back to Tantallos no matter what. They may be far stronger and tougher than any normal human, but she had an army of trained guards to fend them off. And a kuvi of her own certainly did not harm her chances against these enemies of the crown. "Sorry for that outburst," said Daina. "Hardly fitting someone of my station and responsibility. But don't think I'm weak or anything; it's just been a rough time."

"It's all understandable," said Aleksei. "You're unused to such stress, and I would feel similarly if I knew a group of villains planned to kill my mother and I had little time to save her. But everything you describe is quite interesting. I'm not a Summoner but I'm familiar with the process and the ingredients needed to perform the ritual successfully. First ingredient is the gaze of the enemy, and then the next three are the bones of the mother, flesh of the father, and blood of the daughter, related to both parents. Which leaves the question of what they intend to summon; I thought such summoning rituals were considered taboo by the Church of the Goddess."

"They are," said Daina. "And I can't grasp how such a devoted follower of Her could lower himself to using such means for any purpose."

Aleksei thought of something. "You're a princess, and I imagine you have many guards and servants waiting on you. How were you caught alone by these knights, even after twilight?"

"They began their chase at such an hour when all the servants would be asleep in their quarters in another part of the castle," she said. "They cut me off from going down the staircase, so I tried to get away from them by running out of the castle and onto the walls. I thought a long, straight path would tire them out and allow me to escape; running's one thing I'm actually good at. But I was an idiot. I didn't know what they really were at that point. They effortlessly kept their pace with me, even with their full suits of armor weighing them down. Then one of the knights started jumping from building to building and the others generated wings and flew around me! The four knights were actually kuvis, similar to you..." She stopped to take a breath. "They caught up to me quickly at that point, incapacitated me and took a vial of my blood."

"That's all very horrible, but you should be thankful they didn't decide to kill you and consume your flesh right on the castle walls," said Aleksei. "Many kuvis don't have a lot of self-control and a hungry kuvi will eat almost anything."

"Anything?" she asked.

"Yes, and I still regret trying to eat a cud plant," he said. "I found a better taste on the pieces of metal I gnawed on as a child for my claws."

"I guess your claws need metal from somewhere," said Daina.

"One more question before I'm finished," said Aleksei. "Kuvis have one of nine vices; you can tell by the rings of our eyes. Did any of these kuvis have especially large third rings? Did any of them show an overwhelming, obsessive desire to consume your flesh after you were cut open, especially if he or she had not tasted you yet?"

One of the kuvis matched that description perfectly. "Definitely," she said. "He was the scariest one of the four. His partners called him Jurek."

Aleksei stared at her in interest as he mulled this over. "I... don't know any kuvis who go by that name. Most kuvis tend to keep to themselves, except for our woodland friend. He had repeatedly tried to eat me as a child, but I think he regrets that now. If his soul still exists, given how the Goddess treats us. But never mind that; what else can you tell me about this gluttonous kuvi?"

Daina thought for a moment. "This is just a theory, but I think he may be none other than the Red Light Murderer."

Aleksei raised an eyebrow. "Red Light Murderer?"

"Sorry, I should explain," she said. "When I was but a little girl, there was a killer who roamed the streets of Tantallos. He was discovered to be a kuvi. He killed dozens; pretty sure he killed thirty-eight women and their families before he was finally apprehended and thrown out into the Decay. He was a cold, heartless and brutal kuvi, not civil and reasonable like you are. I may not know this Jurek well, but he made remarks about eating girls my age that are on the opposite end of the economy. The farthest away from a princess would probably be a prostitute, and the Red Light Murderer primarily targeted prostitutes similar to my age. And though I didn't see much of his face besides his mouth, you're proof that some kuvis are human enough in appearance to pass for one, provided your eyes and claws are disguised."

Aleksei took all of this in before coming up with a response. Daina did not expect it. "How can you be so sure that this Red Light Murderer was evil prior to his banishment?" he asked. "I cannot deny that many kuvis are evil and feel no sympathy toward those they consider inferior, such as humans. But there are several other kuvis who only kill because that's how we're designed to live; they kill just enough to survive. If you've been stranded in a location with one kind of food far more abundant than any other, what would you choose to feed upon?" He continued before Daina could respond. "Keep in mind no kuvi is stupid enough to attack a prey he doesn't think he can get away with taking down and feeding upon. Whether it's a human or a pack animal that has strayed from a herd, no kuvi wants to go after a target that may trigger the wrath of its kin, whether the punishment is being stampeded or being forced to live out in this dead landscape. No creature would want this fate. Perhaps if someone had just given this kuvi a sandwich every now and then he would not have resorted to killing humans."

"If I could have done such a thing, I would have," said Daina. "At least, if I found him starving I'd have given him some food. I don't know. My subjects love to proclaim that I'm kind and selfless and such, but I don't think I really am. Would I have helped him? I think I might have read some evil into his situation that wasn't there. I do that all the time. I can only think of one instance where I helped someone without hesitation or thought concerning myself, honestly. There are few people I let myself trust, and I can only think of one kuvi among them."

"But it's the one kuvi who will remain steadfast at your side and protect you until you're back in Tantallos, safe and sound, and I'm hidden away in some back alley so I can rest without worrying I might be attacked while sleeping," he said. "And if we do encounter this red murdering kuvi, I'll do what I can to keep him at bay. I just hope he's not as powerful as you make him out to be."

"I'm sure he doesn't stand a chance against you," she said. "I know I'd be terrified if I was in a fight against you. But I'm not, so I thank you from the bottom of my heart for doing this, even if it's more for yourself." Even though he was a monster in the eyes of everyone else, he was the best bodyguard she could have at her side.

CHAPTER 13

*Don't let yourself quiver before the might of a creature that has forsaken Me.
As long as you remain faithful to Me, you shall be the one with the greater
reward at the end while they have nothing but oblivion at My hand.*
-From the Teachings of the Goddess.

Vikenti paced back and forth frantically in front of his throne, going
about so rapidly he was almost wearing holes in the carpet as he awaited the
return of the searchers he had sent off. Alkin sat in a chair nearby, hand on
his chin as he tried to imagine the circumstances that would bring Daina to
seemingly disappear from the castle and all nearby areas. The Captain of the
guard was also nearby, quietly ordering about guards who came to him so to
not disturb either of the other two.

No one had seen her since last night. The entire castle had been
searched, revealing nothing, and now every castle guard was going through
the city to look for her. Even the servants had been excused to aid the guards.
Goddess forbid that the population grows as frantic as Daina's father and
tears Tantallos to the ground in their search for her. What in the greatest
nightmares of the Goddess could have happened to her?

All three people jumped as the throne room doors were loudly opened
and two men quickly walked in. One was a castle guard and the other was an
older man with a bushy gray mustache. They hurried up to Vikenti as he
calmed himself down and sat on the throne, doing his best to keep his posture
despite his fatigue.

"You had better have some damn news if you're going to come in so
loudly," he said curtly. "So what is it? What can you tell me about what
happened to my daughter?"

"A few moments ago I had been walking on the walls when I came
across some slight bloodstains, your highness," said the guard, keeping
himself calm despite the king's anger. "These stains had undoubtedly only
shown up recently or the rain would have washed them away. I then met this
man, who claims to have witnessed what happened from his house window.
He would have come to you earlier but what he saw made him afraid for his
life. I can't say I blame him, honestly. It's fortunate he even came to tell me;
we could still be as clueless as when we began."

The older man was handling the king's wrath more poorly. He nervously stepped forward ahead of the guard and bowed quickly before the king. He brought himself back up, trembling all the while. "Your most gracious majesty," he said, "I saw the beloved Princess Daina running across the walls last night. It was unspeakably late and I would have been asleep any other night if not for the excitement of the day, with the new arrivals and such. At first I thought it was odd that the princess would be running so late when she usually does so during the day, but then I saw her pursuers.

"She appeared before my spot in the moonlight only moments before four men caught up to her with unholy speed and captured her; I never knew one could move so quickly. It was like they just appeared around her, they were moving so fast. I couldn't see them very well in the darkness so I couldn't tell you what they looked like or what they were wearing, but they were definitely large men. I thought about calling for help, maybe distracting them long enough for her to escape, but I thought they would only send one of them to silence me while the rest ensured she didn't get away. They grabbed her, held her still for a time while I heard some groaning noise and then one of them took off with her. She and her captor went right into the Decay from the walls. I was about to leave for the castle when I noticed something horrible; it all became so much worse."

"How could it get any worse than that?" asked Vikenti. "What did you see?"

"I wouldn't have seen them all if they hadn't been glowing," said the man, "but three of them had... demon wings."

Vikenti's eyes widened and he jumped up from his throne, the man backing away in fright. "Demons are in Tantallos?" he roared. He turned to the Captain of the guard, who stopped talking to a servant and snapped to attention. "Put everyone, and I mean everyone, on full alert immediately! Even one demon is enough to defeat countless guards, and we have three of them among us! Do everything you can to inform people concerning Daina's kidnapping. We have to risk a riot for her sake. Have the gates opened so people can search through the Decay, but only if they want to. If enough people are out there and armed with whatever they can find, hopefully the monsters won't jump them." The Captain quickly bowed, issued some orders out to the nearby guards who had been fixated on Vikenti's fury and ran off to find anyone else who was not aware of the situation.

"I just hope there's enough left of her to find," Vikenti said to himself. He knew just how likely it was that she was now nothing more than a pile of bones picked clean by the demon, but he did everything he could to keep the mental images at bay. She was alive. She had to be. The Goddess or perhaps something else intervened and saved her from such a horrible fate. He looked to the side door of the main hall and saw three of the Tulroy knights, including the red one, walking in as Abdaas came off the staircase into the main hall. Vikenti quickly made his way to the four as they approached, resulting in everyone converging by Alkin. The prince got up and moved in front of Vikenti.

He got down on one knee and put his right hand on his heart. "Your highness," he said, "I volunteer my services so I may join the search for Daina in the Decay. I'll talk to my partners and see if they cannot assist us in some way. Perhaps they can help organize search parties or fight off the creatures of the Decay. And, if any of us find her, rest assured she will be brought right back into your arms. If anyone else finds her, one of us will know."

"I graciously accept your offer and extend all courtesies to aid you," said Vikenti. Alkin stood back up. "Thank you so much for your help, Alkin. Already you're about to save my daughter again." Something then occurred to Vikenti. "Tell me, Alkin, what sort of weapon do you prefer to use?"

"I am an unparalleled swordsman and can wield a blade as well as a demon can wield its claws," said Alkin. One of the knights made a slight snort, resulting in a glare from the red knight through the visor. "Truth be told, I lost my sword in the Decay on the trip to Tantallos, but my fists are more than enough for any monster."

"Undoubtedly for any creature of the Decay," said Vikenti. "But while I'm sure you could punch a mire beast as massive as the one above me into a bloody mess, you are up against demons. Not just one, but several. If you're going to even stand a chance against them you need something much, much more powerful."

Alkin and Vikenti bid farewell to Abdaas and the knights, who went off to the bedroom hallway to, according to them, plan their course of action. At the same time, Vikenti led Alkin to the other side of the castle. Alkin soon found himself in Vikenti's own room, where the king moved over to an incredibly dusty display case on a dresser; the dust was so thick the item inside was obscured. He took out a key and unlocked it. Inside was the largest two-handed sword Alkin had ever seen. It was almost as long as a typical citizen of Tantallos and was made of a bright, shining metal similar to iron. The hilt had the names of soldiers who had been killed in the wall collapse carved into it, and the blade was devoid of decoration. Even from a distance both of them could see that it was still very sharp and free of corrosion. Not that a sharp edge was needed; the blade was undoubtedly so heavy it would obliterate any limb unfortunate enough to be in the way.

"This is my old sword, cared for and used by members of my bloodline since before I can remember," said Vikenti. "No other blade like it exists in Tantallos. With it I killed the mire beast on my wall and countless other creatures of the Decay after the wall collapse. It is so heavy my soldiers call it the Back Breaker. I used it effectively in my younger days, but now I'm far too old and weak to even lift it. But, if there's a single soul who can wield it, it's you. Take it into the Decay and rip through those demons like paper."

Alkin nodded and stepped forward to the sword. It glistened in the light, almost beckoning to him. He grabbed the sword with both hands and slowly hoisted it up out of the display case, careful to keep himself from dropping it on his feet. It was very heavy, but Alkin was used to such immense pressure. Vikenti found its sheath and aided Alkin in placing the sword inside it before they tied it to Alkin's back. Already Alkin found himself adjusting to its weight. "It is nothing I cannot handle, I assure you," said Alkin, "but I can see that your sword earned its nickname."

"Indeed," said Vikenti. "I pity the poor guard who actually tried to lift it on a bet, but that incident is in the past. Now, please, go into the Decay and save my daughter."

"She will be back in your hands, alive and with all her limbs, soon enough," said Alkin. He bowed and left the room, making his way to the castle entrance that connected with the wall so he could stop in with Abdaas. He did so and Abdaas agreed to share this news with the knights; they had a lot to discuss.

CHAPTER 14

Anyone who kills men, violates women and enslaves children in My name is
no servant of Mine. I can only hope that, by your destruction in My depths,
your essence is used to create something much better for the world.
-From the Teachings of the Goddess.

"I can't believe you would do something this idiotic!" yelled Abdaas.
"You fools! You monstrous, moronic, dog-toothed fools!" He glowered at
the three armored kuvis in his bedroom, angrily pacing back and forth in
front of them, fidgeting with his fingers as he saw the seams of his plan come
undone. "What were you thinking in killing her? Yes, she overheard us and
yes, I know you fiends love eating the flesh of innocents, but the princess is
rather necessary for this plan to work!"

Jurek did not notice any such faults in the plan; to him, it was still going
well. "Don't let yourself get so flustered, Abdaas," he said. "First of all, the
one we sent off to take care of her never came back. Wesan went to his
territory and found him dead and the princess gone. It's possible, however
unlikely, that she's still alive." He held up the vial of blood carefully in his
oversized hands. "Second, we already collected the blood of the daughter so
she's useless to us anyway. Give us an hour in the ossuary and a minute in
the main hall and we'll have gathered every ingredient you need. Besides the
one you said was a guarantee."

Wesan nodded in agreement while Tulsan busied himself with a
wineskin. He funneled the edge of the skin through the bottom of his helmet
while raising the other side up in front of his face. He dare not lower the
mouth cover lest an inopportune servant burst in and see what was lying just
underneath the suit of metal.

"Yes," said Abdaas. "Desecrate their queen's grave and then murder
their king on his own throne. We'd only inspire every soul in Tantallos to
chase after us as we flee into the Decay. Jurek, leave the thinking to me. Yes,
the blood you collected will work if we have to use it, but the ritual would
take much longer as a result. This is a great task set to me, and it's important
that nothing be risked. It's, as you would say, possible, however unlikely, that
the Tantallos citizens could reach Tulroy by that time or one of Alkin's
subjects could work to sabotage our taboo endeavor. She might also be

slightly weaker than usual after the summoning, something best not chanced, and all that's only if the other ingredients are of the highest quality. If you want the ritual to go smoothly the blood needs to be pure. It has to be the last drops of innocence."

"Blood is blood no matter where it comes from," said Jurek. "What sort of blood could you possibly be talking about?"

"I need the blood of her maidenhead," said Abdaas.

Tulsan spat up his drink, sending him into a coughing fit as he tried to clear out his throat. The wine ran down the inside of his helmet and dripped down onto his chest-plate while the skin emptied out onto the floor from his hand. All three knights looked at Abdaas in shock. "Her what?" Jurek asked angrily.

"You know exactly what I said, Jurek," said Abdaas sternly. "Your hearing is better than mine, is it not? Gather it by any means necessary, and I do mean any means necessary. My church forbids me from partaking in such pleasures of the flesh, but your soul's already doomed if you remain in this world. What do you have to lose?"

"My complete respect for myself!" said Jurek. "*Mirke dal mi Prosopsei*, no!" Beneath his helmet was a face that looked like it could throw up at any second.

"Don't speak your hellish language in my presence," said Abdaas.

"Then don't demand such a request of me!" said Jurek. "Would you lay with a pig or a chicken or any other animal you feed upon? No! So why do you expect me to do as much?"

"Because if you don't do it, no one else will," said Abdaas, "and this ritual could very well hinge on you collecting it. And it's not like I'm asking you for an extensive, inconceivable amount of effort. She's a weak girl, not even twenty years old and with about as much strength as me. Surely you can catch up to her again and apprehend her, can't you? And once you've collected her blood feel free to kill her and dispose of her body in any way you see fit. I'd imagine you would find her taste pleasing or at least decent. I cannot say for certain; I've thankfully never tasted the blood of another human."

"To think you humans share a similar viewpoint to most kuvis in that regard," said Jurek. "And both groups lose so many opportunities by not eating their own. The breasts of a human are the finest meat I've ever tasted, bar none."

"If that's the case, then feel free to indulge yourself once you've collected the blood from her," said Abdaas. "Just bring the vial to me beforehand so I can begin the ritual. Do that and before you can even finish your snack I'll be done with my end of the bargain. The entire populace of Tantallos could appear at the front gates of Tulroy and it would be of no consequence to us."

"I guess it's good that you're so confident with your plan," said Jurek. "My thoughts concerning the matter get worse every day." He looked to Tulsan. "You're staying here to look after things while Wesan and I go out into the Decay to find our little princess."

All three kuvis then got up and left without another word to Abdaas, who glowered at them as they walked out. Wesan went on ahead of Jurek, who took a moment to step into Daina's bedroom while no servants were nearby. Once inside he quickly swiped a scrap of her clothing. He caught up to Wesan and, while walking down the main street to the front gates, raised the piece to his visor and breathed in deeply, taking in the exotic aroma. He licked his chops at just the smell but stopped himself from losing control. He had to find her. He only hoped that no monster, or kuvi, had gotten to her already.

CHAPTER 15

Only animals consume their own kind; you are above them and should act as such.
-From the Tomes of the Huntmaster.

Outside of the safety of Tantallos what little life there was continued as it normally did: just barely. As the afternoon went on the sun sank further and further down, though no living being could tell through the thick layer of clouds. Even through the overcast layer the foggy landscape was illuminated, though Daina doubted the desolate wetlands would look any better if the sun was out. She and Aleksei continued their journey to the mountain on the crumbling road. Already she was feeling much better than she had when she woke up. Daina walked alongside Aleksei, who was using his superior eyesight to look out for threats through the slight fog. The rings shifted themselves about, focusing as he gazed at specific areas of interest and potential danger, seeing through the thin piece of cloth like it was not even there.

Daina thought for a moment and turned her head to the kuvi. All things considered, with his maddening gaze covered up by the white band, he was surprisingly easy on her eyes. This apparently runty hunter of hunters had been forged into a lean, strong creature by his environment. His hair alone was undoubtedly more than enough to deter most predators, but even with such hardened qualities there were still some gentle features on his face; it was completely devoid of facial hair and probably incapable of even growing it, though he still had eyebrows as red as his quills. And although he had little experience at doing it, he had a nice and friendly smile. When he was smiling he did not look half as threatening. Then she would look at his claws and this fantasy would be immediately ruined. Friendly or not, he was still a hunter. There was no better reminder for that than his claws.

But beyond all that, here she was with one of the most powerful creatures walking the face of the world, a member of a race that may be one of the greatest in all dimensions of existence. Surely he would be open to more talking and it wouldn't hurt her to ask. So much could be learned. "Aleksei," she said.

Aleksei turned his head to look at her. "What is it you need?" he asked.

"Nothing, really," she said. "Just a small, minor question. I was curious about your age. You look about my age but I am unfamiliar with kuvis; you may very well look this way when you have children or even grandchildren."

"Huntmaster's mercy, no," he said, smiling in humor. "My quills would have started turning gray by that point. I cannot give you an exact age down to the day as I'm not very familiar with the calendar of your world, but I wasn't even seven years old when I was dragged into your world." He raised a claw to his chin as he thought things over, his smooth flesh durable enough to remain uncut from accidental contact with the tips of the blades. "I'd say that, by your calendar, I'd be turning eighteen years old within one cycle of the moon. Give or take a few days. With all the clouds it's hard to tell at times."

"You're young," she said.

"You cannot be that much older than I am," said Aleksei. "How old are you, princess?"

"I'm nineteen, quill-head," Daina responded proudly.

"You're not too much older than me at all," he said. "And it's not like age plays a significant role, now, does it? I've witnessed male humans going after females much younger than themselves. Though not nearly as much the other way around. Wouldn't you naturally want a mate of similar age for better compatibility? I'd imagine a sizable age difference would result in less shared passions."

Daina thought about the age of her own fiancé and decided to move on from the conversation. "How about we talk about something else?" she asked. Aleksei nodded. "The other kuvis I've encountered have not really proven themselves to be kind and courteous, but are there any kuvis that you're friends with, perhaps some female kuvis? I can't speak for them, but you seem to be attractive enough for a human if your eyes are covered up. Even the quills aren't that unsightly since they're so thickly grown in."

"I appreciate the compliment," he said. "But no, I do not have anyone particularly close to me out here. My summoning seemed to have been a botched effort; while Tantallos seems to largely deal with children, most of the kuvis summoned to this world are adults. They are much more powerful than a runty juvenile with little combat experience and thus more likely to live. There are exceptions besides my own, but that's what seems to be dominant. Females aren't any less capable than male kuvis; they're weaker yet faster, but they don't seem to be summoned as often. I last saw a female kuvi some time after being dumped into this swamp."

"Who was she?" asked Daina.

"Felaem," said Aleksei. "She was about ten years my elder. She came across me shortly after I had been expelled from Tantallos. I think she saw me as the younger brother she never had. She assisted me in adapting to the

Decay and helped train me to fight. She also taught me more about Proso and fine-tuned my human language skills. I had been capable before then, but often missed some details."

"She did an excellent job," she said. "You're as fluent as any Tantallosian."

"Thank you," he said. "We spent a lot of time working together. We hunted and trained and it wasn't long until I was holding my own against her. She noticed my *Ateni* early on and helped me better learn to use it."

"You mentioned that earlier," said Daina. "What is it?"

"I'd imagine the kuvi skill-set is very confusing to one unfamiliar with it," said Aleksei. He raised up a claw. "An arch kuvi controls one of five alignments; I control *dal Kafteros*." His claw glowed white and burst into flames. Then his claw went black and the flames died.

"So fire," said Daina.

"I think the literal translation would be 'of burning,' but I'm unsure of that," said Aleksei. "And outside of these five are the Mediators, or *dal Olokanos*. Mediators have no alignment of their own but can disable any kuvi from using their own element. They also have one of two abilities, gifts of the Huntmaster. These gifts are *Ateni*, gaze, and *Lias*, fury. There's also *Briko*, roar, but no living kuvi has access to that ability. I'm one of the very few non-Mediators who can use one of the two gifts; if it wasn't for that I might have lost that fight in the forest."

"Continue," said Daina. "What's special about *Ateni*?"

"I can read any movement, analyze any fault," he said. "Try and punch me. Use your speed. Try to punch any part of my body."

Daina looked at Aleksei oddly and then shrugged; it's not like her little jab would cause any lasting harm. She aimed a punch at Aleksei's gut, so fast she was barely aware of her movement, but she was knocked off-balance as Aleksei's own arm moved hers to the side, her momentum nearly making her lose her footing. She regained her posture and looked at Aleksei. "I guess I wasn't fast enough," she said.

"It wasn't so much that," said Aleksei. "But your body gives you away. I can read the slightest movements you make and use that to tell where you're striking. Then it's only a matter of blocking you, and with my speed I can stop a blow in the blink of an eye. I can even predict fake-outs most of the time."

Daina's eyes widened. "No wonder you were flying circles around that other kuvi. You knew every move he was going to make!"

"I knew when he did," he said. "His armor made it difficult to predict strikes, but fortunately he was a slow target. *Ateni* also helps me find weaknesses. For example, you tend to favor your left leg when you make a move, probably due to the additional cuts you had received there from my improper handling."

"Don't feel bad about that," she said. "Between your *Ateni* and this Falaem training you, you must be an unparalleled fighter."

Aleksei paused for a moment. "To an extent," he said.

"I'm guessing your modesty concerns why we haven't encountered Falaem yet," said Daina. "If it's a painful memory, don't feel pressured to tell me."

"No," said Aleksei. "It might help you to know. She was killed by another arch kuvi, the only one I know of more powerful than myself. Whether or not he's one of the kuvis working with the priest, I could not possibly say, but I pray to the Huntmaster he's not the same one, for both our sakes. He was a terrifying foe, massive, strong, and very fast on his feet. He was also a third-ring kuvi." Aleksei gestured to his eyes. "And his rings were glowing so vividly he must have been starving."

"You don't mean he..."

"He jumped us while we were trying to hunt," he said. "We tried to fight him but he defeated us effortlessly. He easily bested me, keeping me alive, but killed her and feasted upon her flesh. Ate her down to the bone, then broke the bones open to get at the marrow. I did everything I could to fight him off, try to save her, but he had no trouble in taking me down." He sighed and looked down. "He was *dal Tinagmos* and used his control of the earth to defeat me as easily as you could defeat a housefly. I tried using my *Ateni*, but that does not help when your opponent can use it himself. Maybe if he had been *dal Afxanos*, wood, or *dal Spazos*, metal, the situation might have been different. But no." He sighed again and shook his head.

"Chin up, quill-head," said Daina, coming up to Aleksei's side and rubbing his upper back. He flinched at the touch but quickly calmed and raised his head. Daina's hand retreated and Aleksei smiled a little.

"Thanks, princess."

"Just one more question concerning him," she said. "What did he look like?"

"He was over a foot taller than me," he said. "He had smooth flesh the color of clay, a broad nose and quills that were black, black as oil. But the things I remember most about him were his wings. His wings were so gigantic, so intimidating. The sort of wings whose maker you would never want to get in the way of; no kuvi with such wings could possibly be weaker than you are, after all. It was rather fitting; he was so violent, so dominated by his vice that he would kill you just for a snack."

Daina took this all in as they continued walking through the Decay. Such an entourage of horrors surrounding them, and the one nice person that this kuvi had known had been killed by a gluttonous cannibal. "Are most kuvis like that?" she asked.

"Most of the ones that I call my neighbors," he said. "Like the one I killed for you last night. When you're surrounded by nothing but the scum of Proso, you tend to enjoy your own company. We kuvis can be solitary creatures, so it's not... that tough on one."

Daina wondered how tough it was on a young boy who had just been torn away from his mother, a young boy who had already survived getting swallowed alive when all his peers had been slowly killed below him. She felt a sickening feeling in her gut. "And to think I hate that people want nothing more than to be around me and treat me kindly. To think I try to avoid all those who adore me and view me as a hope for the future... and here you have been living with no one at all. Even now you're alone, save for one spoiled princess."

Aleksei awkwardly brought a claw around Daina's shoulders, none of the digits touching so as to not accidentally hurt her. "Spoiled or not, at least that princess takes the time to actually talk to me when she could easily remain silent," he said. "That alone is so much more than how most of the sentient creatures I have encountered have treated me. Even from the beginning of my time in your world. Even then, I had no one. I hate to continue this conversation about myself, but I need someone to talk to about that day I came here."

"I don't mind at all," said Daina.

"Thank you," he said. "I remember it all too well. I was with my mother. We had killed this stray *baro* juvenile who was dying from exposure already. We were busy eating when suddenly the fabric of the world around us tore open. I can't even really describe what that was like; it was a massive black space that just appeared behind me. I don't do it justice. We stood up and looked at it in fright and then I felt myself getting pulled toward it. I tried to struggle against it, fight back and keep myself firmly on the ground, but I started floating in the air. My mother let out a scream and rushed forward, grabbing me by my claws as my feet rose above my head and faced the gap in the world. There was nothing inside that gap; nothing more than a blackness reaching out to me, dragging me ever closer even as my mother tried to pull me back. She found herself getting dragged alongside me." He sniffled.

"But even she, in all her might, could not stop it. I remember the look on her face as I slipped out of her grasp and disappeared feet-first into that rip. It was complete shock and grief, and the only look that came close to rivaling it was the one on my face as she disappeared from my sight. What followed next is as much a mystery as anything else. I was dragged from Proso to your world, with nothing of my own. All I had were the clothes on me, the icon of Prosopsei around my neck and the bit of His spirit in my heart. I seemed to be moving between worlds for an eternity, all while being smothered by something; or perhaps it was a nothing smothering me. It was like I was being completely enveloped by a massive thick, black blanket, or perhaps it was like being buried alive. I could barely breathe and every time I tried to scream nothing would come out. I could hardly even move as I drifted through this gap between worlds.

"Then all my senses came back in an instant when I landed painfully on a flat stone dolmen. I winced at the light and took in every breath of fresh air I managed to get like it would be my last. It very well could have been at that point, for all I knew. Then I heard a voice; I couldn't understand exactly what it was saying, but I could tell it was angry and disappointed. I looked to the voice in confusion and locked eyes with an old man, the one who had summoned me. He used one word in particular while pointing at me; '*demon*,' he said repeatedly. He said it with such hate. Then like so many others he got lost in my eyes and collapsed onto the floor, dead, unable to withstand my accidental glare. My relationships with humans did not improve after that initial meeting."

"I cannot even imagine what that must have felt like," said Daina. "But I do feel even pettier now. To think you're unfortunate enough to be stuck looking after me. You deserve someone nicer."

"Don't be so hard on yourself," he said. "You're nicer than almost all other humans I've met, and kuvis are used to being alone as it is. As are most predators, I'd imagine. And not even a young kuvi will ever shed a tear over his own fate. When I cried that day it was over my mother losing her only child and being left with nothing." The grim mood was interrupted by a loud grumbling coming from Daina. She put a hand over her stomach and felt it growl loudly again.

"Not now," she told it.

"You're hungry already?" he asked. "I'll look out for possible food."

"I'll persevere through it," said Daina. "It won't be pleasant but I'll go hungry for as long as it takes. We need to get to Tantallos as fast as possible. Once I get there they'll feed me as much as I want."

"That is a long time to go without any food," said Aleksei. "Tantallos is quite a distance away. We still need to cross this mountain before the city walls even come into sight. To say nothing about all the Decay we'll have to go through. You'll want to be healthy and strong when you get back home."

"Then perhaps something quick," she said. "Something that doesn't require thorough preparation to avoid making me throw up." She looked at a nearby cud plant. "What about cud plant seed pods? Some of my tutors said animals eat cud plants."

"There is no amount of preparation that will make those things edible," he said. "I can't let you subject yourself to them."

"There must be something else," said Daina. "Perhaps we could..."

Aleksei stopped cold and shushed Daina immediately. He ran behind her in the blink of an eye and grabbed her around the waist, finishing with a claw around her mouth to further stifle her. He looked around rapidly and spied a copse within only a dozen feet. He hurried her over to them as fast as he could and got inside to the deepest, most obscured place. Daina did all she could to avoid gagging on the burnt taste of his claws as she looked around for what had disturbed him so.

She looked at the ground for a moment before lifting her head upward to spy two flying shapes heading toward them. She felt Aleksei tremble a little as they came closer into view; his eyes widened at an all-too-familiar sight. One was Wesan and the other was unmistakably Jurek, his massive, jagged wings beating the air as he slowly passed over the land. He turned his head rapidly left and right, scanning the terrain for signs of his quarry. Daina and Aleksei remained motionless as the kuvis eventually landed at the spot they had been at just moments ago. Wesan looked around while Jurek got down on one knee, picked up a handful of dirt and smelled it.

"I can find traces of her scent," he said. "Weak, but definitely there. There's also another scent just as prevalent." He took another sniff and then chuckled sinisterly. "Oh, isn't this scent a welcome reminder. And just as excellent as ever, I must say."

Wesan looked at Jurek in confusion and a little fear. He constantly worried when Jurek got into such a state. "What is it?"

"Kuvi scent, no mistaking that," said Jurek. "Specifically, a runty juvenile kuvi. I encountered him and his older sister many years ago. It's been so long I can hardly remember. I killed big sis and ate her. I would have eaten him as well if he hadn't gotten lucky. Damn kid had the *Ateni*, same as me." He grinned. "But now that little boy's all grown up and probably fuming with rage over what happened to his sister. He was of the fifth rings."

"Any kuvi with two pieces of brain to rub together would capitulate to you," said Wesan. "And he was a runt as well? He'd be wise to not even try fighting back."

"It won't spare him any pain to do so," said Jurek. "I have certain matters I need to settle with him before I finally let him die." He stood up, moved a few spots away from his first position and knelt back down again. Daina felt Aleksei relax some as Jurek moved further away. "These tracks are fresh. If the human scent was stronger I could find them in an instant but the girl's been in the Decay for too long. The kuvi scent doesn't help, either."

Aleksei rotated his head to the right. The mountain had been looming over them for some time, but now it was within a relatively short distance; a human could run it. He looked around and saw the ruined path that led into one of the caves dug into the base of the mountain. The cave entrance was small and cylindrical and went inside an unknown distance. Aleksei had always gone around it rather than risk disturbing something possibly living inside. But that would not work this time. Even if he did not have Daina, he could not fly away. Not with Jurek pursuing him. It was only a matter of time until Jurek found them. Even though they'd been lucky to escape notice inside the dense copse, they'd be discovered eventually.

Aleksei made a decision and inched his way out of the back of the copse, all while holding onto Daina as carefully as he could. She kept herself from wincing every time his claws accidentally scraped against her flesh, anything to avoid falling back into the claws of Jurek. Aleksei and Daina only moved when one of the kuvis moved so the clinking and clanking of their own armor covered the noise they made; Daina's feet were on top of his to further reduce chances of disturbing the two kuvis. Each second seemed to last an eternity as they backed away, slowly emerging out of the back of the copse. Then Aleksei's foot found a fallen branch and snapped right through it.

Wesan and Jurek immediately shot up and turned to face them. Aleksei let go of Daina and moved himself in front of her as fast as possible to better protect her. They turned to face the two kuvis as they quickly made their way around the copse to confront them. Daina backed a couple feet away from Aleksei, who sprouted his wings and displayed them prominently. He made them glow even brighter in an attempt to make himself look as large and intimidating as possible.

"*Mi Prosopsei*," said Wesan mockingly. "Your wings are so beautiful! Too bad they're on a male!"

Aleksei said nothing. His and Daina's backs were to the mountain.

"They are really cute," said Jurek, grinning. "So elegant and graceful, a complete mockery of what kuvi wings should be, and you're honestly trying to look threatening with them? It would be funny if it wasn't so pathetic."

Aleksei remained silent and continued slowly strafing around them. It was slow progress but each step brought them closer to the path that would lead them straight to the cave. Was it close enough, though?

"Not talking," said Wesan. "Perhaps you should kick him around some, Jurek. I'll provide tactical moral support. I suspect he's *dal Kafteros*. What does he actually use?"

"He uses powers that are absolutely useless against me,"said Jurek. He planted his feet firmly in the ground and focused, his grin fading away, leaving his face as solid as stone. Aleksei's eyes widened and he moved away from Daina.

"Go, now!" he whispered to her before she could get close to him again. "Get to the cave while I keep them busy! I'll be right there!"

Daina nodded and took off for the cave, doing all she could to focus solely on speed and not on what was about to happen. Jurek pointed a claw at

Aleksei's feet; the claw seemed to have become immobile and non-malleable, unable to bend or make articulate motions. Aleksei barely managed to leap and fly into the air before a spike of rock erupted from where he had been standing. Wesan took to the air as well, slowly gaining altitude with every beat of his wings. He was not as fast as Aleksei, though. Aleksei looked between them rapidly, keeping track of his enemies and diving and soaring as more spears of rocks came out of the ground. One almost skewered him through the waist had he not sharply inclined upward.

"It's just as much fun as I remember it being," taunted Jurek. "Only thing better was our hand-to-hand fight, *Ateni* against *Ateni*. No, the best part was skewering your partner. I remember it like it was just yesterday." Jurek knew his adversary all too well; it took just the right comment to provoke him. When provoked he wasn't half as strategic and would predictably charge him in his rage. He would be stronger, perhaps, but definitely not enough to overpower him. "If it makes you feel any better, she was delicious."

Aleksei's rings started glowing so brightly they showed through the band of cloth. "Shut your mouth!" he yelled, bringing his claws away from his body. They glowed white and became enveloped in flames. He dodged another series of spikes and then dived at Jurek before letting fire flow from the palms of his claws like a river. Jurek saw all the moves coming and made a motion like he was dragging something up from the ground. A wall of earth erupted upward, blocking the fire. Aleksei ended his attack the moment he noticed the motion and swerved upward to avoid hitting the wall.

Then Wesan exploited this moment to dive down feet-first, hitting Aleksei on the shoulder and knocking him off-balance. Wesan failed to recover from his attack and landed roughly on the ground, but Aleksei had fared no better. He flapped his wings in a vain attempt to recover and landed headfirst. He tried to pull himself up but in moments bonds of earth wrapped themselves around his feet, leaving only his hooked claws exposed. He let his wings disintegrate into the air lest they get damaged. Jurek walked up to Aleksei, smiling in self-satisfaction as he grabbed him by the shirt. He pulled the young kuvi up to his eye level and then let go. Aleksei was still more than strong enough to keep himself up; it would take more than Wesan's attack to defeat him. But any attempted attack against Jurek now would be fruitless.

"How nice to see you again after all these years, kid," said Jurek. "I'd love to catch up with you, but I must ask. Why the eye cover? It's almost like you were traveling with someone who'd be affected by the glare of a kuvi. A human, perhaps, a human who managed to escape in our little scuffle because Wesan was a damn moron and didn't think to get her." Wesan looked at Jurek in shock but then immediately began looking around for Daina.

"You've had enough flesh in your life, *te trogo*," said Aleksei, spitting the last two words as an insult. "And all for that girl? I've tasted her blood. She's not worth half the amount of effort you've put into getting her back."

Some distance away Daina was watching from the cave entrance, fear growing inside her as she saw Jurek unscrew the mouth cover on his helmet. She felt helpless as she watched, thoughts whirling through her head as she caught a glimpse of Jurek's teeth. They were just as frightfully white and pearly as she had remembered; how could they stay so clean, given how much he eats? Wesan gave up on his search and moved closer to them, possibly suggesting some other torment for Jurek's captured plaything.

She felt Aleksei's quill in her pocket. She could not do this. Aleksei certainly would not stand by if she was the one being threatened; she had to at least try something. But she could hardly fight them off herself; how could she make a difference and save his life? Perhaps all it would take was one little action to make that difference. She could not do much, but she could certainly do something. She looked around the cave entrance, checking for the things she needed for her idea. Not to fight the kuvis, but something that might help almost as much.

"I do love sharing some banter with my prey," said Jurek, salivating madly. Aleksei looked at him in revulsion, not wanting to fathom what was about to happen. "Kid, you may be annoying, weak and undersized in addition to being just plain worthless, but you'll still make a great little snack. I haven't had kuvi flesh in so long. Do you have any idea how tough it was for me, with my partners never going off on their own while I was not busy?"

Wesan immediately turned his head to Jurek. "I knew it!" he yelled. "And I'm really surprised you didn't at least try to eat Tulsan."

"Shut up, Wesan, or I might change my mind!" Jurek yelled back. He quickly turned back to Aleksei, who was slowly struggling to loosen the earthen bonds on his feet while Jurek focused solely on his face; the kuvi's arrogance was betraying him. "No matter; the arch kuvis always taste the best. You agree, don't you? You would if you've had the pleasure. I've had all variants and fire's probably the second-best. Water might be the best one; it's a tough call."

"Neither are the best," growled Aleksei. "I think earth is the best kind. At the very least it's the most satisfying to obtain. Allow me to demonstrate, you dirt-faced abomination."

Jurek whistled. "I'm an abomination just because I like to chew on people from time to time," he said. "Kid, you have quite the little temper. Nothing but fire in you, burning for vengeance. Tell me; does fire leave a great aftertaste, a spicy little note that lingers in the mouth and leaves one wishing for water? I can't remember." Suddenly there was a noise coming from the side of the mountain. Off in the distance something snapped, soon followed by another similar noise. Jurek dropped Aleksei and turned toward the sound of the noise. "That wasn't what I think it was, was it?" he asked Wesan.

Wesan looked to the cave entrance but did not see the princess. "Sounds like she just made a couple clumsy steps; hard to tell with all that dead brush," he said. "Maybe if you had stopped talking about your longing to violate one of the Huntmaster's teachings we'd have kept better track of that damn princess."

"The Huntmaster has no presence here, so stop with that dogma," said Jurek. "And if you had ever had the pleasure of consuming your fallen opponent you'd understand. Now go get that royal pain or your blood is going to be my chaser."

Wesan took off into the air without another word and flew toward the noise while Daina carefully observed from behind a large rock at the entrance. She carefully threw another rock to a place by the area the first two rocks landed to help keep Wesan occupied; any amount of time she could afford to buy would serve her well. Jurek sighed; it was probably nothing more than a facade. He turned back to his plaything but instead found two small holes in the ground while Aleksei sprinted toward the cave entrance. Jurek yelled in rage at his own idiocy and brought his stiff hands up, as if he was a hellish conductor readying an orchestra. Each movement of his claws brought stalagmites shooting up out of the ground at his quarry, Aleksei dodging and darting side-to-side to avoid them. Jurek attempted raising spikes and walls in advance of Aleksei but he always dodged opposite of the side Jurek had chosen.

Jurek was getting nowhere with this. The kid had obviously grown at least some brains since last time. He then looked up and observed the mountain. Something clicked in his head as he examined it. He grinned and focused on a mass of rocks above Aleksei. In an instant the rocks became free and started tumbling down the mountain. He treated himself to a laugh as the avalanche got closer and closer to the bottom. Once it landed his target would be trapped and buried under it. The rocks wouldn't kill him, but keep him pinned long enough for Jurek to deal with him at his own leisure. He had a lot more he wanted to say to the runt.

Aleksei forced himself to move even faster as the distance between the ground and the falling rocks narrowed as quickly as the distance between him and his goal. Soon he was running at a speed above even the fastest of humans. Daina stepped out from behind her rock and urged him toward the entrance as she felt the mountain rumble all around her. Then he was in the tunnel with her, wrapping an arm around her waist, pulling her away from the entrance as rocks fell and barricaded them in. In moments they were in complete darkness.

Jurek sighed as he saw his nemesis disappear into the tunnel before it was covered, obviously able to get out of the dangerous area. But he did not feel any less accomplished; he could not remember the last time he had so much fun with a weaker arch kuvi. His hands limbered up and his summoned spikes sank back into the ground as he regarded his handiwork. Even if the runt made his way out of the caves to an entrance on the other side he would be trapped inside for some time. Jurek could relax for a bit, even leave and come back for him if he wanted. Wesan returned to Jurek, landing at his side and saying nothing. Jurek turned to face him. "I may be mistaken, but you don't seem to have the princess in your grasp," said Jurek. "Silly of me, I know, but it appears to be the case. Don't you think you should be getting her?"

"I can't believe we fell for her trick," growled Wesan. "This must be what Tulsan feels like all the time. Nothing more than a little noise to distract us while your plaything took the opportunity to escape, and both of us just stood around like human's pets looking for a small animal that just ran past."

"I won't tell anyone and you certainly won't," said Jurek. "You take one side of the mountain and I'll take the other. We'll search the nearby area for her, just in case she didn't go into the tunnel. If you do find her, bring her back to me so I can get this accursed job over with." He shuddered. "I'd rather be forced to have that weakling kuvi for a mate than go through what I have to."

"Seems like a waste of time," said Wesan. "Most likely she's trapped in the mountain with him. And I'm sure you don't think so much with your stomach that you've completely dismissed that possibility. At least, I hope so. Tulsan and I are too weak to spearhead this plan."

"You won't have to worry your small heads with responsibility any time soon," said Jurek. "If she is, then she is. All the more time to weigh down our friend and keep the two of them busy. If your sweep is fruitless find an entry way into the mine on the other side and hide by it. Take them by surprise if that's how they leave."

Before Wesan could fly away Jurek grabbed him by the neck and pulled him close. Wesan could feel Jurek's panting breath. "But I get to kill that runt," growled Jurek. "No one escapes from me; not twice." He pushed Wesan away and let go of his neck. Wesan immediately took to the air and began looking around for their target. Jurek turned the other way, sprouted his massive wings and slowly rose into the sky. He slowly flew over the landscape, landing frequently but always getting back into the air after just a second. He painstakingly looked over every copse and ditch for the small female human. She could not possibly hide; not with hair such a bright shade as hers.

Aleksei looked away from the collapsed entry way and let himself fall against the side of the cave wall, panting heavily as he lay propped against it on the ground. Daina took a seat by him, stumbling over seemingly every little lip and edge on the floor as she made her way to his side in the blackness. After a few minutes of catching their breath and collecting their thoughts, Aleksei mustered the energy to speak. "Thank you so much for that distraction," he said. "I dare not fathom what was about to happen to me."

"No need to thank me," she said. "It was the least I could do. I couldn't let you die at the hands of someone as awful, as horrible as that."

"So if someone that was still horrible but not quite as horrible as him was to try and kill me you'd let that person do so?"

"That's not what I meant!" Daina slapped herself on the forehead. "Poor choice of words. I'd rather not have my only friend in all of this hardship get killed at any particular moment in the near future. It's not like you're that Goddess-forsaken murderer who almost ate your face. No one should die at the hands of that thing. Not even you, quill-head." She gently nudged him in the ribcage with an elbow, making him flinch slightly.

"Hopefully not many more will, princess," said Aleksei. "Even someone as small as me can take down a great foe, like the hero who fought an evil god's stripe-faced giant. Can't remember that kuvi's name." He sighed. "It's not important. Perhaps one day I'll fulfill this daydream of mine. I pick him right off the ground he loves so much, take him high up into the air and squeeze him so hard his back snaps. Then I tear off his limbs and propel what remains of him back to the ground, obliterating him."

Daina liked the idea, even if it was a bit excessive. "Would you eat him?"

"I hope I never do such a thing, even with Jurek," he said. "And it's not like I'll be able to kill him on my own to begin with. You saw him, the power he wields. I can't compete with *dal Tinagmos*. All I can hope is that when a whole city learns of what he's tried to do to you twice they'll help me by unloading a few hundred bolts into his body."

"He would kill many before he fell," she said. "I'm not even sure all of Tantallos could take him down with its weapons."

"All kuvis like him have a very crippling weakness. Exploit it and they're nothing in a fight. It's just doing that little bit that can be so hard, especially with someone as massive as him."

The two of them sat there for a moment, breathing heavily from the excitement. The stale air of the cave did not help matters. Daina got onto her feet. "Do you feel good enough to walk? I don't want to wait around for him to open up this blocked passage and get at us in an area surrounded by earth."

Aleksei stood back up quickly, already feeling much better. He recovered from the punishment far faster than any human would have. "I'm fine," he said. "Can't see anything in this place, though."

"I thought you had great vision, so great you could see in the dark," said Daina. "At least well enough to fight that one kuvi in the dead of night."

"I still need some light to do that," said Aleksei. "Do you see any of that around here?"

"I see a kuvi who can create and control fire," she said. "Use one of your claws like a torch."

"Created by me or not, fire still uses up a lot of air," he said. "Unless you humans don't need to breathe to survive, it seems like a very bad decision. I certainly know that I need air to breathe, though it would take quite some time to kill me."

"I did not mean anything by it, Aleksei." Daina said this lightly and slowly. "You don't need to set your whole hand ablaze. Just make a very small amount of fire, enough so you can see. I'll follow behind you."

"All right..." Aleksei focused and one claw started dimly glowing white. Then a few flames the size of match fires sprouted up along the digits. The remaining cold claw reached back and found its way onto Daina's shoulder, making her jump a little. "Hold my claw so we don't get separated."

"Wise," she said. She carefully moved the claw into one of her hands, placing her grip by his thumb to better avoid getting cut. Aleksei slowly moved through the cramped tunnel. His direction was something the near-blind Daina could not fathom, but if he could not get them out the other side, who would?

CHAPTER 16

Do not forget the words I tell you. So long as you remember what I taught you, even if you don't remember Me, I shall be satisfied with your actions.
-From the Tomes of the Huntmaster.

Although things had calmed down for Daina and Aleksei, the other side of the mountain was a bustling wave of activity. As the sun finally slid below the horizon, hundreds of people started funneling back into Tantallos. Not because they wished to, but because the king ordered them to for their own sake. Many of these people would rather continue their search through the night, but even after just one day many of them were feeling the deteriorating effects of the Decay on their bodies. No one had died from the rot, though a few fell victim to creatures roaming the swampland, but many people would awake the next morning to find clumps of hair on their beds and rotted teeth falling out of their mouths. Only one person remained completely unaffected.

Alkin was the last person to come back inside Tantallos before they closed the gates, Back Breaker holstered but seemingly not weighing him down at all. The hardy, double-edged blade was covered in blood from the amount of usage it had seen that day. He quickly walked up the city's main street and made no deviations on his way to the castle. But it was not enough to avoid staring into several sad faces, faces that had sacrificed so much and had received absolutely nothing for their losses. He felt hollow looking at them.

He breathed a sigh of relief when he finally arrived back at the castle. Rather than head for his quarters to collapse on his bed he took the main entrance into the gathering hall. He walked up to the elevated throne area and found Vikenti sitting at a long table by himself, surrounded by trays of food. Although no dish was the same, it was all comfort food, delicious juicy meats and rich, succulent desserts. Alkin could hardly recognize any of the exotic dishes. He went up to the king and took a seat by him. Vikenti stopped eating for a moment.

"There's no need for you to be here," said Vikenti. "I already have all the information I need; it came to me some time ago. Not a trace of Daina. If she was dropped into the Decay last night then she's undoubtedly dead by now. She's probably rotted so much that..." He stopped himself before he could even consider those thoughts and went back to trying to fill the empty feeling inside with food.

Alkin took this in and tried to think of something positive to say. "Your majesty, I believe she still lives in the Decay," he said.

Vikenti swallowed and grabbed a chicken leg. "I appreciate the thought, but it's not much of a comfort," he said. He tore into the leg and ate half of it in one bite, skin and all. "Your believing can't make it so. But, please tell me that I at least managed to help you with something. I can't help my daughter, but did I succeed in helping you? I need to hear this. Please. Let me know I've done something worthwhile on this awful day."

"Your gift was an unparalleled benefit for me," said Alkin. "Not a single beast stood up to more than one blow from this sword and many of your subjects were spared from their jaws. Back Breaker sliced through the fiends like butter and smashed their bones into bits like dried twigs. This blade will be instrumental in saving Daina from the monster that has her in its grasp."

"Listen to the words you say," said Vikenti. "If my daughter was unfortunate enough to fall into the clutches of a monster then she's already dead."

"Not if the monster's an intelligent foe," said Alkin. "If part of a demon can keep me from rotting in the Decay, I'd imagine the same goes for a demon that still lives. She could be alive if a demon is holding her captive."

Vikenti's face lit up a little and he put down a spoon of pudding. "I can see that... No." His smile quickly faded away and he resumed shoveling the pudding into his mouth. "Why would a brutish demon want to keep a human around? Several demons have appeared in Tantallos in the past and not one of them showed any desire to preserve human life."

"But I doubt any of those demons ever met Daina," said Alkin, smiling a little. "Every human loves her; perhaps a demon will feel a similar devotion after a conversation with her."

Vikenti managed to smile again. "I thank you for everything you've done," he said. "But even so it has been a horrible day. I can't let my subjects rot themselves half to death again. I'm going to have to make sure the gates stay shut and no one goes out into the Decay in a doomed attempt to find her. Even if she claimed to not really care for her subjects that much –I don't believe that but she keeps saying it–she would not want them all to die uselessly for her." He sighed and stared down at his empty plate and bowls. "I... I don't think I'm ever going to see her again."

"You will see her again," said Alkin. "You still have one person at your disposal who can go into the Decay without fear of rotting away." He pointed a finger at himself. "I'll go out into that death-ridden land, shove this sword down the throat of the demon holding her prisoner and carry her back to this exact spot to deposit her in your arms. If the Goddess is kind she will be unharmed."

"Strong words," said Vikenti. "And I expect no less from a man as mighty as yourself. You're strong enough to back up those words; I have no doubt. A man like you, devoid of faults of any kind. No wonder Daina took to you so quickly."

Alkin stopped for a moment and mulled over something in his head before deciding against it. "To be honest, I do have one fault," he said. "No hero is devoid of faults and I'm no exception. At least everyone would see it as a fault. But I won't trouble you with that for now; it won't hinder my quest for her. It will only need to be revealed when I bring her back to you alive."

Alkin got up from the table, bowed and left for the nearest staircase. He immediately made his way up to his room and barely managed to get Back Breaker off of himself before he collapsed onto the bed for some much needed rest; he needed every bit of energy he could muster for the morrow.

Daina had absolutely no idea how long she had been trailing behind Aleksei, holding his claw the whole way. She had tried to keep track, counting the seconds as they faded into minutes and in turn melted into hours. But eventually she lost her train of thought and failed to accurately recall the number. She just gave up; not like time mattered in this tunnel. It had to be dark outside, but she would have no idea at all until she came out the other side. The tunnel kept winding up, down, left, right; a convoluted and confusing path that vaguely reminded her of the Tantallos catacombs. Without the walls of bones, of course.

Aleksei worked his way down the tunnels slowly and deliberately, stopping for some time at each intersection to investigate every option available. He felt in the air for the slightest of telltale breezes, failing to come up with any decent indication of wind more often than not. Daina sucked on her finger for a bit and then raised it into the air, feeling the cold wind against it. "There's a slight breeze from the tunnel on your left," she said. "I may be mistaken but it seems just a bit stronger than last intersection."

"Thanks for your help," said Aleksei. "I certainly couldn't feel anything. Maybe soft human skin isn't such a bad thing after all, in some cases."

"Can't you feel the wind?" asked Daina. "It's not strong, but it's somewhat evident."

"Over seventeen of your years I have been enduring various forms of discomfort, and ever since I came here it's been a constant battle with the wind and cold," said Aleksei. "I've become dulled to such things for the most part. I couldn't feel the blow of a maul through my claws. They're the same metal that covers the Huntmaster; nothing can break, dent or dull them, not even magic. More than likely that striking maul would just shatter. A single one of my claws weighs several hundred pounds."

"Certainly puts you at an advantage in a battle," said Daina. "But I'm not sure if I could live with them. I would miss such slight feelings like wind, even if it's often cold and biting."

"I'm hard-pressed to miss things I've never had to begin with," said Aleksei. "Such as color. You humans see something around you that I never will, but as I will never know what separates red from green I will never miss it."

"Kuvis have great night vision while humans are near-blind in the dark," said Daina. "I may not miss it as I never had it, but I do wonder what it would be like to experience."

"We may have similar feelings," said Aleksei. "But I'd rather focus on what I can do rather than what I can't. I recommend you take a similar outlook, improve your strengths rather than dwell on your weaknesses."

They fell silent after this, Daina not wanting to discuss it. They continued on in this dead silence for a long time until it was broken with a yawn. "Pardon me," said Daina. "I'll try to stop myself next time."

"You're just tired," said Aleksei. "I understand fully. It's been a long and eventful day for both of us." He stopped walking. "We'll stop here and rest for the night. It's as good a place as anywhere else in this tunnel." Daina let go of his hand and he moved to the nearest wall, where he carved an arrow into the stone pointing the way ahead. "We can get back to our never-ending walk through this cave tomorrow." He extinguished the light on his claw and sat against the wall below the arrow. Daina walked to the wall and felt her way down it. She lay against it, finding a reasonably soft spot of earth. But her head found no such comfort on the hard wall. She moved it about, trying to find a nice spot to rest against, but failed. Then her cheek touched something tough, but smooth and very warm.

"I hope that's just you on my shoulder," said Aleksei. "I would not put anything past this tunnel."

"It is me," said Daina. "You're toughened and dulled against the elements, but you're still more comfortable than anything else here."

"You may want to reconsider doing this," he said. "What would your fiancé say if he was to see this? If it was me I would be very angry and definitely jealous."

"You being angry is the norm, quill-head," she said. "And Alkin is a good man. Also, I don't think he fancies me enough to become too maddened, if at all. It's not like this is a particularly intimate act."

"If you insist," said Aleksei. "It's on your conscience. But let me adjust my arm first lest you put it to sleep from your position."

"All right," said Daina. She lifted her head up a little and felt something moving behind her. She resumed a place close to her old one and felt a warm arm drape around her shoulders, with a cold piece of metal on the end of it. It was all so comforting; she felt old memories surface up inside her of scary nights as a little girl. She had rushed down the halls of the castle and made her to way to her father's room. There he had always kept her safe from the raging storms just outside. It was a lot like that. All it would take is one more thing to make it complete.

"Will you tell me a bedtime story?" she asked, humored by her own words. She allowed herself this moment; who would Aleksei tell?

"We've already discussed this, princess," said Aleksei. "I don't tell stories. Stories are for the old and dulled who have nothing else to do while taking care of the children, not for the strong and vicious like me. I'm too busy hunting and killing and tearing living things apart."

"We don't have one of those old and dulled people here to tell a story for you, quill-head," she said. "And keep in mind a princess old enough to marry is asking you for a story. I'll make sure not to tell anyone if you promise not to as well."

Aleksei sighed. "If you insist I'll entertain you," he said. He could not disguise a slight happiness as he said this. "Which leaves you to tell me what sort of story you actually want to hear?"

"I don't want to hear anything from this world," she said. "Tell me a story from Proso. You kuvis must have some great fables."

"Most of the stories I sadly cannot fully remember," said Aleksei. "The Cold One's Fall, the Battle with the Stripe-Faced Giant, I cannot recall great portions of those tales. But I do know some of the stories from the Tomes of the Huntmaster. *Prosopsei's* teachings. I learned these tales in depth while I was on pilgrimage to Proso Center."

"Tell me whichever one you want."

"I'll tell you the first one in the Tomes. It's called '*The Arrival of the World Guardian*.'"

In eons long since past, there existed a foul, godless and unconquerable world. It was a harsh place home to nothing but the most wicked and fierce of creatures. Nothing soft or kind would survive to see a second sunrise in this world. All of this changed on a day millennia ago. The skies of this world cracked open, destroying the world's ceiling and leaving nothing but the great white rings. All this heralded the arrival of a massive shape, red and covered in black plates.

It descended down to the ground; one of its feet touched down on a mountain and flattened the top. It quickly made its way to the lands below this mountain, where it paused to observe the desolate landscape before it. It was a creature so horrid, so terrifying that even the monsters of this land scattered away from it in fear. "Greetings, creatures of this savage world," *said the being with a voice deep, powerful and wizened. It was like the roar of the biggest of monsters.* "I have come to claim this realm as mine and mine alone. Any who dare to approach me, come forth and speak."

Every creature living in the world heard this proclamation and every creature was horrified by the thought. Not even the mightiest beasts could force themselves to get closer to this colossal entity, lest its cavernous mouth effortlessly swallow them whole. None even dared to get close enough to see it for fear of its many, many shifting hands that could reach impossible distances. Many of them tried to get so far away as to not feel the being's footsteps. Even the creatures who had only heard its voice could not fathom getting close enough to find out to what horror the voice belonged.

In all of the world there was only one exception. On a small island in the ocean, one unique creature heard this voice and felt something no other animal did toward it; curiosity. It was a creature much smaller than the mighty hunters of the world, with only two claws on its feet and a quill-covered scalp to protect itself. It sprouted its wings and flew over the water, daring to get close to this voice. As it flew further away from its home it watched countless other animals cower in fright, animals that had so many times tried to eat it. This only fueled its curiosity; it had to see this entity that scared those that frightened it in turn.

This creature flew across the land for many days and nights, eating only the worst of prey and whatever it could scavenge as it had always done. Its effort brought it to the border of the land the being wandered. It crossed over the final hill and saw the entity in all its presence, facing away, its many hands moving about as if they were looking at the surroundings. The creature, although scared, was not deterred. It traveled some more and eventually made its way to the top of the mountain in the center of the being's land; there it would confront the entity. It walked to the edge of the flattened top and faced the being. The divine being was facing away from the creature's place.

"Unrivaled entity from a land unknown to me!" *called out the creature. Its voice was light and high, so unlike the deep voices of the other monsters.* "I ask, no, beg, for your attention!" *Even as it said these words it could feel the fear rising in its throat. This fear only grew as the entity turned to face it. The countless hands came forward and surrounded the mountaintop, the fleshy protrusions reaching in and enclosing the creature, who marveled at the metallic claws with an oddly-placed toe on each one. This odd, small toe moved with a flexibility no other creature could even attempt.*

"This world is full of fierce, savage creatures that would be unmatched on other worlds and yet you're the only one who dares approach me?" *said the being. Its voice made the weak one's knees buckle, sending it collapsing to the ground. It did all it could to keep itself from fainting.* "Tell me, little one. What is your name?"

"I call myself Kuvigos," *said the creature.* "Although others flee from your presence, I had to see you with my own eyes. I know I cannot hope to stand against you, but I beg of you to spare this world of your rage. Although any one of these creatures would kill me, I do not feel they're worthy of death at your many hands. I implore you, if you demand sacrifice, please take me instead."

The entity laughed, a deep emanation that shook the ground. Kuvigos was afraid, but the laugh was not one that would worry it even more. "Do not trouble yourself, Kuvigos," *said the being.* "I did not come to this world to demand sacrifice or to kill the undeserving. I have simply come to find a place of rest, a home I can exist in and defend from worse beings than myself. For I have no land of my own and no company."

"But you are so powerful!" *said Kuvigos.* "You're strong enough to create a world of your own! You needn't this wretched land!"

"I do not blame you for thinking such things," *said the being,* "but that is one thing I cannot do. I can take that which already exists and mold it to suit me, such as my scavengers. But I cannot create something from nothing, like the others similar to me can."

Kuvigos felt something inside of it as it looked at this fearsome being; a god, unparalleled in strength and skill, possibly mightier than other gods, and yet it could not do the one thing it truly wished it could do. "I cannot help you, mighty god, and I can offer you no more than my sorrow. For I too am unable to do what I wish. I want to live in safety and stability, but I cannot possibly compete against the other creatures."

"They may seem stronger than you now, but you have done what none of those creatures would dare do," *said the god.* "And for that, I shall reward you." *The god's hands then shot toward Kuvigos, picking it up gently in several spots and bringing it closer to the face of the mighty being. As it got closer, Kuvigos stared into the creature's pure-black eyes with its own black-and-red eyes. The hands suddenly tightened their grip and an energy started to flow into Kuvigos from them. Kuvigos' fear melted away and was replaced by a sense of calm, a sense of affection for this monster taking an interest in it. A sense of caring that nothing could break.*

The empowering feeling did not end, even as the god moved it back onto the top of the mountain, as gently as one would move their child. It found itself placed on its feet as the power finished flowing into it. It then became aware of the many different powers this god had gifted it with.

"Both your bravery and sense of curiosity have touched me," *said the god,* "and as such I have made you a hunter like no other in this world. You shall have my gaze, my fury and my roar. You shall control the five elements as well. You will shake the ground, make the water flow, call upon the minerals in both, twist plants to your will and destroy all in searing flame. But none of these can compare to the greatest gift. I have given you intelligence. With it, you shall accomplish feats that no other creature can do, because no other creature can fathom doing it."

Kuvigos stood before the god, amazed by the transformation it felt. Already it found itself looking at the world in a completely different way. It got down onto its knees and bowed before the generous deity. "I thank you from the deepest reaches of my heart, god," *it said.* "When I hunt, it shall forevermore be in your name, all-powerful world guardian. I ask only one more thing of you, and that is the name I shall praise when I make my kills."

"I have no name, but you may call me by my role," *said the being.* "I am the guardian of your world. I am the Huntmaster."

"And from that moment on, we kuvis have served as *Prosopsei's* diligent hunters," said Aleksei. "*Prosopsei* means '*world guardian*' and means '*huntmaster*' as well. With the Huntmaster's gift of versatile powers and intelligence, we began to grow and thrive. Now we live all across Proso, and no matter how far we stray from the Center, the Huntmaster travels alongside us in our hearts."

"He didn't give you your claws?" asked Daina. "I thought for sure He would have then. And your god just wanders about your world?" She felt her eyelids start to droop as she relaxed.

"He granted them to kuvis when faced with the threat of the Stripe-Faced Giant," he said. "As an act of balancing, since the Giant's god had also given him powers to help defeat us. And the Huntmaster tries to keep Himself removed from our world; He wants us to look after ourselves. He resides in a fold in space and time, connected to Proso by a portal on the mountain where Kuvigos first met him. I suppose a kuvi could step through it, or His claws could reach out, or He could tear another rip in the fabric of the world and move about that way. I cannot say for sure. I've only seen Him once."

"You've seen your own god?" she asked. "What was it like?"

"Much like in the story," he said. "He's everything you'd expect; terrifying, yet not. There is something comforting about Him. He looks vicious and brutal but there is a gentleness and understanding to Him. This was when I was on pilgrimage to the Center with my mother."

"No living human has ever been fortunate enough to see the Goddess," said Daina. "I guess it's just a difference in how these deities run their worlds." Her eyes closed and she let herself lean more against Aleksei, who felt a different sort of burning in his cheeks. "Do you have any nightmares?" she asked.

"Sometimes they start as such, but they never end as nightmares," said Aleksei. "I guess that bit of the Huntmaster expels them from my mind. He doesn't talk to me but I know He's always with me. Only He can protect me from the enemies I carry up here." He tapped his forehead with his free hand.

"Could you ask Him to chase away my nightmares as well?" asked Daina. "I'm tired of having them every night, especially after the nightmare I had last night."

"Huntmaster willing, you won't have to worry about nightmares," said Aleksei. He shut his eyes as well and sleep finally found both of them.

CHAPTER 17

Beware of your power; while it may raise you above two of the other elements, it also puts you below the two that remain.
-From the Tomes of the Huntmaster.

Alkin breathed a sigh of relief as he finally emerged from Tantallos, blinded by the morning sun directly facing him. In light of the damages the citizens of the city had suffered he had chosen not to stir them up into a frenzy by leaving through the main gate. Even now there were countless people at the portcullis, several partially rotted from yesterday, begging to be let out into the Decay. Alkin had considered traveling down the wall until Vikenti suggested a different option.

Though he had certainly not been enthused by it; the very idea of an ossuary disturbed him. Even as he had walked through the carefully stacked and sorted walls of bones in the Tantallosian catacombs his skin had been crawling the entire time. It was so macabre to him, all of it; Tulroy burial rights consisted primarily of being wrapped up in cloth or, for the rich, packed into a casket. They were then left to sink into one of the bogs in the Decay, gone and hidden from the monsters. Only the uppermost royalty were preserved within the stone of the city; the dead had no need for the finite space within Tulroy.

Though even he couldn't deny that Tantallos' ossuary made for a convenient secret way out of the city. And the entryway into the Decay was very well-hidden in an especially thick copse; it was highly unlikely a demon had ever come across it. However, one would be hard-pressed to get back in through it. Alkin had to tie a rope to get down to the Decay level and the knot had become undone by the time he reached the bottom. He certainly was not getting back into Tantallos that way, not unless he could fly. He thought he had seen something in the corner by the ledge but it had been too dark for him to tell what it was. All of that was of no matter. Daina was going to be back within the walls of Tantallos by the end of the day. He could feel it in his bones.

He walked southward in the direction of the main Tantallos gates. Once beyond them he started his trek to a great mountain he had passed coming to this city. It was an impressive specimen in comparison to the others, but the interesting part of the mountain was the multitude of holes bored into it; it must have once been a mine before the Decay took it over, however long ago that was. If Daina was alive, it would have to be in there. The Decay may not have as much an effect in the shelter of a mining shaft. Daina was unlikely to be the only one considering this benefit. Several demons might also be living in the mountain's dark holes, coming out to feed on the unsuspecting when they let their guard down. But demons did not worry Alkin any, not as long as Back Breaker was in his hands and ready to slice them to pieces. If he could overpower a demon and its metal claws with his own leathery hands, how well could any demon fare against the blade he carried?

Daina ran down the halls of the ossuary as fast as she could, the mire beast only a few feet behind her. The chase had gone on for longer than usual, but she still kept her breath. The mire beast was just as persistent, and this hall was not slowly getting smaller. She risked a glance over her shoulder. The mire beast was still keeping up. But then something flashed before her eyes; thick lines of red appeared for fractions of a second and disappeared faster than she could blink. The ossuary began crumbling, but only behind her. She continued running away from the mire beast but the creature stumbled. It let out a yelp as the ceiling of the ossuary caved in, burying it in rubble.

Daina stared at the cave-in then looked back to where she was going. The path led to someplace bright, someplace warm and with a blue sky. She walked outside of the ossuary and found herself standing at the base of a steep hill. Before her was a vast, dry field with only the occasional bush or scrub. Then she noticed it in the ground; a circle of rocks. Eight spikes formed of stones shot inward, creating a shape she now recognized. The icon Aleksei carried with him. That was it. That was why the tunnel collapsed on the mire beast and killed it after so many years of the dream always ending horribly. The Huntmaster had protected her.

Two clawed hands sprung up out of the ground on red tentacles, the back of them covered with black plates of metal like the shingles of a roof. The claws did not scare her; they reminded her of a feeling she had felt many years ago when comforted by her father after hurting herself. The claws came forward and she made no effort to move away from them. A claw gently touched her cheek while another held her shoulder. She let herself relax in the claws' grips.

Daina slowly woke up; she could not even remember the last time such a thing had happened. More often than not, waking up consisted of her shooting upright and breathing heavily. She remained wrapped up in Aleksei's arm; the kuvi was still asleep, or so she guessed from how he sat motionless against the wall. She could not tell with the band of cloth still wrapped tightly around his eyes. Daina thought about what little of her dreams she could remember. Not nightmares; *dreams*. Never before had such things happened in her dreams. It must be true; the Huntmaster protected the dreams of kuvis, and now He had deemed a human of deserving the same. Had the Goddess ever done something so simple for Her devout followers?

No. She stopped her thoughts right there. She could not think such things. The Goddess created this world. It was Her decision what She did or did not do. She felt a shuffling as Aleksei stirred. She propped herself up, letting him retract his arm from around her shoulders. He brought it up alongside his other arm, raising both into the air and stretching while letting out a yawn. "Good morning, Daina," he said. "At least I assume it's morning; can't hardly tell in this mine. Did you sleep well?"

"Yes," she said. "Better than I have ever slept before. Can you give the Huntmaster my thanks when you pray to him?"

"No need," he said. "You've given it to Him yourself just by saying it. He's right here with us, after all." He patted the spot of his chest just above his heart. Daina wondered if the Huntmaster was even closer, now in her own heart, or if He was just in Aleksei. However, that thought was broken off when both of them heard two low growls. They each felt their own stomachs. "I guess we had best start again, princess. We still have a lot of ground to cover before we can get out of this mine."

A loud, angry growling made Jurek open his eyes. He felt his gut as it continued its protests. He shot up into a standing position in an instant, moving faster than any human could in such armor. He stretched a little as he surveyed the landscape just outside of his sleeping spot, scanning for any potential easy meals. Everything in the Decay was as dismal and depressing as it usually was. All around his hiding spot creatures were stirring from their nightmare-ridden slumber, unaware that the apex predator was soon going to be eating several of them. After all, not many like him were hungry enough to stomach their half-rotted flesh. He would even eat cud plants if he needed to; anything to stay satiated. He had done so on countless occasions, even if they at times made him sick.

Jurek let out a quiet sigh as he looked at the meager opportunities. It was never like this in Proso. Back in Proso there was always more than enough food, even for him. Almost daily he would help his uncle fight animals big enough to eat him in one bite, and then he would kill them and consume his share of the corpse within days. He even helped take down a trogo once; that was a satisfying meal indeed. After every kill he would encase the carcass with a barrier of stone to keep opportunists away. Any who dared get close he would kill, and then he'd encase that body in stone as well. He could not possibly pass up seconds. His stomach growled again. It had been far too long since he had indulged himself with such a bountiful feast.

Then he saw a glowing red shape coming toward him. He moved out into the open and watched as Wesan landed in front of him. Wesan knelt in submission before getting back up, always sure to keep his eyes on Jurek. "I took the liberty of checking all the mining entrances on this side," he said. "No scent of either of them yet. They must still be deep inside the mountain."

Jurek did not feel disappointed or angry; if anything it gave him time to do other tasks rather than immediately hunt down the princess and the runt. "Then perhaps you should stop talking to me and instead look over your entrances," he said.

"I wouldn't even be here if it wasn't for something approaching one of my entrances," Wesan replied. "You might enjoy the sight of it. I find it rather cute, to tell the truth."

Jurek and Wesan secretly observed from their hiding spot a few dozen feet up the slope of the mountain. It was a cramped, slanted, enclosed structure with small horizontal slits for windows; Jurek had created it himself just for this sight. They watched attentively as a lone, tall, muscular human approached the mountain with a massive sword holstered on his back. He walked along the pathways, suspiciously eying any monster near him. His right hand quickly moved to clutch the handle of the blade as mire beasts and other fearsome predators tested him, moving quickly in and out, trying to get him to pull his blade too early.

"At least it would be adorable to a Tantallosian," said Wesan. "He's traveling through the wasteland all by himself to rescue the one he loves. Wonder what those idiotic humans would think if they knew he had no such feelings toward the princess."

"Though the princess cannot say the same," said Jurek. "She'd gladly take a union with him, even if it's just an obligation for him. I truly cannot understand how so many human females are excited by him; he may be powerful for a human but he is far too soft in appearance. How he managed to kill a kuvi escapes me."

"He probably killed someone like Tulsan," said Wesan. "I hope that fool hasn't gotten himself exposed."

"If he does it'll give the Tantallosians someone to kill so the populace calms down. I doubt Tulsan has the mental capacity to reveal us as kuvis, so no worries. But what should we do about Alkin?"

"As long as he's here we need to stay hidden," said Wesan. "If we kill him as well the city will go into a frenzy and we'll never get a chance at the king's flesh, so let's let him finish his search. He will check most every tunnel entrance but I doubt he'll enter any of the tunnels as he has no light source. We only engage him if absolutely necessary."

"That will work for me," said Jurek. "I could use some spare time to get something to eat." Wesan backed away a little. Jurek grinned. "Not you, Wesan. You're useful to have around on projects like this. I might go kill a mire beast instead. You are not welcome to join me, either."

Jurek bent his digits, relaxing his hands and allowing the earthen structure to collapse around him and Wesan. Jurek effortlessly pulled himself out of the wreckage and aided Wesan's struggles to free himself. Both were careful to make sure Alkin did not see them, but the prince was too busy watching the predators all around him. Both kuvis slowly climbed down the mountain and walked off to sections of dead forests before taking off into the air, too far away to be identified by prying eyes.

Alkin found himself looking at the two glowing demons as they flew off. Their flight paths did not take them any closer to him or to Tantallos, but just seeing the sight of them made the hairs on the back of his neck stand on end. They were not the only demons out in the Decay; one of them had Daina even as he was standing there. He could not leave Daina at the mercy of such a creature for any length of time.

Daina and Aleksei continued their slow and clumsy walk through the twisting tunnels, hand firmly in claw. "It never seems to end, does it?" asked Daina. "How much longer do you think we have in here before we finally see sunlight again?"

"None at all," growled Aleksei. "Can't you feel the warm light coming down on your face? Can't you taste the fresh air? Can't you feel not completely surrounded by earth threatening to bury you alive? Can't you feel not in a place that, if you added some acid and moisture, would be startlingly similar to a stomach you nearly died in?"

"I did not mean to offend you, quill-head," said Daina. "You're not the only one who can't stand being trapped in these dark tunnels. But it all does make me wish I could create fire like you can, or at least had some way to see what's all around me."

"If I had known it would take this long I would have had you grab a lantern and some candles from my home before we left," he said. "But there's nothing of interest, anyway. Just rock walls, dirt, some mole with a piece of wood stuck in its eye, and a..."

Aleksei froze in place, nearly making an unsuspecting Daina bump into him and trip. She slowly walked up to his side and tried to see what had made him stop. "What's wrong?" she asked. "Is the area up ahead collapsed?"

"We need to turn around immediately," he said hurriedly. He was breathing more and more rapidly.

"What is it?" asked Daina, worry growing in her. Aleksei increased the flames on his hand enough to illuminate the object of interest, only a few feet away. The tunnel was partially filled with water for a stretch, several dozen feet, before dry land returned. The water did not appear to get more than five feet deep and there was still plenty of emptiness above the stagnant pool. It did not look drinkable, but Daina and Aleksei had been sustaining themselves on the canteen Daina brought. The fear in Daina immediately died. "It's just some water, Aleksei."

"Yes, princess. That's the problem," he said, slowly backing away. Daina tightly gripped his claw and tried with all her might to keep him from moving away from the still pool. She had little success, but Aleksei did not move far.

"I can't believe it took me this long to understand this," she said. "You're afraid of water." She thought this over and it took her no time to figure out what was wrong with this phobia. "How could you possibly be afraid of water? You're surrounded by it every day! For the Goddess' sake, you live in the Decay!"

"Are you sure you want to explore that realm of reasoning?" he growled. "Because I am certain that you spend every day surrounded by people you'd rather not be around, yet you continue to hate them."

"Never mind that argument, then," said Daina. "But this is still the best route to take. Can't you swim? Can't you put up with a little water?"

"Did you seriously just tell a kuvi *dal Kafteros* to put up with water?" he yelled. "You have to know what water does to fire! If I go into that and my claws get wet, I can't ignite any more fire until they dry out! My claws will dry out very quickly, yes, but those will be precious moments where I'll be blinded. And perhaps that water is much deeper than it looks! Maybe it collapses at some point into a tunnel below it so it's deep enough for me to sink in! Do you think I'm a good swimmer with these massive claws on my arms?"

Daina sighed; knowing Aleksei's temper, this was getting dangerous for her. Perhaps making herself seem just as poor at swimming would calm him down some. "Aleksei, I share your feelings. I can't really swim either but..."

"Don't you dare try to say that," said Aleksei. "Unless you sink faster than a rock or a creature with two metal weights on his hands you're a better swimmer than I am."

"I'd appreciate if you'd let me finish my sentences before you respond to me," said Daina.

"Daina, for your own sake I'd recommend shutting up for a moment," Aleksei growled back. A red light was shining brightly from beneath the band of cloth. "I've been known to pull limbs out of their sockets when I get angry."

"You can't keep threatening me with death and expect me to cower in fright every time!" yelled Daina. "And you can't expect me to be scared of someone who's too afraid to even go into some water!" Before Aleksei could react to this outburst she immediately ran to the water's edge and jumped as far away from the shore as the could. She quickly sank below the surface and felt the soft ground at her feet; the pool was just as shallow as she had expected. She bobbed back up to the surface about twenty feet from Aleksei; he still stood by the shore. Even in the barely existent light she could see him fuming, his gleaming white teeth exposed in a vicious snarl as he paced back and forth, his normally lax quills standing up on end and every which way. It was as if a person had completely filled up a pin cushion. She felt regret at what she had done, but she had to commit to it now.

"What are you waiting for, coward?" taunted Daina. She desperately hoped Aleksei did not do as he had warned once he got to the other side. "It's just a little walk out here from there, Aleksei! You're tall enough to walk along the bottom! A child with one arm could swim this space!" She splashed the surface of the water some, making noise. Aleksei let out an incredibly loud roar in frustration and slowly forced himself closer and closer to the water. He jerked back in fright when it lapped up against his toes but eventually brought his feet to the edge again. Then he finally entered it, his rage instantly turning to fright as the water slowly reached above his ankles. Daina dog-paddled further away from him as he sluggishly moved deeper into the water; he looked like he was about to faint when it reached above his waist. His breathing became extremely rapid as the water got near his shoulders. He made sure his torch claw was raised well above his head so there was not even a chance of it getting wet.

Once Aleksei reached the halfway point Daina moved herself back onto dry land. She carefully shook herself as she watched the horrified face get closer and closer. Once the land started sloping back up Aleksei made his way out of the water as fast as he possibly could. In seconds he was dripping in front of her, back on dry land. His fear melted away and the rage returned with a vengeance. Daina made the mistake of blinking and her eyes opened back up to find Aleksei right in front of her. His metallic digits wrapped themselves around her throat, the glow from behind the band of cloth seemingly getting brighter with every passing moment. He lifted her up with one hand and forced her against the wall. She looked at him in fear, watching him fume, pondering how he was going to exact his revenge on her.

"I want to apologize to you, Aleksei," said Daina, Aleksei's grip lax enough to let her speak. "I'm so sorry for what I did to you. I know you're far too mad for those words to mean anything, especially after what I just made you endure, but I had to think of a way to get you through this water so we didn't have to take a massive detour. It was mean of me, so unfathomably mean of me, and I'm amazed that I did it at all. I understand if you despise me until I die and I wish I could have avoided doing it. I accept whatever you do to me as punishment."

She watched worriedly as Aleksei's snarl faded slightly. Aleksei released his grip on her and let her drop to the ground before him. His eyes still glowed fiercely. He then moved to the other side the tunnel and slammed his claws into a massive piece of stone like he was trying to chop it. Bits of rock flew everywhere as he pounded fiercely away, roaring in rage the entire time. Daina dashed about ten feet ahead to get to a safe distance as Aleksei obliterated everything in sight. She glanced nervously at the ceiling; hopefully it wouldn't collapse. The noise faded away as Aleksei stopped slamming against stones; the only remaining sound was his slight panting as he regained his breath. After a moment he walked back up to her, both claws at his sides.

"You have no idea how dangerous that was for you," he said. "I could have killed you in that state. You were this far away from getting ripped to shreds." He held up a claw and made a small distance between the thumb and index digit.

"I was scared, but I don't think I truly believed you would kill me," she said. "Maybe inflict punishment upon me, but nothing that would kill me. I trust you."

"Moments like those make me wish you wouldn't," he said. "I certainly wouldn't. But now that we're through that... unpleasant experience, let's continue on, shall we?"

The two continued their trek through the tunnels, eventually drying out due to time and Aleksei's burning claws. They carefully drank from the canteen to satiate their thirst, but that did nothing for their stomachs, which growled more and more as time went by. Aleksei's eyes darted toward Daina as he reflected upon the taste of her blood he had gotten on his claws. He immediately backhanded himself across the face, causing Daina to turn toward him.

"What was that awful sound?" asked Daina. "What are you doing to yourself, quill-head?"

"Nothing you need to worry about, princess," he said. "Actually, you may want to worry a little. Tell me; you wouldn't happen to not want one of your arms, would you? One arm's just not good enough and you can't stand having it attached any longer? I'd gladly cauterize the stump for you. I'd rather not, but I'm afraid I can't eat dirt. So would you let me have one of your limbs?"

Daina looked at her arms and then at Aleksei in a mixture of shock and jest. How does one react to such a question? "Anyone else and I'd assume they were just joking," she said, "but the answer is no. I like each arm equally and would rather keep both; I'm quite attached to them after all these years. And you can't have one of my legs, either. And definitely not my head, so don't even bother asking. Why don't you join me in going hungry for a little bit longer?"

"If you're going to act in such a way I guess I don't have a choice," he said. "But why do you have to be so selfish? You only need one arm; you don't need two. Weren't you taught that it's better to give to those in need?" He smiled a little; he was improving at the act.

"Did the angriest resident of the Decay just make a joke?" asked Daina, a smile appearing on her face as well. "You are truly a creature of many emotions, and little time spent switching between them. I have no idea what you'll surprise me with next."

"A strong kuvi learns to keep his vice from always dominating his will," he said. "I'd like to imagine that I'm adequate at such a job. Though it doesn't help I have the unfortunate pleasure of having that vice indicated on the outside." He pointed to his eyes.

"I find your eyes to be very fascinating," said Daina. "Even if my one glance made me faint and endure the worst nightmare of my life. They are very impressive and foreboding. If only an artist had the stamina to paint a portrait of a kuvi."

"It would undoubtedly have to be a human painter rather than a kuvi," said Aleksei. "Not many artistic types among us, for the same reasons I kept resisting telling you a story. Not to say there are none; I'm certain I've talked about Malek *dal Spazos* with you..."

Aleksei stopped immediately at a particular sight ahead of him, and

Daina halted at his side. Far ahead of them, small but unmistakable, was a sliver of light. Their steps sped up as they walked toward it, their smiles growing as the sliver of light did. Their faces started to beam as much as the sunlight as they ran up to it, closer and closer. Then they finally arrived at the exit of the mine, Daina letting out a cry of joy.

"I never thought I would be so glad to be outside again!" said Daina, basking in the comparably warm glow, eyes shut as they worked to adjust to the light. The sun was even slightly out of the cloud cover as if to greet them. Aleksei held a claw up above his eyes but brought it down within seconds as his eyes adjusted.

"Don't be too loud, Daina," said Aleksei. "Jurek knows exactly where we are and where we're likely to escape from the mine. He's probably watching one of these entrances right as we speak. If he's observing this place we are in unfathomable trouble. If it's his partner we have precious minutes before Jurek shows up."

Daina nodded and fell silent. They both slowly looked over the surrounding area, seeing nothing of interest. But then Aleksei found his eyes drawn to something moving off to the side of the mountain, so far away a human would barely notice it. He could not see it clearly, but it walked on two legs and had a short-cut crop of hair on its scalp. "Daina, I know you said no to me eating a part of you, but what about someone else?" he asked. "I don't recognize him, but there is a man approaching us from some distance away."

"No eating humans while I'm with you," she said. "And I'm not about to commit cannibalism, no matter how hungry I may be. We'll just eat any of the other creatures living out here. We can go hunting together. I'd rather not be the bait, but I can't see myself serving as much else in this place."

"Are you certain you won't change your mind?" he asked. "He looks like he comes from very good stock, well-fed and physically active. I'm very surprised Jurek didn't jump him by now; he must not have noticed him, and if a kuvi's going to kill this man, you'd want it to be me. I'd slice his jugular or stab him through the temple or heart. It would be quick in comparison to what the others would do."

"One of many conversations I never thought I'd have until I met you," said Daina. "I forbid you from eating this man." A thought then occurred to her. What would a man be doing out in the Decay all by himself? "Describe this man for me."

Aleksei sighed but did as she asked, focusing on the approaching person. "He is a tough-looking human, roughly five years older than you or me. He's carrying a massive sword on his back and has hair similar to yours in shade. He looks reasonably clean, too. Impressive, considering where he is right now."

Daina's eyes widened as she heard this. "That sounds like Alkin!" she said. "Please don't attack him!"

"Alkin?" asked Aleksei. "The man you're marrying?" He looked again. "Exactly how much older is he than you?"

"That's not important right now," said Daina. "We need to go and talk to him!"

She was about to run forward but found an arm wrapped around her waist, holding her back before she had even taken the first step. Aleksei's *Ateni* had caught her motions. "Very, very foolish idea," he said. "You might not have noticed this, but humans don't take kindly to us kuvis. And I don't think he'll be pleased to see me so close to you. He'll undoubtedly perceive me to be a threat and attack me. I don't want to kill him if I don't have to."

"Alkin's killed kuvis before," said Daina. At the very least he had killed one. She did not know. Had he killed more than one kuvi? "Don't treat him so lightly."

"I'd be willing to wager my left claw that he's never fought and beaten an arch kuvi," said Aleksei, "especially one with *Ateni*." He let go of Daina, easing his claw back so as to not cut her. "Here's an idea. We'll both approach him, but I'll stay back and keep myself hidden so you can ease him into meeting me. But friendly relations or not we're going to convince him to let me into the city under the pretense that I'm just some blind fool. Understand?"

"You still think so lowly of me?" asked Daina. "I would never betray you in such a way. I wouldn't ruin my relationship with one of the few beings in this world I can trust."

"Apologies," he said. "But thank you all the same. Go in front. I'll be watching over you." He ran off and made his way into a copse of dead trees nearby. Red quills aside, he blended in surprisingly well. Daina took a deep breath and began her trek around the side of the mountain toward Alkin. She had no idea why she felt an anxiety brewing in her; Aleksei could not be even more than fifty feet away from her, easily able to defeat any monster interested in her. All the same she looked about warily, watching for any animal that might be considering her for a snack. The dismal nature of the Decay did not help the feeling, either. It was just as depressing as ever, and clouds had quickly covered up the light.

She only saw Aleksei for fractions of a second at a time as he moved from one hiding spot to the next. He moved deftly and quietly; one would be hard-pressed to even notice him. A part of her mind then started wondering if Alkin would fall unconscious after a look into Aleksei's eyes.

CHAPTER 18

If you follow me you will have nothing to fear. Those who have forsaken Me shall meet an end on your world by your hand and an end in the afterlife by My hand.
-From the Teachings of the Goddess.

Alkin noticed a person also walking through the Decay from quite a ways off and started making his way over. He then sped up as she came closer and closer, becoming all the more familiar in her shape and color. In a few moments he was close enough to see her clearly, her golden hair catching his eye; even the Decay could not dull it. He took off toward her, and she toward him. In moments they found themselves together. Daina expected more but only received a soft hug from Alkin.

"I'm so glad to see you alive and well!" he said. "Your entire city has been worried half to death! How have you managed to survive in the Decay for so long with its effects and all the monsters? What exactly happened when you found yourself out here? Please, don't spare any details!"

"Calm down, Alkin," said Daina. Alkin quickly released his grip on her and returned to his straight stance. "It's quite a long tale; shame I'm not a storyteller. I was captured by this horrible kuv... I mean demon while on the city walls and he brought me all the way out into this wasteland. He even flew me over that mountain to his lair." She gestured to the mountain near them. "I found myself in a dead forest that obeyed his every whim and once he had finished tormenting me he had been about to eat me alive."

"I can see," said Alkin. "He certainly cut you heavily and deeply; those scars will never go away." Daina felt her cheeks, forever altered. They did not bother her as much now; after all, what could she do about them? "Rest assured, you're still beautiful, even with those matching cuts. But how did you manage to escape from such a foul creature? Did you kill it? It takes immense strength and skill to kill a demon."

"The demon was killed, but not by me," said Daina. "I was fortunate enough to attract the attention of someone nearby in the Decay. He heard my cries and then came and rescued me, slaying that awful beast with an unmatched tenacity."

Alkin raised an eyebrow. "Another person able to survive the Decay and also able to take down demons on his own? I need to thank him if I ever meet him. Where is... did you hear that?" He looked toward a nearby cluster of trees. He could not see what lay inside but he could hear slight noises coming from it. He focused more on the sounds and started to hear a slight clinking. And then he saw a scalp of red quills, bristling up, standing on end and looking like a massive pin cushion.

"Get to a safe place, Daina," he said, stepping away from her and placing himself in between Daina and the cluster of trees. He pulled Back Breaker out of its hilt and held it carefully. "Reveal yourself, demon! I see you clearly, foul creature!" He ran toward the cluster of trees, and then dashed to the side as a raging shape blasted out of the dead woods. It turned on a coin to face him, its face in a look of fury, its claws raised up and poised to strike. Beneath the band of cloth its eyes were glowing brightly.

"Don't call me a demon, stupid human!" roared Aleksei, charging at Alkin at an impressive speed. Alkin swung Back Breaker surprisingly quickly but Aleksei went into a roll while Alkin was still starting his swing, safely going underneath the slashing blade. He made for Alkin's legs but quickly retracted his hands when he saw Alkin's legs moving, leading to him dodging to the side. Both of them turned around almost instantly and looked at each other with equally angry expressions.

"I don't know if your human shape makes you less or even more horrid," said Alkin. "What foul atrocity would make a demon contort into such a form?" Aleksei's band of cloth glowed ever brighter until the kuvi finally tore the band off his face and pocketed the strip. The rings in his eyes shined intensely as the fifth rings expanded even more, pushing the smaller rings together and to the corners and insides of his eyes. Alkin was unimpressed. "Don't waste your time using that eye trick on me. I've endured the look of a demon before and did not even feel dizzy while all the others around me fainted."

Aleksei snarled. "Stop calling me a demon!" he yelled as he charged forward again, but soon he saw the motions, stopped and raised his claws to block and catch a menacing cleave from Alkin. As Aleksei held the blade, both of them put more and more of their strength into their weapons, whether they were attached to their bodies or simply treated as an extension.

Alkin started sweating as it became harder and harder to force down the sword. All it would take was his foe to redirect the blade to the side, then he could dash in and shove a claw into his gut before he could respond. He must be so irate he wasn't even thinking of the possibility. But the speed, the strength, the near foresight of Alkin's blows; this was far greater than any foe he had ever faced. And Alkin could tell Aleksei had just gotten started. Then his eyes widened as Aleksei's claws started glowing white. Fire blossomed on the claws, slowly moving up to the kuvi's shoulders. The flames licked around the blade of the sword as if looking for a grip, their temperature rising.

"Please, both of you, stop fighting!" yelled Daina as she ran toward them. She moved herself in between the two of them, risking possible death to stop the fight before Aleksei melted the blade and tore Alkin to bits. Alkin immediately backed off, only saved from death by the human shield. Daina quickly turned to face Aleksei, who looked ready to charge straight through her, and gazed directly into his eyes. An intense anxiety quickly started to grow inside her as she stared down those contorted, glowing wells. She watched as the fifth ring in each eye began to slowly, slowly shrink itself to normal size. Still slightly bigger than the others, but at least its light had faded.

The calmed Aleksei immediately caught Daina as her knees buckled and she fell, unable to stand but still conscious. He carefully laid her on the ground face-up, doing the best he could not to cut her, and got back on his feet to look at Alkin. The prince stared at them both in shock.

"Wait a minute," said Alkin, gawking in disbelief. "*This* is the person who saved you from getting killed?"

"His name is Aleksei dal Kafteros," said Daina, pulling herself up into a sitting position despite how woozy she felt. "He's not a demon at all. He's a kuvi; an arch kuvi, to be exact. He fought off the other arch kuvi with greater skill than he used on you and he saved my life. He's hot-blooded but friendly. He won't hurt you if you don't make him mad. His temper is his vice. And don't ever, ever call him a demon."

"Not if you want to live, pretty boy," growled Aleksei.

Alkin took all this in, slowly thinking it over as he examined Aleksei. He glanced at Daina for a quick moment and then looked back at Aleksei. After a few seconds of thought he took Back Breaker and shoved the blade into the ground. He stepped away from it, holding up his empty hands to show he had no other weapons.

"And I fully understand that you de... I mean, kuvis are incapable of disarming yourselves, so I trust you not to turn those claws on me," said Alkin. "You have no reason to accept this, but I want to apologize to you for my brutish behavior. I was deathly worried you might have been a kuvi of a less favorable nature. It may just be my perception as a human of your kind, but I hope you understand my motivation." He looked sincere as he extended a hand toward Aleksei.

Aleksei stared at the hand for a moment before raising his corresponding claw to Alkin's eye level. "You don't want to shake my claw," he said. "You'll cut your hand to ribbons."

Alkin shook his head before stepping forward and carefully grabbing Aleksei's claw. He shook it heartily before releasing his grip and pulling back his hand; not a scratch was on it. "I may not have metal hands like yours, but a lifetime of hard work has made mine tougher than leather." He grinned. "Though I'll never get a head of hair like that. Is it naturally that dark a red or do you use it in combat and those are just stains? Every limb of your body is as dangerous as the others, it seems."

"My hair is always this shade," said Aleksei. "Be it my family blood or my enemy's blood." He folded his claws across his chest. "So, what are you doing out here all by yourself? Looking for your soon-to-be queen, I suppose?" A slight snarl formed on his face; Alkin didn't make much of a note of it.

"That was my mission, though it seems the need was not as urgent as I thought," he said. "Not with someone as strong as you watching out for her. I've never fought such a powerful adversary, even in comparison to other kuvis. How's your wingspan? Assuming you have wings. If they're anything like your power they must make an impressive sight."

"I'd rather not discuss my wings with you after just meeting you," said Aleksei, his small snarl quickly turning into a look of embarrassment.

"Apologies, Aleksei," said Alkin. "I did not mean to delve into more personal matters." An awkward silence fell on the group as they simply stood there for a few moments. Alkin thought up a new question to break the dead air. "I am in no way complaining about your actions, mind you, but what made you decide to save Daina? You are the first kuvi I've ever met who would rather save a human's skin than eat it. Assuming you eat the skin of animals. Some humans peel it off and just eat the meat. But don't let me ramble."

Aleksei sighed. "It's no problem," he said. "But if you must know, she was going to get me into Tantallos. But now that you're here it doesn't look like that plan will work."

"I can't see why it wouldn't," said Alkin. "No other kuvi would cease attacking me to have a conversation, even if Daina was the one who calmed you down. If that's any sign, you're civil enough to live among humans. Maybe with both Daina's blessing and my own you can be allowed into Tantallos. All else fails, I'll tell everyone that I can easily incapacitate you and you can come live in Tulroy. The citizens of my home city have viewed me as the strongest creature in this world since I was sixteen."

"Really?" Aleksei asked halfheartedly. "What did you do?"

"It's actually a very interesting story," said Alkin, enthusiasm growing on his face. "I went into one of our biggest dining halls in the dead of night and fought against this giant monster that kept terrorizing it. Tore one of its arms right out of its socket, too. Then for a finale I went out into the Decay and decapitated its mother at the bottom of one of those disgusting ponds. I doubt it compares to your greatest triumphs, but it would have been a sight for you to see."

Aleksei shuddered at the imagery of anyone spending so much time in a pond, let alone one full of foul Decay water. "You've certainly accomplished a great many feats for a human," he said. "So I'm sure you'll be able to protect Daina well, keep her safe from all possible harm once she becomes your queen."

Alkin pondered this oddly fixated statement. What was brewing just underneath this kuvi's thick skin? He looked at Aleksei's claws; he was dragging the palms rapidly up and down his forearms, rubbing tightly against them. The action was making him wince and bare his teeth from the self-inflicted pain. "Don't think so much of it, Aleksei," he said. "It's something anyone should hope to do. I think this needs to be discussed more thoroughly back in Tantallos. I'll get you in, buy you a drink, and then we can discuss the state of the relationship between Daina and..."

Alkin's words were cut off by a massive lump of rock shooting out of the ground and hitting him in the back of the head. He fell forward, unconscious, and landed on his face as Aleksei looked around rapidly for the single person who could have done such a thing. His hair, which had just finished lowering itself, rose back up immediately as he scanned the landscape for the one foe he had hoped to avoid above all others. Daina was looking around rapidly as well, trying to watch everything at once as she pulled out her dagger. She felt her breath get faster and faster as she slowly moved closer to Aleksei. He was all she had; she dare not get separated from him. Not now.

Then came the sound that made them both jump, a deep, loud laugh from above the nearest cave entrance. They turned toward the source of the noise and gazed upon Jurek, still clad in his red armor with the mouth visor of his helmet down, exposing a massive, gleaming grin. "How nice to see you both again," he said. "I hope you enjoyed your reprieve in the mine. It's been unbearable waiting for you two. I've been working up a massive appetite. I could eat four of you both."

"What is your obsession with eating us?" asked Daina.

"Some call it my vice but I find it doesn't hinder me at all," said Jurek. "That and humans and weaker kuvis are delicious creatures. Don't waste your time resisting me and I might kill you quickly. Whatever gets this over with faster, especially considering what I have to do to you, princess."

"You won't do anything to her!" yelled Aleksei. He did not need his *Ateni* to see the pointlessness in trying to fight Jurek; he was too far away to even attempt an attack and could easily counter any assault from his higher location. Instead he turned around, generated his wings and wrapped his arms around Daina tightly. He took off into the air fractions of a second before massive rock spikes shot out of the ground around him; had he taken a second longer they would have trapped him and Daina.

Daina winced as Aleksei's claws easily cut through her clothes and dug into her flesh, but she bottled the pain and did all she could to hide it from him. Any moment he spent adjusting his grip might make her slip right out and plummet to the ground. He would have to stop to adjust her, giving Jurek plenty of time to catch up to them. Aleksei gained altitude as quickly as he could, his wings releasing lots of heat as they glowed even brighter. He swerved rapidly to avoid the rock spikes, the tips of his wings barely missing them at times. As he continued his dodging he slowly rose into the air. Jurek snarled and concentrated harder, his claws going stiff as boards as he dug his toes into the ground. Aleksei paid this no mind and continued his direct charge to Tantallos.

Alkin lay on the ground, still unconscious from the blow, undisturbed by anyone or anything throughout this whole ordeal. He would remain that way for hours, but no living being would be foolish enough to bother him lest he wake up and fend it off. Jurek watched Aleksei and Daina fly off toward the city and ceased his assault; already they were too far away for him to manipulate anything to attack them. Instead he generated his massive, spiked wings and took flight, but rather than chase after them he made his way to Wesan's area. He was in no hurry to get them. Tulsan was a moron and would definitely have not thought of it, but Abdaas was not so dense. He would undoubtedly have made sure a surprise was waiting for the two.

CHAPTER 19

It only takes one mistake for the one you hunt to become the one hunting you.
-From the Tomes of the Huntmaster.

The battlements were alive with activity as guards walked all about them, each one carrying a readied crossbow. It was truly a boon for them to gain the resources and knowledge of another head priest of the Goddess. Abdaas had enlightened them all of horrible facts concerning demons; how they poisoned the minds of humans unfortunate enough to meet them, how they tricked them into believing outrageous falsehoods. Such actions are nothing more than feeble attempts to convince others they are civil despite knowing nothing but lies and deceit, he said.

He also spoke of demons disguising themselves as those they had recently eaten, but none of them wanted to even consider that possibility. If Daina had met a demon, she had simply been tricked and brainwashed by it. No one could perfectly imitate their princess, especially some evil demon. This knowledge further weighed on each guard's mind, especially given the recent string of gruesome murders and countless missing people. If only one person could be spared from being torn to pieces, it would be a relief for them all.

Although three of the knights had gone into the Decay in search of the princess, one had remained nearby. He was walking along the outside of the walls, right at the bottom of the steep hill from which the stone bricks rose out. He looked toward the sky, still completely covered in his plated armor. Abdaas had him placed around the edge on the off-chance Daina was being flown back home. The knight could not fly but he could certainly catch her if she fell. Then a group of guards saw it, flying toward the city at a speed over twice as fast as the greatest sprinter. Its glowing, graceful wings made it easy to find against the overcast morning sky. Soon they had a better view of it, and it did not take long to see the poor soul the monster was carrying.

"It's a demon!" yelled one of the guards. "And it's carrying the princess in its claws! Alert all guards immediately!" The fastest guard in the group ran to the nearest horn and blew into it with all his might, drawing every person armed with a crossbow to them. Soon dozens were watching the demon as it came closer and closer to the city. Abdaas ran up to them, huffing and wheezing from the effort.

"Aim for its wings," he said between pants. "Demons may be unique in how they fly, but a shot through those glowing wings will make it lose its balance and cause it to plummet like any frail bird. It's likely that it will drop its clutch while trying to correct itself or brace for landing, in which case my loyal guard will catch her." Soon the demon was close to the city, close enough to be in range of the crossbows. Everyone aimed and made sure they were ready to fire.

"This is why I didn't want to fly you back, Daina," said Aleksei, aware of Daina's groaning. "We're almost there. You'll be all right." He then swerved to avoid a sudden barrage of crossbow bolts. The bolts flew past him, missing his legs by only a few feet.

"T-They're firing on us?" asked Daina, stifling her outcries as best as she could. Each swerve sent Aleksei's claws into her ever so slightly. "The guards are well-trained and very accurate, but why would they aim for you when there's a chance they could hit me?"

"I fear someone told them the secret to shooting down a flying kuvi," said Aleksei, diving and swooping upward to avoid a second onslaught of bolts. "And I can't use the trick I exploited while fighting the kuvi in the forest; you'd surely slip out of my grip!"

All this was not enough to chase another worry from his mind. Even as he struggled to avoid the missiles sailing at him through the air, a part of him kept worrying about two more foes that were undoubtedly coming after them. But one development shoved all thoughts out of his mind; Daina was slipping out of his grasp. He looked around rapidly for some sort of reprieve, even the slightest break that would give him time to readjust his grip, but he found nothing. His maneuverability was worthless so long as he had to compensate for Daina. She tried to hold on tighter to him but found it hard to keep her grip as her hands got sweatier and sweater from the fear coursing through her veins.

"Look for a small entrance at the bottom of the wall!" she yelled, even as the rushing wind struggled to drown her out. "It's hidden by some trees! We can get into Tantallos through there!"

Aleksei picked out the spot in seconds and turned to face parallel to the wall. "I see it!" he said. "It's right down..."

A lucky bolt pierced part of his right wing near the end, shattering the pane of energy like glass. The part that had broken off immediately dissipated into the air as what remained flapped away uselessly. Soon the unharmed left wing disintegrated as well. Aleksei began his descent to the ground, still traveling forward at incredible speeds, doing aileron rolls from his loss of balance. Both of them screamed in fear for their lives as the ground rapidly rose to meet them, the dead forests clearing away to reveal a massive stretch of muddy plains. Aleksei struggled to keep his back facing the ground as he held onto Daina tightly.

Only a few rotted trees broke their descent before they finally collided into the muddy ground like a meteor, traveling for a short distance and leaving a trench through the earth. After a second that seemed to last forever they finally stopped. Aleksei let go of Daina and allowed his claws to fall onto the ground without resistance, all while Daina lay on him, attempting to recover.

After a few breaths Daina got off Aleksei and pulled herself to her feet, disoriented from the crash but surprisingly fine save for shallow claw marks. Aleksei had taken almost all of the impact. It amazed her he was still alive. "I'm grounded for the next few hours," he said, strength still in his voice. "It would be pointless to generate my wings before then. Daina, you might want to go on without me. You're close enough to the ossuary entrance; I'll just regain my breath for a few moments. Had I fallen without you in my grip I'd be back on my feet already."

"I'm not leaving you to die out here, Aleksei," she said, offering her hands to him. "If you're tough enough to survive that fall, you're tough enough to walk with my support. Once we get to the ossuary we can take a break. The place is a labyrinth; no one will find us."

"This is not about my current state," he said. "I'll be up in no time at all. But there's undoubtedly a kuvi on your trail even as we speak. Those guards would not have shot us down unless they knew someone was waiting to '*save*' you."

Right behind them a twig snapped. Daina turned around instantly and saw a sight she did not want to see. "Damn, he's fast," said Daina. "I'll come back for you!" She instantly took off toward a collection of bogs as her pursuer chased after her, passing by Aleksei without a second look. She was not running nearly as fast as she should have been; the wounds and the lack of food were finally taking their toll on her. All the same she kept running, focusing on nothing more than the current path and getting her dagger ready as a last resort. She held it carefully, the blade going up her arm so to obscure it from sight.

She could not see the one chasing her, but she knew who it was by simple elimination; Tulsan, the one who had been jumping on the walls. The dumbest of the four, or at least viewed as the dumbest by the rest. Wesan and Jurek were still too far away and the fourth one was nothing more than a skeleton by now. She risked a glance behind her and confirmed this. Tulsan ran unbelievably fast despite his bulky armor, easily keeping up with her. As she continued down a straightaway he looked to be gaining precious steps on her. Daina ran down the flat, open area between two bogs desperately but then saw another bog coming up in front of her. At the edge of the bog she turned on a coin and ran to the right; another step more and she would have fallen right in.

She continued running as Tulsan's bulky armor kept him from making the turn, still propelling him forward. Instead he leaped over the bog, making a spectacular jump of around two dozen feet. He landed sloppily on the other side, falling into some mud. Daina stopped for a moment to catch her breath and watched him recover from this. Then an idea clicked in her head. It was unlikely, but she had no other options. Even Tulsan would be too much for her in a fair fight.

She finished catching her breath and resumed her run as Tulsan continued his chase. She kept her breath as she ran, deeply thankful for every jog around the walls she had made throughout her life. It was not strength or toughness that would save her; it was her agility. In a few moments the kuvi was almost on her, but then she made a tight left turn to avoid another bog. Tulsan again failed to redirect himself and instead jumped over the foul body of scum, landing on the other side and colliding into a copse of trees around a series of rocks. He pulled himself up, shaken-up but largely unharmed. A lucky rock had bent his helmet, trapping the mouth guard downward. This exposed his fang-lined mouth and the edges of his skin, cracked and lined like dry dirt.

Daina smiled on the inside, even as her mouth was busy taking in every breath it could. She felt a stitch at her side as Tulsan got closer to her again. She adeptly swerved once more and the kuvi went sailing through the air, this time slamming into a large half-rotted tree. He picked himself up faster than the past two times and let out a roar of indignation. "*Uza mi gevmo!*" he yelled in the rough kuvi tongue before resuming his chase. Daina did not know the words but they meant exactly what she thought they meant. "You are my dinner!"

Daina looked around in surprise as the landscape opened up around her. Fewer and fewer bogs were lining the sides of her path, instead being replaced by sparse trees. Tulsan was an idiot but he could plow through trees like they were twigs. She could not. And even as she continued running, the stitch in her side grew more and more painful. All it would take was one misstep, one second to catch her breath. That would be more than enough time for her chaser to catch up to her. Catch her, haul her back to the city and let Abdaas perform whatever detail he had missed the first time. That or he would just kill her now and eat her out in the open. Then she saw her salvation right in front of her. Tulsan ran at her, getting within a few feet of her before reaching out. His eyes focused solely on her, naturally drawn to her long hair of that distinctive light shade, flowing behind her and within inches of his grasp. So beautiful, so easy to grab and pull back. He was about to reach forward that final bit when...

Daina turned so sharply she tripped, landing roughly on the ground but in the end getting no more than a little muddy. Tulsan let out a yelp as he sailed forward, only getting a few feet off the ground due to the lack of time to execute even a remotely decent jump. He went through the air but quickly fell down into the colossal bog, shattering the surface and splashing around frantically in the fetid water. Daina slowly pulled herself to her feet, coughing and wheezing from the exertion of the greatest run of her life.

As she stood still, resting her hands on her knees to recover, she watched the bog water for signs of movement. She looked away and glanced around at her surroundings; where was she? She quickly checked inside her pocket with her free hand; Aleksei's quill was still inside, so she had nothing to fear about being rotted by the Decay. She moved her focus back onto the bog as it shook and rattled, undoubtedly from the drowning creature just below its surface. She stepped back as the cover at the shore broke away, revealing a soaked Tulsan. He pulled himself onto the comparatively dry land, coughing and sputtering as he got onto his hands and knees. He then stopped moving and started vomiting. Not a single part of his body was dry, and lots of the disgusting bog water was still trapped in his armor. He placed a claw over his gut as the other one propped him against the ground, all while heaving and retching. He expelled every bit of bog water that had gotten inside his mouth and continued throwing up past that.

But despite his current condition Tulsan still managed to hear a slight squishing noise growing louder; something was approaching him. He weakly looked up just in time to see Daina squatting down onto her haunches before him. "Maybe you can keep this down," she said before forcing her arm forward, shoving her dagger into the helmet and piercing Tulsan right through his mouth. Tough skin of a kuvi or not, he could not endure the stab of such a sharp blade through his unprotected maw. Daina slightly pulled out the blade, tilted it upward and stabbed in again, piercing bone and penetrating the kuvi's brain. Tulsan made gagging noises and twitched uncontrollably. Daina pulled out her dagger moments before he finally collapsed face-first onto the ground.

Daina shook the blade some to get the gore off it before deciding to wipe it off on Tulsan's claws. She stood back up, staring at her work, then at her dagger. She slowly realized what had just happened by this bog. She had killed a kuvi, the most feared creature in the world.

No one else had even helped.

Nothing more than her dagger and a long run.

Just her.

A conflict of emotions soared through her alongside this revelation. She had to keep herself steady as it all dawned on her. She stared at her little dagger in wonder, marveling at the gore she had failed to get off the blade. She moved a muddy hand to her face as she spent more time thinking it all over. All that time she had lived, thinking she was a pitiful creature at almost everything physical. Weak, she had called herself over and over. Unable to even consistently hit a dummy. And yet now she stood above the corpse of something only a few humans could even say they have fought and survived. Not even her father had fought one.

No more beating herself up for her perceived faults. The Daina who thought she had them was not the same person who had just stabbed a kuvi through its mouth. She finished collecting herself and decided on her next goal. She reached down toward Tulsan's body and felt along the outside of his armor for a chink or gap. She found one at the shoulder guard, made even larger by the kuvi's numerous collisions after jumping over bogs. She stuck the dagger in and began cutting away, the blade slowly working its way through the tough kuvi flesh.

It took several stabs to get the bone out of its socket, but eventually she succeeded in severing the arm. She cleaned her dagger off and put it away before picking up the arm with both hands. It was incredibly heavy, but it might make a nice trophy. Even as she held it the claw seemed to be flaking off. Tiny shreds of metal blew away from it with every breeze or simply fell to the ground. No matter to her; what remained would be testament enough.

Aleksei picked himself up, the damage from the fall quickly fading away. The soft mud had helped him deal with the impact. He did not risk generating his wings to check their condition, but he knew it would still be some time before he could use them. His clothes were torn and ripped in several places but still effectively protected his modesty. They did not expose any telltale signs of his true nature as his skin was smooth in appearance like a human's, but no less durable than the crevice-ridden flesh of other kuvis. He tried to recollect which direction Daina had run off to, looking at the nearby footprints when he heard a noise behind him. He turned around and saw her carrying the last thing he had expected to see; an arm partially covered in armor with a menacing, oversized clawed gauntlet on the end. Already the claws had receded by two inches per blade, the mixture of lesser metals blowing away into the wind.

"That's definitely an item I never thought I'd see you carrying," he said, "though I'm glad to see you alive and our enemy dead. Least I assume it is. Kuvis can survive terrible blows."

"I shoved my dagger into his mouth," she said. "I don't think it likely he survived. But could I request your help in getting the armor off? I think I just want one of his bones. A little memento, since his claw is rapidly degrading. Then again, I don't know. Would keeping a bone as a trophy make you uncomfortable? I'd certainly be terrified if you had a collection of human bones lying around your home."

"It does not bother me," said Aleksei. "It's not like it's from me or someone I care about; it's just some villainous kuvi's bone. But before we do that I think it's important we take cover in the ossuary. Who knows how long it will take Jurek and Wesan to track us down." His ears perked up as he heard several somethings stomping toward them. "And I'd wager that several humans have entered the Decay in an attempt to find us. I'm sure you could talk to them, but they'd likely lead you to Jurek and lead me to a torture chamber. Will they enter the ossuary?"

"Just inside there's a tall stone shaft," said Daina. "Unless they can fly or climb walls they'll be unable to get to us once we climb up, assuming they even come across the entrance to begin with."

"Works for me," he said. With that they started walking toward the city, aiming for a small hole at the bottom of the hill, somewhat hidden but outlined by stone supports. Once they arrived at it they quickly went inside, finally escaping the Decay.

CHAPTER 20

The only creature you must truly fear is the Cold One; resist her alluring
promises and rewards, for deals are always in her favor.
-From the Tomes of the Huntmaster.

Alkin slowly regained consciousness at the sensation of something nuzzling against him, sniffing loudly. He shot up, the quick motion making his head explode with pain. The movement startled a small, fat animal with cloven hooves and a large snout that it had been rubbing against him. It let out a squeal and took off into a nearby copse, content to forage for food there instead rather than deal with a still-living creature. Alkin let out a groan as he slowly brought himself up to his feet. He walked over to Back Breaker and returned it to its place on his back. With the added weight and current disorientation he struggled to keep balance while also collecting his thoughts.

First he found Daina, that was certain. Then he nearly got overwhelmed in combat with a demon... no, kuvi; they're actually called kuvis. He had a conversation with the kuvi and was preparing to help get them back to the city and into it safely when something happened and he fell unconscious. He looked up to the sky but the sun was nowhere to be seen; so much for that indicator of how much time had passed. Daina and the kuvi could be anywhere by now. Or dead. They had not stopped to save him, so something chased them off in quite a hurry. This unknown threat could have killed them, presumably after incapacitating him from behind so there was one less element to worry about.

But how could there possibly be such a dangerous threat? The kuvi he had fought against – Aleksei, he believed his name to be– was by far the toughest and most tenacious opponent Alkin had ever faced, and even then Daina had managed to hold him back. It would take something unimaginably powerful to chase him off. Alkin turned toward the city and walked back as fast as he could despite how much he ached. Daina and Aleksei were headed there to begin with, so perhaps he could meet with them before the Tantallosians tried to harm Aleksei. He would hate to see such a mighty combatant get killed just because he was what humans perceived to be a monster. And, under the quills and claws, he seemed like a good person.

It was hard for Daina to see anything in the dark shaft that connected to the ossuary above them, but what Aleksei saw did not aid matters. The floor above was in sight but still out of reach. He guessed that the next level was around thirty feet off the ground. A burning claw helped illuminate things so Daina could provide judgment as well. She came up with a similar guess. "I hate to question a gift like this, but why does the city ossuary connect to the Decay?" asked Aleksei.

"No living person knows precisely," said Daina. "It just always has connected to the outside. Some people have theories that there might have been a time when the Decay did not exist. No Decay and more cities near Tantallos. Humans are easily-angered creatures, so these cities might have attacked and besieged each other. If they did such things this shaft could have been a sort of one-way escape tunnel. Down a ladder or something similar. I'm just thankful it exists. The chancellor sends a repairman down to this entryway monthly to keep it in working condition. '*You never know,*' he always said."

"It's good that it works on the other end, but that doesn't help us," he said, "and unless you recently gained the ability to fly it might be hard to get you up there."

"You can't fly right now, but can't you climb it?" she asked.

"*I* can climb it," he said. "You can't, and I need both my claws to climb so I can't hold onto you. I don't want to risk you riding on my back, either; you'd gouge your eyeballs out on my quills. Once I get up to the top I'll find something to help you. Just stay here with your trophy." Aleksei sized up the wall, his eyes rapidly scanning to detect weak spots and already-existing holes to use. The crumbling stone face was covered in such points and soon he had settled on a specific stretch to climb. He jumped onto the wall and dug his claws into the rock, the metal blades effortlessly piercing it. The claws on his feet came out to further aid him in latching onto the stones. This done, he quickly made his way up the wall and in just a short moment he pulled himself onto the above floor.

He lit up a claw like a torch and looked around, quickly finding a rope harness of sorts tethered to a sturdy anchor. It looked brand-new, undoubtedly the handiwork of the Tantallos chancellor. How fortunate for them that he had thought to do so. Daina looked up, listening to the shuffling going about above her, and then moved to the side as a harness fell downward. Shortly after it landed on the ground she picked it up and tied herself securely to it. She gave it a couple tugs to check her knots and then called out the affirmative to Aleksei. He hoisted her up to his level quickly and in moments they were standing by each other. Daina undid her knots and tossed the harness back into the place it had been stored.

"Now that we're technically in Tantallos you'd best stay close to me," she said. "I've no doubt the citizens will think to look through the ossuary soon enough; there may be people coming to this entrance as we speak. But there's one area they won't dare to look."

"Where could that possibly be?" he asked. "A tunnel in disrepair...?"

"Not at all," she said. "It's the royal tomb. Kings, queens, princes and princesses are stored in their own coffins permanently. Normal citizens are in coffins only as long as it takes for them to become skeletons. Then they get stacked up on the walls to save space." She gestured to the walls as they passed them. It was a macabre sight to say the least, stacks and stacks of human bones sorted by size, type and abnormalities. The irregularity of the tunnel's width did not help matters, and at one point the two found themselves nearly squeezed by two piles of femurs. Curious, Aleksei grabbed a grinning skull and pondered it for a moment, assessing the intricacies in its design. So unique, but among the other skulls it looked no different. He put the skull back on the stack of bones he had gotten it from and kept following Daina, holding his torch claw high enough to light the way for her. He found his pulse quickening as they got closer to the surface, so close he could pick up some of the noise from above.

Any minute now a group of unwary Tantallosians might come around the corner and see him, his eyes uncovered and ready to suck them into its pits. Some would fall in and faint. Others would be overtaken by the hysteria, collapse and go into seizures. And a few others would still have enough sanity to run off and warn the whole city that he was right under their feet. They would hold up their promise; if he came back, they would kill him by torture--though that was only if they found him again.

After some time Daina and Aleksei arrived at a massive stone door and stopped. It was engraved with a coat of arms that, while once intricate and detailed, had become so worn that it was barely decipherable. Along the edge of a side of the door was a depression, a small gap large enough for several men to slip in their fingers and get in a grip. It would take several of the city's strongest to quickly move the door but one kuvi would be more than enough for the task. Aleksei latched onto the stone carefully, making sure his claws were not digging into the stone so he did not lose his grip. That done, he pulled the door open; it was slow but much faster than if a group of humans had tried to do it. Daina cringed as the door scraped against the stone tile surrounding it and she prayed to the Goddess that no one should hear them from elsewhere in the ossuary.

Aleksei finished pulling it open, having created a space just large enough for both of them to fit inside. Once they got in he pulled it back as much as he could without completely sealing them in. He moved the door back to almost the same position; hopefully no one would notice the slightly bigger gap. He walked back to Daina and followed her into a small, bare chamber separate from the other chambers. Only a single coffin was in it, placed against the far wall. Daina stood before the coffin, staring at it in sorrow.

He looked at her and then to the coffin. He put the pieces together easily.

"It's been so long since I've visited her tomb," said Daina. "I never felt the desire to. She may be my mother and my namesake, but I never knew her. I wonder; how much different would I have been if she had survived giving birth to me? What would she have taught me that my father and tutors did not?"

"I think all children with one parent ask that same question at some point," said Aleksei, thinking of the father he had never known. He walked up to the coffin and inspected the writing on the cover, able to read it albeit clumsily. "Was she a good woman? I know her daughter is."

"I appreciate the thought, but I'm not that nice," said Daina. "I pretend to be nice, and I'm damn good at it. I have genuine feelings toward so few people, and the rest of the time I'd rather let those people I'm kind to burn. I'm surrounded by so many whores and traitors, all trying to get me to love them to further their own desires." She brought her head downward. "Father always told me that mother was nice to everyone, loving them as dearly as those closest to her. She loved all her people and simply wanted the best for all of them. Maybe she could have helped me be like her."

"Are you sure you're so different from her?" he asked. "You befriended a creature believed by your people to be the ultimate evil, the greatest spit in the face of your deity, a monster so horrid that his soul is consumed by the Goddess alongside all the sinners after he dies. But you quickly started trusting him and even let yourself place your life in his unfeeling hands. If you can trust a... *demon*, you can find it in your heart to at least accept these other people who surround you."

"One would think so, but you're different in some way; I can't say exactly how," she said. She worked on a way to change the subject and eventually settled on the arm she was still carrying around. "This is a bit old, but do you want to eat it? You're hungry."

"That's cannibalism, princess," he said. "I'll fast. I'd think you'd want to eat it instead. You're not a kuvi so it wouldn't be a crime against your kind. You're just as hungry as me and you aren't used to the pangs."

"Thanks, quill-head," she said. "I certainly could not cook a human, but would you light a fire so I can cook the meat? I'd rather not throw up in this place."

"I'll cook the meat," said Aleksei. "Just let me peel off the armor first."

Daina and Aleksei sat against the wall next to each other. Aleksei lay propped against the stones with his arms folded while Daina sucked on her fingers some to get the last bits of juice off them. As... *exotic* a meal as it had been, it was a blessing after such a long time without food.

"Perhaps it was just my hunger, but that was beyond delicious," she said. "You kuvis taste better than any other meat I've ever had. Do you find that worrying?"

"Not at all," he said. "At least, not as long as you don't try to get a taste of me. I've had enough creatures try to eat me in my time, and Huntmaster knows that one even succeeded. And don't spread the word to other humans; we lose enough dignity in death without ending on your dinner plates as well. I can see the craze sweeping Tantallos: kuvi kabobs, kuvi pies, kuvi flanks grilled medium-rare, and what remains getting turned into kuvi sausages and black pudding."

"I'll be the only human to ever know the taste," she said.

With the meal finished, the two of them just sat there, resting, grateful for the opportunity to relax as they heard shuffling all around them. Large groups of people walked past the entrance to the royal tomb not twenty feet away from where they sat. Almost all of them figured the door was so heavy no one could have moved it to get inside, let alone moved it back into place. But each time a group stopped by their door they expected it to get slowly dragged open, a dozen or so citizens waiting to come inside and search. What seemed like eons later the noise finally died down. Daina noticed a cold pressure on her hand and looked to see that it had ended up in Aleksei's claw. He had gripped onto it fearfully as the groups of humans had become larger and more frequent in their trips past the door. He controlled his strength and avoided harming Daina, who did not mind the claw's embrace.

"Rest assured, Aleksei," she said softly, "they won't find you in here. And if they do I'll latch onto you and protect you."

"Who's worried?" he asked.

Daina smirked a little. "This may not be the best moment, but I'm not sure how much more time we'll have together before we go our separate ways. I've been meaning to ask you something. It's something I've been wondering ever since I first talked to you. I hope you don't mind."

"What's your question?" he asked.

"Why do you hate being called a demon so much?" she asked. "I understand it's not something you'd want to call anyone, but that word in particular makes you express seething rage every time you are called it, even when you call yourself it. What makes that word worse than any other?

Surely a kuvi living in a human city has been called all sorts of things; monster, abomination, and countless other flattering titles. What makes '*demon*' more hurtful than them?"

Aleksei sighed. "You deserve an explanation," he said. He put one of his claws on his chin as he pondered it. "In Proso we do not have any demons. No supernatural forces representative of good and evil, at least not like in human theology. The mortal creatures we fight are fierce enough for the minds of kuvis without us creating new, more evil ones. Many villains like the Stripe-Faced Giant are not inherently evil; the Giant acted on his god's accord. The only real comparison I can think of would be to the Cold One, Kriothanatos, and that truly horrid beast is a discussion for another day.

"But then I came to your world as a terrified little child, wracked with grief over being separated from my mother. On Proso almost any parent would have been sympathetic to me and have offered me even the slightest of comforts. Most males are inherently protective of weaker kuvis, be them old or young. But as I fell around a bunch of odd-looking kuvis with weird eyes and no claws they said one thing to me.

"The first word out of the mouth of the first human I ever saw was '*demon*,' and that word was further uttered by all the humans that followed. Each one of them took a single look at me and decided right then I was an instrument of evil, a twisted mockery of a human child. I scared them, and that fear made them angry and urged them to destroy me. Even though I was just a child, a child whose claws had only just become hard enough to be an effective hunter. I had not even killed anything on my own yet. I had been taught to take down prey and deliver blows that quickly kill, but learning and doing are two very, very different things."

He let go of Daina's hand and brought his claws up to just below his eye level. He stared at them, the palms facing him. "My first true kill was a human," he said. "And I had not wanted to even do it; it was all just a blur of actions and reactions. All kuvis are born hunters, but I was unfortunate enough to be made into a killer. I've been forced to kill so many wastefully in self-defense." He reached into his pocket and pulled out the band of cloth, left in there for hours. He tied it around his eyes before looking right into Daina's. "I've wanted nothing more than to protect, to find those who would treat me justly and look after them if they needed or wanted me. But it seems that will never be, not as long as I'm in your world."

Daina grabbed Aleksei's nearest claw and held it with both of her hands, bringing it closer to her. She gripped it carefully to avoid cutting herself. "You've done wonders to protect me," she said, "more than anyone else could. More than I deserve. I just hope I can repay the favor in some way. I'll do what I can to protect you from my people, but you can't kill them."

"Thank you, Daina," he said. "And I hope to never do so again, not unless it's in defense of someone close to me."

Time passed by as they continued waiting for crowds to die down. The excitement finally got to Daina, who let herself fall asleep against the wall. Aleksei gently moved her onto the floor before standing up, careful to avoid making any noise while he did so. He turned to the coffin and walked toward it, eventually stopping right in front of it. He looked at Daina to ensure she was sleeping before he made his next move. He brought his digits along the side and slowly got a grip on the lid, relying more on sight than on feel. This done he ever so carefully lifted the lid up, an eye constantly darting back to Daina as she still slept. Soon he brought the lid up high enough to fit one of his claws in.

He looked inside, examining the skeleton that was Daina's mother. She appeared to be undisturbed save for her torso, which was missing a rib. It was broken off close to the sternum but just enough had been left protruding to catch his eye; it was not just a birth defect. *The bones of the mother*, he thought. Abdaas and his minions have been in the city for some time now. He or any of his minions could have collected it during that time.

He pushed these thoughts to the side and reached his right claw in, making for the remaining bones in the hand; something easily hidden in a pocket without being obvious in shape. He picked up several of the phalanges and some other parts of the hand as well, holding them as carefully as he could given the motor limitations of his claw. He slowly brought the claw, palm up, out of the coffin and quietly shut the lid. He closed it slowly to avoid making too much noise, still glancing rapidly toward Daina as he did so. Once the coffin was shut he put the bones away in his pocket opposite Daina's lock of hair.

Aleksei let out a sigh of relief; he had executed it without disturbing Daina. He walked over to her, pondering just how soundly she was sleeping. The day must have made her wearier than he had thought. He got down and reached around her, picking her up by the back of his claws. The grip was awkward but Daina stayed asleep, muttering nonsense as she dreamed. Aleksei's single-edged claws wouldn't cut her as long as he carried her this way. *I'll make sure you're safe*, Daina, thought Aleksei, *but there is something else I need to do. I'll find you once I'm finished with it.*

Daina looked around her; she was not in the ossuary like she was most nights. Instead she was on a massive, flat rock. A plateau, one of her tutors had called it. A landmark she had never seen, but her tutor's books and what little artwork there was to be found in Tantallos had painted a vivid picture. She was incredibly high up, so high she could almost reach out and touch the perpetually overcast clouds. But the plateau was not bare, not at all. Countless slabs of granite lay about the landscape. They were all uniform in their circular shape and smoothness, only varying in size. They were dolmens, summoning platforms. Tantallos once had such rocks but they had all been destroyed upon discovery. This plateau housed two massive ones in particular, perfect discs each large enough to fit a house. They were located on opposite sides of the plateau.

And one of them, the one she was closest to, had a man in a hooded robe standing by it. She made her way up to the man and found herself standing by him in an instant. She saw him place the summoning ingredients out before him; a bowl of flesh stripped off the skeleton, bones so clean they were white, an eyeball in a jar of preserving fluid, and a vial of blood. He moved the flesh, bones and eyes out of their containers and onto the dolmen, and then smashed the vial on the dolmen, starting the ritual. She watched as the ingredients slowly dissolved into a paste, seemingly evaporating as the dolmen called for a creature.

"You!" she called, going up to the man's side and grabbing his shoulder, shaking it a couple times. "What creature do you intend to bring into this world?"

The man turned to face her and she immediately recoiled in horror. It was a rotting skeleton, missing one of its eyeballs while the remaining one was dominated by cataracts. Flesh fell off its face in clumps and the exposed bone cracked and crumbled.

"I am summoning your doom," it said. "It has come time for the world to end. This creature shall do so and all those who are worthy shall go on, while the rest are doomed to a painful destruction."

She let out a scream and tried to run away, but suddenly she could not get herself to move. The decomposing skeleton man simply stood there looking toward the dolmen as a gleaming white hole in the fabric of the world tore open above it. As the hole increased in size she felt a fear greater than anything else she had ever felt surface up inside of her. The skeleton man was right; she was about to be destroyed. But then the ground shook, nearly making her lose her footing. She turned around and saw something appearing at the opposite side of the plateau; another hole, equal in size to the one near her. The presence inside filled her with as much fear as the one she was by, but something emerged from this new hole. As it did, she felt her fear melt away. Coming out of the portal were red tentacles covered in black plates, each one ending with a black, metallic claw.

CHAPTER 21

You may break My rules and you may forsake Me, but I shall always be with you and I shall always accept you back if you decide to change. I love you too much to force My will upon you.
-From the Tomes of the Huntmaster.

Daina awakened by something grabbing her shoulders and shaking her while calling her name. She opened her eyes to find herself looking at one of the wall guards. "Princess Daina!" he exclaimed. "Forgive me for shaking you so roughly, but I was worried you were dead. But you're not! This is truly a sight to behold!" Daina kept her confusion hidden from the guard and smiled. She looked around and realized she was on the Tantallos walls, only a few dozen feet away from the castle entrance to the walkway. It was well into the night and the nocturnal guards had started filing out. The guard grasping her had either just started his shift or had been just about to end it.

"What?" she asked. "How did I get here?"

"I'm afraid I do not know," said the guard, letting go of Daina's shoulders. She pulled herself up to her feet on her own, refusing the hand of the guard when he offered it. He got up alongside her. "I had just been on my way back to the castle when I discovered you lying here, hidden away in the shadow of one of the battlements." He gasped as Daina's cheeks came into a better light. "What manner of horrible beast has scarred your face in such a way?"

"It was a ku... I mean, it was a demon," said Daina. "But that foul creature is long since dead. Did you see anyone else on the battlements before finding me here? A man slightly taller than me with red spiky hair and a band of cloth over his eyes?"

"I saw no one at all, milady," said the guard. "Sorry I cannot help you with your friend. But now I must take you to King Vikenti! He has been so distraught since you disappeared! He and Prince Alkin will be so elated to see you alive and well!"

"Lead the way," said Daina. She let the guard take her back to the castle, all while wondering about Aleksei. Why did he leave her here? Where did he go off to? She only wished she knew.

Vikenti's face immediately changed into a massive smile as he ran forward and wrapped his arms around his daughter, holding onto her in a tight grip she had only felt a few times in her life. All those times had been when she had recovered from sickness or injury.

"Oh, Goddess be praised!" said Vikenti, tears of joy streaming down his face. "I was afraid I would never see you again!"

Daina returned the hug to the best of her ability but soon found herself struggling for air. "Can't breathe, father," she managed to say.

"I am so sorry," he said, slackening his grip some. "But these past days have been the absolute worst of all my life. I can think of none that compare." He looked Daina in the face, taking a note of her scars. "But it's so great to see you alive, even if some despicable fiend had the audacity to scar your cheeks. You look like you're starving; I have the cooks preparing a bountiful feast and every bit is just for you, cooked just the way you like it."

As if on cue the doors connecting the main hall to the kitchen swung open and an armada of cooks emerged, each one carrying a different dish. Vikenti let go of Daina and let her take a seat at the main table. He sat down across from her and watched as she stared at all the various meats, pastries, breads and drinks placed before her. It all looked like nectar and ambrosia after her meals and lack thereof the past couple of days. She could not hold herself back for a moment longer. She descended on the bounty with an unmatched tenacity, devouring massive amounts of food in minutes. She would have a stomach ache for sure but it was a small price to pay. Once she finished stuffing herself she pondered how she had always taken such spreads for granted before her journey into the Decay.

"Never in all my time raising you have I seen you eat that much," said Vikenti. "Never have I seen monsters in the Decay eat that much. But I should have expected it; I can only imagine what disgusting things you were forced to eat out in the Decay to survive."

"I certainly ate some things I never thought would ever enter my mouth in my life," she said. "But I should be thankful I was able to eat anything at all, given how little edible food is in the Decay. I just wish he was here so I could thank him properly."

"Who's 'him?'" asked Vikenti.

Daina thought carefully; this conversation could prove very dangerous for Aleksei. "You would not know this man," said Daina. "He is just over a year younger than me. He has an incredibly fierce temper but he is strong, fast and smart enough to fight off the creatures that wanted to eat me." She pointed to the scars on her cheeks. "He even killed the demon that had done this to me, absolutely annihilated him. If it had not been for him I would've been consumed by that monster days ago."

"Sounds like a truly admirable and powerful man for one so young," said Vikenti.

"He's not that young," said Daina. "I told you, he's not even two years younger than me."

"Nevertheless, I wish I could have thanked him myself," he said. "Where is he now?"

"That's one question I cannot answer," said Daina. She let her head fall downward. "Though I do wish I could. He's not used to other people and he's unfamiliar with the city so I can only imagine what sort of torment he is going through right now. You see, he's... heavily disfigured. People would react in horror to him if they saw him."

"You have the resources of the whole kingdom at your disposal," he said. "I could have the guards search for him and have them inform the citizens that this man is to be rewarded at the castle. I must commend his good deed."

"He'd hate the attention," she said. "I'd imagine he'd rather remain unknown to the people."

Something occurred to Vikenti, something that he had completely forgotten in his euphoria. Something that dampened his spirits. "Daina, I need you to be completely honest with me," he said, looking her straight in the eyes. "Throughout the day I've been listening to reports from the crossbowmen which patrolled the walls today. This savior of yours... is he a demon?"

"He's not a demon!" she said. "He despises being called that. His kind refer to themselves as kuvis, not demons."

"You shouldn't believe anything he says, Daina," said Vikenti. "This demon or *koobie* or whatever he calls himself tricked you to satisfy his own goals. He poisoned your mind to make you subservient to his will and used you to get in; I have no doubt he'd have used you as a hostage if he found himself cornered. You should be fortunate he did not kill you and eat you once he was finished using you."

"He didn't poison my mind at all, father!" said Daina. "He may be a hot-blooded person but he is not a threat to this city!"

"I also took the liberty of asking the guard who found you about all details concerning when and how he found you," said Vikenti. "He reported seeing nothing unusual, but he had plenty to share about what you were saying. He said you were talking about a man with a band of cloth over his eyes and red, spiky hair."

"Notice the band of cloth? He's taking measures to keep himself from harming humans!" said Daina. "He protected me and fed me, father! He never willingly hurt me and kept me safe from far more dangerous creatures!"

"It's the comment concerning red hair that piqued my interest, Daina," he said. "Almost no other demons have hair like what you described; most don't have any at all on their scalps. I had reviewed reports of all the demon expulsions of the past twenty years while you were gone from the city, and this color detail allowed me to single out a similar-looking demon. About eleven years ago a demon had been exiled from the city, and he had the exact same hairstyle, color and habit of wearing cloth over his eyes as he approached his victims."

The details did not spur her memory, but the date did. Soon Daina was recalling her birthday night. "You can't possibly mean to say..."

"Daina, you helped bring the Red Light Murderer into this city!" said Vikenti. "But I cannot punish you or even hold you responsible; it was the fiend's will that twisted its way into your mind, making you into his slave. A demon could subjugate any unfortunate person and leave nothing in its wake but faulty memories.

He let out a loud sigh. "Believe me, nothing makes me happier than to see you alive and well again, but I must urge you to not go in search of this monster. Ever. Under no circumstances should you. He does not need you anymore, and if you are not careful he might make you his thirty-ninth victim." Daina took it all in, staring ahead blankly and sitting silently at the table. She reflected upon her conversations with Aleksei, trying to grasp how the pieces worked together. How could he be the Red Light Murderer?

I've eaten dozens of humans. My first true kill was a human.

I wasn't even seven when I was dragged into your world. I'd say that, by your calendar, I'd be turning eighteen years old within one cycle of the moon.

But how could it be?

"Before I forget," said Vikenti, "one of the guards found a trophy by the spot you were at on the wall. They assumed it had some tie to you and your journey through the Decay, so it's waiting for you up in your room. I'd rather not ask how you obtained it."

"The kuvi's arm bone?" she asked.

"That's what it was?" he asked. "No matter. Go up to your room immediately. You are not to leave this castle until after we've captured the demon. If you have any respect for what I say and what I do for this city you will listen to me."

She found it difficult to have such respect when he was dismissing all possibilities of a friendly kuvi without a second thought, not even bothering to call him a kuvi. All the same she stood up from her chair and nodded. She then walked across the hall and ascended the staircase without another word. Vikenti remained at the table, pondering his daughter as she walked away so silently. Abdaas said the memories were faulty and poorly faked, but she had seemed so insistent and truthful with her statements. And she had been so protective of a beast she claimed to have been saved by. But more noticeable than that; she now called him *"father."*

Once he finished thinking this over he stood up from the table and signaled to some servants nearby to come and clean up the table. He slowly made his way to his bedroom, cane in hand. Along the way his mind devised and broke down plans to capture and contain the demon he now had the task of dealing with. But not killing, not in the dead of night. He needed to see the creature himself before he could decide on an appropriate punishment.

Daina quickly arrived at her room, opened the door and stepped in before shutting the door behind her. She lit some candles, illuminating the lavish chamber. She walked over and flopped onto her bed face-up. She let her head fall to the left side, facing her toward a white, thin and long mass on a piece of cloth. The kuvi bone. The claw portion had finished disintegrating, leaving only part of the bone left. The metallic claw extended well up the bone of the claw under the skin, evident from the leftover grooves and depressions where it had once been. It made her wonder how the bone endured the punishment and pressure the claws managed to resist. She guessed it was another part of the claws being a divine gift, same claws as the Huntmaster and such. Quite an edge in a fight.

She picked up the bone, moved off the bed and took it to her dresser. She shoved all sorts of worthless trinkets and baubles to the side to make room. This done, she went back to the bed and lay down on it, looking up. The bed was far softer than anything else she had slept on in the past couple of days. Even so, she felt a longing for one of the surfaces she had laid her head on. So warm and comforting.

All of Daina's thoughts ceased and her eyes grew wide. She missed him. She missed Aleksei. But he was an evil, foul creature. He was the Red Light Murderer. But he was not. He had just been a scared and isolated child trying to survive by any means necessary. Anyone would do the same. But he brutally killed people, dozens of them. Not all of them were killed for food. But he killed them solely for survival. He did it to live and even so he was regretful for his actions. He hated what he had been forced to turn himself into.

She shot upright, her back stiff as a board. Even as she sat on the bed she felt one of her biggest weaknesses come crashing down around her. She could barely comprehend herself as she tackled thought after thought. Every time her mind brought up a reason to hate Aleksei it came up with a response that defeated it. A creature with metallic claws, sharp quills for hair and the ability to create fire had succeeded where dozens of handsome, courteous and socially powerful nobles had always failed. She trusted him, faults and all. It took her some time to recover from this revelation, but once she did she moved herself off the bed and pulled out his quill, still as tough and sharp as ever. She put it and her dagger to the side of the bed as she changed into a set of less-ravaged but similarly casual clothes. She placed her dagger back on her person and pocketed the quill as well. She then extinguished the lights in her room and walked out.

This sent her straight into Alkin. "How great to see you back on this side of the walls, Daina!" he said quietly, cautious not to disturb anyone else in the castle. "Goddess be praised. I was worried you and Aleksei had been killed by whatever had knocked me out."

"I'm amazed the kuvis didn't kill you," said Daina. "Though I'm glad they didn't."

"Perhaps they had their eyes out for only one member of royalty," said Alkin. "I don't pretend to understand or even know anything about the race besides their being vicious fighters. Speaking of which, where is Aleksei? I really need to speak with him."

"I wish I knew the answer to that," said Daina. "I had been preparing to leave for the kennel to get a hound, actually. I have this." She reached into her pocket, carefully grabbing the quill and pulling it out. She showed it to Alkin.

"That will work," said Alkin. "Let's not waste any more time. Goddess knows what sort of acts he's involved with right now, or how the citizens are reacting to him."

"We can't be certain until we get a hound," said Daina, "but I'd guess he's hiding in the poorer sections of Tantallos. He'd be comfortable and familiar with those streets. After all, he was the Red Light Murderer."

CHAPTER 22

Consider your actions before you do something immoral. It may extend your life today, but necessity does not change the fact you committed a sin against your fellow people and against Me. Many sins can never be forgiven, and those who commit them deserve a torturous death.
-From the Teachings of the Goddess.

Some moments later, Daina and Alkin emerged from the castle and made their way into the streets of Tantallos. They walked along the sides of the street, Daina holding the leash of a slow-moving hound. It was a long-bodied, wrinkly specimen, with ears so long and floppy Daina wondered how often the dog tripped over them while following scents. Despite the anxiety in the humans walking it the dog made no efforts to hurry. It kept its nose close to the ground, sniffing this way and that for traces of the distinctive scent Daina had given it to smell. However, as it continued tracking the scent the dog led them closer and closer to some of the worst sections of the entire city.

"I really hope he's taking us in the correct direction," said Daina. "I don't want to stay out on these streets for long. But the kennel master said Dom was the best tracker."

"He'll track down Aleksei," said Alkin. "It's just a matter of how long it takes him. I hope we reach Aleksei's lair before sunrise, at least. We don't want another massive search for you after everything that's happened."

"Judging the state of these neighbors it cannot possibly take that long," said Daina. Then something occurred to her. "By the way, thank you again for coming along with me. This would be a lot more dangerous for me without you at my side."

"You're welcome, but I highly doubt it," said Alkin. "You calmed him down from a blind rage. He would never harm you intentionally, though he would probably be rather possessive of you. He's very jealous of me; if anything I should be the one in danger."

"The danger was more in reference to any criminals or vagrants that also happen to be awake at this time of night," said Daina. She stared at the dog woefully as it continued dragging its muzzle across the ground, nearly stepping on its own ears several times. "I found out he was a famous murderer, a person I had vowed to never trust on the night of my birthday. But tonight, when I discovered that, it didn't change my perception of him at all." She sighed. "I missed him as much after I found out as before."

She looked to Alkin. "Alkin, I know you expressed a desire to keep our marriage simply political, but I'm afraid I can't even let it be that. I just cannot marry you anymore, even if it's for appearances. You may not feel for me in such a way, but I hope you're not mad over my decision."

"I'm not hurt at all by it," said Alkin. "Though I am worried by what the noblewomen back in Tulroy will do once they hear I am coming back without a bride. But besides that it's not a problem in the slightest. Tantallos and Tulroy can become steadfast allies without an arranged marriage, though it may take some convincing to call everything off. My father's been urging me to find a wife for over half my life."

Daina became flooded with relief; Alkin was too kind a soul to hurt over such a development. But then she looked at Alkin oddly. "I cannot lie; I thought you would be a little disappointed. Hope I don't seem smug about my own worth."

"It's hard to be disappointed over something I was barely aware of," said Alkin. "I only knew you an evening before you got kidnapped. It would take me more than a single conversation to feel something greater than the slightest attachment. Not that you're an inadequate choice; it's just..."

He started messing around with his fingers while his eyes darted about rapidly. "Honestly, there are a lot of your reasons; our age differences, a lack of similar interests assuming we share any at all, my preference for red hair over golden hair. And..." He stopped himself. "I'm afraid our relationship simply wouldn't have worked."

Daina regarded this with suspicion but had bigger concerns at the moment; Alkin's hesitance to explain himself could wait until much later. She pushed the thoughts aside as the hound sped up some. She let the dog lead her further onward when she decided to bring up something else.

"Different subject," she said. "While journeying to Tantallos, did you ever suspect that those knights were kuvis in disguise?"

"I had my suspicions," said Alkin. "I suspected that something was odd from the moment I first laid eyes on them. No Tulroy soldier wears so much armor. But Abdaas has a significant amount of influence in Tulroy, similar in power to my own, and he seemed to have control over them. I was a fool back then. I thought because I killed one apparently very weak kuvi, I could dispose of any of them that were ever foolish enough to cross me." He looked upward, scanning the roofs of buildings. "But Aleksei had been about to defeat me almost effortlessly. And Jurek is an even stronger adversary than he?"

"It may not be so much a matter of combat prowess but a matter of alignment," said Daina. "Jurek's elemental alignment bests Aleksei's. Perhaps if they fought each other without using their elements the results would be different, but they'd likely have to get airborne for such a setup. I haven't once seen Jurek leave the ground while in combat. I'm thinking precisely because of his alignment."

"But he must have a weakness," said Alkin. "Aleksei mentioned as such. Kuvis *dal Kafteros* can't use their power if their claws are soaked in water, right? There has to be a similar way to separate a kuvi *dal*, what was it, *Tinagmos*, I think you said, from his power. Perhaps instead of coating him in an element we take him off the one element he never leaves."

"It's possible picking Jurek off the ground would give an opportunity to exploit his weakness," said Daina, "but we don't even know what that weakness is nor how to exploit it properly, and it would be difficult for Aleksei to pick up Jurek, between the bulky armor and Jurek's own size."

"Honestly, if that armor is forged from what I'm certain it's made from, we should be amazed Jurek is even able to fly," said Alkin. "Strong or not, if you tie a weight to a bird's legs it won't be able to fly. And such durability; I doubt all the guards in Tantallos could defeat him so long as he wears that suit. It doesn't rival kuvi claw metal, but it's more than a match for anything we humans use. I've seen steel blades shatter on it." They both sighed and let their gazes fall to the ground, focusing on the ground and the shuffling hound as it continued its tracking. Both of them started to feel like an animal that had just realized it had walked into a trap. But even as the creature turned around the gate fell downward, sealing it in.

"They continue to worry me, and I can do nothing but wish I knew what could be done about them," said Daina. "Jurek, Wesan, even Abdaas to a lesser extent. What will they do when they find out I'm still alive, if they haven't heard from Abdaas already? I certainly can't kill either of the kuvis, and how well would Tulroy react to the news that the Tantallosian princess killed the head of the Church of the Goddess?"

"It is no good worrying about such problems at the moment," said Alkin. "It's better to focus on finding our best chance against them. But perhaps in the meantime we could enlist a large group of armed guards around you at all times; force our foes to wait for the perfect moment that never arrives. All else fails, they still have to get through me, and Tulroy would never believe that a kuvi had killed me. The populace would immediately suspect Abdaas and the knights of foul play. At least that's how they should react. Considering how much I've done for the city, anything else would be disrespectful and they know it."

Their conversation was cut short by the tugging of the leash. The dog further sped up until it was running, or as close as it could get to running given its short and stumpy legs. All while continuing to sniff, smelling its way toward a tall building of questionable safety, on the border between the city and the farming areas. The structure looked to be of older design and was tall enough for someone on the top floor to look out into the Decay. Nothing seemed too destroyed or smashed on the outside, be it the doors or windows. The dog ran up to the steps of the building and stopped. It howled at the building while Daina and Alkin looked at the structure, then at each other. The location did not seem to be the sort Aleksei would seek out, but they both felt it in their gut. This was definitely the place where a kuvi was hiding.

Daina knelt by the dog, which continued to howl. She shushed it and pet it behind its comically large ears. "Good boy, Dom," she said. She folded the leash and slipped it under the dog's collar, tying it slightly so it would stay under and not fall out halfway home. "Very good boy. You go back home and tell your master you did a good job. Okay, buddy?" The dog licked Daina's face once and then started walking back to the castle, leaving Alkin and Daina alone at the steps of the building. Even as they looked at it they noticed a disturbing lack of activity. None of the building's windows had light, save for one on the top floor. And they could hear no sounds of life inside.

They slowly walked up the steps, in sync with each other. With every step they half-expected the building to collapse on them. Daina reached forward and, slowly and carefully twisting the handle she opened the door. In a second the hall was open before them and the structure still stood tall. They continued onward, feeling slightly relieved.

It was a tenement, like most Tantallosian buildings similar to it in size. However, it appeared to be completely abandoned. Daina and Alkin methodically checked every room on every floor and failed to find anyone, or anything for that matter. What they did find was more than enough to occupy their minds. Most of the rooms had not been moved out of but rather vacated as fast as possible. Stools and chairs lay toppled by tables, as if the people using them had leaped off them and had not stopped to pick them up as they fell. Beds remained unmade, the linens getting ravaged by moths. The insects were almost an encouraging sight as they were the first living things they had seen. Another room featured a table with various dishes still on it, though the food had rotted away long ago. A massive layer of dust covered everything they came across; nothing had been touched in years, not even by looters.

But none of that could have prepared them for one of the rooms near the top floor of the building. Daina opened the door to the small, one-room apartment, peering in while holding a candle she had found in one of the first rooms, and immediately shut it before getting Alkin to come and look. She slowly opened the door and they examined the horror inside together. The entire room was red, blood red. The floors, the walls, and even the pieces of furniture were covered in faded crimson stains. All of the furniture had been torn to pieces, strewn about randomly. They shared no words concerning the cause; they both could guess what had happened in this room eleven years ago.

"This seems to be a bit far away from the Red Light District," whispered Alkin. "Perhaps this building was abandoned because of a kuvi scourge prior to Aleksei? He can't have been the first kuvi this city's ever feared."

"He's not by any stretch of the imagination," whispered Daina. "Jurek for sure came from Tantallos as well. But I'm very sure this was the building where he claimed one of his victims. Though I can't imagine him being able to do such things." *Or I won't*, she thought to herself.

"Kuvis are like any other creature, be it human or monster," whispered Alkin. "Willing and able to do anything to survive. And to be fair to him, it's not cannibalism unless the other creature is your own kind. He refused to eat the kuvi arm you had been carrying, correct?"

"Could we please stop this conversation?" asked Daina, still whispering. "I'd rather not discuss Aleksei's eating habits, especially after seeing his handiwork. I just want to find him for now and we can talk about the rest of this later, all right?"

"My apologies," whispered Alkin.

They shut the door and both of them vowed to never open it again for any reason. They continued up the tenement, but neither of them managed to get the room out of their minds. However, as they moved upward they found nothing but more dusty, uninteresting rooms. Finally their search took them to the topmost floor of the tenement, which seemed to be a single apartment separated from the stairwell by a wooden door. Daina inspected the door and spotted claw marks against the wood by the handle.

"He definitely came in through this door," said Daina. She looked at the bottom of the door and saw the dim light coming from inside the apartment, the same light they had noticed outside of the building. "Kuvis have great night vision; he wouldn't need a candle. And he opened the door as carefully as he could instead of just smashing it to bits. Someone else must be here."

She stood up tall and rapped her knuckles against the door, hard enough to be noticed but not hard enough to seem urgent. She and Alkin waited patiently as someone inside walked up to the door. The door swung inward to reveal a middle-aged woman with the brown hair, pale skin and short stature typical of most Tantallosians. She looked rather weary and was dressed in casual garb with her hair down. She took one glance at the two people outside her door before falling to the ground and bowing in respect. "Princess

Daina and Prince Alkin!" she said. "Words cannot properly describe the honor and inadequacy I feel in having you both visit me, The same can be said for my confusion, if you will pardon me." She got back up onto her feet. "What would compel your majesties to come to this decrepit building, especially at such an hour?" She looked at them both in confusion. As Daina looked at this woman she could not help but feel a sense of familiarity with her. She knew her, but where could she have possibly met her?

"I beg your pardon for disturbing you so late, ma'am," said Alkin, "but we are searching for someone and our hound led us to the steps of this building. And having searched all the lower floors of this building I must admit I'm very, very interested as to what happened here."

"I may be unworthy but I dare not turn away royalty waiting at my doorstep," said the woman. "Please come in and take a seat at my table. I'm afraid I have little in terms of refreshment to offer you at this hour."

"That's no problem, ma'am," said Daina. "Hopefully we won't keep you for long." The woman's face drove her crazy as she wracked her mind for a memory that featured her. Why did she seem so familiar? The woman stepped to the side and let them enter the apartment, whereupon they moved to the table and took their seats. The apartment was not very big but it was well-maintained. Their current room was a combination of living room, dining room and kitchen. A small wood stove stood in a corner, an original feature of the building as its chimney was integrated into the structure. The table they currently sat at featured four stools. Two archways without doors led into two other rooms that were not lit. One appeared to be filled with stuffed shelves and the other looked to be a small and rather Spartan bedroom.

"Very cozy apartment," said Alkin. "And well-kept."

"I'm sure you're both used to much greater and grander accommodations, but I hope it will do for your visit," said the woman. "I do apologize, I haven't even introduced myself. My name is Anesha. I work at the Tantallos library and whittle various items on the side. I sell my products from a stand I have just off the main street."

"It's a pleasure to meet you, ma'am," said Daina, "but I feel like that's not the case. I know you from somewhere. Something about you... I just can't place it."

"I'm not sure if you would want to," said Anesha. "It's an awkward topic, for you in particular."

"No, please," said Daina. "Do not hold back on my account. If anything, this would keep me from continuing to ponder it. Were you one of my servants when I was a bratty little child?"

"Of sorts," said Anesha. "I was your wet nurse after the queen had passed away. I had just lost a child of my own, shortly after he was born, while I was a common servant at the castle. King Vikenti heard of this and asked me to to see to you."

Daina could not say anything besides "*oh*." She looked oddly at the woman in front of her for a few moments but then worked to keep the thoughts in the back of her mind. It was not something she wanted to think about as an adult.

"Never mind such things," said Alkin, thankfully breaking the rest of them away from the uncomfortable topic. "Again we apologize for disturbing you so late, Anesha, but it's important that we find this man we're looking for."

"There's no man here, I can assure you," said Anesha. "But if you wish I can tell you if I have seen him. What does this person look like?"

"He's handsome in his own way," said Alkin. "He's a bit taller than Daina, but hardly towering. He's rather muscular but not excessively bulging. He tends to look fairly angry. He also has long, blood-red hair. Impossible to confuse with someone else."

Anesha took this all in and looked at the two with suspicion. "I know of who you look for," she said, "but this man has not been here in over a decade. I'm sorry, but I can be of no more help to you. I hate to ask such things but I must request that you let me get to sleep. I have a very busy day ahead of me and I'm sure you both have important things to attend to tomorrow."

"Please hear us out, ma'am," said Daina. She pulled Aleksei's quill out of her pocket and showed it to Anesha. "His hair is like this. We are well aware of what he is and we mean him no harm, not that we could harm him if we tried. We just want to talk to him. Please, It would mean so much to both of us."

Anesha sighed; she could hardly chase two royal family members out of her apartment with a broom. She thought things over for a bit and Daina caught her glancing toward one of the other rooms. Anesha then knocked on the table once, which was responded to with three knocks from the room full of shelves. Daina and Alkin got up from their stools and looked toward the shelf room. Nothing inside stirred but their eyes soon noticed the outline of something deep within the shadows. Daina picked up her candle from the table and slowly walked closer to the room, watching the presence carefully. As she arrived at the entryway she could make out the unmistakable shape. She smiled a little.

"Aleksei," she said. "Don't worry. It's me, Daina. Please come out. I want, no; I need to talk to you."

"I fulfilled my part of our bargain," said Aleksei. "I brought you back like I said I would. Please, let me be. I have a long list of issues to deal with that I've been waiting to tackle for over a decade."

"I have no doubt you do but I also have some unresolved matters I need to discuss with you," she said. "Please come out and speak to me, just this one time. Once we're done talking I'll let you be for as long as you'd like. Even if you never want to see me again." She hoped that would not be the case. Aleksei thought it over for a few short moments before making a quiet snarl. However, he soon shaped his face into something less angry and stood up from his spot. He slowly walked out of the darkness, straight posture making him seem taller than usual. His wings were not generated and his foot-claws were retracted as well, but Daina could see a glowing light coming from the pulsating rings in his eyes as he looked at Alkin.

He pointed the index digit of a claw at Alkin. "He stays up here or he waits outside."

Alkin nodded. "I suspected as much," he said. "I'll stay here and let you both be, though I wish to talk to you as well, Aleksei."

Aleksei bared his teeth but nodded. "Whether we talk or not depends on my mood," he growled.

"Acceptable," said Alkin.

Aleksei resumed his nonchalant face and looked to Daina. "Let's go down a few floors. No, better yet, outside," she said.

Aleksei nodded. The two of them took their leave, Aleksei following Daina out of the apartment. He moved to shut the door but Anesha did it for him. Once she finished she turned back toward Alkin.

"Your lack of fear at seeing a kuvi suggests you're quite familiar with him," said Alkin. "An obvious observation, perhaps, but I felt I had to make it. Do you often encounter kuvis?"

"Aleksei is the only kuvi I have spent a fair amount of time with," said Anesha. "Please, take your seat again." Alkin sat back down on his stool and Anesha moved one of the other stools out to the middle of the room in front of him. She sat down upon it, facing the prince. "Feel free to ask whatever you wish. It feels good to finally be able to tell somebody about all of this."

"How did you meet him?" asked Alkin.

"It was around eleven years ago," said Anesha. "More specifically, a few days before the so-called 'Red Light Murderer' unleashed his terror on the poverty-ridden streets of this city. Those days were very tough and food was very expensive. I was living in one of the smaller rooms downstairs. But not *the* room. I was a floor above it." Alkin nodded, listening attentively.

"Well, on that night I had just gotten back from my job as a seamstress. I placed the groceries I had bought in a cabinet and relaxed as much as I could, same as most nights. It was very late, but so few lived in this apartment back then so I didn't really worry about disturbing anyone. I often wished that there had been, I was so lonely. My husband had died a few years back and all of my children died in childbirth or as infants. It constantly weighed on me." She continued. "The night goes on and then, as everything else is settling around me, I start to hear something creeping around the tenement. The tenement front door had no lock so we were all encouraged to make sure our own door was. At first I thought it was just one of the people downstairs being louder than usual, but I kept hearing the noise in varying locations for several minutes. It never stayed in the same place for long. It kept randomly walking about, making just enough noise for me to hear it without waking up any of the other tenants. I started wondering who was making all the noise. I worried that there was a burglar in the building looking for an easy target.

"So I worked up the nerve to open my door and look out, candle in one hand and iron dagger in the other. I saw a small shape at the stairwell, climbing up the steps. He was gripping the steps with his hands as well as walking up with his feet. But he was far enough away for me to see little besides his outline. I called out to him to ask who he was and he jumped up in the air like a frightened animal. He moved back and tried to hide from me. But I calmed him down by talking to him quietly and gently, like I would have to one of my own children.

"I convinced him to approach me and I promised not to hurt him. That's when I realized he was not a human child. I saw the claws and the prickly red hair, shorter than it is now. His eyes were thankfully covered in a cloth, otherwise I might have fainted. A part of me wanted to recoil in horror but another part of me realized how scared and distressed he looked. He wasn't an evil monster; he was just a child. He didn't appear to be crying but he was in bad shape and looked to be starving." She said. "So I bottled my fears and let him come into my apartment; he was so timid and kind. I gave him a little of my food to eat and talked to him. He said his name was Aleksei, Aleksei dal Kafteros. He was slowly saying his words, stumbling over them like he wasn't used to saying them. He said he was a kuvi and he was completely alone. He had just been taken to this world some days ago and he was still distraught over being separated from his mother. I imagine he will always feel that way.

"I told him I'd let him stay with me on the sole condition that he would keep himself hidden from the other tenants. He thanked me and then asked if I had any metal. I showed him my iron dagger and he asked if he could eat it. I was taken back by this, but I let him gnaw on it some. He actually shredded off bits of the dagger and swallowed them."

"Kuvis do have metal claws, even if they aren't made of iron," said Alkin. "And he was a growing child. I guess he needed the extra nutrition to grow his claws. Only a kuvi could actually evolve to digest metal."

"He explained that to me later on. I let him eat my dagger until it was just a hilt. I spent time with him, teaching him about the world he was in and about the royal family. I taught him to read basic words in just one day; it was stunning how fast he learned to do it. I helped him with his speaking as well.

"But the days of pretending I had a son quickly came to an end. One day I lost my job. I didn't have the money to buy enough food for myself, let alone a kuvi who eats twice as much as a human child would. One night I had to leave him in the apartment so I could go to a meeting concerning a possible job. I didn't even get it in the end, but that was nothing compared to what happened at this building."

Alkin felt a chill ride up his spine. "That night," he guessed. "That was when it began."

Anesha nodded. "I came back some hours later to find the entire building in an uproar. Guardsmen flooded the place and all the tenants and the landlord were waiting outside. Most were wearing what they slept in rather than their working clothes. I talked to them and found out that something had killed the two girls who lived a floor below my room. Tore them to pieces and ate part of the older girl's body, they said. Took one of her legs and both her arms as well. I was dumbfounded.

"But horrible murder or not, I resolved to find him that night. I walked the streets of Tantallos until the sun rose, calling out Aleksei's name, alternating it with *"quill-head,"* my nickname for him. As horrified as I was by what he did, I needed to talk to him, to know why he did it. And to tell him that I still loved him like my own." Anesha sighed and looked downward. "I did that for several nights and never found him; eventually I had to return to work lest I ended up starving. I never saw him again until tonight when he showed up at my door. After the murders, people believed this place was haunted by his victims. Most of the tenants moved to other buildings and then my landlord passed away. I was making more money at my current job by this point, so I moved into the top apartment.

"I was happy to see him, of course, and greeted him like I would have my own son. He was a changed person; a man, almost. He asked me to help him find more information concerning Tantallosian summoning techniques so I unearthed some of my books and helped him read them."

"I guess he wants to go back home?" asked Alkin.

"It's all he wants, but our search through these books proved fruitless," said Anesha. "There is nothing in any of the books concerning the creation of a portal that pulls something from this world into another world. All of the books said it could not be done. Nothing short of divine intervention could force something through the opposite direction like that."

Alkin mulled over all this, feeling a sense of pity for the kuvi. "If only there was such a way," he said. "The top of the plateau that contains Tulroy is littered with summoning dolmens, remnants from days long past. If it could have been done, I would gladly have helped him reach them and use them. Whatever to keep him from destruction at the hands of the Goddess."

CHAPTER 23

I then crafted a creature similar to My image, like the ones before Me.
However, I tore the evil from her heart and destroyed it. I then sent her down
to live with the lonesome one, and while other couples fought and feuded
they remained loving and true. She was the first angel.
-From the Teachings of the Goddess.

Aleksei and Daina stood facing each other just outside of the building, no one in sight for blocks and no lights on in any of the buildings nearby. All that separated them was a few feet. They were lit up by Daina's candle and a small ball of fire in Aleksei's right claw. He appeared to be fidgeting with it, moving it between his fingers. Daina searched for a way to start the conversation.

"I've never seen you do that with fire," she opened. She could not get herself to tackle the bigger issues just yet.

"It's a control exercise," he said. "The ball explodes into a blanket of flame if I don't keep it suppressed. If I was better at it I could make larger ones and throw them in combat."

He tossed the ball to the ground, a few feet away from them. It exploded upon contact and covered a small area in fire that quickly died without anything to fuel it. "Never mind my fireballs and never mind how you managed to find me," he said curtly. "Why did you find me?"

"I mean you no harm at all," she said. "I just wanted to speak to you. So much has happened these past few days, both good and bad, and I wanted... no, needed, to speak to someone I trust deeply about it all."

Something glimmered behind his eye cover. "You still trust me?" he asked. "After seeing... *that* in the apartment building?"

"I still do," she said. "I just want to let you know that, even though your past is dripping with blood, I still feel safer with you than anyone else in this world. You've done so much for me, and I can never even hope to pay you back for it all."

"Do not say such things," he said. "Truth be told, you are not in debt. Not in the slightest. As far as I'm concerned, I still owe you so much."

Daina could not think of this in any way that did not cause confusion. "I'm just a useless princess," she said. "I haven't contributed meaningfully. I pointed you to the secret entrance through the ossuary but I'm sure you could have found that on your own. For most of the trip I felt like a fifth cart wheel. I suppose I helped here and there, but for almost all of it..."

"No," said Aleksei. "I'm not talking about what you did on our journey through the Decay. I'm talking about something that happened long ago. Something you have no reason to remember, but I have every reason to. And I still do, clear as day."

He grabbed a nearby bench, presumably tossed out by one of the neighbors for someone to take and put to good use, and moved it back to Daina. They both sat down on the bench and kept facing each other. He sighed, working up the will to share the story. "I may hate being called a demon, but there is a better side to that name. If demons exist in this world, then there are undoubtedly angels to balance them."

"The Church does mention angels," she said. "They live among the mortals, their mere presence making us better people."

"Precisely," he said. "And I've had the fortune to meet one of them."

Daina leaned forward somewhat, all of her attention captivated by Aleksei. "You've met an angel?" she asked. "A real angel? Are you certain?"

"I have no doubt she was an angel," he said. "Everything about her suggested nothing less, although I didn't know she was an angel until Anesha explained them to me. And, like some of the ones in the Teachings, she came at my darkest hour."

"Please, go on," said Daina. She did not try to hide her intrigue.

"It was about a week after I had been summoned, a couple of days before I met Anesha," he said. "At that time I was still aimlessly wandering the streets, feeding off whatever I came across that looked edible; dead animals, rotting discarded fruit, and several other things you would never want to eat. If I didn't have the stomach of a kuvi I would have died. I was scared, lonely and miserable. I had found various rags to bundle myself up with, hiding my eyes and claws. Every day I hoped no one would get a close look at my hair and realize it wasn't simply clumped in spiky shapes.

"But not even a kuvi can eat such a horrible diet. After so much time eating garbage I grew very weak; my body needed better food. It progressed so much I could barely move from my hiding place. I just lay in an alley, slumped against a wall, hoping that I'd find a little strength so I could move and get something to eat lest I starved. As time went on it only got worse, and then I finally consigned myself to a slow, drawn-out death. I started to wonder if what the humans around me said was true, if kuvis like me had no afterlife and were just consumed by the Goddess after we died. It horrified me, especially after spending so long in the stomach of a creature already.

"That's when the angel appeared before me," he said. "I had become so weak I couldn't even move when I saw her walking in my direction from the corners of my eyes. She looked to be about my age, not even two years older than me. She was clad in a dress that was both beautiful and simplistic, and she was surrounded by several muscular guards. I remember her perfectly, though more than anything else I remember her hair. Unlike other humans, it was a very light shade. Similar to the shade of gold."

Daina's eyes widened as his story brought up memories of her own. "Two of her guards stepped toward me and ordered me to move, but I was too weak to respond in any way," he said. "Their voices grew sterner and in little time they were threatening to hit me if I didn't move out of the royal daughter's way. A part of me wondered if their following punishment would knock off my disguise and they would take the time to give me a quick death. But before they could the girl with the hair like gold spoke up and asked them to let me be; I was clearly too weak to move on my own."

"What?" she asked, jaw dropping slightly. "That was you?"

"She weeded her way through her guards and approached me, getting onto her knees to give me her own food and drink," said Aleksei. "She patiently fed me every last bite, even though I barely had the strength to chew and swallow. Thoughts of my disguise didn't even occur as I let her care for me. Only once I had finished each bit of her food did she get back up and go off with her guards. I used what little energy I had to say '*thank you so much*' to her as she got up. Even today I wonder if she had heard it."

"She had," she said. "It made her feel so good about herself."

"When I was at my worst and no one even gave me a second thought, you saved my life," he said. "That meal was enough to give me the strength to get back onto my feet. As I walked away from that alley I swore to myself that I would repay the favor to you countless times over. Over a decade went by, the extent of my interaction with you being the occasional glance as you ran the walls, but I never forgot the promise I had made. And then I saw you getting kidnapped by that kuvi *dal Afxanos* and I knew what I had to do despite my fears. I just regret not arriving in time to keep him from scarring you."

"Scars mean little to me, especially considering the great things you did," said Daina.

"It all comes together as a confusing mess," said Aleksei. "Traveling with you, looking after someone precious to me as I had always longed to do, took me back into Tantallos and back into contact with humans. Beyond the fact I've been forced to consume them, they are also the main ingredients in summoning rituals."

"You wouldn't want to summon a kuvi," said Daina. "What did you want to call forth?"

"I wanted to make a rip in the world that would drag me back to Proso," he said. "As I traveled with you and learned you were due to be married, that revelation did something to me, tore me up inside. I don't know how to explain it; I had never felt it before. It pushed me further to executing this plan. I will not begrudge you if you hate me for what I did, but while we were in the ossuary I took bones from your mother's coffin."

"I have no doubt that such desecration is blasphemous, but I am no priest," said Daina. "And I never knew my mother so I can't and won't hate you for your actions. Even if I did, it's not her but just her remains. But... what about the other ingredients?"

"If only the other ingredients would be as easy as the bones," said Aleksei. "It would not be too difficult to get the eye. I'd steal one of the eyes of that giant mire beast everyone admires your father for killing all those years ago." He paused for a moment. "But... even as I held you, asleep in my arms, I couldn't bring myself to harm you. Even though I've cut you countless times on accident, even though my rage nearly killed you in the mine, I couldn't get myself to hurt you and collect your blood. To say nothing about harming your father. I could not do that, either. Not after all I've done."

Aleksei looked away from Daina and focused on the ground ahead of him. "I finally found a person I could protect who would also let me protect them, but to get back home I would need to betray that same person's trust," he said. "So instead I placed you on the castle walls in a place I expected a guard would quickly find you. You would be safe for the moment while I tracked down the one other human I can trust in this city. She gave me books on summoning and helped me read through them, all to learn that I cannot escape... my soul is doomed to be destroyed by a deity proclaimed to be kind and loving, just because I have quills and claws instead of hair and hands."

Daina grabbed one of Aleksei's claws with her hand and held onto it, lifting it up off the bench some. "She will do no such thing," she said. "Even if my soul has to travel alongside yours so I can talk to Her and spare you from Her wrath."

Aleksei felt a warm feeling inside, not a flame he had generated. "Thank you," he said. He turned his head and looked down at Daina's hand in his own. She had generated the warmth. "It truly makes me feel better, knowing you'd offer to help me in such a way. Though if I should die before my time it is best if it was to save your life."

"It won't be a matter of one of us saving the other," she said. "We will look out for each other, doing what we can to make sure the other is safe."

They stood there in silence, saying nothing out loud. Nothing needed to be said between them. They just enjoyed the company of each other for a few moments, up until Aleksei forced himself to break the silence. "I hate to tell you of this," he said, "but it is important. You said when Jurek and the others attacked you on the walls they harvested a vial's worth of your blood, correct?"

Daina nodded.

"When I took some bones from the coffin in the ossuary I noticed that some were already missing," he said. "Abdaas' plan is progressing. But he still has to get some of Vikenti's flesh, and I presume one of the rival's eyes. I fear he will use one of his own eyeballs for that step, but if the Huntmaster's kind he will not think of that. But severing a person's limbs would make one quite the enemy."

"That is important to know, but I'd still rather not think about Abdaas doing such a thing to my father," said Daina. "We should just retrieve Alkin and make our way back to the castle. We'll devise a disguise for you and I'll take you straight to my father. Once he sees you in person and talks to you he'll realize you're not a threat anymore. I know he will."

"There isn't one kuvi alive who's not a threat to weak creatures like you humans," said a voice by them. A spike of rock shot up out of the ground, right through the middle of the bench. It sent the two of them flying away from each other and leaving nothing but pieces of kindling in its wake as it sank back down. Aleksei jumped back onto his feet in an instant, tore off his eye cover and quickly scanned the area. Daina lay on the ground, unconscious from knocking her head on the cobblestone path but healthy otherwise. Before he could run over to her to ensure she was all right another sharp stalagmite shot up from beneath his feet; if not for a dodge to the right he would have been impaled.

He jumped up into the air as another spike erupted and generated his wings to stay airborne. He immediately focused in on Jurek, standing in the middle of the street before him. "If you injured her with that attack I will tear you to pieces!" Aleksei yelled at the older kuvi.

Jurek chuckled as he sized up his opponent; still as runty and weak as ever. "You remind me of my pet krio back in Proso," he said. "She would bark a lot but when it came to attacking her jaws couldn't even break through skin. You shouldn't have gotten involved, kid. But, your stupidity is my gain. My hunger continues to grow, and the humans in this city have been doing a poor job of satiating me."

"I've escaped your jaws on three separate occasions, Jurek," said Aleksei. "Even with all your strength you don't have the speed needed to catch up with me, and as long as I can fight I will ensure you never get a bite."

Jurek reached up and gripped his helmet, perfectly placed to hide his entire head. He loosened the grips at the neck and in just a few twists the helmet was wobbling. "Perhaps it's time for me to give you all the facts, kid," he said as he struggled with his helmet. It had been much easier to get on than take off. "I stalked these same streets, doing the same thing you did, for about nine years before you showed up. I doubt I was even three years older than you were at the time. But the biggest difference was that I was not the only kuvi; there were probably five of us hiding, all of us children."

He finished loosening the grips but the helmet still would not come off; the connecting areas had gotten bent and permanently locked together. Jurek growled in annoyance and dug his claws into the helmet, tearing it apart with his unprecedented strength. "I killed and ate every single one of them," he continued. "I don't think even one of them was younger than me, and two were arch kuvis. Age or alignment, none of it kept them alive. They all said I'd never get a bite of them, but I always did. And if you will recall, there was a kuvi between our ages who gloated I would never get a bite of her. I think you were there when I followed that first bite with countless more."

Jurek finally ripped the helmet to shreds, pieces flying in every direction. Only tiny little pieces remained, still locked into the top of the breastplate. The head under the helmet was a vicious-looking face with smooth flesh like Aleksei's that was reddish-brown, similar to clay. The teeth were bright, pearly and humanoid with the exception of two extra canines in the top row. The quills were just as well-kept as Aleksei's, but much shorter and as black as oil. Four massive scars ran along his face from one high cheek-bone to the other, parallel and equally spaced.

"The only thing that separates you from the rest of my victims is that your *Ateni* landed you a blow," said Jurek. "But I have it as well, and prey can only run for so long. I always get my kill, no matter how long it takes, kid."

"My name is Aleksei!" roared the young kuvi, his claws glowing white-hot and fire springing up all over his arms as he prepared to dive at his foe.

CHAPTER 24

Don't let strength intimidate you. Even before I came you could endure more punishment than any other creature your size. Don't fear taking a blow if it allows you to strike with three of your own.
-From the Tomes of the Huntmaster.

Alkin shot up from his seat as he felt the tremors. Anesha looked around worriedly, half-expecting the poorly-maintained tenement to collapse. "What in the name of the Goddess caused that?" asked Anesha.

"That wasn't caused by anything the Goddess created," said Alkin. "When I battled with Aleksei I noticed he could generate fire on his claws. Do kuvis have power over other elements in addition to fire? Daina only mentioned one other."

"They use a five-element system as opposed to our four-element one, but yes," said Anesha. "Five alignments and three gifts, he said when he explained it to me. You don't think a kuvi *dal Tinagmos* did that, do you?"

"I can't think of anything else that could have done it," said Alkin. "Aleksei's going to need help, unless fire is able to reduce ground to ashes. Thank you again for your openness and aid, but now I must leave. You'll want to escape as well. This tenement was not built to last." He made a quick bow and dashed out of the apartment door, scaling the steps downward at a dangerous pace. Anesha did not move from her spot and just relaxed. She could not possibly change the situation, and if she was to lose everything she owned she would rather be taken along with it all.

Jurek stared at the kuvi preparing to dive at him, a grin forming on his face. Such courage, such diligence in the face of certain failure. It made him want to cry a little. "Your mother must have eaten some *famko* berries before choosing such a lengthy name," he said. "Far too long to bother learning, especially since you're about to die." He pretended to think for a second. "How about I call you '*Idiot*' instead?" He laughed, watching as Aleksei's eyes glowed ever brighter. "Yes, Idiot. That's very good, that's very good indeed. Well, aren't you going to attack me... *Idiot*?"

"I'm not letting you goad me into a blind rage," growled Aleksei, fighting against his vice, trying to maintain control. "You're not taking away my mind."

"That's a shame, Idiot," said Jurek. "What about '*Coward*?' I think it's a better name."

Aleksei's eyes shined brightly and he dived down at Jurek, mind working at incredible speeds to break down the fight. Jurek was much stronger and had an advantageous alignment. In addition, he had *Ateni dal Prosopsei* and was well-trained with it. *Ateni* could be trumped by a much faster opponent also with the gift. Aleksei was faster, but he still needed to get in close, bypassing Jurek's defenses. The armor would have to be destroyed or removed in some way so to not require blows to Jurek's head and Jurek's head alone. Jurek saw Aleksei diving, claws straight ahead of him in preparation of skewering his foe. He rolled to the side and brought up a massive wall of earth, Aleksei expecting this and quickly pulling himself up before he collided into it. He performed an aileron roll as he sailed over Jurek, turning himself to face his older target quickly before unleashing a stream of fire. Jurek brought up pillars of ground around himself as he turned to face Aleksei.

Aleksei swore mentally. He had expected Jurek to need eye contact with the ground he was manipulating. "Cute trick," said Jurek. "Let me show you mine." Jurek let the earthen pillars and wall sink back into the ground save for one. The pillar broke into two, the pieces falling to the ground and rolling away from each other. The ground curved up at the edges of the rocks and they began spinning forward like wheels, becoming perfect spheres and gaining incredible momentum before the curve transformed into a ramp that pointed them right at the flying kuvi.

Aleksei saw the rocks coming and killed his fire to better focus just on physical strikes. As the boulders neared him he bashed them away effortlessly, chopping them into halves with a move from his claws. The pieces landed on the ground and shattered into smaller ones, which then developed their own slight curves holding them in place as they grated against themselves and began to hum with Jurek's control over them. Aleksei heard them humming up behind him, glancing between the dangerous rocks and the more dangerous Jurek. The rocks did not solely aim at Aleksei but rather every which way, creating a ridiculous spread range. Any area was a dead zone, guaranteed to shatter his wings.

Jurek chuckled and allowed the rocks to fire themselves into the air. Aleksei waited until the last moment before disintegrating his own wings and he dropped to the ground, landing on his feet with not a single rock embedded in him. The rocks sailed away, bombarding the nearby buildings and shattering countless windows. "Neat little maneuver," said Jurek.

"Though I do wish you were more enraged. It's so cute when a weak kuvi like yourself gets mad. It's like watching a child throw a tantrum because he wasn't allowed to have any *glik* berries before dinner." Suddenly his ears perked up as he heard something approaching him from behind. He brought earthen bonds over Aleksei's feet before turning around.

Alkin launched himself at Jurek from the steps to the tenement, letting out a loud yell. Jurek prepared to strike with the sharp side of his claws but hesitated when he realized who it was; he let the human grapple him with both his leathery hands, sending him backwards onto the ground. As more of him came in contact with the cobblestones he felt more vigor flow into him. "I should have known you were a kuvi this entire time!" yelled Alkin, trying to get his large hands around Jurek's throat. "I may have been stupid enough to miss it then, but I'll make up for that right now!"

Jurek laughed and moved a foot onto Alkin's chest; the metallic boots prevented him from extending his foot-claw and disemboweling the human. He pushed with half his strength and launched Alkin off him, sending him skidding dozens of feet away. Both of them got to their feet almost instantly and Alkin moved back within a few feet of Jurek. Alkin strafed around the kuvi so Jurek was facing him and the tenement. "You honestly think you have a chance against me?" asked Jurek. "I've heard the stories about how you bravely fought and killed a kuvi, all by yourself. Not impressed. You killed a normal kuvi; cracked skin, no hair, no secondary gifts, not even an alignment." Jurek pointed his rigid claws to the ground surrounding him, spikes of rock jutting up around his sides. "Do you *really* think you even have a chance against me?"

"Not in the slightest," said Alkin. He glanced to something behind Jurek but stopped himself from doing so too late. Aleksei charged forward as quietly as he could, wings generated so he was not so much running as floating toward Jurek. He ran bent over, claws facing forward like the pikes that had skewered him as a child. Thanks to Alkin's mistake Jurek managed to turn around in time and brought his claw out in a backhand. He stepped in between Aleksei's claws and delivered a powerful backhand across the young kuvi's face, sending him flying off to the side and breaking one of his wings against the ground. Before he was propelled out of reach Jurek grabbed his clawed foot and swung him around like a bull-roarer before letting him sail over Alkin's head, crashing into the base of the tenement.

Anesha felt a powerful rumbling as the building began to shake all around her. Her apartment floor seemed to tilt for a moment before it gave away, the building collapsing. *It truly figures*, was all she managed to think before she died.

It was somewhat excessive, but Jurek admitted that there was something satisfying about watching an entire building collapse and crush the kuvi he had thrown into it. It was far too fascinating to look away. Alkin struggled to move out of the way in time but Jurek brought up a slight earthen mound that tripped him, keeping him from escaping pieces of falling rubble that knocked him unconscious. At the same time Jurek raised walls of rock around himself to keep the collapsing building from even scratching his armor. As soon as the collapse had begun, the tenement was reduced to nothing more than a pile of broken stone and rotted wood.

Once the destruction was finished Jurek lowered his protective barrier. He let out a laugh as he walked forward, the rubble moving to make a path as he searched for his quarry. The alterations he had made to the street fixed themselves, even the cobblestones going back into their original places. Soon all it looked like was that the building had collapsed. A few feet away Aleksei unearthed himself from a pile of stones and got back onto his feet. He breathed heavily, claws hanging low at his sides, back bent over. Jurek raised an eyebrow as Aleksei approached him, claws glowing white. He struggled to generate significant amounts of fire but could not do so. Jurek approached calmly; Aleksei knew as well as he did that this battle was over.

But still Aleksei raised his claws and swung at Jurek, surprisingly fast despite all the punishment he had taken. Jurek blocked the claw swipe with the metallic arm guard extending from his claw and backhanded Aleksei across the face with his free claw, sending the young kuvi back down to the ground. "I'll admit," said Jurek. "That was impressive, kid. Next time I need to throw you into a bigger building. You're definitely tougher than I thought, though that was not a high expectation to begin with. Tough for a runt. It'll be satisfying to finally eat you." Aleksei looked at his rival as he lay on his back, too worn out to move.

"Or perhaps not," he said. "They need someone to execute for all this death, destruction and endangerment of the princess." He looked away from Aleksei, whose head fell to the side. This gave him a perfect view of Jurek as he used his alignment to sift through the wreckage. He used his claws to move away pieces of wood, eventually revealing his replacement meal. He reached forward and pulled out Anesha's corpse. "Not much meat on her, but she looks like she'll hold me over for now," said Jurek. "What do you think, kid? I don't even know why I'm asking. Not like what you think matters. But farewell; the humans will be far worse than I would be to you." Jurek threw the body over his shoulder.

"And just to twist the claw in your gut, rest assured about your beloved princess you were gushing over. Abdaas asked me to gather the blood of her maidenhead; a disgusting task for any respectable kuvi, so you're excluded. But I'll be sure to kill her quickly after I finish and I'll enjoy a nice snack." He placed the side of a digit on his forehead and then brought it out while clicking his tongue. He then ran off into the network of streets, headed toward the nearest abandoned tenement to consume his discovery.

Aleksei could barely clench his claws in anger. He felt it brewing up inside him, making his eyes glow. But even his fury could not possibly keep him from finally succumbing to the damage he had taken. He fell unconscious just as people started appearing in his line of sight.

CHAPTER 25

Although you may wish to forget, your dreams will always remind you of what you must never do again. It is I who makes them just as horrid as the original time, and it is I who makes them come every night. To forget is to invite the mistake again.
-From the Teachings of the Goddess.

Daina opened her eyes to find herself in her bed with a splitting headache. She quickly shot upright and immediately let out a groan of pain. She clutched her forehead tightly as it gave its response to her fast motions. She clenched her teeth, trying to control the pain as she slowly moved herself out of bed. Someone had put her in one of her nightgowns. She gradually moved to the dresser, where she put on some more appropriate clothes. Once she finished dressing she headed toward the door.

It opened before her and Vikenti stepped into the room, Daina backing away to give him some space. Vikenti's two attendants remained outside. "It's good to know that you're well now," said the king. "You were unconscious when we arrived at the destroyed building. That demon caused an incredible amount of damage."

"I don't remember that much about what happened," she said. "I was talking to him, and then suddenly this giant spike of rock shot out..."

"Calm yourself, Daina," said Vikenti. "No spike of rock shot out of the ground, not anywhere nearby. We arrived at the place and the road was completely intact save for some extra dirt here and there. The same could not be said for the tenement; it had fallen down to the ground, not a stone left standing. You have no idea how worried I was that you had been caught in that disaster when I looked upon it."

"How did you know where I was?" she asked. "Not even I knew my destination when I set out from the castle."

"No one knows you better than your father," he said. "Whenever I tell you not to go somewhere for your own safety you just ignore me and go there anyway. I did not think for a second that my warning would have kept you from going back to the demon, though I had hoped it would for once. I'm just fortunate I was able to arrive at the place in time. We only had one scout following you and Alkin for most of the trip, from a distance so you wouldn't notice him. He came back to alert us once you entered the tenement."

Daina stared at her father in shock, her feelings of betrayal only rivaled by her feelings of revulsion. "Father," she said, "you used me."

"I did what I had to do to protect my people," he said. "Part of ruling is doing what you know is right no matter what."

Daina tasted something foul in the back of her throat. What he knew was right, or what he thought was right? "Where is he now, Vikenti?" she asked. "Did you execute him at the place you found him?"

"I am your father, Daina," growled Vikenti. "Address me as such. And no, I did not have him executed in the rubble. The demon is currently locked away in the dungeon, his belongings stored nearby. A macabre collection of items, to say the least. We were fortunate enough to find him unconscious. The specifics are still undergoing discussion, but his fate is sealed. The promised punishment for a demon re-entering Tantallos is death by torture. I never thought we would ever perform such retribution, but his actions have forced us to."

"You would kill the person who has protected me, cared for me, done more for these past few days than most have done in the past nineteen years," said Daina. "He may have a criminal past, but he is not the real enemy. There are two other kuvis in this city, and one of them is beyond dangerous. He's able to manipulate the earth..."

"Ridiculous notion," interrupted Vikenti. "Demons aren't masters of disguise. Any demon would have been noticed upon entering Tantallos, unless they had been traveling with you and the demon we do have captured. Even if there were any nearby Tantallos, Abdaas said his guards would take care of them. I doubt even a demon could tear through their armor."

Daina then thought back to how both Aleksei and Jurek ripped through the armor, and then of herself piercing a chink in Tulsan's suit. "Just leave me alone," she said. "I need some time by myself."

"Continue throwing your tantrum," said Vikenti. He turned away from Daina and walked back out into the hallway. Before he shut the door and turned back to face Daina. "Hate me as much as you want for my actions, but leading a city means making difficult decisions. As it stands, a killer is behind bars and the city can now calm itself down."

Daina turned her back on Vikenti. "Talk to Aleksei," said Daina. "Talk to him, just once. Let him speak, and treat him like a real person. He's not the monster you think he is." Vikenti made no response to this request and let go of the door, allowing it to swing shut.

Aleksei felt something vacant. He was alone, stuck in a black space.

Deep inside of him, he knew what was coming. Not even the Huntmaster could brighten the terror he was about to endure, surfacing back up from his darkest memories. He slowly moved about the tenement's hallways, looking around warily. He kept his claws close to his body and his foot-claws retracted so they did not click against the floor. The darkness kept him obscured. Anesha had warned him to stay away from the other people in the tenement, but as he listened to them every day while Anesha was gone he grew ever more curious about them. They were kind people, with friends and family, who had endured losses not unlike his own.

He descended the staircase and got off on the floor right below his own. He saw a door at the end of the hall, slightly ajar. He was most familiar with these people as he easily heard them through the floor. They were two sisters trying to survive in Tantallos. Anesha would not tell him what they did for money, but she said the older sister helped make men feel good about themselves. He did not know what that meant, but his stomach continued to growl loudly. Anesha did not have any food and he had nearly finished off his piece of metal. He needed something to eat. If only he could meet that angel again; Anesha said her name was Princess Daina and that she lived in the castle. The angel deserved nothing less for her kindness, but the castle was no place for him. He did not have a chance of seeing her again.

He slowly approached the door, carefully choosing his steps to avoid the squeaky ones. He was familiar with each squeaky board's placement by now after several bouts of walking the tenement hallways in the dead of night. Once adjacent to the door he placed an ear against the wall, listening intently and seeing what he could of the inside of their room. A single candle burned inside, creating a small bit of light he made a note to stay away from. He did not need the light to see; the moonlight coming in through the windows was more than enough. He just listened as the sisters talked about how much money the older one was making. They were all set for the next shopping trip. They were going to celebrate by splurging on some meat. Meat...

Aleksei's mouth watered at the very word. He had been feeling the primal urge to taste flesh building up inside him, ever since he had started living with Anesha. Her food kept him alive and filled him up, but the need continued to grow, driving him mad. It was so intense it made him itch at times. Mom had said this would happen if he ate like a plant-eater; he could eat starches and vegetables for years but he was still a predator. Every part of him was built to hunt. Mom had never let him hunt on his own, but he had been too young for that. Now his claws were developed enough, but he could not hunt them. They were humans; humans are not for eating. Maybe they would share some of this meat with him if he asked nicely.

He worked up the nerve and called out to them, ignoring Anesha's warnings. He asked them if he could have some of that food because he was so starving and had not eaten meat in so long. He heard the big sister get up from her chair and approach the door. He stood up from his crouching position and tried to make himself look as harmless as possible; claws at his sides with the palms backward, quills relaxed and down, foot-claws retracted and eyes covered up with a band of cloth. He still was not sure why his eyes made people faint, but at least they did not make Anesha faint. He moved his claws behind his back instead of at his sides; even Anesha kept her eye on them. You could poke somebody's eye out with those, quill-head, she would say.

The girl opened the door and walked into the hallway. She turned to face him, seeing him despite the darkness; she could not have been even twice his age. She looked at him for just a second before she started screaming. She backed into her room in horror, recoiling at the sight of him, absolute terror all over her face. He rushed forward, claws moved to his sides. He begged with them, pleaded with them to listen to him. He asked the big sister to please calm down and stop screaming. He would not harm her. She did not listen. The big sister yelled at the little sister to hide as she tried to fight it off. She called him an "it." He was a "he," not an "it." He urged her to calm down and let him explain but between her yelling at him to go away and the little sister's shrieking in terror his pleas were drowned out. Go away, you evil demon! Leave us alone, you monster!

She held a thick piece of wood in both hands and swung it at him, trying to hit his head. He blocked the blow with the back of a claw and sloppily grabbed it; his fingers were so clumsy compared to a human's. He tried to pull it out of the big sister's hands, disarm her so maybe she would actually listen to him, but when he pulled forward she was pulled along with it. The momentum made her fall onto him even as he held out his other claw palm-first to stop her. Anesha did it when he tripped once and it had kept him from falling.

He felt something warm and sticky splatter onto his face as the big sister started gurgling. He pushed her off him and stared at his claw in horror, blood covering his blades and dripping downward onto the tips of his digits. Then he looked at the gaping hole in her torso and felt a surge of adrenaline go through him. He just continued looking between his bloodied claw and what he had done to the big sister, who continued to spit up blood. She somehow pulled herself back onto her feet, a hand holding herself together before she launched her body at him again. He held his claws forward again to stop her and they sank into her body, but this time they got stuck. He struggled for a moment to tear them free but even as he pulled them out they were still skewered through many long, tube-like things inside her. No, one long tube-like thing that stretched far longer than he would have thought. He panicked and tried to force the tube thing off his claws, tearing it into smaller bits and flinging them every which way as his mind started racing.

He started hyperventilating as he looked at the big sister. She was no longer moving. He had killed her; no, he could not have. He was not supposed to kill humans. He told Anesha he could never kill humans. But he had, because she kept attacking him. Why did she keep attacking him instead of stopping? Why did she make him kill her? Then the growl within him came back in full force, his mouth salivating like a wild animal as he stared at the carcass. He tried to fight it; humans are not for eating. Anesha was a human. The angel looked identical to a human. But the instinctual urge kept coming back, each time stronger than the last. His eyes kept staring longingly at the corpse as his mouth remained open. He panted heavily.

No one would ever see him eat her. He would take a few pieces of her away, far away, and eat them someplace where no one else was around. No one could see him doing this; it had to be hidden. But the little sister kept screaming, shrieking for her sister to get back on her feet, for her sister to still be alive. He looked at her, huddled away in the corner. He could not let anyone know about him. He could not let anyone know what he had done this night.

CHAPTER 26

Never cry over your own fate. Only cry over the fates of others, for they
cannot change what must happen to them. You are a kuvi; you can.
-From the Tomes of the Huntmaster.

Aleksei came to in a kneeling position, unable to move a single limb. His head was the only part of him free to move. Although his eyes were covered with a different band of cloth, he was still able to see. He looked down at his bound claws. Both were tied to massive balls of iron, so heavy he doubted he could lift them up at such an awkward angle. More balls held down his limbs at the elbows, knees and feet, forcing him into his current position. He did not bother struggling; not even his strength could lift all the weights.

He raised his head and looked about, gazing at what was beyond his small cell. There were numerous cells in the dark, dank dungeon, but the ones next to and across from him were empty. As the cells got closer to the single entrance of the dungeon they steadily filled up with prisoners. The cell furthest away from him was completely stuffed.

He watched as the prison guard approached him. He was a tall, muscular man of typical Tantallosian complexion. He did not look angry or disgusted, though. He looked more curious than anything else. "You're awake," said the prison guard as he moved to a spot right before him. "I was wondering when you would come to. You were unconscious for so long despite all of our moving you about."

Aleksei found himself puzzled by the neutrality of the guard toward him, but made no comments about it. "Are so many prisoners foolish enough to think I'm still dangerous?" he asked the guard.

"Most of them are," said the guard, looking down the hallway. "Most of the prisoners not in the cramped cell are there because I'm not willing to fit more in that one." He looked back. "And, even if you had a more selfish reason for your actions, thank you for saving Princess Daina and bringing her back to Tantallos alive. Don't tell anyone I gave you a compliment, though. My career would be ruined."

"I doubt anyone who talks to me today besides you will give a damn about what I have to say for myself," said Aleksei. "They won't give me a trial, even a show trial. If anyone comes, it's to mock me prior to my execution. How terrible a death has been planned for me?"

"I'm unsure of the details so I'll have to leave you in suspense," said the guard. "I hate to do this but I have to get back to my post. I don't want my captain showing up and scolding me for talking to you."

"I understand," said Aleksei. "Huntmaster forbid that anyone learn anything about the creature they plan to kill." The guard nodded and walked back to his post, glancing back at the bound kuvi several times once he arrived there. The guard had approached him under the pretense that Aleksei would have all the communication skills of a raging beast, a mindless monster that wanted nothing more than to kill humans and eat their bloody remains.

After finishing his third glance he looked back to see an unexpected guest stepping in front of him. He straightened his posture and patted down his tangled hair before bowing lavishly. "Truly a pleasure to see you alive and well, Princess Daina," he said. Down near the other end of the dungeon Aleksei's ears perked up; he turned to see her and felt a weight lift slightly from his heart. "I'm afraid this place is as dirty as ever, certainly not a place for someone of your status."

"It's no problem," said Daina, her nose wrinkling some at the foul smell. The cramped conditions in the nearby cells did not help this. "Prison should be an uncomfortable place for those who deserve the punishment. I'm guessing that Aleksei is in one of the cells at the other end of the dungeon."

"Aleksei?" stupidly asked the guard, the connection becoming apparent a split-second after he said it. "Oh, him. So that's his name. Fitting for an exotic creature like him, I suppose. But don't mind my rambling, princess. He is indeed near the end of the dungeon. Would you prefer my presence while you visit him?"

"I'd rather approach him alone," said Daina. "I have matters to discuss with him, private matters. But first, I must ask you something. Has King Vikenti come down to the dungeon and visited him yet while he's been awake?"

"Goddess, no, princess," said the guard. "I haven't seen anything of his majesty this whole morning. He's undoubtedly busy working with the guards to help calm down the citizens, or some other similar project. I'd imagine our famous guest's reappearance has several people worried."

Daina felt little more than disappointment at this. "I suspected as such," she said. "I'll walk back to you when I am done visiting. Do not worry; he will not harm me."

"He couldn't harm you even if he tried," said the guard, "but I share your feelings. He didn't seem half as bad as they say he is when I talked to him, even if it wasn't a long conversation."

"I'm willing to wager that you've talked to him longer than almost everyone else in this city," she said. "Thank you for your complacency. Please make sure no one disturbs us while I'm busy talking to him."

"I'll do what I can, milady," he said.

Daina did a slight bow to the guard before she walked down the hall, arriving in front of Aleksei in less than a minute. She moved down onto her haunches, getting to eye level with the kuvi. She felt something warm up in her as she watched his face light up.

"Daina!" he said, smiling. He had gotten far better at the expression. "It's so good to see you're alive after that fight. It had looked like a horrible blow to your head."

"It was a horrible blow," said Daina; the headache was still present but thankfully weaker. "I doubt I'd even be alive right now if it wasn't for my favorite kuvi in all of the world, so thank you." She looked at his numerous bonds. "They certainly took every measure possible to keep you from moving, didn't they?"

"It was not that excessive a precaution," said Aleksei. "Their placement on my limbs has me pinned. I can't even scratch my nose. I'm not even certain I can make a fire hot enough to melt the metal without alerting the guard. He'd have to go for help and then I'd have an armada of soldiers ready to try and fight me. So unless I want to fight and possibly kill a lot of people I'm stuck here until they decide to execute me."

"Abdaas' damage has been done," she said. "I cannot convince anyone to take what I say concerning you seriously; they all tell me I've been brainwashed. Not even the king could be convinced by me to visit you and talk to you. He didn't even listen." She sighed. "And I doubt he would even listen to any plea to spare your life. I'm sure he will do something awful to you. I'm still looking for a way to help, but the king has taken away all of my options."

"Do you usually refer to him as the king rather than how most daughters would call their fathers?" he asked.

"I refuse to believe I'm related to someone so closed-minded," she growled. She did not want to even think about how she had been such a way prior to Aleksei opening her eyes. "Especially after his betrayal of my privacy. I almost wish..." She stopped herself and shook her head to dispel the thought. "No, I don't wish it. I can't wish it."

"What did you almost wish for?" he asked.

"I almost wished that he actually did get attacked by one of the kuvis planning to harvest his flesh," said Daina. "I almost wished him killed. Oh Goddess, I'm horrible."

"Don't tell yourself that," he said. "You're not horrible. Jurek is horrible. Abdaas is horrible. Wesan is horrible... I'm more horrible than you are."

"Don't you tell yourself that, either," she said. "You are the greatest guardian for this city's king as well as its princess. And they are going to kill you despite needing you more than they could ever fathom. I don't want to become queen of Tantallos, not so soon."

Aleksei sighed. This was going to be painful. "Daina," he said, "it gets worse than just his death. Far, far worse. Worse than anything you in particular would want to comprehend."

"How could this matter possibly get worse than murdering my father?" asked Daina. "They already have my blood and apparently my mother's bones, and I'd wager that Abdaas would take his own or perhaps Jurek's eye as the gaze of the enemy."

"They aren't done with you yet," said Aleksei. "They still need you."

"But they no longer have a reason to kill me," said Daina. "I know of their plans concerning regicide, but even the king thinks that you brainwashed me. Any of my testimony against them would be useless."

"Daina, listen to me, damn it!" yelled Aleksei, his eyes glowing under his band. He caught himself almost immediately after saying the words and attempted to calm himself down. "I'm sorry. It's just that there are varying grades of summoning ingredients; various degrees of quality. The blood of a royal daughter is excellent, yes, but it's so much better when it is gathered after something that happens only once in her life."

Daina thought this over, trying to ponder what it could be. She quickly figured out what it was and went cold, her pale face losing even more of its color. "You cannot possibly mean..."

"I'm afraid I do," said Aleksei. "They plan to collect the blood of your maidenhead. Jurek... Jurek said he was the one who was going to violate you. Then, once he was finished he would kill you and eat you."

"Oh, Goddess," said Daina, refusing to fathom Jurek cornering her, forcing her to submit to his will, violating her and violating the Teachings of the Goddess. "He... he wouldn't dare. He would never even get the chance. I'll always be in the company of guards, and Alkin and King Vikenti."

"He can kill whole armies with just his alignment," said Aleksei. "No place is safe for you while he lives. I endured a living Punishment when he kept me prisoner, preparing to kill me once he had finished with Felaem."

"He is an unstoppable force," said Daina. "How did you manage to best him, even that one time?"

"It was all because of a foolish mire beast," said Aleksei. "He had just finished eating Felaem down to the bone and had broken some of her limbs open to get at the marrow." He held his head low and looked pale and sickly, as if he was about to vomit. "He had to have been satiated and his movements were slower than before, but despite having eaten an entire adult kuvi he still felt the need for more.

"That's when a mire beast approached his lair. Clearly the creature had never encountered a kuvi before; few do who live to learn from the experience. While it occupied his attention I worked away at my earthen bonds and managed to free myself. After he had killed it with a rock spike through its chest he turned around to see me freed.

"Before he could react I attacked him, slashing across his face with my claws and giving him a dreadful scar. He was unused to pain and had been stunned, giving me more time to let out a stream of fire. The fire alone did not kill him but it kept him occupied long enough for me to run out of his cave, sprout my wings and take off. By the time he had recovered I was long gone, and I had been fortunate enough to not see him again until now."

"All it takes is one opening to leave him vulnerable," said Daina. "When that happens I'll stab him between the shoulders with my dagger. He will not do such things to me."

"You can be tough when you let yourself, but I fear your resolve won't be enough," he said. "I don't even want to imagine it."

"He'll never violate me," she said. "I'll kill myself before I let him use me in such a way." She reached a hand into the cell and lightly grasped Aleksei's chin. She raised his head so he was looking her in the eyes. "At least, if it comes to that, we'll see each other again."

"I'm afraid not," said Aleksei. "The Goddess would never consume one of her angels. Where I'm going, there will be no return. I will be completely destroyed and you will be beyond this world." He felt a bulge grow in his throat and sniffled a little. "I wish I could do something, anything, to change that."

Daina looked at him and felt something give way inside her. The Goddess she had devoted her life to, the only deity she had ever known, would swallow his soul just for not being Her creation. There was no pity in Her heart for a kind albeit hot-blooded being which had only ever killed out of necessity. An entire race fated to a short and painful afterlife, no matter how good they actually were, just because they are kuvis and not humans. She could not revere such a deity.

Daina looked back to Aleksei and stared in shock. Something was sneaking its way through the band of cloth around his eyes, accompanied by noises coming from the kuvi, despite his attempts to stifle them. The thing rolled its way down his cheek, leaving a glistening trail in its wake, and soon other wet things just like the first one were following it downward. The kuvi was crying. "Please don't cry, Aleksei," said Daina. "Please, don't. I promise She won't do that to you. You'll be fine."

"But you won't be," said Aleksei, stifling a heaving. "That's why I'm crying."

Daina retracted her arm, unable to think of anything to say. She just reached into the chamber, grasped Aleksei's head with both hands carefully, brought it down some and kissed him on the forehead. She brought his head back up and stared at him in the eyes. He did what he could to stop his crying as she felt her own eyes water a little. But the moment came to an end when she heard a clomping coming from the other end of the dungeon. She glanced toward the entrance and saw a heavy-footed servant talking to the guard and gesturing toward her. She grew crestfallen as the servant approached her with the guard.

She let go of Aleksei and moved her arms out of the cell. "Goodbye, quill-head," she said. "We'll see each other again, alive, if the Huntmaster wills it."

Aleksei let himself smile a little as Daina got back onto her feet. The servant arrived at her side but made sure to stay several feet away from Aleksei's cell. He kept glancing toward the kuvi anxiously. "Your highness; what in the Goddess' name are you doing here? His majesty gave a strict order to keep you from entering the dungeon to avoid precisely this!"

"I'm sorry, your highness," said the guard. "He was insistent and threatened to come back with my commander. I hope you had enough time."

The servant ignored the guard. "Your highness, I must ask that you come with me immediately," said the servant. "Please refrain from sharing any more words with that foul demon lest he ensnare your mind once again!"

"That's rather harsh, considering you've never met him," said the guard. "He's not foul; he's just a predator. I'd imagine that chickens call us foul creatures when they cluck to each other about where one of their friends went."

"This does not need to become a major issue," said Daina. "I will obey the king's orders, even if he has not even considered my one request of him." She turned toward the guard. "Thank you for your compliance. Please treat him kindly in his last days."

"I will to the best of my ability, milady," said the guard, bowing.

"Don't waste your affections on the demon," said the servant, turning to leave as fast as he could. Daina followed the servant down the hall and then up the stairs, back into the more pleasant areas of the castle. The guard remained by Aleksei's cell for a few short moments, pondering the kuvi as his head followed the princess up until she disappeared from sight. As he looked closer, he saw something he did not know could be done. He saw moisture glistening on the sides of Aleksei's cheeks in lines; the guard's eyes widened as much as they could when he realized what they were.

He broke himself away from the sight and made his way back to his post, pondering this development the whole way. He glanced back to Aleksei and saw that the kuvi's head was hanging downward, like he had gone limp. Stifled sounds came from him, but not so stifled that the guard could not tell what they were. His own children had often made them. They were sobs.

CHAPTER 27

Don't waste the effort of turning your claws on yourself, no matter how tragic circumstances may seem. Doing so would deprive yourself of opportunities to put your claws to better use.
-From the Tomes of the Huntmaster.

The servant calmed down as he left the dungeon, leading Daina onward at a more casual pace. As she walked down the hallways leading to the bedrooms she looked about for Alkin's face but found it nowhere. However, she did unfortunately pass by Wesan and grew cold as she imagined the fiend's black-and-red eyes staring at her, deciding upon what part of her was the best to eat first.

Right after Wesan came Abdaas; the servant halted to address the fat priest. "A very good day to you, Father Abdaas," he said. "I do hope you've been enjoying your stay thus far. Is everything fine or at least satisfactory? Please tell me if there is anything you would like."

"Nothing too much at the moment, said Abdaas. "But do you mind if I talk to the princess for a short moment?" The servant shook his head and moved to the side, allowing Abdaas to walk up to Daina. He looked at her, his expression full of kindness. Daina gazed into his eyes and saw something much more sinister just underneath his cheery facade. Abdaas checked the servant's distance; he was about ten feet away and the hallway was so busy the servant would be hard-pressed to hear their conversation, even if he was trying.

"It is truly a blessing from the Goddess that you are back with us, Princess Daina," he said. "I was among the many that had feared the demon had done away with you, or finally brainwashed you to the point of turning you into a mindless husk of a person. It is fortunate Vikenti's party arrived by the collapsed building when it did."

Daina said nothing. She kept a stony look on her face to mask her disgust while she searched her mind for an appropriate response. She found nothing fittingly biting. "Where are the other three '*guards*' of yours?" she asked. "Wouldn't they be near you? Alkin doesn't require the protection."

"One is more than enough for me," said Abdaas. "So instead I asked the red guard to go out into the Decay, scout out our planned path for any huge monsters and kill them while they're still groggy. I assume he took the other two guards along with him. Why do you ask?"

"When I was out in the Decay with Aleksei I encountered one of them," said Daina. "We found ourselves disagreeing. I have a memento from him, though. It was a massive gray gauntlet with knives embedded into each digit. Incredibly durable, though it started flaking away the moment I got it from him. It looked so similar to Aleksei's claws that I could have sworn they were the exact same thing."

Abdaas' friendly demeanor vanished instantly. Instead, a snarl made its way across his face. "You are fortunate that I'm too happy to let your accusations hinder my spirits," he said. "I shall forgive you for suggesting I would associate with demons, though such comments give me ample grounds to accuse you of heresy."

"You may lead the Church of the Goddess in Tulroy, but such status will do you only so much good in Tantallos," said Daina. "Every citizen of this city knows I am a devout follower of the Goddess. Or, at least I was." She smirked a little. "There is an easy way to solve this matter. Perhaps we should have your guard take off his helmet around these good people, show that he's just as human as we are? I can't imagine he's gotten a chance to take off that suit the entire time he's been here. It must be horrid in that thing."

"Smells worse than you can imagine, princess," said Wesan.

"Silence!" hissed Abdaas. "It would be a waste of time, Princess Daina. He is leaving the city to join the other guards in reconnaissance for our upcoming trip." He grinned. "Unfastening the helmet alone takes so much time, to say nothing of the rest of the suit. It's best if he leaves his armor on for now. Otherwise, I'd be more than glad to have him prove his innocence."

"Wesan's as innocent as a mire beast by a fresh kill," said Daina. "I know precisely why you want me, Abdaas, and I'll kill myself before I become a participant in your schemes."

"Strong words from such a young girl," said Abdaas. "And to think just days ago you were tripping over yourself while running down a slick wall near a deadly drop. But don't think that I bid you any ill will."

"Perish the thought," said Daina. "You would never do such things. You need me alive, after all."

"I and the cities of Tantallos and Tulroy need you alive," said Abdaas. "You are a symbol of prosperity, of utmost purity." He grinned sickly again. "And by your grace and sacrifice a new age shall be ushered in. An age where the Decay ceases to be a problem, an age where all demons face their destinies once and for all."

Daina grew cold. She glanced at Wesan but got nothing from the fully-armored kuvi. She looked back at Abdaas. "I guess we shall see," she said. Abdaas shook his head while grinning and turned away from her before walking off to his own room. Once he was several feet away the servant returned to Daina's side and gently urged her to go back to her room. Daina agreed and followed the servant back.

Daina searched all of her drawers but each one was completely empty. Already the servants had packed up her clothes in preparation for the trip and new residence at Tulroy. The only things in the room not packed up were her personal possessions and mementos. Small wooden carvings she had whittled herself back when she had still been trying to be an artist; a scrimshaw made from part of a mire beast tusk with her name engraved in it; a hound plush doll she could remember having ever since she was a toddler. And placed beside them in stark contrast were the two latest additions to her knickknacks; the bronze dagger and the kuvi arm bone.

As she stared at the bone she felt anxiety growing inside, gnawing away at her soul, barely suppressed. She was going to die. Perhaps it would be during this afternoon, or maybe later once the sun fell, possibly even tomorrow if she was lucky, but in the end she would die by Jurek's claw. After he finished violating her, of course. The thought of that alone was enough to doubt her faith in everyone, not just the Goddess she no longer revered.

She moved to the dagger and grabbed it by the hilt. She moved away from her dresser and looked at it as she held it gently. Ever since she had gotten it for her birthday it had helped her so much, killing a foe she would never have imagined herself taking down. Even after all the punishment it had taken it remained sharp enough to pierce flesh and kill. Sharp enough to stab a girl through the stomach, twist once inside and kill her.

Yes, of course. What better way to foil Abdaas' plans?

Daina moved both her hands around the hilt of the dagger, gripping it tightly. She brought the dagger downward, the blade turned to face her stomach. All it would take is one stab through her gut; one quick motion from her hands to insure her death. A death she had only read about in the tales of warriors of old, warriors who would rather die than face dishonor. It would be far more painful than any other experience she had ever felt, but it would spare her the humiliation she would suffer if Abdaas or Jurek managed to detain her.

She brought the blade closer, within but a few inches of her stomach. Her hands started to shake as she breathed in and out heavily, closing her eyes, working up the nerves to bring the blade forward. Bring the blade forward for one split second and foil Abdaas' plans forevermore. No! Her eyes opened and her grip loosened, letting the dagger slide out from her hands and clatter on the stone floor. She stepped over the blade and sat down on the bed, putting her head in her hands. She could not do it. She was no warrior, not like the ones in the stories. She had fought for her life, but anyone can do such a thing. She did not defeat Tulsan in some brutal death match; she killed him by running away and dodging his pounces. And she lacked versatility; she could not even hit the walls of her bedroom with her dagger if she threw it.

She sighed before getting back up and moving to the dagger. She picked it up off the floor and put it in its normal place, hidden away. She moved back and knelt down on the floor while facing it. She placed both palms on the mattress, a bit more than a foot of space between them, and bowed her head. "My Goddess..." she began, but then stopped herself. It did not feel right. She could not hail such a deity, so how could she expect herself to pray to Her? Her people suffered; they endured constant nightmares despite dreams being Her preferred medium of communication, they got rotted by a plague never once mentioned in Her Teachings. She could not devote herself to that.

Yet there had been a god with a more personal touch. A god far more kind and forgiving than Her. It was a god just as misunderstood as the creatures who worshiped it. She made up her mind and kept her praying position out of habit. "*Mi Prosopsei*, great Huntmaster, world guardian and protector of the kuvis," she said. "I apologize to you; I have no ideas or knowledge concerning how your followers pray to you, if they pray like humans do. But forgive my informality; I just wish to beg that you look after Aleksei, who has been imprisoned by my misguided people. I am no hunter like the ones who worship you, but if there is some way I can save him by other means, I ask that you help me to do so. I have no idea whether or not you can even heed this plea in my world when your kuvis come from a different one, but if you can, please do so. I beg of you."

She raised her head, brought her hands down to her sides and stood back up, rubbing her knees after the cold time they had spent on the floor. She felt a satisfaction in saying her first prayer to a god she found more suitable for her, but a worry grew alongside it the more she thought of her faith. The Church of the Goddess had often stated that She was the only true deity in the world and all others were false idols. How would She take to a formerly devout follower praying to the deity of another world entirely, let alone turning her back on Her? She pushed those thoughts to the side. Hopefully she would not be meeting the Goddess anytime soon... hopefully.

Or perhaps the Huntmaster would somehow save her, though that seemed a lost cause. Her thoughts were interrupted when a servant came into the room. "I'm so sorry, your highness," said the servant. "I hate to disturb you, but the caravan for Tulroy has finished their preparations. Do you need any assistance with your personal belongings, and do you have a demon relic for the trip?"

Daina checked her pocket; Aleksei's quill was there, still intact, partially embedded into the cloth but not her skin. "I already have a relic in my possession and all the things I want on me," she said. "Please lead me to the caravan." The servant nodded and moved to the side of the room, holding the door open for her. She stepped out of the room and the servant followed, shutting the door behind him. Daina would never see her room again.

The crowds pressed in tightly against the caravan, consisting of a cart pulled by two men and a platoon of guards around the royalty and clergy. The guards managed to keep the excited citizens at bay, but only barely. Past their lines Vikenti walked toward the city exit with Abdaas at his side. Daina followed them while walking alongside Alkin. The people of Tantallos cheered loudly, flowing banners from the buildings and showing their love and support for the royalty. At the same time Vikenti's advisers took over the throne, ensuring their king that everything would be well taken care of until he returned. Almost no trained guards were present to control the bedlam, as they were at the castle to keep an almost-forgotten threat under control. Most of the guards at the scene were volunteers and squires, though their work sufficed.

"They really do love you," said Alkin, yelling just loud enough for Daina to hear him over the cacophony. "And rightfully so. I'm not even sure I get this much praise."

"You deserve the praise more than I do," said Daina. "I just hope I live long enough to give my people a reason to love me so. Aleksei's gone. He cannot help us now, and without his help I don't see how we can deal with both of... them. Or how you could; I wouldn't be of much help."

"We can discuss this matter more thoroughly once we leave Tantallos," said Alkin. "For now, let us just maintain the illusion that we are still in love and getting married." Alkin gently grabbed Daina's hand and raised it to the sky, inciting a roar from crowd as they took in the sight with glee. People exclaimed in both joy and jealousy and countless gossipy mothers expressed a gladness that Daina had finally found someone worthy of her. No one argued whether or not she was deserving of him.

Daina smiled and waved with her free hand, gazing upon the crowd with the trained expression she had worn countless times before. She looked at them all, so many of which she could not have even imagined enduring for hours at a time just a few days ago; now she knew of no other group she would rather have surrounding her in trying times. After several minutes the caravan finally arrived at Tantallos' main gates. The ancient mechanism worked slowly, creaking and groaning every inch of the way as the portcullis was hoisted upward. Everyone watched as the gates reached their highest height, exposing the caravan to the Decay. No one worried, though; it was common knowledge that everyone on the caravan was carrying a demon relic.

After another few waves goodbye the caravan left the city and began their journey into the Decay. The gates shut behind them, never to open again. The guards spread out and away from those inside their protective barrier, forming a spacious perimeter. Something then occurred to Daina. She walked up to Vikenti and Abdaas, who had just finished saying something to each other.

"What relics are all the guards carrying?" she asked.

"Each guard is carrying a small vial of demon blood," said Abdaas. "I had the blood drawn from the foul creature that had almost killed you while it was still unconscious. I would have gotten some for you as well but you apparently already have a relic."

"Yes," she said. She did not want to think of them slicing up Aleksei's flesh numerous times to get enough blood for all the guards, but still the thoughts came up in her mind. "I do."

"Abdaas was gracious enough to loan me his relic for the trip," said Vikenti. "He is using some other relic for now, and I must say the one he gave me is impressive. Second most amazing preserved eye I have ever seen."

"Second most amazing?" asked Abdaas. "What could possibly upstage the gaze of a demon?"

"Only the gaze of an especially large mire beast," said Vikenti. He reached into his clothes and pulled out a small, sealed jar containing an intact mire beast eye. It was a large, white orb with a green iris and a massive, black slit for a pupil. The eye was contained in a jar of vinegar; although the vinegar had pickled the eye it was still identifiable. He put the jar back in his coat. "I had the jar specially made, so durable I could drop it and it wouldn't even crack. It's my good-luck charm."

"Quite a remarkable token," said Abdaas. "Does the eyeball's story relate to the stuffed mire beast head hanging above your throne?"

"It certainly does," said Vikenti. "I'll tell you its story once we finally arrive at your city. I am anxious to meet your king."

CHAPTER 28

Never use your claws unless you intend to kill. Instead strike with the back of them to knock out an adversary.
-From the Tomes of the Huntmaster.

It had been over an hour and Aleksei had not moved an inch since Daina left. The guard continued watching him from his post by the entrance, still trying to comprehend the noises he had heard at that time; Aleksei had since ceased making them. A demon had been crying. But no demon has ever cried. Every story ever told in Tantallos concerning demons made this clear. They never wept. They existed only to kill and feed upon the unsuspecting.

At the same time, every story ever told concerning demons had been written and spoken by those who had only fought against one, or run one out of a city. No stories had ever been told by those who had met a demon face-to-face and talked to it. The guard had no doubt that Princess Daina would have a story worth telling concerning demons. But despite his fascination with his most dangerous prisoner he still had to deal with the inmates behind him begging for food. He finally gave in and grabbed some buckets of gruel and hardtack. He provided the food to all the inmates as evenly as he could to shut them up, averting his eyes as they greedily, noisily and messily gorged themselves on every last bit. They even consumed the pieces that had fallen on themselves, on the filthy ground, on each other. If he forced himself to sit down and watch them eat even one meal he would never be able to feed himself again.

He faced opposite the eating prisoners and again found himself looking down the cells to the demon. He had been under orders passed down from Vikenti to not feed the demon, that the monster has consumed enough flesh in its time. Then again, all the guards in the castle were stationed throughout the building rather than down here with him; no one wanted to spend time in the same room as the creature. He had not minded the job. He decided to quickly go to the kitchen and grab lunch. He rushed up the stairs and through the networks of hallways as fast as he could, carefully dodging other guards and avoiding his superiors like the plague lest they asked where he was supposed to be. Soon he ran out of the kitchen clutching a loaf of bread and a thick, juicy piece of meat.

He returned to the cells in almost no time, wherein he ate the bread upon arrival. He ignored the groans of the inmates as they watched him eat it. They did not dare anger him by throwing something at him; he controlled their food, after all. He held the piece of meat up to his mouth but before he even took one bite he again found his gaze drawn to the demon. The demon had not been fed anything since he had arrived at the cell, so the latest he could have eaten was last night. He was undoubtedly hungry and certainly needed to consume flesh. Like it or not, predators live on flesh; mire beasts are not known for eating fruits and vegetables. And kuvis are more tenacious hunters than even the fiercest mire beasts.

The guard sighed, his pity finally getting to him. He let himself get up from his chair and walk toward the poor demon, clutching the piece of meat carefully. In moments he stood by the creature. He moved down onto his haunches, waiting patiently until the sniffling demon noticed him. It took the demon some time because of how distraught he was but eventually he looked up. The band of cloth around his eyes was completely soaked through.

"Anyone would cry in my position," said the demon. "If you mock me for it I'll tear you to pieces." Its voice was higher than normal and wavering; the statement was more a plea to be left alone than a threat, even an empty one.

"I was not planning to do anything of the sort," said the guard. "You have a lot on your mind, after all. Your name's *Ah-leck-seh-ee*, correct? Sorry if I butchered that. I only somewhat heard it from Princess Daina."

"You said my name correctly," said the demon. "What are you doing here?"

"I believe that everyone, even someone other humans view as an embodiment of evil, deserves a final meal," said the guard. He held up the piece of meat and Aleksei's eyes immediately focused in on it, following it as it slowly swung back and forth in the guard's hand. They both heard a loud growling coming from the cell. "And you can hardly eat this meat without help so I thought I'd kill some time by helping you with it."

"Almost no human has ever been this kind to me so soon after meeting me," said Aleksei. "Why are you doing this?"

"Just eat the meat," said the guard. "I'll explain once you start eating. Don't try and bite me when I bring my hand in." Aleksei nodded and the guard slowly moved his arm into the cage, an apprehension growing in him as he moved his exposed fingers closer and closer to Aleksei. Soon he had the piece of meat dangling in front of Aleksei's face. Aleksei reached forward slowly so to not startle the guard. He sank his teeth into the slab of meat, his incisors and canines cutting through the cooked flesh with little need for pulling against the guard's sturdy grip.

"I guess I owe you an explanation," said the guard. "My family has a bad history concerning... when you or another of your kind refers to yourself, what do you say you are? Like how I would call myself a human."

Aleksei chewed and swallowed, salivating in anticipation of more delicious meat. So much tastier than his normal diet. "We're kuvis," he said before going in for another bite. It was a struggle to keep himself from moving quickly, ripping into the slab of meat viciously.

"Between my brother's family and my own wife and children we have a bad history of encountering kuvis," said the guard, unpleasant memories surfacing in him. "My brother's almost ten years older than me. He used to have a family, a wife and several children. They were all so friendly and kind; few were as gracious and generous as them."

Aleksei snapped out of his lust for the meat and focused on the guard while still eating. He reflected on the humans he had encountered, particularly the ones he had been forced to kill for food. He had never attacked a whole family; after having to kill the two young sisters his victims usually only had one other person there, a sibling or a friend.

"It happened about twenty years ago, well before your time in Tantallos," said the guard. "Kuvis were more common then and we kept finding dead ones. It was because of one especially vicious kuvi in particular, not like you at all. He was a fierce, gluttonous monster with quills as black as oil."

Aleksei knew just from the quill color: Jurek. He nodded to the guard.

"My brother worked as a night guard at the time," said the guard. "He arrived home late from work one night to find his apartment torn apart and entire family ripped to shreds and partially eaten. Not one of them was spared; not his wife, not his eldest son, not the twins, not even his month-old daughter. The guards determined it had been a kuvi attack and the hunt began." The guard told him. "As awful as what happened to his family was, they were but the first of many to find that kuvi visiting them late at night before he was finally apprehended. That vicious kuvi turned out to be a young boy, not much older than you were when you were exiled from Tantallos. Never before could I have imagined any creature being so ruthless at such a young age. I hated kuvis as much as everyone else did.

"And then nine years later you appear in Tantallos. The city is overrun by fear, myself included. I buy a weapon for my wife and two kids and make sure all three know how to use it in case I'm gone and the kuvi decides to target my family. Every few days another body or two is added to the kill-count, ever increasing while the guards have no clue where the kuvi is. Every night shift at my job I worry that my family will be next. Would I end up like my brother, those I love torn away from me?" He continued as Aleksei took another bite. "Then one night I hear they managed to capture you and have banished you from the city after you wreaked havoc upon my neighborhood.

Fear overtook me like a disease, caught from the guard who had told me. My superior excused me from work so I could rush back to my home as fast as possible. I jumped up the steps to my floor and arrived quickly, finding the door wide open, the windows broken and the place in shambles.

"But, as my heart was in my throat, I saw them," said the guard, smiling slightly. "My family lay on the floor, dazed but all right considering the creature they had just encountered. The children woke up from apparently horrible nightmares and my wife had gotten a bruise from her fall, but besides that they were unharmed. My children said they had seen a frightened person in their apartment standing over their mother and looked at his face before they found themselves collapsing."

"I never mean to make people faint, nor drive them insane with a glance," said Aleksei. "It's just something my eyes do to most humans. Few can resist it."

"Their fainting did not matter to me," said the guard. "I was just so happy to see my family alive and, all things considered, well. I knew that the kuvi from nine years prior would have killed them all just for being in his way, but you had sidestepped them as you ran away from the guards. It was then I realized that you kuvis are not all the same, that there was something deeper to you all than a primal urge to hunt and kill."

Aleksei took the final piece of meat away from the guard, who removed his hand from the cell and wiped it on his clothes. "And from what I heard of your conversation with the princess, it sounds like she is in incredible danger. Who is this '*you-wreck*' person you were talking about?"

"Jurek is the kuvi who killed your brother's family twenty years ago," said Aleksei. "He's incredibly dangerous, controlled by his vice, and he means to perform acts equally as horrible to Daina and King Vikenti."

"I know everyone proclaims Alkin as an unparalleled hero because he apparently killed a kuvi once, but after seeing the results of just your gaze I can safely say I don't believe it," said the guard. "At least not enough to trust him with Daina's life. Hold still for a moment, will you?"

The guard got up off his haunches and reached into his left pocket. He pulled out a comically large ring filled with keys. He moved his fingers through them before selecting the one he wanted. He moved it so it was by itself and placed it in the cell door's lock. After one twist of his wrist the door swung open before him. He walked into Aleksei's cell and got down on his haunches again before leafing through his keys once more. Soon he had another key, much smaller than the first, in his hands.

"I'm not sure if you still desire flesh, but I do ask that you don't kill me once I unlock your claws," said the guard. "I'm taking an incredible risk by doing this. Helping one of your kind is enough to get me drawn-and-quartered, at the very least thrown into one of these cells."

"Why would you unlock one of my claws?" asked Aleksei in disbelief. "Are you letting me go?"

"I'm doing no such thing," said the guard. "I am just a weak-willed human who was brainwashed by your malevolent and conniving mind into opening the cell door and unlocking one of your claws." He moved his hand toward one of the claws. "Left claw or right claw? Which do you generally favor?"

"Almost all kuvis, myself included, are ambidextrous," said Aleksei. "Choose whichever one you wish."

The guard came to a decision, placed the key into the right claw lock and popped open the shackle. "Then, after I obeyed your orders to the letter you stared me straight in the eyes and caused me to faint. I fell unconscious before you and you took the key and finished unlocking yourself. You undoubtedly left claw marks on the key and area by the shackle locks to prove my case."

"Are you certain about this?" asked Aleksei. "I've seen humans after collapsing from my eyes and I am well acquainted with the nightmares they're forced to endure while unconscious. The most common nightmare is of a giant monster that swallows you whole."

"You felt it was an easier way to take care of me than wasting time ripping me into pieces," said the guard. He took the key off the ring and dropped it into Aleksei's freed claw. "Princess Daina, Prince Alkin and King Vikenti will not live unless they have you fighting for them. Even if that other evil kuvi is stronger than you, perhaps you'll be just enough to turn the tide of the battle." He pointed to a small wooden box by the staircase. "All of your possessions are in that box; the odd icon, the lock of hair, the bones, all of it. Don't forget to grab it all after you free yourself from your bonds."

Aleksei let himself smile some. "I wish there was a way to pay you back for all of this," he said. "I'm forever in your debt."

"Don't think much of it, Aleksei," said the guard. "Just bring back the princess alive and I'll hold your debt paid in full. Now I think it's time for the vicious, scheming kuvi to make the foolish guard faint after he managed to overpower the kuvi's brainwashing abilities."

He reached forward and carefully grabbed the band of cloth around Aleksei's eyes to avoid piercing himself on the kuvi's quills. He ripped it off Aleksei's head and let go of it before looking into those black, red-lined wells. In seconds he felt himself grow sweaty, and then other sounds slowly faded away and were replaced with a growing buzzing. He could not break off his gaze even if he had wanted to. Soon he fell to the side, unconscious and awaiting the nightmares.

"You may have just saved Daina's life," said Aleksei, "and I never even learned your name."

He disregarded that and instead focused on the key, trying to trap it between two of his clumsy digits. The blades of his claws kept striking against each other, constantly keeping him from getting a good grip. Through the solid plating he could not even feel how much pressure he was applying to the key. He had no idea how close he was to snapping the small key in two. For not the first time and not the last time he wished he could trade in his claws for some small, soft, pink human hands.

After an embarrassing amount of time he finally caught the key between his index digit and thumb, held carefully between the two by the loop. Even as he held the key he thought he saw the loop stretching outward, moments away from snapping into bits. He kept himself from worrying about it, moved the key to the lock on his left claw and slid it in. He pinned the loop between his middle and index digits and ever-so-slowly turned the key until he heard a click.

He grew elated as he lifted his left hand away from its shackle. He moved the key from his right hand into his left and started working on the numerous remaining weights holding his right arm down. The process took much, much longer than it would have for a human in the same position but he still felt so proud. Each time he heard that click as a shackle unlocked he felt a slight pride, increased by the key not breaking once. Soon both of his arms were completely free, and then one leg, and then the other. After what felt like ages, the last lock popped open. He was free.

He pulled himself to his feet and stretched slightly before looking at his hands in awe. Never before had they demonstrated such precision and gentleness in anything not related to combat. They could do much finer and more delicate things than he had ever imagined. He was definitely not an artist, even by kuvi standards, but he could do great things with this new-found talent.

Though a small metal key does not bleed. When a key gets a scratch it is not harmed. It would take longer than a single session of dealing with locks to give him the skill needed to ever hold a human without making wounds. He pushed those thoughts to the side; focus on the victory. He walked out of the cell while moving the guard into a more comfortable position. However, even this small act cut through the guard's clothes at certain points. Aleksei sighed and felt his opinion of his new skills plummet; not even training would make his claws gentle.

He made his way down the hall and crouched to open the chest by the staircase. The inmates to his right cowered in horror, too frightened to scream. Grown men begged him and pleaded with him for their lives; many of them were crying. Aleksei looked at them and let them stare into his eyes; soon most of them fell unconscious and the rest of them knocked each other out in their insanity. The dungeon grew incredibly quiet as he picked up his belongings and placed them back into his pockets. He pondered the icon of the Huntmaster for a few moments, holding it gently.

Mi Prosopsei, he thought, *please let Daina survive. Let her stay unharmed long enough for me to reach her. Even if the choice becomes me or her, I ask that you protect her and leave me to my fate. I beg of you, Huntmaster, heed my prayers.*

This done, he pocketed the icon and reached into the box one last time to pull out the final item; the lock of Daina's hair. He put it by itself in his other pocket and stood back up, evaluating the dungeon. Very small windows, too small to fit through. Relatively thick stone; not impossible to break through with blows, but the noise would undoubtedly attract attention and the damage may cause a large section of the building to collapse. Aleksei sighed. He would have to go through the castle.

He walked up the stairs slowly, constantly glancing around for guards. He moved as quietly as he could, foot-claws retracted, eyes barely glowing as he kept himself calm and collected. He carefully moved up the stairs and felt a relief when he saw that the hall stretching before him had no guards. Perhaps this would not be as bad as he thought, even if stealth was not one of his skills. Then he looked to the left and saw a servant screaming in terror. He grabbed the servant by the shirt and pulled him close, looking him in the eyes until he fainted. But the damage was done; the chance of escaping unnoticed was gone. The doors burst open and guards flooded out of the rooms wielding pikes. Aleksei thought back to his wound all those years ago at the tip of one of those. Not this time.

He ran forward, looking the guards dead-on. A few fainted, but many were too hardy to fall victim to such a trick. Unbeknownst to Aleksei, several had gotten themselves drunk in order to dull their sense of impending doom by kuvi claw. But no matter; no human could match him. But could an entire army of humans match him? He stopped by the guards and his claws turned white-hot, followed by a cloak of fire spreading up his arms and connecting between the shoulders. The guards stabbed with their pikes but he saw each and every jab coming. He easily sidestepped each one, his claws slicing through both wood and metal like paper. Each guard that brought a pike forward pulled back a splintered piece of wood. Their superior numbers were useless in the close quarters of the castle halls.

The disarmed guards came back wielding swords and axes. Aleksei charged into the soldiers, shoulder-barging his way through and sending many of them to the side. They kept moving themselves into his path, so he let his claws cool down in an instant in order to back-hand each one across the face. Every swing sent another guard flying to the sides, out like a snuffed candle. Aleksei made his way through the group of guards and ran to the staircase. He entered it quickly, went down a single flight of steps and stepped out to the left. He entered the main hall, all the dining tables moved to the sides.

This was to make room for an armada of soldiers passing the time by training. The soldiers turned to face Aleksei and the kuvi heard the guards from the room above coming down the staircase to get back at him. All throughout the castle groups of soldiers moved to focus on the kuvi. Aleksei looked about rapidly and saw only two other passages out of the room; the door opposite him and the main doors. The opposite door was already filled up by guards.

He heard slight clicks and twangs from the main group of soldiers and dodged to the side as a wave of crossbow bolts came flying toward his direction. He got back up onto his feet and sidestepped several more, using his claws to deflect the ones that would have hit true. The bolts that did not shatter on impact had their tips flattened against his indestructible appendages. The guards not busying themselves with the reloading of their crossbows charged forward with their pikes and blades. He leaped into the air to escape the mob and attacked them from behind, continuously delivering powerful backhands that sent the guards flying. In such close combat many were stunned or incapacitated by just his eyes alone, and the ones that were still conscious felt their morale slipping away in seconds.

The guards wielding crossbows held their fire for fear of hitting their fellow soldiers, all while Aleksei continued knocking them out effortlessly. Some guards came close but he continued to keep his eyes on all of them at once while wading between their swings, stabs and slices. Their numbers continued to fall as piles of unconscious bodies formed at the sides of the arena. Finally some of the guards started fleeing, begging the Goddess to forgive their cowardice and protect them from the demon. Aleksei felt his eyes glowing but suppressed his anger; he could not let himself go wild. Not now. He had to keep his calm. Now and forevermore.

The guards attempting to fight him in melee finally disbanded, scattering to the staircases and leaving Aleksei open to attack from crossbows. He turned to the sound of firing bolts and continued to dodge and parry the missiles. One crossbowman fired his bolt later than the others had; Aleksei took the moment to catch the bolt in mid-air. The guards' eyes widened as they saw it in his hand. He dropped it to the floor, the tip of the bolt clinking loudly.

The late crossbowman dropped his weapon. "I quit," he said. He fell to the floor, gripping his head with his hands. Several other crossbowmen did the same and others moved out of the way. Aleksei sighed in relief; he had a moment to think of a way through the doors. Opening the doors would be simple enough, too simple. He had demonstrated his control and lack of desire to harm; not a single blow he had landed had been fatal. Damaging, undoubtedly, but none of the guards had been killed by his claws. And they had been put to shame by his trumping their entire arsenal.

But a demonstration of power to the militia would not be enough. He had to show it to the city as well. It would leave them cowering in fear, but with Daina vouching for him they would be convinced that he is a worthy asset for Tantallos. And not one to ever be trifled with. He thought things over, all while generating a ball of fire in his hands and twirling it between his digits. He looked to the ball, then to the wooden main doors, and nodded. He focused some, growing the ball in diameter until it was about two-thirds the size of a human skull. He hurled the fireball at the door and it exploded upon impact, blanketing the door in flames. The fire greedily ate away at the wood, weakening the door quickly and scattering the guards who had curled up by it. But that was not the main objective; that was just to make the next move more likely to succeed.

The castle's main doors exploded outward as a shape engulfed in flames burst out of it, claws pointing straight ahead like a series of pikes. His wings regenerated themselves in an instant after his flying collision with the door, allowing him to raise himself into the air and fly over the equally amazed and horrified crowds. People exclaimed in fright as Aleksei soared over them. People cowered as he flew down the streets, making his way to the portcullis. A few dozen feet before them he halted his charge, killing the flames over his body and just focusing on another fireball in his hand. Once it was generated he hurled it at the top of the portcullis. It landed and covered the top of the structure with flames while Aleksei resumed his flight over the wall. In moments he was back in the Decay, wherein he moved closer to the ground and slowed down so to make less noise.

The flames on the portcullis worked quickly, melting the chains connected to it. The workers who attempted to pull it up so the citizens could chase after the demon and warn their king and princess made matters worse, the weakened chains breaking and leaving them powerless to open the entrance to Tantallos. The flames did even more damage by melting the parts the chains connected to; it would be impossible to open the gates by just replacing the chains. The portcullis was down for good.

Inside the castle the guards slowly recovered from the fight. Many pulled themselves to their feet while issuing groans from how much they ached. Others stayed down; they were trapped in the nightmares of a kuvi. Messengers came to them from the Tantallos gates, revealing that they were trapped in the city to the chagrin of all. The Captain of the guard stood in the main room, overseeing the lining up of the wounded for medical treatment. A soldier came up to him. "I counted up all the dead, sir," he said.

"How many?" asked the captain. He braced himself for the answer.

"None, sir," said the guard. "Incredibly high amounts of wounded and dozens of people going through nightmares but no casualties."

"What about the prison guard?" asked the Captain.

"Unconscious but very much alive," said the guard. "It is the same with all the inmates."

"He didn't kill anyone?" pondered the Captain. But he was a demon. Demons kill. Everyone knows that. They do not have any mercy or pity in their black hearts. Why did the demon kill no one? There was something deeper to all of this. "Send any guard still standing out into the city to restore order," said the Captain. "Make sure no one tries to enter the Decay to find the king and princess. They're not in as much danger as we think."

"Sir...?"

"Think about it," said the Captain. "This demon escaped his cell by some means and ran through the castle, encountering well over a hundred guards, and he did not kill a single one. He's a demon, so he has a pair of claws unmatched in their brutality, and he did not turn them on any of the guards trying to impale him. I'm starting to wonder if the princess' stories concerning the demon being friendly are true. Red Light Murderer or not, no one died by his claws while he was escaping. That has to mean something." He sighed. "If I ever see him or the princess again I'll need to discuss this with them."

CHAPTER 29

Your greatest advantage over your predators is your intelligence; use it to
turn their brute strength against them.
-From the Tomes of the Huntmaster.

"I know how it sounds," said Daina. "I know it's incredibly bizarre and... uncomfortable, but that's what Jurek said to Aleksei. I'm still not entirely sure what to make of it."

"Unfortunately for all of us, and you especially, it holds up," said Alkin. The two of them walked near the end of the caravan, just in front of the cart. They talked quietly to each other so neither Father Abdaas nor the nearby guards could overhear them. Vikenti and Abdaas were still walking at the front of the protective circle, leading the way to Tulroy. With each step Tantallos disappeared further from sight; soon they were starting to round the mountain Daina had been taken both over and under in the past few days.

"It does?" asked Daina. "Really...?"

"I'm not very knowledgeable concerning summoning and I've certainly never done it myself," said Alkin, "but I still know a fair amount about the subject. The blood of the maidenhead is the preferred kind for summoning. As horrible as what Jurek plans to do is, it might be the one thing that has kept him from just killing you already."

"Why is... *that* blood preferred over normal blood?" she asked.

"If I remember correctly maidenhead blood drastically speeds up the opening of the portal," he said. "By using it instead of normal blood the summoner does not have to worry about someone sabotaging the ritual by taking an ingredient off before it is has at least sunken halfway into the dolmen. It gives you quite the advantage if you're competing with a summoner making his own portal, and considering the quality of the planned ingredients, it's safe to say Abdaas would never have a second chance at this. Especially if he uses one of his own eyes for the gaze of the greatest enemy. The trauma from having even one eyeball removed might kill him, let alone both."

"I shudder to think about what horrible manner of creature they are going to summon with such ingredients," said Daina. "I mean, what would they choose to call forth? Aleksei sometimes mentioned a Kriothanatos but never went into detail about it. Could that be it?"

"No possible way," said Alkin. "I doubt Abdaas even knows what that creature is. I certainly don't. Assuming that there even are more worlds besides our own and Proso, he may be trying to call forth a creature from one of those. Or perhaps something from this world. Summoning creates tears in the fabrics of two worlds and moves objects between them. Perhaps he could create two tears in this world and accomplish the same."

"That's far more likely," said Daina. She raised a hand to her chin and thought it all over for a moment or two. In the end she could come up with nothing that Abdaas could, and would, plausibly summon. Not unless there was some great being besides the Goddess in this world that he wished to call forth, something that indeed would require such prime ingredients. "Hopefully they don't make their move until Tulroy. Then you could talk to your father and get the city to expose Abdaas for the heretic he is. Right...?"

Alkin sighed and looked down slightly, breaking his eyes away from Daina. "I wish I could guarantee that," he said. "While many people in the city adore me and view me as a hero, a champion of men, Abdaas has just as much influence over the people as I do. The people of Tulroy believe it to be the holy city of the Church of the Goddess. We believe that on the rocks above us She stepped into our world and that She went below-ground to rest in the same place. If the king denounced Abdaas many people would side with him and fight against the crown."

"And Abdaas' side has two kuvis fighting for him," said Daina. "As it stands right now, I am doomed to a horrible death. You're strong but you can't compare to Jurek; maybe Wesan, but definitely not Jurek. And I certainly couldn't fight him off. Not so long as he's covered head-to-toe in that armor."

The stench of rotted filth had been increasing steadily over the course of their conversation, and Daina finally took the time to look around and see the source of the odor. "Lots of bogs and other fetid pools around our path; they had been key in my killing Tulsan. But both Jurek and Wesan can fly. I can't possibly trick either of them into jumping into one and nearly drowning before shoving a dagger through their mouth."

"I'll do what I can to keep you safe," said Alkin. "You're my friend." He pulled Daina into a protective but lax embrace. Daina returned it gently. They shared this hug, a platonic gesture interpreted as so much more by the unknowing guards.

"I just wish Aleksei was here," said Daina. "He could keep both of us safe. He'd probably try to leave you to fend for yourself, but I think my insistence would change his mind. And you probably get tired of me talking about him all the time, even if we aren't going to get married anymore."

Alkin let go of Daina. "I really do not mind," he said. "It's important for you to find someone you can trust, someone who cares for you so strongly. That, and there's another thing. You see..." He stopped himself. "I really have no idea how to say this, and the very thought of sharing it with anyone is terrifying me. It's something... Please lean forward. I'll whisper it."

Aleksei's sense of pride and energy vanished instantly. Something squirming in his body, some sort of malignant parasite, twisted his heart and tore it to bits, leaving nothing but an aching hole in his chest as he watched the scene unfold from a distance. Alkin and Daina, walking side by side, talking. About what, not even his ears could tell, but he could see them staying close to each other, bride and groom. Then came the move by Alkin, pulling Daina close, embracing her warmly and protectively. The pain in his chest worsened at this particular part. Then he whispered something in her ear, something that made her look at Alkin in surprise and slight confusion. What Alkin had said, Aleksei did not care to find out.

He had seen more than enough. He continued to follow them, frequently stopping in trees and observing them as he played through scenarios with Daina in his mind, scenarios that placed him at her side instead of Alkin. Each time he tried to perform the same move, holding her lovingly, but then his claws got in the way as they always did. He pierced her in so many different ways, sliced her to ribbons, left her bleeding and shrieking in pain as he panicked and accidentally cut her even more. Nothing managed to expel the images from his mind.

It was a struggle for Daina to comprehend such a revelation, but she eventually nodded and accepted it. "It explains so much," she said. "Makes me wish even more than Aleksei had been here to hear it. Would have made him much less jealous of you."

Alkin sighed. "I know," he said. "If we ever see him alive again, or if I go to the same place he does when the kuvis kill me, I'll tell him myself. Only tell him if I die."

"Don't worry," she said. "It's definitely something that should come from you." She then looked over her shoulder and watched as Tantallos finally dipped and disappeared from sight. She felt an odd feeling inside her, like she would never see it again. *Of course I'd feel that way,* she thought. *It's very likely I won't live to see another sunrise. Depends on when Abdaas and those kuvis make their move.* "I'll be right back, Alkin," said Daina. "I want to ask my murderer something."

"By all means," said Alkin. "Though he wouldn't let your blood be on his hands, not when two kuvis are willing to do his dirty work."

Daina nodded and hurried up to the front of the caravan, where Vikenti and Abdaas continued walking forward slowly to accommodate for Vikenti's slow pace. She got onto Abdaas' side and did not even acknowledge Vikenti, taking steps to avoid his gaze. "Father Abdaas," she said. "We're far away from Tantallos now. When will all four guards rendezvous with us?"

"You have to be patient, Princess Daina," said Abdaas. "Give them a few moments. Sweeping through the Decay for dangerous monsters is a difficult and extensive task."

"Not for your guards," said Daina. "They put everything that lives in the Decay to shame. Monsters recoil at their mere presence. Any of the four of them could kill even the toughest mire beast. Perhaps not the weakest one, he strikes me as slow in the head, but the other three would have no problems. The red one is so strong he could kill the entire population of predators living by Tantallos."

"They are indeed powerful and well-trained, but even so we may only be joined back by two of the four," said Abdaas.

"Only two of them?" asked Daina. "It must be because Aleksei killed one and I killed another, correct?"

"Daina, you murdered someone?" asked Vikenti, eyes widened.

"I've never killed anyone, Vikenti," said Daina. "I killed a kuvi who was chasing after me while journeying back to Tantallos. The four guards are kuvis; that's why they all wore full suits of armor, to hide in plain sight. And from where do you think I got that part of a kuvi arm?"

"I'm your father, damn it," growled Vikenti. "And you keep saying '*kuvi*' instead of '*demon*.' I do question your choice of that particular nonsense word. You honestly think a creature as evil and fearsome as a demon would choose to call its race something that meek-sounding rather than the name we humans call them?"

"The word '*kuvi*' is short for '*Kuvigos*,' the first of our race that all of us call our ancestor," said a voice behind the caravan. "When you insult her name you insult all of us, and thank you for bringing such a small selection of guards. I almost worried it would take some time to harvest you."

Every member of the caravan, including the cart pullers, quickly turned around. The guards all formed a protective barrier between the royal family and the two horrors they saw; even the cart pullers picked up makeshift weapons and joined the lineup. Jurek stood before them, eyes uncovered, the third rings glowing brightly. He still wore the rest of his armor, even if his helmet was long gone. A moment later Wesan landed at his side, his wings dissipating into the air. He tore off his helmet as well, revealing a hairless head covered in erratic depressions like cracked ground. His eyes gazed at them as well, the outermost rings slightly larger than the others. His teeth were far less evolved than Jurek's, resembling the jaws of a dog more than those of a human.

"If Aleksei has taught me anything, it's that the more fearsome a kuvi looks the weaker it actually is," said Alkin. He reached behind his back and gripped the hilt of Back Breaker tightly. Vikenti moved away from the line of guards while also making for a short sword sheathed at his side. Daina watched in horror, hand going for her dagger, well aware of the damage two kuvis could do to a group of humans and how quickly they easily do it. Abdaas moved to the side and folded his arms.

"Could you two have taken any longer to finally arrive?" asked Abdaas.

"Shut up, you fool," growled Jurek. "We had to make sure we were far enough away so no one could see us. Excessive, maybe, but it was worth the wait. I've built up quite the appetite."

Abdaas observed the glow in Jurek's eyes. "It certainly seems that way," he said. "Deal with the guards as you like."

Jurek chuckled. His claws became rigid and he pointed one at the three people standing away from the rest. The feet of Daina, Vikenti and Alkin all sank into the ground, bound in place by earthen snares. They struggled in vain to move their feet as Jurek and Wesan turned their focus to the guards separating them from their quarry. "Don't let them intimidate you!" yelled Vikenti. "Attack them with everything you have before they kill you!"

Wesan backed away and let the guards surround Jurek, pikes out straight and ready to stab forward. Jurek saw each slight movement coming, reacting to them with split-second timing. He ducked down just fractions of a second before they stabbed and slammed the side of one of his claws against the ground, causing the earth all around him to shake. The ground dipped at where he had slammed it and spread outward in all directions like a wave of water, followed immediately by massive spikes of rock shooting up out of the ground, piercing several of the guards and sending the rest flying.

Jurek let out another chuckle. He loved showing that move off. Even as the guards struggled to pull themselves to their feet and regroup Jurek and Wesan moved to the sides of their makeshift formation. They charged forward, lacerating the poor humans with ease, ripping through their armor and weapons with no resistance. The guards still alive panicked and flailed their weapons about rapidly in a desperate hope to hit something, anything, even if by accident. Wesan stayed back and let Jurek dart in between their random blows, slicing through the wooden shafts and disarming each guard before Wesan rejoined him to finish gutting them all.

Daina watched in horror, unable to avert her eyes. Vikenti felt the memories resurface from when he had spent seemingly an eternity defending the broken wall; the spilled blood of humans falling to monsters from the

Decay, the cries of pain from the wounded moments before they were silenced. Alkin took it all in with equal amounts of fascination and horror. The kuvi he had killed had been nothing compared to these two; Jurek was so much greater it was almost mystifying. Abdaas grimaced at the slaughter but felt no guilt; it was all for the greater good.

Before a minute had passed all the guards and the two cart pullers were dead; some had been torn to shreds, some disemboweled, some beheaded, but most had been reduced to pieces of bloody flesh that Jurek feasted on greedily while Wesan watched over the remaining humans. Jurek stuffed himself sloppily, like a wild animal feeding on a fresh kill. He stood back up while breaking a bone to get at the marrow contained inside it. "Each mouthful is sweeter than the last," said Jurek happily. "It's hard for me to hate humans when you taste this good. And I think a full stomach will help keep me from eating what I tear off you, Vikenti. I wonder what little Jurek twenty years ago would have thought if he knew he would eventually get to kill the king of that accursed city."

Vikenti ignored Jurek's taunts and looked to his daughter. "Daina, I'm so sorry for not believing you," he said. "I know it's far too late for you to accept it, especially since we're both about to die, but know that I'm truly sorry with every part of my being."

"You're not both about to die, Vikenti," said Abdaas. "I require Daina to be alive for a short time after you're dealt with. Once Jurek has appropriately harvested her then she shall be killed. Don't think me evil; I represent a much higher will than that of a petty, earthly king."

"You give me no reason to not think you evil, as that is all you stand for," growled Vikenti. "No, you're worse than evil. You stand for evil that thinks it's doing good."

"Your words mean nothing to someone as blessed in purpose as me," said Abdaas. "You may as well be a street urchin calling me fat. But while your thoughts are harmless, your interference may have doomed your soul to being consumed by the Goddess when your life ends." He looked to Jurek. "Now's the time. Collect his flesh; I'd prefer part or all of one of his arms."

Jurek grinned evilly and walked slowly toward Vikenti, intentionally dragging out the sequence for greater pleasure. In his arrogance he let the bonds on the group's feet weaken, allowing Alkin to pull his feet out of the ground as the kuvi approached his quarry. Alkin looked to Daina, who also managed to unearth her feet as quietly as possible. Jurek was too focused on Vikenti to notice or care. They both readied their weapons and moved to block the path to Vikenti. Jurek stood just a few feet in front of them. With two backhanded swipes from his claws he swatted them to the side, no more a nuisance to him than a couple of buzzing houseflies.

Wesan grinned and readied to pounce; ever since he had heard of Alkin he had wondered just how tough he really was. He was no arch kuvi, but that was of no matter to him. He was still more tenacious and menacing than any human. And what better trophy than the head of a kuvi killer? Alkin rolled with the impact on the ground, somewhat dizzy but largely unharmed by the blow. He came to a stop lying face-up, Back Breaker in the mud by him. Before he could move Wesan leaped onto him, pinning his arms against the ground. Wesan caught Alkin's scent wafting up to him and could not help but salivate; this would be a very delicious victory.

Daina pulled herself to her feet, several dozen paces away from her father as Jurek moved ever closer to the immobile king. She had kept her grip on her dagger, but any charge against the kuvi would be fruitless. He would sense her coming and hit her to the side again like the nothing she was. If only he did not have most of his armor on; maybe then she could at least throw her dagger into his back. "That was one of the cutest attempts to stop me I've ever seen," said Jurek, pretending to wipe away a tear. "It would have been funny if it hadn't been so pathetic. Now Vikenti, which arm would you like me to tear off first? You might want to use one in your last moments for whatever reason, and I don't need a specific one."

"I'd rather use both my arms to shove this sword down your throat," said Vikenti, holding his blade forward. "I'm well aware I stand no chance against you, but that doesn't mean I won't try to keep you from ever harming my daughter."

"The bonds of family," said Jurek. "I won't lie; it's something I've missed these past twenty years away from my own. You found my soft spot, your majesty, so I don't think I'll desecrate what remains of your body by consuming it. Plenty left around here to nibble on anyway." He brought up his claws and Vikenti readied his sword. Jurek moved back a few paces so he had plenty of space to charge. Suddenly a blazing light soared over the Decay. It covered the ground at twice the speed of a fired crossbow bolt, barely identifiable as it came closer. The light showed no signs of slowing down until it embedded itself in Jurek's back and exploded.

Jurek cried out in pain as a blanket of fire wrapped itself around him, smaller flames flying off him in the direction the fireball had been traveling and dying out on the damp ground. He continued howling in pain as he collapsed to his knees while everyone else looked in the direction the light had come from. A creature with glowing, graceful wings barreled through the Decay to them, turning slightly to charge claws-first into Jurek while emitting a high-pitched yell, sending him flying forward while the attacker did a loop and landed on the ground. He let his wings dissipate into the air, his eyes glowing brightly, the fifth rings much larger than the others and a snarl firmly planted on his visage.

"Aleksei, you're alive!" yelled Daina, smiling happily. Tears of joy started forming at the corners of her eyes. "I had feared the worst!"

"Amazing entrance, Aleksei, and impeccable timing!" said Alkin. "We really need your help!"

"You're the great kuvi-killing prince who is beloved by all his people and hailed as a hero," growled Aleksei. "If you live up to half your name I'm sure you can fend off a normal kuvi by yourself. Wesan doesn't even have any quills." He glared at Daina and Vikenti. "I'm here to help the ones who need my assistance; the kind, understanding and open-minded king and, of course, the truthful and loyal princess."

Daina was taken aback by this hostility and looked at Aleksei in confusion. "Aleksei, what are you..." Jurek let out an incredibly loud roar, slamming a claw against the ground and knocking everyone off their feet. Aleksei regained his footing in a heartbeat, back bent forward and claws facing ahead at his sides. Alkin took advantage of the tremor to push Wesan off him with a leg, giving him time to roll to Back Breaker. He picked it up and got back onto his feet as Wesan recovered and stared at him angrily, taking a stance similar to Aleksei's. Daina fell down again but was quick to pull herself up before rushing over to Vikenti and helping him back up, the earthen bonds broken; age was betraying his body.

Everyone looked at Jurek, who was crouching behind them and sending waves of earth onto himself to extinguish the flames. Balls of mud shot up from the ground and hit him all over, coating him in a cooling layer. In moments he was completely enveloped in dirt, and as soon as it finished covering him it fell off to reveal the charred creature beneath. His face was horribly burnt but his body was largely fine. It had been protected by his armor, which was now warped by the intense heat and broken by Aleksei's charge. The dirt took the destroyed pieces off his body and they sank into the ground. His plated legs had largely escaped harm, however.

"Two hits for one," said Jurek. "A daredevil charging strike and a surprisingly well-executed alignment ball. That's too good for you, kid. I am going to relish making you pay." He forced his eyes open despite the lids being burned; the pain did not matter. He pushed it down, controlled it. It could wait until after he killed Aleksei. "I see numerous bogs and the like all around us, kid. How would you like a tendril of rock to drag you into one?"

"You've beaten him multiple times; he's not a threat!" yelled Abdaas. "Pay him no mind and gather Vikenti's flesh!"

Jurek's neck painfully moved to look at the priest. "Gather it yourself, you pompous bastard," growled Jurek. "The kid and I have some personal matters to settle." He turned to face his younger opponent. Their eyes locked, each one sizing each other up, waiting for that first move. They both assessed the other's strengths and weaknesses almost instantly, though it was largely unnecessary. They knew each other's combat skill so well. But both noted an attitude change; Jurek was far too infuriated to underestimate Aleksei, and Aleksei was too collected to not fight strategically. Both would be unmatched in their tenacity.

Abdaas grumbled about relying on demons under his breath, reached into his robe and pulled out an iron dagger. The hilt of the weapon was shaped in the symbol of the Goddess, the dolmen part connecting to the blade while the beam of light was the handle. He ran to Vikenti despite his bulk when Daina stepped in front of her father, dagger at the ready. "I've killed a kuvi; a fat priest will not be an issue," she said. "So go ahead and try to hurt my father. I dare you, Abdaas." The priest charged at her and stabbed forward, Daina sidestepping the blade with ease and preparing a strike of her own.

Alkin and Wesan circled around each other warily, black and red eyes locking with white and green eyes. Alkin held Back Breaker snugly in his hands, cautiously waiting for the right moment to strike. Back Breaker was a very heavy weapon and would take a lot of time to swing. Wesan had no such restriction; despite their indestructible nature kuvi claws seemed as light as claws of keratin.

Wesan dashed forward as fast as he could, catching Alkin off-guard and knocking Back Breaker right out of his hands. Wesan grabbed the blade and threw it off to the side, far out of reach. He laughed triumphantly and sliced at the human with his claws, intentionally missing Alkin's face by a hair. Alkin felt the breeze as the claw rushed past him.

Wesan grinned. *A great hero indeed. He must have killed a kuvi on the level of Tulsan, and nothing of value had been lost when the princess had stabbed him through the mouth.* Though Wesan could not help but feel disappointed; he had hoped Alkin would have gotten one swing in before he started toying with the human. He prepared to stab Alkin through the chest. Alkin dropped to the ground, narrowly avoiding Wesan's stab. Wesan readjusted himself to stab downward but only embedded his claw in mud. Alkin rolled onto his feet and stood up in an instant as Wesan pulled his claw out of the ground, shook it to get the mud off and faced his prey. Alkin's eyes darted toward Back Breaker, but it was still too far away. Wesan would jump him and tear him to shreds before he even got close to it. Or so he thought. He still had to try.

Alkin dashed toward the blade and Wesan charged at him, bent over and claws facing straight ahead. Alkin faked to the left and successfully dodged the kuvi as he pounced at Alkin, but Wesan recovered almost instantly after hitting the ground and made more slices at Alkin's face. He backed away, barely avoiding the bloodstained claws. Wesan snarled. The thrill of the fight continued to wear off each time Alkin evaded an attack without making one of his own. Not even a single punch for Wesan to block. "Face your death and fight me, coward!" he yelled. "I had been aiming for your jugular, but I'm going to kill you slowly if you don't start fighting back!"

"I'll fight back if you can actually manage to catch me!" taunted Alkin. He evaded another claw swipe from Wesan, but the kuvi's movements were getting faster and faster as he grew more agitated. Each dodge Alkin made moved him further way from Back Breaker. The blade still lay on the ground, glimmering as Alkin glanced at it, but it was impossible to reach as long as his opponent stood in the way. Wesan made for a slice across Alkin's waist but changed up quickly and instead backhanded Alkin across the face with his other claw. The blow sent Alkin flying to the side, eventually landing on a slope and slowly rolling toward the shore of a bog.

Alkin stopped himself from rolling in just inches away from the pool of rank fluid. He watched warily as Wesan slowly, cautiously walked closer to him with his claws at the ready. Alkin pulled himself back onto his feet, balancing precariously on the slope. The bog was but one false step away, and once he fell in he might as well let himself drown in the fetid waters. Unarmed and in a terrible defensive position. He had no hope unless he managed to obtain a weapon. His fists could not possibly stand up to a kuvi claw, as tough as they might be, and Back Breaker was far out of reach. Then Alkin looked at Wesan's claws. They were certainly in reach.

Wesan attempted a stab, but Alkin sidestepped the attack before reaching forward and grabbing the claw, relying on Wesan's balance to keep himself from falling into the bog. His leathery hands barely felt the pain as the blades slightly cut into him while he moved onto better footing. He pulled Wesan closer to him and proceeded to punch him repeatedly in the face with his free hand, landing blow after blow on the toughened, cracked surface. The continual pushing and pulling disoriented Wesan enough to make the attempted swipes with his free claw worthless. Several of Alkin's punches made their way into Wesan's mouth, shattering his teeth and leaving gaping, bloody holes where they used to be.

Wesan managed to free himself from Alkin's grip and brought his other claw forward again in a swipe, but Alkin grabbed it and brought it upward, stabbing Wesan through the jaw. The kuvi gave less of a yell and more of a garble as he staggered backward, letting out incomprehensible moans of pain as he attempted to pull his own claw out of his mouth. Wesan stopped himself, focusing and succeeding in removing the blades from his jaw. He howled in rage; Alkin could not possibly do this! He was just a weak human! He should have died by this point!

No retreating; he was going to kill Alkin no matter what! Wesan howled in rage and charged blindly at Alkin, who stood ready several feet away. In his rage he neglected to see that Alkin had picked Back Breaker up from the ground and had readied it so the blade faced directly ahead. The blade's great weight made the move difficult, but Alkin still managed to stab ahead just as the kuvi got within striking distance.

In his blind fury Wesan completely failed to recognize the attack and his own momentum impaled him upon the sword. He traveled far up the blade before coming to a stop at the hilt. He spat up more blood; it trailed out of his mouth as Alkin grimaced. The victor twisted the blade and let go of it, watching as Wesan fell to his knees and then collapsed on the ground. Another kuvi slain by Alkin; no small feat. Alkin walked up to the corpse and kicked it across the face, ensuring Wesan was dead before he reached for the hilt. He placed a foot on the dead kuvi's face as he attempted to pull the blade out of the body. He dug his heel into Wesan's visage as he worked to free Back Breaker so he could help the others.

CHAPTER 30

You [of Burning] can create and control the hardest-to-tame of destructive forces, and survive all its attempts to strike back at you. It cannot feed on your flesh and its fumes are like sweet air to you. But like this force, you can be drowned and smothered, and enveloping torrents steal your control.
-From the Tomes of the Huntmaster.

Even as the battles around them waged, the arch kuvis paced back and forth evenly, watching each other, the longing to make that first blow brewing in both of them. "That's the second time you've managed to catch me off-guard, kid," said Jurek. "But we both know very well that you need the element of surprise to do any damage to me."

"You know damn well my name is Aleksei," growled the young kuvi. "You'd think you would remember the name of the one prey to ever escape you. Surely, despite all evidence to the contrary, you're intelligent enough to remember such a small detail?"

"All those years ago I figured there would be no point to remembering your name," said Jurek. "I'd catch you soon enough and make you pay for scarring me, as slowly as I could manage, and now you've gone and added some burn marks to the scar. You also destroyed a well-crafted breastplate."

"You'll experience much worse than destruction of your bulky armor when I sink my claws underneath your shoulder blades," said Aleksei.

"That's what you keep on telling me," said Jurek. "Just like all the other fighters who found themselves at odds with me. And then I ate each one. I think your little friend said something very similar all those years ago, but instead of her harming me I ended up using one of her severed digits to pick her flesh out of my teeth."

Jurek watched, grinning in satisfaction as Aleksei's eyes glowed even brighter. Aleksei worked to control his temper, focusing clearly on his goal to keep his anger at bay, and his eyes died down some. Jurek thought for a short moment, devising a new plan of action. "And to think all this time you could have been on my side," said Jurek. "I certainly thank you for keeping the princess alive for me, but now there's no need for all this."

"You can't honestly expect me to believe you," said Aleksei. "You still need her blood."

"It is still preferable for the ritual, I won't deny," said Jurek, "but you don't have to die by my claws. Work with Abdaas and me. I know the mere thought irks you but what I'm working on with that pious fool will ensure that kuvis everywhere will be safe from having their souls destroyed when they die. If you're like me then you've feared that event since the moment you were dragged to this world as a child."

Aleksei's eyes lost some of their glow. "What?" he asked caught suddenly between his curiosity and his distrust of Jurek.

"I fear I have said too much for now," said Jurek. "But my offer still stands. If you come over to our side, I won't lay a claw on Daina. I'll even give you the task of... collecting her blood, since you're perverted enough to lust after her."

Aleksei did not think it over for even a second before his eyes blazed brightly. "I'll never do such a thing," he spat. "I love her too much to hurt her, no matter how or why. The only way you're getting to her is through me."

Jurek did not look disappointed. "I must admit I was hoping you'd feel that way," said Jurek. He generated his wings and made them glow even brighter, further emphasizing their massive and jagged appearance. Aleksei generated his own wings in response, displaying them prominently and brightly to make himself look as big and threatening as possible. Jurek's gigantic wingspan dwarfed Aleksei's. "You'd better make this battle a damn satisfying one, Aleksei."

He hardened his claws and pointed them at Aleksei's feet. Rock spikes shot out of the ground but met air as Aleksei disintegrated his wings and dashed away, getting some distance from Jurek. Jurek continued bringing up lines of spikes, focusing on slowly getting Aleksei caught in a semi-circle so he could better aim at him. Aleksei's *Ateni* and excellent sight took note of each subtle movement by Jurek's claws as he pointed them at target spots. All the while he focused on his hand, generating fire and shaping it carefully.

Jurek snarled; this was going nowhere. He disintegrated his wings as well, just in case an unfortunate incident should destroy them. His own *Ateni* was proving ineffective at guessing Aleksei's movements; the faster kuvi cleverly faked dashes and dodges right when Jurek thought he had guessed his next move. All around him the other duels continued to rage, Daina and Abdaas both having to move out of the way as mud balls started to hum as he prepared them.

Jurek tweaked their expected trajectory while using his other claw to continue sending spikes upward; the spikes were enough to keep Aleksei from escaping the zone despite his noticing that one claw was facing backward. Many of the spikes in front of Aleksei sank back into the ground to make way for Jurek's projectiles. Jurek sensed the wetness of each mud ball judging by how much less control he had over it; the wetter it became the more influence he lost over it. He eventually found one so wet a kuvi *dal Richtos* could have easily taken control of it from him. He crouched down, the drier mud balls firing off to surround Aleksei while the wettest one aimed directly for the young kuvi.

Aleksei saw the mud balls coming. The ones aimed to the sides and above guaranteed he could not dodge or take flight without getting bombarded. Instead he jumped forward and lobbed his fireball at Jurek right as the wettest mud ball fired back at him. Between the spread of mud balls and Jurek's slower speed both kuvis could only raise their offhand claw in defense. The fireball exploded, again blanketing parts of Jurek and scorching his already black quills. Almost immediately he started getting the dirt to throw itself onto him to extinguish the flames. The mud ball behaved similarly, sending parts of itself all over Aleksei. His left claw was completely blanketed in wet mud and most of his right claw had also become coated. He felt fear rising in him, easily detected as his rage was kept down; Jurek had done worse than usual. All the other times Aleksei had always had his fire, even if it had never really worked.

"You can dodge my spikes all day long and balls of earth are more annoying than deadly," said Jurek. "And now it looks like you're deprived of fire. Come and fight me up close, claw to claw, the way it should be!" Aleksei said nothing as he dashed toward Jurek, bent forward, arms out and back, claws facing ahead. Jurek braced himself, assuming a similar position as the distance between them closed in seconds. It was his strength against Aleksei's speed. He looked forward to completely overpowering the young kuvi.

Aleksei made a quick swipe forward, aiming for Jurek's head. Jurek parried it inches away from his scalp and pushed the claw away with his sheer strength. The force knocked Aleksei off-balance, sending him reeling away while Jurek readied a claw strike of his own. He stabbed forward but Aleksei let himself fall to the ground, evading Jurek's attack.

He rolled to the side moments before Jurek stabbed downward with both claws, embedding them in dirt. Aleksei got to his feet quickly and made for another blow at Jurek's head, but Jurek hardened a claw and raised up a wall of earth between him and Aleksei, stopping the attack. Aleksei snarled and tried to dash around, faking as much as he could to trick Jurek, but Jurek extended more of the barrier to protect himself.

Daina and Abdaas watched each other carefully as they paced back and forth. Jurek's barrage of mud balls had obliterated the land they had been fighting on, leaving nothing but a muddy terrain littered with holes. Daina struggled to keep her feet from getting caught up and from taking a false step into one of the holes; she needed every bit of agility she could muster. Although old, Abdaas was a surprisingly capable fighter and clearly had extensive training. "Long have I known that I was to make great changes to this world," said Abdaas. "Even as a child I knew I must keep myself strong and train myself vigorously in the art of combat. Priesthood has dulled my skills and physical prowess; I'm not half the fighter I was in my prime. But I can still take a weak little princess like you."

Daina paid his words no mind; they would not matter once she killed him. She instead looked for an opening. She glanced down for but a second and spotted a somewhat-dry patch she'd have better footing on. She dashed forward, planting her feet on it as she stabbed at the priest. Abdaas backed away, nearly set off-balance by his own weight. He recovered quickly and sliced horizontally at Daina, but the limber princess easily jumped back and avoided a cut along her stomach that would have spilled her intestines. Abdaas stabbed forward again but Daina knocked the blade away with her own. Abdaas was slow, and despite all his training he proved to be rather predictable.

"You may be fast on your feet but eventually you'll have to actually hit me," said Abdaas. "And you won't so long as the Goddess' fortune favors me. I sure hope you're not wasting your time praying to Her. She would never grant such a privilege to one who even now attacks Her messenger."

"I don't pray to the Goddess anymore," said Daina. "Instead I pray to the Huntmaster, *Prosopsei*."

"Pro-soap-se-what?" asked Abdaas, stumbling over the syllables.

"He is the god the kuvis follow," said Daina. "Given the creatures that worship Him, I'd imagine He would have far more influence over the outcome of a fight. And if you're the messenger of the Goddess, then Her falling from my favor is complete. She is not the righteous deity I was raised to believe She was."

"Infidel!" yelled Abdaas, slicing madly at her, overcome by his rage. Daina parried the mindless blows, the force nearly making her lose her grip on her dagger, and reached for the priest's own weapon. She grabbed what little of the hilt extended out of Abdaas' grip and yanked it out of his hands. She threw it to the ground behind her, leaving Abdaas completely unarmed, but before she could strike the priest pulled a new blade from his robes, almost exactly like the dagger on the ground in design.

Jurek finished recovering and brought his earthen barrier down in an instant, catching Aleksei off-guard and making him waste precious time turning to face his foe. Jurek spun around and connected a powerful backhand to Aleksei's cheek, knocking the young kuvi off his feet and sending him spinning some before landing on the ground face first. He struggled to pull himself back onto his feet but the blow left him dazed; any other part of his body and he would have gotten back up in a heartbeat. Jurek dashed over to him and stomped his back, Jurek's foot forcing Aleksei down into the mud. His metallic boots had been removed alongside other pieces of destroyed armor. He moved the foot to Aleksei's head and extended the claw until it was touching the young kuvi's temple.

"Remember this position?" said Jurek. "I recall forcing you into it. I think it was right after we first met. I had kicked you around some, largely just humiliating you and wrecking your confidence in your abilities, the norm for me. It also made your friend surrender. She sacrificed her own life to save yours."

"Shut up," growled Aleksei. Jurek was purposefully dragging it all out solely to appease his own arrogance and torment Aleksei some more.

"And what exactly will you do if I don't?" asked Jurek. "Your friends are busy fighting their own opponents. Actually, Alkin somehow managed to kill Wesan and is trying to get his corpse off that massive sword. I expected better of Wesan, but it can't be helped. Vikenti is still laboring over his decrepit body and Daina's locked in combat with Abdaas. They're all busy and you can't get out of this situation alone. If you even try my foot-claw will sink itself into that air pocket between your ears."

"*Mirke dal mi Prosopsei*, shut up!" yelled Aleksei.

"Last time I checked the Huntmaster was not here," said Jurek. "Nor will He ever be here save for the pieces supposedly in our hearts. Our god is weak, so weak He could not create His own world. And unless you give your allegiance to a more powerful deity you will never leave this accursed world."

"The Goddess does not want our allegiance," said Aleksei. "She consumes our souls."

"I think She will be kind to the kuvi who helped wake Her up," said Jurek.

Aleksei's eyes widened. The stolen bones from the ossuary, the intense desire to get the best of Daina's blood, the current attempt to get a large amount of Vikenti's flesh. It all clicked; such royal ingredients would work especially well, so well they might summon a certain particularly powerful creature with a penchant for swallowing souls. "Now I actually have said too much," said Jurek. "I tend to keep talking when I'm with weaklings. But tell me; which arm do you want me to tear off first?"

Daina ducked, dashed and weaved through Abdaas' strikes, narrowly avoiding the iron blade rushing through the air in front of her. She stabbed forward and sank her dagger into the robes covering Abdaas' chest, only to be stopped by something hard. Something metallic.

Abdaas grinned and stabbed forward, sticking the dagger into Daina's left shoulder. She cried out in pain, stunned long enough for Abdaas to raise a leg and push her away with it. She fell into the mud, Abdaas keeping his grip on his dagger so the momentum forced it out of her. It had not pierced her deeply but it still was no less painful for the victim.

"I may be fat from so many years without proper training, but it doesn't help that the armor adds a dozen or so pounds," said Abdaas. His free hand reached into his robes and brought up something bright and glimmering. Daina saw a cluster of interconnecting metal rings in his fingers, extending back into his robes and undoubtedly covering his whole torso. "This chain mail is made of the same material as the plate armor I gave the demons. You should be amazed your little bronze butter knife didn't break upon impact."

Daina huffed frantically as pain went off throughout her body, though especially in her left arm. She could barely move it on her own and the slightest touch to it sent more excruciating waves of pain through her. What little she could do with it was sluggish. Her eyes darted across the battlefield, seeing how the other combatants were faring. Alkin was struggling to remove the corpse of Wesan from his sword. Vikenti was moving closer to her, but slowly. And Aleksei's head was right under Jurek's clawed foot. She brought a leg up and kicked Abdaas as hard as she could in the shins, ignoring her wound. The priest fell back a little, wincing in pain nowhere near equal to what Daina was enduring. She forced her torso upright, twisting to face Aleksei and Jurek with her dagger in hand, fingers carefully grasping the blade before letting go as she hurled it at Jurek's head.

It went too low by mere inches and instead landed in the back of his right shoulder. Jurek yelled in pain and stumbled slightly, giving Aleksei the opening he needed to escape from under Jurek's foot. He rolled away quickly, leaving Jurek to fall to the ground. Aleksei found himself next to Alkin, Back Breaker ready for action and a hand outstretched toward his ally.

"I don't need nor want your help," growled Aleksei. He pulled himself onto his feet as Jurek hardened a claw and pointed behind himself. An earthen spike rose out of the ground and contorted itself so it bent toward him and ended with a hand. The hand grasped the hilt of the dagger and Jurek let out a yell as the spike pulled the blade out. The spike let go of the dagger and it fell to the ground before the spike returned back down into the earth.

"That... that's my limit!" roared Jurek. "I've had enough of this!" He charged forward, tackling the weakened Aleksei and pushing him underfoot. He trampled the smaller kuvi and, once past him, turned around quickly and grabbed him by one of his legs. He brought him over his shoulder and slammed him into the ground, and then a second slam in the other direction, topped off with a third slam at the same spot as the first. Jurek then spun around a couple times before letting go of Aleksei and hurling him like a living discus into a bog several dozen feet away.

Alkin recovered from his shock and readied Back Breaker, the blade facing outward like it had before Wesan had skewered himself on it. He prepared to attack but Jurek slammed the ground with a rigid claw, sending up the waves of spikes like he had done to kill the guards. Alkin escaped getting skewered but was still sent flying by the tremor, dropping Back Breaker in the process. Before he even landed on the ground Jurek had grabbed one of his feet. He slammed the human on the ground only once before he spun around and hurled him in the same direction that Aleksei had been tossed. Alkin landed only a few feet away from where Aleksei sank below the surface. Daina had watched it all with a look of horror on her face. She struggled to get to her feet as Abdaas stared in shock at the enraged kuvi. Jurek moved forward and stood in front of Daina as she finally managed to get back up. She pressed her right hand on the wound in her shoulder in an attempt to keep the blood in. Jurek snarled before smacking Daina across the cheek with a powerful backhand. Daina fell to the ground, unconscious.

"Never before have I seen you fight like that," said an amazed Abdaas. "Even for you, that was fantastic. Truly you are the apex of your species."

"That's the least you could say, damn it," growled Jurek. "The kid getting me twice across the face, fine. He's an arch kuvi with *Ateni*. He's tougher than he looks. But I won't accept some stupid bitch backstabbing me."

"Don't you say those things about my daughter, you vile creature!" yelled Vikenti, holding his sword out, still struggling with his weakened body.

"She certainly is," said Jurek. "And as unfathomably disgusting as it may be I'm going to have to violate her shortly after we arrive back at Tulroy. But don't worry, king; you'll be dead long before that happens."

"How dare you!" yelled Vikenti. He charged forward with every ounce of his strength, ignoring his pain as he swung his sword at the kuvi. Jurek effortlessly hit the blade out of Vikenti's hands before grabbing him by the jugular and hoisting him into the air like he weighed nothing. As he held the king up. his free hand went toward one of Vikenti's arms.

Jurek let go of Vikenti, who fell down to the ground bleeding profusely. The kuvi held onto the king's arm, pulled completely out of the socket.

Vikenti howled in pain as Jurek handed the bloody limb to Abdaas. The priest stared at the thing in revulsion but held it carefully, wrapping it up in a cloth from a pocket inside his robes.

"This arm's not going to keep," said Abdaas. "We need to get back to Tulroy as soon as possible." Jurek nodded and sprouted his massive wings. He reached down to the ground and wrapped a claw around Daina's waist. He picked the unconscious girl up and worked his arm around Abdaas to get a similar grip; Abdaas' chain-mail allowed Jurek to be less delicate when holding him. He jumped and let his wings take over, beginning their flight along the same path as before.

He flew onward quickly, always making sure to stay low to the ground. His wings beat rapidly to keep him airborne as he traveled across the air but he frequently slowed down while flying. Before he even crested the horizon he had touched back down on the ground several times. Only for a moment, but it was enough to make his flight seem more like a series of long jumps. An instant after each stop he leaped back up into the air, reinvigorated. It would be a long flight back to Tulroy, but Jurek would have no problem accomplishing the feat before the sun fell.

CHAPTER 31

Your gifts give you incredible skill at destroying, but don't neglect to use them for more civil purposes. Each gift is versatile enough to build or destroy.
-From the Tomes of the Huntmaster.

Vikenti lay on the ground, going into shock, paralyzed by the intense pain. His crown had fallen off his head and rolled into a nearby bog, never to be seen again. Some distance away the surface on the edge of another bog rattled. The rattling grew ever more violent, and then an arm broke through the surface and sank its digits into the ground. The arm pulled itself forward, freeing the body it was attached to from the foul water. The body gasped for air as it dragged more of itself and something else in its other hand out of the bog. Soon the body got its feet back onto dry land, and both hands worked to finish dragging out a sputtering, humanoid but distinguishably different shape.

Alkin let go of Aleksei after pulling the nearly-drowned kuvi out of the bog. Aleksei barely managed to get back onto his feet before placing his claws on his knees and bending over. He vomited, expelling every drop of disgusting water that had made its way into his mouth while he had been drowning.

He finished retching and stood back, wiping off his mouth before making his way to Vikenti. Hhe started heating up the drier of his two claws, reaching intense temperatures quickly and boiling away the water on the blade. Once at the dying king he got down onto one knee and placed the white-hot claw where Vikenti's arm had been, cauterizing the wound.

"Th... thank you," heaved Vikenti, his words barely audible, even to a kuvi.

"Don't speak," said Aleksei. "You can't afford to waste energy, especially if you want to see your daughter again. I have no idea what I'm even going to do with you but it will undoubtedly require you to have as much strength as possible."

Vikenti nodded, letting the fatigue catch up with him. "Tell... later," he mumbled before he finally fell unconscious. Aleksei sighed before standing up. He looked off into the distance, scanning the horizon for clues concerning where Jurek had traveled. He found the initial take-off spot, a depression left from when Jurek had jumped into the air. Off in the distance he saw a series of similar depressions; a perfect bread crumb trail to follow. Jurek clearly thought Aleksei had died in the bog or he would have landed in less obvious spots. Alkin ran behind Aleksei and picked up both Back Breaker and Daina's dagger. He ran back up to the kuvi, holstering Back Breaker and placing the dagger in his breeches for safekeeping. He stopped at Aleksei's side, out-of-breath from the excitement while Aleksei kept his normal composure. "We can't possibly reach Tulroy by foot before nightfall, not from this point in the Decay," said Alkin. "Especially with Vikenti like he is. You'll have to pick us both up and fly us there. You're a fast flier, right?"

Aleksei turned toward Alkin and stared at him in contempt, eyes glowing brightly. His jealousies throughout the past couple of days, coupled with his recent failures, culminated at this particular moment. "Surely that won't be necessary for someone so prestigious, so unparalleled as you," he growled. "You're quite the accomplished hero; slayer of terrible monsters and barbaric demons, heir to a mighty city and the exact sort of man who gets all the women swooning over him. You don't need a lowly murderer like me to aid you."

"Aleksei, you may hate me but I need you to calm down," said Alkin, backing away slightly. "There's something I need to..."

"I'm not going to calm down, damn it!" yelled Aleksei, swinging a claw and obliterating a nearby dead tree. He looked back at Alkin, his eyes brighter than the daytime sky. "I've endured enough torment these past few days. Being a kuvi in this decrepit world is bad enough, but I've taken more punishment than any human could endure. I'd love to see any human survive getting crushed underneath a building! To say nothing of how many times I've nearly been killed by both humans and kuvis alike! At least prior to all this my life was calm and quiet. The extent of my excitement was going out and killing a mire beast instead of some other creature every now and then. It was empty and lonely, but there was a familiarity in it."

"Aleksei..."

"Shut your damn mouth!" He paused for a moment. "And then I meet a princess, the same girl who had saved my life over a decade ago and restored my will to live. But of course she would not feel anything remotely toward me, not when she has a much more handsome man like you right at her side. A man with actual hair instead of quills, a man who probably sees colors and can appreciate whatever her hair's color is. But her unwillingness to make this favoring clear... It's just... it's too much for me to deal with at this point." The glow in his eyes completely died down, replaced by a very different emotion as he turned around and walked toward a fallen log. He checked that it was not too rotten before sitting down on it. He looked downward, unaware or uncaring that Alkin was walking toward him and taking a seat near him on the log.

"This kuvi has never had anyone really care about him," he said, his voice cracking slightly. "Not since he was forced into this world. There was a human, but she saw him as a replacement for her lost child. Then a kuvi, but she saw him as a stand-in for a brother. Attachment, yes, but not something that felt whole. And it's hard for him to display his feelings when just a single gaze into his eyes makes almost everyone faint or go mad. I'm unsure about this, but don't humans refer to the eyes as the gateways to the soul? What does that say about me, if my gateways cannot even be entered by most humans? What horrors are laying just past the entrances?"

His head fell even further ahead, hanging lower. "This kuvi has never truly had someone like him or care for him in that way he had always felt missing, and then he comes across someone that might actually be able to fill in that vacant place in his heart. But then he sees her going off, being held by another. It tears him to shreds inside. He knows he's stronger, more loyal, able to protect her better than anyone else in this world, and so willing to pay her back for what she did all those years ago that he would die before he saw her come to harm."

He raised his claws a little and looked at them. The palm faced him so he could better examine the sharp inside edge of the blades. "But then he sees these massive, clumsy things on the ends of his arms and he realizes exactly what the other one can do that he never can. These claws weren't made for being gentle; they were made to kill. Any motion, no matter how civil the intention, would only kill."

Aleksei let his claws fall to the ground as he looked downward. Alkin took this all in, working over his next words in his head. Then came the moment where he forced himself to say something. It came much easier to him than it had with Daina but it was still tough. "Aleksei, I meant to tell you this a while ago, but..." He stopped himself, struggling a little more before finally saying the words. "I'm not attracted to women."

Aleksei stopped and sat up straight to look at Alkin. The sadness in his eyes was replaced by a slight confusion. "What do you mean?" he asked.

"Exactly what I said," said Alkin. "I'm not attracted to women. I find myself more attracted to those of my gender."

Aleksei tried to comprehend this; the concept was foreign to him, but not inherently malignant. "You..." he said. "You don't like women?"

"I feel no attraction toward them in any way, no matter what they look and act like," said Alkin. "I never have. I liked Daina as a friend but I never wanted to go any further with her than just something platonic. I first realized this part of me at around my tenth birthday, but even then I knew what standards my father and my whole kingdom had for me, let alone the condemnations for it in the Teachings of the Goddess. You cannot fathom the outrage that would have been unleashed upon me if anyone had discovered this and had revealed my secret. My father would have disowned me, the Church would have shunned me and my citizens would have banished me to the Decay." He continued. "And as soon as I noticed this part of me I realized that people were becoming suspicious about my complete lack of interest concerning courtship and noblewomen. I was twelve and royal girls of similar age were pleading for my attention, quite literally in some cases, but I felt nothing beyond friendliness toward them. There were good souls among them, but I had no urge to develop a relationship further.

"So I decided to turn myself into a human of peak physical conditioning, engaging in as many tough, masculine physical activities I could find so the public could never associate me with my orientation. After all, what man attracted to other men could accomplish such heroic feats? How could he completely lack any interest in women when he's carrying one of the fairest maidens of Tulroy in his arms out of a burning building?"

"You were due to be wed to Daina, though," said Aleksei. "That's the cover reason for why you were being taken back to Tulroy. Weren't you to be married?"

"Not because I would have wished for such a thing," said Alkin. "I told her from the very beginning that I wished it to be solely a matter of politics. I didn't want her to become attached to me in such a way; it would not have been good for either of us. If it hadn't been my royal duty I would not have agreed to it. My father and my people would have expected me to marry the princess of the only other kingdom we've found in this world, and such a goal was the one reason I had managed to maintain for why I had not married one of the noblewomen in Tulroy. If we had been brought together in matrimony, Abdaas joining us before the Goddess instead of trying to murder us, I would have explained my secret before we walked down the aisle. I haven't even so much as tasted her lips, Aleksei."

"But what about after the fight you had with me?" asked Aleksei. "I had nearly defeated you before Daina had stepped in, so you did some boasting to make yourself seem stronger, talking about your diving into the Decay to kill creatures with your bare leathery hands. Didn't you do that to impress her?"

"That was to impress you!" said Alkin. "I had hoped some entertaining anecdotes would make me seem more than some foolish human to you. And I fully understand if you find this rather unsettling, but I'm going to be honest with you." He looked directly into Aleksei's eyes. "You are not ugly. Don't you ever tell yourself that. You are not ugly. Quill hair aside, you are actually rather handsome. All the boasting was just to make a good impression on such an amazing fighter." Alkin sighed and looked off into the distance. "Of course, it all seems so petty now. I overheard what Jurek was giving away to you about the plans to summon.... *Her*. Life as we know it is going to end unless we do something about it. We need to get to Tulroy and we need to get there fast."

He looked back to Aleksei and extended a hand. "I know you still want to save Daina, even after everything you have witnessed," said Alkin. "And if we work together we can stop that kuvi from violating her. You love her, and she definitely loves you as well. With you, her, Vikenti and my subjects, we'll stop Abdaas from calling forth the apocalypse."

Aleksei thought for a moment and then grabbed Alkin's hand with his own, shaking it gently. His claws did not cut into Alkin's skin at all. "It would be my pleasure to work with you," he said. "I feel awful about it all. I've been so curt to you, so hostile, and all that jealousy extended from nothing. I hope you can forgive me."

They released their grip and stood back up from the log. They walked back to Vikenti, who had not moved an inch. Alkin reached down and pulled the king up out of the mud. He tightened his grip around Vikenti's waist but not so much as to hinder his breathing. "It is fine," said Alkin. "I'm not hurt. As I said, who would have suspected it?"

Aleksei moved behind Alkin and worked to grasp him in such a way so he would not fall once Aleksei got airborne. It took some time but he eventually managed to find a suitable grip. "If we manage to get through all of this alive, I'd like to make this all up to you in some way," said Aleksei.

"You don't have to, but we can come to an agreement after we save the world," said Alkin. "And the longer we wait the harder that task will become." Aleksei nodded and jumped, taking the other two pairs of feet off the ground along with his own. He generated his wings and heat emanated off them with incredible intensity, keeping him airborne. He struggled only slightly under the weight he carried; even the weakest kuvi is significantly stronger than a human. The heaviness of his heart being gone also helped matters, giving him more confidence and sense of purpose.

Soon they were soaring above the dead trees and endless bogs, following the broken trail of depressions as it slowly led them to Tulroy. Jurek's landing spots also indicated shortcuts not accessible via the path. The creatures of the Decay looked up in interest, spying something their half-crazed brains could not recall ever seeing before. Even the oldest of mire beasts did not know what to make of it.

"Please don't drop me," said Alkin. The prince became somewhat queasy as he looked at the ground rushing away below him; the typical stench of the bogs did not help matters. "I haven't moved this fast since I tripped and rolled down the longest staircase in Tulroy."

"Exactly how long was this staircase you tripped on?" asked Aleksei.

"And how did this even happen to begin with? You usually seem careful and precise in your movements. You have to tell me how this came to be."

"I'd rather not," said Alkin. "The story's just as stupid as it sounds."

"I could use something light and stupid between everything that has happened today," said Aleksei. "And it doesn't help we have only Huntmaster knows until we finally arrive at your city. Please share it; the reality of what's about to happen is already setting in."

"You twisted my arm," said Alkin. "It all happened when I was fifteen. I was chasing some bandit into the upper levels of Tulroy when..."

CHAPTER 32

*The original couples settled around the site of My arrival, living within the
walls of the cave below. I aided them by hollowing it out more, making it
large enough to become the city it was destined to be. Though staying close
to my entrance to the world would not spare the sinners from their justly
deserved punishment. No sin is too small to be overlooked.*
-From the Teachings of the Goddess.

Jurek continued flying, only stopping to touch the ground and never
spending more than a second in contact with the earth. He traveled through
the Decay as fast as he could, old priest in one arm and unconscious princess
in the other. For hours he flew like this, making his way through the rotten
land before finally seeing his destination. A colossal plateau stretched out
before him, going on in both directions for miles. The side of the plateau was
surprisingly green and featured a series of holes and ledges. Even from this
distance he knew that hundreds of Tulrians were walking about the thin paths
the holes connected to, tending to the numerous vines the city cultivated so
high up in the air and collecting the eggs of the birds that lived among them.
He licked his chops as numerous memories came back to him. All too often
clumsy farmers found themselves plummeting to their deaths, but then were
stopped in mid-air. They then realized that, luckily, they had been caught.
Unluckily, they had been caught by Jurek.

"When you get closer, land by the main gates," ordered Abdaas. "I need
to speak to my cohorts stationed there. Few in Tulroy know of you besides
me."

"I'd imagine that Tulroy reacts to kuvis the same way all the other
human settlements react to us," said Jurek. "Though, I can't say I blame them
when it's me they encounter."

"Their opinion of you doesn't matter in the slightest," said Abdaas. "My
opinion of you is what matters, and with my blessing they'd let you bed their
mothers. Just do what I say, damn it. I'm so close to finally completing my
life's calling!"

Jurek said nothing; soon enough he would no longer have to worry
about the fat old priest. He arrived in front of the giant stone doors and
landed gently. He let go of Abdaas, who quickly ran up to them while the

kuvi held Daina in both arms. "This is Father Abdaas!" he yelled. "I demand that you open these doors at once!"

"Yes, father!" called out several guards just behind the doors. In a few seconds a group of guards were pushing the stone doors open. Jurek grew impatient and hardened a claw, facing it toward the doors and influencing the stones to move forward faster. Eventually they were fully opened, revealing a well-lit tunnel through the rock that led deeper into the plateau. Jurek smiled a little; rock and earth all around him, just the way he liked it.

A guard rushed up to Abdaas. "It is such a relief to see you... what is that demon doing here?" Jurek let out a loud snarl in response, chuckling a little as the guard cowered in terror.

"Pay him no mind," said Abdaas. "He goes by the name of Jurek. He saved my life moments before a mire beast would have torn me to shreds. Treat him as you would the king and his family, and send a messenger throughout Tulroy that he is to be left alone. He doesn't take kindly to nosy humans."

"But where is our exalted Prince Alkin?" asked the guard. "Please tell he has not come to harm! He couldn't have! He has defeated de..." He glanced at Jurek. "...terrible creatures no human could hope to!" Jurek thought about Wesan, his corpse rotting away in the Decay while his soul was destroyed in the depths of the Goddess. That would not be his fate, though.

"Nothing of the sort has happened to Prince Alkin!" Abdaas lied. "He and the guards I had hired are still at the city we discovered. It was a truly fascinating place, a city of stone towers surrounded by a thick wall. I give it no justice, but perhaps Prince Alkin will be a better storyteller than I when he arrives back home. May we please come in? This girl needs help."

"Of course," said the guard. He gestured to the other guards and they all moved out of the way, careful not to get within five feet of Jurek. His black quills stood on end as he got closer to a concentrated group of humans. His presence was enough to distract people from the arm-shaped bundle Abdaas was holding, and no one thought any more of the girl he held.

"I have a contact just beyond the main gates," said Abdaas to Jurek, careful to make sure the guards did not overhear. "I need to speak with him and get another command out. The king has been suspecting me of something for some time now and I will need to create a distraction so the ritual succeeds. While I'm preparing the other ingredients, namely the gaze of the enemy, get me her blood. I'll use the vial we already collected but only if you don't show up in time. That blood may be the difference between a successful summoning and a botched one."

"I'm not so stupid as to need the explanation," growled Jurek. "Kuvis aren't beneath humans in intellect. Getting you the blood won't take long, I assure you. I'm not going to drag this disgusting task out." He prepared to move away but then looked back at Abdaas. "Don't expect me to ever forgive you for making me do this."

"Whether or not you forgive me won't matter by the end," said Abdaas. "Once I'm done you'll never have to see me again and you can go back and surprise your uncle by being twenty years older."

Jurek nodded; never dealing with Abdaas again was definitely a plus. He ran ahead of the priest with Daina in his clutches. In moments the cramped tunnel opened up into a massive cavern; this cavern was the majority of Tulroy. Numerous cylindrical tunnels went upward along the edges of the main chambers, each one housing a flight of circular steps that connected to every level of the city. Homes and stores were built right into the rocky walls, from the bottom floor all the way up to the roof. Hundreds of lanterns lit up the chamber, illuminating the king's palace, the Church of the Goddess' bastion and the giant aqueduct that ran down to the central fountain from the aquifer just above the bastion.

While most kuvis would feel confined and perturbed by the sight, Jurek felt right at home as he gazed at it all. He jumped into the air and ascended upward quickly, getting high into the air so he could find an appropriately secluded place. He did not want anyone to see him finally perform his disgusting duty.

"And make sure it is taken care of as quickly as possible," said Abdaas. "Every second counts and I will not get a second chance at this."

"Yes, father," said the messenger. The limber young man ran off at top speed toward the palace, ready to initiate a secret plan Abdaas had arranged years ago for when his greatest work finally came to a close. This dealt with, Abdaas turned back to the guards stationed at the main gates.

"I hate to worry so much about him, father," said one of the guards, "but do you know when Prince Alkin will return home?"

"It's hard to say, given how the other city functions," said Abdaas. "The politics of it are slow, monotonous and convoluted beyond all measure. There's no way he could come back to Tulroy within the next day or so. Which reminds me of something else; it's important that you take it into account."

The guards all focused heavily on Abdaas, moving in slightly closer to better hear him. "While on our way from Tulroy to the other city we were set upon by two horrible demons," said the priest. "One looked like my companion except shorter and with red hair, but the other one was a dead ringer for the prince himself. Jurek threw them both into a bog, assuring me they drowned, but I have little doubt that they will emerge from those foul waters and make their way here. When they arrive you are not to let them in under any circumstances and you are to get the entire city on full alert. Those two must be killed on sight for the good of all."

"We understand, father," said the guard. All the other guards nodded in agreement, their faces stern. "Rest assured, they will not get into this city through these gates. We will die before they get in."

"I thank you greatly for your diligence in these trying times," said Abdaas. This done, he cradled the bundled-up arm carefully and started his slow run to the Church's bastion. He had a much longer trip ahead of him and, prior to that, an incredibly painful sacrifice to make.

The dreams came different from before. They were less organized and stable. Daina found herself drifting through them randomly, unable to wake up. But they were unified by the horror they conveyed, and each one was worse than the last. She saw Vikenti getting ripped to pieces by Jurek, his remains left to be picked apart by the monsters of the Decay. She saw Aleksei and Alkin struggling for air in the fetid bog water, eventually drowning and sinking to the bottom, their bodies destined to be preserved but never seen again.

But as horrifying as their deaths were, they did not compare to the devastation she witnessed spreading to everything she knew and loved. The walls of Tantallos fell to pieces as earthquakes shook the land, the formerly stable ground beneath the fortifications falling away. The already crumbling buildings of Tantallos followed suit, reducing themselves to rubble and raining down upon the innocent people in the streets, to say nothing of the ones inside the structures as they collapsed. In just a few minutes every last building in the city had been torn to the ground, not even a stone remaining in place as Decay creatures climbed the hills to pick off the few people who had survived.

Then the vision ended, leaving her drifting through a blackness. It was not an empty blackness; rather, it seemed like she was almost swimming through the blackness. Though her breathing was not hindered in any way, so Daina did not know what to make of it. In front of her a series of vague outlines formed. They made a thick circle with eight fang-like projections going inward. The lines on each side were parallel to each other. It was identical to the icon Aleksei had; the symbol of the Huntmaster. The lines on the inside of the circle seemed to be pulsating, moving in and out as if the circle was breathing. Like the mouth of a monster. No, not the mouth of a monster; the mouth of a god.

It makes sense I would imagine you as such, said Daina. *I could not possibly have known what you would actually look like, after all. Aleksei never described your appearance in-depth.* She thought it over some. *To think you've been living in me, ever since that night I spent sleeping in Aleksei's arm. Then again, you're not really the Huntmaster. I mean, you are, but you are just a small part of Him. I don't know. I'm not certain of anything anymore. All I do know is that I'm about to be raped by my father's murderer and this world is going to be destroyed because of it.*

She heard no other voice in the blackness besides her own but she felt a wave of emotions come over her, seemingly from the outline. The strongest was hope. Right after the emotional assault she fell into a new vision. In this one Aleksei flew over the landscape, holding onto Alkin and Vikenti so carefully he was not even cutting them. He was flying toward a massive plateau at an incredible speed, similar to how fast he had flown with Daina while dodging the crossbow fire.

It's a great weight off my heart, but I'm afraid it won't be enough, said Daina. *I can't believe it took me so long to figure out what Abdaas plans to do with the royal summoning ingredients. He undoubtedly thinks the Goddess would end all of our suffering once She arrives back on the surface, but at what cost? And who is to say life as we know it is over? We humans still survive in the Decay despite all odds. And Her arrival means the complete destruction of your innocent kuvis. But what can I do? Abdaas is probably starting the ritual right now and I'm still unconscious.*

She felt another wave of emotion emanate from the outline, this one dominated by confidence. Shortly after it overcame her an idea come to mind. *It could be done,* she said, *as much as I hate to drag even more from your world to this one. But I have to save Aleksei. He's gone through enough torment in his life without my former Goddess consuming his soul just because he's not Her creation.*

She felt nothing but happiness, courage, approval, and dedication. Then the outline faded away to nothingness, leaving her to finally wake back up.

"Damn it!" yelled Jurek as he dropped Daina onto hard ground. She opened her eyes and looked around in shock. She lay on the roof of a building near the ceiling of a monstrous cavern. All around her lanterns flickered, and when she glanced over the edge of the roof she shied way from the sides in horror. Even the one look gave her a horrible case of vertigo. She stayed close to the edge of the building that was only ten feet above the roof of the structure bordering it.

"It's truly amazing!" yelled Jurek. "It's almost as if you innately seek to make my life all the more miserable, even while you're unconscious! Couldn't you have just stayed that way for a few more minutes? This was an embarrassing enough task for any self-respecting kuvi to do. But I figured I'd be done and you'd be dead before you could wake back up. But of course you would wake up right after I land on this damn building, and I do mean *right* after I landed. Now I have to deal with your struggling and screaming before I can get some pleasure out of tormenting you."

"Jurek," she pleaded, "you don't have to do this anymore. No more violating me, no more listening to Abdaas. I've just received a vision that could help us all!"

"You are going to shut your mouth right now and not open it again until you're letting out your final screams," growled Jurek. "I'm sick of dealing with you."

CHAPTER 33

You [of Shaking] can make the ground you walk on bend to your will, and you can endure incredible pressure beneath its surface. But, the torrents can wash you away and creeping roots can hold you firm. And while your strength on the ground is unmatched, the moment your feet leave it your strength will fade away.
-From the Tomes of the Huntmaster.

Aleksei gained altitude while maintaining his fast speed, making his way toward one of the farming ledges lining the side of the plateau. "Are you certain about this?" he asked. "We're completely reliant on your information."

"There is no way Abdaas did not warn them about us approaching," said Alkin. "I wonder what lies he fed them. It's meant to delay us; he knows it would never actually stop us. Or at least stop you. Did you really catch that crossbow bolt as it flew past you?"

"Bigger issues at hand right now," said Aleksei.

"Of course," said Alkin. "The farmers out on the ledges may not have received the warning yet. We could hopefully get past them without spilling any blood. With me at your side they'd let you take their sisters out to dinner."

"That's fine by me," said Aleksei, baring his teeth. "There are only two creatures at the moment that I am going to rip to shreds." He slowed down as he neared a particularly wide ledge and once he was hovering over it he let go. Alkin and Vikenti landed safely on the ground, much to the shock of the farmers tending the vines nearby. They all gathered close to their prince while Aleksei landed a reasonable distance away, covering his eyes as the farmers near him backed away in fear.

"Your majesty!" proclaimed a farmer. "It's a pleasure to see you alive and well, but what horrible events have driven you up here and have forced you to consort with no less than a demon?"

"First," said Alkin, "he's not a demon. He's a kuvi. Second, Abdaas has turned traitorous against the royal family. He tried to kill me and it was only because of this kuvi that I still stand alive and well. I need you to alert every messenger within range and tell them to warn everyone; my father, the nobles, the guards, the soldiers, even the servants who clean the halls. They must be warned of this treason at once before Abdaas manages to surprise them!"

The farmers nodded, dropped their tools and took off immediately, each one headed toward a different messenger who would be able to run much faster than they could. Alkin got an arm around the barely-walking Vikenti's shoulders and helped him move toward the hole that would take them into Tulroy. Aleksei ran up next to them.

"I'm headed for the palace," said Alkin. "I need to see if my father's all right. I can take care of Vikenti, so don't worry. How are you going to find Daina, let alone save her? Tulroy is massive."

"You speak to a creature whose species name means '*hunter*,'" said Aleksei. "I will have no trouble finding her. I can track her scent easily, and Jurek will probably be at a place where few can see him. Most likely high up so he has a good view of the city."

"Best of luck to you when you find them," said Alkin. "That Jurek is a menace, so impossibly strong."

"Only while he's connected to the ground," said Aleksei. He moved in front of them, emerging into a more open part of the tunnel that overlooked the city. Sniffing the air, he caught a whiff of the scent he wanted. Without a moment's pause he leaped off the side of the path, sprouting his wings and soaring over the city in Daina's direction. Soon he reached the ceiling of the cavern, and Aleksei thought hard as he continued closing in on the scent. Each move he had used against Jurek had failed to properly incapacitate him. He had an incredible amount of durability, even without the armor. How could he hit the kuvi *dal Tinagmos* with enough force to weaken him prior to the loss of contact stealing the rest of his strength? Then it came to mind; good that it did as he finally saw his goal far off in the distance. He focused intensely, his claws glowing white as he quietly neared his target, readying himself.

Daina sat sprawled out before the kuvi. She looked around everywhere for a weapon, a rock, anything that she could use against Jurek, but nothing was in reach. The people roaming about were too far below for them to hear her, especially given how noisy the city was in the echoing cavern. She could leap to the roof of the neighboring building, but it would not keep Jurek at bay. And she could not jump off onto the street below without killing herself. She looked back at Jurek, who had started tearing off the plates covering his legs. He ripped off each piece easily but violently before throwing them off the side of the building. He was glad to finally be rid of the stuffy, bulky pieces of metal. Soon the last piece of armor was gone, revealing the torn breechclout he wore underneath the suit of armor. His flesh was much like Aleksei's in its similarity to human skin, but it was far more muscular. She did not even want to think about that body and how it was about to ravage her.

"This was not going to be a drawn-out, painful manner until you had the audacity to shove that dagger into my back," said Jurek. "Now you are in for such a long time with your friend Jurek, at least once I've finished this absolutely disgusting act. Rest assured, princess; it is going to be a long, long time before I let you reunite with your father."

"My father still lives, even if barely," said Daina. "Aleksei saved him by cauterizing the wound."

"I'm pretty sure that kuvis *dal Kafteros* are by far the worst swimmers in Proso," said Jurek. "They somehow manage to be even worse than kuvis *dal Tinagmos* like myself. Even if he somehow defied his lack of ability to swim or if that weak pretty boy saved him I doubt he could reach us in time to save you."

"Then tell me something I've been meaning to ask you," said Daina.

"I thought I told you to shut up," growled Jurek. "I'd recommend you start doing so or I'll--"

"Or you'll what?" asked Daina. "Kill me? You were already planning to kill me as slow as you could manage, so I have nothing to lose by disobeying you. Why do you bother collecting my blood if you object so strongly to having to violate me?"

["You have to know how summoning works by now," said Jurek. "The pretty boy knew how it worked."

"I do, but I want to know why you want to summon... *Her* so much," she said.

"I can't stand another minute in your dying world," said Jurek. "You humans are not worth the cold, hunger and complete destruction we kuvis endure while being forced to live here. Every extra second I can have in Proso, with my uncle and his clan, is enough of a compensation for having to collect your blood."

"Well, it is all the more unfortunate, then, that I no longer have any blood to collect," said Daina. "I've already given myself to another man."

Jurek chuckled, his *Ateni* easily deciphering her face and revealing her as a liar. Though he doubted he even needed them to see through that particular ploy. "Did you, now?" he asked. "Dare I ask who you gave yourself to? Please, surprise me. I cannot possibly fathom."

"Aleksei," said Daina. "I gave myself to him before the fight with you that leveled the building."

Jurek burst out laughing, acting so excessively he even slapped his knee.

"That's a laugh, princess. That pathetic excuse for an arch kuvi never got so far as tasting your lips, let alone bedding you. His scent's not nearly strong enough on you for that to possibly be the case. I actually offered him the task of collecting your blood if he joined me; kicking a dead horse now, though, since he's long since drowned in that bog."

Jurek had not gotten a chance to laugh like that in a long time. His arrogance and enjoyment of the situation blinded him to his surroundings as he focused more and more on Daina. She glanced at something to his right for a second but the kuvi did not take notice. "He did not drown in that bog, and he's going to kill you before you even get the chance to touch me," said Daina. "So long as the Huntmaster is in my heart. This last time you don't stand a chance." Jurek's smile faded before he could respond to Daina's claim. He slowly turned to the right as he heard the low whirring that accompanied the wings of a kuvi approaching top speed.

Aleksei charged directly into Jurek, the massive fireballs he had formed in both claws simultaneously exploding and obliterating everything nearby. Daina leaped off the building and landed somewhat clumsily on the nearby structure. She looked back to see a burning missile carry off Jurek while the entire building collapsed from the explosion. Aleksei adjusted his grip so he wrapped his arms tightly around Jurek's waist, even as he continued flying forward at a speed further increased by his dive. The flames coated both kuvis, burning Jurek all over and sending him through more pain than he had ever felt before. He howled with rage and broke free of the young kuvi's grip but Aleksei grabbed one of his feet before he could fall out of reach.

"Not today, Jurek," growled Aleksei. "I am going to kill you!"

"Damn you to the Cold One!" roared Jurek. He kicked upward with his free foot, nailing Aleksei in the stomach but with significantly less force than he had tried to apply; it was hard to concentrate with each nerve of his body crying out in pain. Aleksei lost his grip and Jurek fell, generating his massive wings and aiming for the nearest surface of any kind. Anything he could manipulate to form a barrier around him while he recovered. Aleksei almost instantly formed and hurled a fireball at Jurek, missing his back by only a couple feet but hitting one of his large and easily-targeted wings. The fireball exploded, shattering the wing and leaving it to dissipate into the air. Jurek fell, flapping his remaining wing uselessly. It soon disintegrated as well from an instinctual habit of preserving what was not broken.

Aleksei dived down, his greater speed and maneuverability allowing him to grab Jurek again with little effort. This time he gripped both feet so tightly his claws started crushing them. Jurek almost bit his tongue from the pain as he struggled, all while Aleksei attempted to move further into the center of Tulroy. Jurek hardened a claw and pointed it at the nearest rock fixture but failed to levitate so much as a pebble. He had been too long away from the ground and was now completely cut off from his alignment. For the first time he felt something that he had no idea how to react to; fear.

He swung himself upward, reaching his increasingly heavy-feeling claws up and grabbing Aleksei by the shoulders. He lacked the strength to squeeze so instead he pulled the young kuvi downward, aiming him so he was diving right at a stone wall. Aleksei struggled with the larger kuvi's grip and managed to break it off with barely enough time to pull up, twist one hundred eighty degrees and loop around. His wings missed breaking against the rock by the width of one of his quills. As he finished his loop he dived forward, moving away from the wall and back to the place he had intended. Jurek once more swung himself up, gripped Aleksei's upper body and forced him into a second dive, curving back around to aim again for the rock face. Aleksei managed to shake Jurek off his shoulders as well, more easily this time, but now it was too late to completely turn around.

The humans watching from below ducked as he flew directly into one of the stairwells, with barely enough room to avoid destroying his wings. For once in his life, Aleksei was glad they were not as big as Jurek's, and their graceful and smooth shape meant no part was sticking outward from the tips to be easily broken. He spiraled up the stairwell before escaping onto the topmost floor, Jurek nearly colliding into some dumbfounded peasants as Aleksei continued to pull him along by his feet. Jurek tried to move his body upward once more, but this time he did not even reach halfway. His claws, normally as weightless and quick as any kuvi's, felt like the massive pieces of metal they really were. They fell downward, Jurek unable to even move a digit, swinging uselessly back and forth as Aleksei brought him back out into the center of the city, over one hundred feet above the ground.

Aleksei swung Jurek upward, once again gripping him around the waist, adjusting him so that they were both facing forward. Aleksei slowed down as he neared the center of the main plaza, his wings soon beating and releasing energy in such a way to keep him in about the same place. Jurek did not have an ounce of strength left in his body. He looked longingly at the ground, everywhere around him but still too far away. Aleksei held him in a vice-like grip, so tight Jurek had trouble breathing. Aleksei adjusted his hold so that only one arm gripped Jurek's waist. "So tell me, Jurek," growled Aleksei, "which arm do you want me to tear off first?"

Jurek let out a final yell of defiance as Aleksei brought his free hand upward, gripping Jurek by the shoulder and sinking his claws in. He dug in deeply, tearing through muscle and separating bone before finally pulling away, snapping the arm right out of its socket and tossing it out into the city.

Jurek could do nothing, too weak to yell again or howl in pain. Aleksei's eyes shined brighter than the sun as he adjusted his grip to tear off Jurek's other arm as well.

Down at the plaza the civilians ran away as fast as they could from the scene while the two limbs hit the ground, splattering blood everywhere. They got what they thought to be a safe distance away and then watched as Aleksei adjusted himself so that both claws held the armless Jurek by the shoulders. Jurek's consciousness had not yet faded away as Aleksei dived down once more, placing his feet on Jurek's back and aiming directly for the ground. A split-second later and Jurek was obliterated, smashed to bits between the kuvi he had for years sought to kill and the surface he had so longed to touch.

Aleksei flared his wings, making them glow as brightly as his eyes as he let out a roar of triumph. He held his bloody claws up to the sky, even while cooling drops ran down the sharp blades. His quest for vengeance had finally reached its end. He let his claws fall back to his sides and both his eyes and wings lost their intense glow. In moments the eyes were back to normal, the fifth rings shrinking and the other eight moving back into their normal places. Most people had scattered by this point but a small group had remained, unable to look away. As he stared at them they did not collapse but instead applauded him, unable to think of anything else to do under the kuvi's gaze. Aleksei paid them no mind and jumped back up into the air, a new urgent goal coming to mind.

Daina pulled herself to her feet, bruised but unharmed by the fall from the collapsing building. She turned and watched as Aleksei quickly flew back to her, landing on the roof in front of her. In moments the blood-soaked kuvi stood before her, his wings disintegrating into the air as he looked at her. She stared into his black-and-red eyes and, for the first time, felt no fear or weakness creeping into her.

"Daina, I want to beg your forgiveness for my accusations of your faithfulness," he apologized. "Once again my anger clouded my judgment and..." He was cut off mid-sentence as Daina ran forward, wrapped her arms around him and planted her lips firmly against his. She broke off, Aleksei completely robbed of words as she continued squeezing him as tightly as she could, moving her head to the right side of his. Both of their faces were a burning red as he slowly and gently brought his arms around her, carefully keeping the inside of his claws from touching her back.

"Daina," he managed to say, "I'm covered in blood."

"I don't care, quill-head," she said, still hugging him, amazed with what she had managed to do. They shared this embrace for a few seconds more before Daina relaxed her grip on him. They broke away from each other, both of them smiling and too embarrassed to kiss again. Even the blood that Daina's clothes had picked up from Aleksei did not register with either of them.

"Never before have I really..." he said, looking away.

"Neither had I," she said, also looking away while still glancing at him. "Just thrilled to see you alive, I suppose." They managed to overcome their emotions and looked back at each other, faces beaming. "So I guess Alkin told you his secret?"

"He told me about his orientation," said Aleksei. "The idea had never occurred to me; it's not something in kuvi society. Or maybe it is, I don't know. But it does make me feel ashamed, considering how I kept treating him. And to think most of it was because I didn't think I was able to touch you without hurting you."

"There are a lot other things you can do to me without hurting me," said Daina, "and some things where I won't mind your hurting me." She giggled a little as she listened to her own words; never had she thought there would be a person she would actually say them to. Then both remembered what had brought them to Tulroy and their smiles faded. "But I'm afraid those things will have to wait for now," she said. "We have little time before Abdaas realizes he's not going to get my blood and he decides to proceed with the ritual. What happened to my father and Alkin?"

"I saved your father by cauterizing his wound," said Aleksei, unaware that Daina already knew. "He should still be with Alkin. Last I saw they were headed to the palace to warn the king of Tulroy of what Abdaas is planning to do." He sighed, shaking his head. "Abdaas means to call forth your Goddess."

"I know," said Daina. "I realized it while unconscious, and I came up with an idea. I'm certain that it will put a stop to Abdaas' schemes and save us all, you especially. But I don't want to share it until we meet up with everyone else. Nor am I sure I want to go through with it."

"We can decide upon that once we reunite with the others," said Aleksei. "And with your own personal arch kuvi that will take no time at all, princess." He reached behind Daina's legs and picked her up like a husband picks up his bride. He generated his wings again, ran to the edge of the roof and leaped off, soaring through the air. Daina relaxed, completely trusting in Aleksei's gentle grip. They flew directly to the palace, Aleksei's claws not so much as cutting through Daina's clothes.

CHAPTER 34

When I do, all souls below the earth shall rise to the surface and no more
shall go on; all will wait for me where I will reappear. And then only the
purest and truest shall return with me to Paradise. The rest, the sinners, the
failures, shall suffer my Punishment.
-From the Teachings of the Goddess.

Alkin helped Vikenti over to a small guard house just outside of the palace. He kicked the door open and the guards inside moved out of the way, watching their prince as he placed Vikenti in an empty chair and grabbed a sword from a nearby weapons rack. He handed the sword to the conscious Vikenti and turned toward the highest-ranked guard.

"Look after him until I get back and make sure he's taken care of," said Alkin. "He's endured a lot today, as you can imagine."

"Of course, my prince," said the guard, bowing. "But before you go, may I ask who he is?"

"He's the king of Tantallos," said Alkin, "and he has not had a good introduction to the people of Tulroy to say the least."

"Not a soul will harm him, my prince," said the guard. "Not as long as I breathe."

"Thank you," said Alkin before bolting out of the guard house. He ran around the perimeter of the palace and rushed into the stone courtyard. He burst in through the main doors, dodging a surprised servant as he made his way to the back of the palace. His goal was the throne room. He barged into the chamber loudly and saw a figure sitting on the gem-adorned throne. "Father!" he yelled. "Are you all right, father? Abdaas is initiating a coup even as we speak!"

He arrived in front of the throne just in time to see the large, golden-bearded king slump over, a sword protruding from his back. Alkin stared in shock and disbelief, unwilling to comprehend what he had just seen, before turning his eyes to a figure standing right behind the throne. "You are far too late," said the man, the symbol of the Goddess hanging from a chain around his neck. "Father Abdaas has given us the order to kill all who would stand in the way of his plans for our world's salvation. You and the rest of the obstructions shall be killed and your souls consumed by the Goddess as punishment for standing in Her way!"

Alkin ran away from the throne as the assassin's lifeless body lay on the floor, his face having been completely pushed in by Alkin's fist. The nose had been hit with such force it had penetrated his brain.

Outside of the throne room Alkin found that several groups of nobles had gathered in response to the noise, their guards and servants following shortly behind them. The hallway was full of the private soldiers the paranoid aristocrats had hired and trained extensively. In moments they were also joined by the king's personal guard, alerted by the servants Alkin had sent all throughout the city. The best fighters in all of Tulroy stood before him in that room. "The leader of the Church of the Goddess has betrayed the crown," said Alkin, burying his intense desire to mourn underneath his anger. "My father was back-stabbed on his throne, and the assassin lies dead at his side."

"Treason!" said one of the nobles. "What could possibly be the mindset of the Church of the Goddess?"

"This was nothing more than a distraction," said Alkin. "They aim to create panic, to keep us occupied while they do something far more sinister than even regicide. We need to get to the bastion immediately and stop Abdaas before he reaches the dolmens!"

"The dolmens?" asked a different noble. "You cannot possibly mean that the Church intends to summon--"

"Rest assured, he's not summoning anything so weak as a demon, or any such creature similar to them in power," said Alkin. "He carries with him royal ingredients and intends to awaken the Goddess Herself, and I don't think any of you need to be told why something like that would be catastrophic."

"But the Goddess would surely punish Abdaas for his traitorous acts and spare all of our souls," said a third noble.

"It is written in the final pages of the Teachings of the Goddess that She will only come back when it is time for the world to end," said Alkin. "No time for atonement, only time for punishment. I know you all well, and many of you have not been given the time you need to make up for your less than exemplary acts."

The nobles made no response to this. Not one of them had a truly clear conscience; even the ones who thought they were good managed to dig up sins to be ashamed of. Their silence and mumbling was broken when a guard ran up into the room, approaching Alkin at top speed.

"King Alkin!" he said, breathing heavily, his eyes as large as dinner plates.

"How could our situation possibly get worse?" asked Alkin, afraid to hear the answer.

"Your majesty, we are about to be attacked!" said the guard. "Even now people adorned with the symbol of the Goddess are leading a mob up to the gates!"

"Fortify the gates and make sure every entrance into the castle is locked up!" ordered Alkin. "I'd rather not have to kill my own subjects, but Abdaas leaves me no choice!" The nobles, guards, servants and everyone else scurried about, going to every possible entryway and barricading each one heavily. Many of them rushed down into the lower levels, reaching the armory and grabbing a mixture of crossbows and composite bows; whichever weapon the person was more comfortable using. Alkin soon stood alone in the chamber, feeling the hilt of Back Breaker still slung on his back.

An uprising, right when he needed every soldier possible to storm the bastion; Abdaas had covered everything, but even with this living Punishment about to rain down upon him his thoughts drifted to Vikenti, hidden away in a guard house that was hopefully far enough away from the palace; Aleksei, flying about in search of the one he loved; and Daina, at the mercy of a horrible monster. But deep down a part of him knew that was no longer the case.

Vikenti sat in the guard house, feeling useless as the soldiers ran themselves ragged barricading the door and windows of the building. Any other day he would have done what he could have to help them but now he felt beyond drained, constantly fighting back the pain of his cauterized wound. Aleksei's handiwork had saved his life, but he knew not for how long. Outside he could hear the approaching mob. Even if their goal was to storm the palace, it was all too likely some of them might decide to target the guard house as well. "How many are approaching the palace?" he asked one of the guards catching his breath.

"Far too many," the guard replied. "They're not at all trained for war and armed with far inferior weapons, but there are so many. Even with all the guards and the nobles' personal soldiers, we're outnumbered at least ten to one. Our only hope is that our fortifications hold them off while we wear them down with ranged weaponry."

"Is there any other way out of this building if we have to retreat?" asked Vikenti.

"There is, but it wouldn't help," said the guard. "There's a door to the roof, but we'd just be trapped up there while they storm the inside. However, they can't get in through there. Not unless they brought ladders or can safely jump down from a fall of at least sixty feet." They all leaped into the air as they heard a thump on the roof. The guards rushed for their weapons and they continued listening to the presence on the roof, moving over to the trap door and tearing it completely out of its hinges before tossing it to the side. Many guards trembled while assembling around the stairwell, spears and swords at the ready as this superhuman fighter slowly emerged into sight.

"Sorry about the door," said Aleksei, holding up his claws, palm forward and digits spread out. "These claws aren't good at locks. Last one I tried opening took me ages."

"Stay back!" yelled a guard, far more of a plea than a threat. Even as he stood there his weapon shook in his hands.

"Don't worry!" said Daina, running in front of Aleksei and throwing her arms out to divert attention from him. "He won't hurt you! We're just looking for my father, and then we'll leave you alone!"

Vikenti perked up at the sound of his daughter's voice and forced himself up out of his seat, leaning heavily on his sword like a cane. His face lit up like a fire as he saw his daughter standing by the kuvi. The guards moved out of the way, lacking the heart to hinder this reunion.

"Father!" yelled Daina, rushing forward and giving Vikenti a warm hug; she did her best to avoid the burnt spot that had been his arm. Even this loss did not take away from her joy. "It's true! You're really alive!"

"I'm so glad to see you in one piece," said Vikenti, tears rolling down his face. He tried to wrap his one arm around Daina but nearly fell over from the effort. Daina held him up as he quickly balanced himself again with the sword. "I just wish I was in one piece as well so I could hold you."

"It's fine, father," said Daina. She broke away from him, her face beaming. "I'm so sorry for my being angry at you earlier today. It was awful of me, and even though it already seems so long ago I want you to know how sorry I am."

"You were right to be mad at me," said Vikenti. "I was an obstinate fool, and now I know I was the one at fault all along. But how did you manage to find me? There are many guard houses like this one throughout the city."

"I tracked you down," said Aleksei. "I carried you for hours, after all. I was able to recognize your scent and follow it here."

Vikenti nodded and slowly approached Aleksei, refusing the help of Daina and everyone else. Each step was a labor to the weakened king but he suffered through it. In moments he was standing before the kuvi. "Aleksei," he said, "I want to thank you from the bottom of my heart for what you have done. Not so much for me, but for my daughter. You have no reason to forgive me for my plans to execute you, but I still beg you for it. If we somehow manage to survive this day I want you to know that you will forever be welcome in Tantallos and welcome in my home. It is the least I can do for your protecting Daina and saving her from that despicable fiend."

"Sir," said Aleksei.

"You can call me '*Vikenti*' if you wish," said the king.

"Vikenti," said Aleksei, "I would be delighted to accept your apology. Given how kuvis, including myself, have acted in your city you were fully justified. But I'm afraid we cannot stay here any longer; we have much larger issues at hand."

"What can we possibly do?" asked Vikenti.

"Daina says she came up with a plan," said Aleksei. "I'm taking us to Alkin so we can discuss it as a group. She's hesitant to share it, but if the plan has even a chance of working then we must do as she says."

"That's more than enough for me," said Vikenti. "Lead the way." He glanced toward the soldiers, who picked up their weapons and left the guard house to join in the conflict. Aleksei nodded and reached an arm around Vikenti, tightening and picking him up around the waist like he weighed nothing. He did the same with Daina and carried them both up the stairwell like so much luggage. Seconds later he was back on the roof of the building, staring at the complete carnage of the siege on the palace.

Thousands of peasants, possibly the entirety of the Tulrian lower class, armed with everything from staffs to vine farming equipment, battered against the walls and gates of the castle. Ladders slowly made their way to the front as soldiers along the walls ran about, pushing them away and sending many civilians falling back onto the weapons of their neighbors. The commoners had little in terms of ranged weaponry, but what they did have they hurled at the soldiers. Anything capable of harm was thrown at the unfortunate defenders. Aleksei looked it all over. The citizens were primarily focused on attacking the walls and front gate. No siege weapons were present, not even a battering ram, so it would take them some time to actually get in. They were hungry for blood but likely so single-minded they would not take notice of him while he flew over them. But where to land?

"I see a parapet at the back," said Aleksei. "There's a single person running about, yelling out orders to nearby men who relay them to soldiers throughout the perimeter. It looks... yes, it's Alkin." He generated his wings and soared into the air.

"I hope he has a moment to spare," said Daina as they passed a hundred feet over the ground. Aleksei continued climbing so to better obscure them; just in case the villagers aimed for him as well. "Huntmaster knows how long before all this manages to get worse."

In Tantallos, it managed to get worse. Back in the walled city people had recovered from the shock of Aleksei's showy escape. The aides of the king watched over the throne in his absence, focusing primarily on calming the populace. The city's portcullis could not be fixed; the aged machinery had been damaged too much by the demon. However, despite the damage people were conflicted concerning the creature's motives. The demon had not killed a single guard. He had wounded dozens of them, but they all were recovering. The throne room's main doors had been replaced already, the fire having not damaged much besides them. All in all, the demon could have done much worse.

And if he went after the princess and king, who is to say he had worse intentions in mind? He would gain nothing by attacking them and he had spent so much time keeping the princess alive. If nothing else, the unparalleled Prince Alkin was still with them. A farmer thought all this over as he moved about his field in a corner of Tantallos, checking to make sure the budding plants were growing as expected. For once the buds were coming in correctly; barely any appeared to be stunted or badly formed from poor nutrition. He smiled to himself, feeling pride in his getting the soil to just the perfect conditions. He checked the irrigation as well to make sure the water was flowing correctly from the above-ground reservoir.

He felt a slight rumbling under his feet, not strong enough to make him fall but strong enough to make him worry. He looked about rapidly but sighed in relief; no buildings nearby had collapsed and the wall still held firm. He felt another rumble of similar strength but did not let it concern him as he continued his inspection. Then he stumbled as his foot got caught on something hard and sharp. He turned around and looked down in confusion; did someone leave a gardening tool in his field? He saw something dark and gray glimmering in the dirt, shifting about, revealing more and more of itself. It looked like a massive gauntlet, with menacing knives fastened to the knuckles of the fingers and thumb, seemingly bending as the digits did.

He gasped in shock, stood up and backed away as another demon claw emerged alongside the first one. The ground moved about as a blue, translucent sight bearing the shape of a bald head emerged from the ground between the claws. The farmer backed further away, a scream caught in his throat as he saw more and more of this phantom come out of the ground. Soon it stood before him, easily seven feet in height, a red glow pulsating from where its heart should have been. It seemed just solid enough to exist, but there was no denying that the claws were quite real. "I'm finally free, but the hunger is still there," moaned the demon. "The hunger! The hunger! I'm so sorry, human, but I just can't stand it!"

The farmer tripped and tried to crawl away as the phantom ran to cut him off. It raised a claw up high, preparing to bring it down in a crushing blow on the human's head.

CHAPTER 35

You can be kind and merciful, but never forget that you are still a hunter.
The desire to hunt and feed on flesh is something that you must learn to
accept or control, for it will always be with you.
-From the Tomes of the Huntmaster.

Alkin continued barking out orders to his designated runners, who then relayed these orders to the nobles and head guards who controlled their respective troops. Servants ran across the battlements, tending to the wounded, bringing ammunition and reloading crossbows for the rangers still standing. The peasants and zealots continued spilling out of the stairwells, forming a sea of enemies around the palace's walls. The old stone structure held firm, no buttressed gate or barricaded entrance giving, but each new arrival of reinforcements further pushed the odds in the favor of the assailants. Alkin felt at least one weight lift from his heart as he saw a glowing red shape in the sky, completely ignored by the angry mob just below. He watched it approach his current position while also yelling directions at his subjects. He finally paused as Aleksei landed gently in front of him, letting Daina and Vikenti get their feet on the ground before letting go.

"It is good to see you all alive, even if we have to meet under such terrible circumstances," said Alkin. "You especially, Daina. I knew Aleksei would win in the end." He looked at the mob assaulting the palace. "Abdaas is going to be executed for this, and by my blade. The zealot killed my father."

"We all have a reason to kill Abdaas at this point, Alkin," said Aleksei. "And with your help I doubt we can lose."

"This collection of nobles, guards and servants won't hold back the civilians forever," said Alkin. "I need to be here to ensure they continue to do so."

"That's treating the effects and not the sickness, Alkin," said Vikenti. "You're far stronger than any other man I've met, even if you're not as mighty as a kuvi. And Daina and Aleksei will need your help to get to Abdaas before he summons the Goddess."

Alkin slowly nodded, as much as he wished he could not. "I will do what I can," he said. "Are we leaving for the bastion now?"

"Not before I discuss something with you all," said Daina. "While I was unconscious I received a vision of some sort, a premonition of what we need to do. It will not only save this world but the souls of every kuvi trapped in it."

"What?" asked Aleksei.

"This is no place for a calm discussion," said Alkin, "or a quiet one. We'll talk about it in the hall below. I trust my subjects to perform well without me during that time." He pointed them toward the stairwell that led back down into the palace. As they walked to it he called out a few more orders to the runners before heading for the stairs as well.

"Where are you going, King Alkin?" asked a runner.

"I won't be gone for long!" said Alkin. "I trust you all enough to keep them at bay without me!"

"Of course, your majesty," said the runner before going off to make sure all the defenders were aware.

Alkin led the group to an empty hallway far into the back of the palace, safely out of the way of the battle. It appeared to be a series of living quarters, reasonably lavish; it reminded Daina of the hallway her room and the guest rooms were located on. "Most of these rooms are just guest rooms, but one is special," said Alkin, gesturing at the door in front of them. "It's not used as a guest room as it contains a passageway out of the palace and into an unassuming location on the edge of the city. We can use it to walk right underneath the angry mob and walk around the back of them to reach the bastion. This would be safer than flying; it would only take one person to notice the pair of large, glowing wings in the sky before they turn their attention on us."

"Sensible," said Aleksei. He felt himself smile inside at his wings being called *large*, even if he had grown comfortable with them being smaller.

"But, before we take this path," said Alkin. "You mentioned getting a vision of what we need to do, Daina?"

"I did get an idea," said Daina, "but the more I think about it, the more I don't think I can go through with it."

"Daina, any plan is better than no plan at all," said Vikenti. "We need to be willing to sacrifice everything to save this world. Share your plan, please."

"Okay," said Daina. "Abdaas is using the royal ingredients to summon the Goddess. The quality of these ingredients is apparently enough to call forth a divine being. I was thinking that we could use a group of royal ingredients of our own to summon..." She paused for a moment. "...to summon the Huntmaster, Aleksei's god, better known to him as *Prosopsei*."

Everyone looked at her in a mixture of disbelief and shock. Aleksei let it all sink in before recovering enough to speak. "*Mirke dal mi Prosopsei*," he said.

"Does it not even have a chance of working, Aleksei?" she asked.

"It should work," said Aleksei. "The Huntmaster is a god of destruction. He's normally forbidden from entering the worlds of beings of creation, like the Goddess. He's only allowed in at the end of days to destroy the world and the being of creation if need be; everything comes to an end but both gods and worshipers can deny it. Since the Goddess' return is an indicator of the end of days, He would be allowed into this world. My disbelief comes from that you would summon Him to begin with."

"I know almost nothing of your religion, Aleksei," said Daina. "I may only know the one creation story, but I know the presence I've felt in my dreams. It's a piece of the Huntmaster like you kuvis carry in your own hearts. In what little time I've had I've come to believe that He is a powerful and kind being. I believe He would be able to reason with the Goddess and return you and the rest of your kind home. That way, none of you would ever have to suffer living in the Decay again. Your soul would have an afterlife and you could finally reunite with your mother after all these years."

Aleksei locked eyes with Daina and put his claws gently on her shoulders, gripping them gently. "I do miss her," he said, "but I'd rather remain with you than return to Proso." He let go. "Though I'm sure none of the other kuvis that still live share my opinion. But how do you plan to call Him forth? I have a basic understanding of summoning rituals but that won't give us the ingredients."

"That's the biggest problem," said Daina. "Do you still have the bones?"

"They haven't left my breeches," said Aleksei. "They've managed to escape harm so far." He reached into his pocket and carefully picked out the pieces of bone one at a time before inspecting each one. Despite the one carrying them enduring so much punishment, the bones had not been so much as fractured. He put them away as carefully as he had taken them out.

"That's one I expected we would have," said Daina. "It's the other ingredients that make the plan fall apart. We don't have the gaze of the enemy."

"Not unless you count mire beasts," said Vikenti. He leaned heavily against the wall, freeing up his hand so he could dig through his robes and unearth the preserved mire beast eye. "Not the smartest of my opponents, but undoubtedly the toughest I've ever fought. I'm reluctant to count the one who tore my arm off as that wasn't a fight. This eye should work well, if I understand the summoning rules correctly."

The group grew silent. Daina looked up at her father, eyes starting to water as the other two men looked at the king as well. "That still leaves the..." started Alkin. "The flesh of the father..."

"No," said Daina, looking at Alkin. "I hate to ask, but isn't your father already dead? Couldn't we use his?"

"I wish we could," said Alkin. "The father, mother and daughter must be related to each other for the ritual to work. Only the enemy doesn't require blood ties."

She turned to her father. "If only you hadn't offered that eye," she said. "You've been through so much today." She walked up to Vikenti and embraced him tightly. "I don't want to lose you, daddy."

"Don't be sad, Daina," he said, pocketing the eye and putting his arm around his daughter. "I'm old, past my prime, and I'm not half as strong as I used to be. Age has certainly crept up quickly on me; I like to blame the broken wall I had stood by for so long, defending my city. But, I've lived to see the best things in the world."

He let go of Daina and used his hand to raise her chin, bringing her eyes to face his. "I've lived to see my only daughter grow up, and now I've lived to see my daughter find someone that she loves." He looked to Aleksei as he said this. "He's nothing like I had expected, but in the end I know he will treat you better than any other, and that's all I want."

"Thank you," said Aleksei.

"Please," begged Daina. "I don't want to kill you. I can't kill my own father."

"Don't worry," said Vikenti. "You won't have to. But as it stands I need to die for the rest of you to save this world. You will be a great queen, Daina. But not a stone in Tantallos will remain if the Goddess starts causing the end of the world. It would be selfish of me to choose my own life over the lives of countless others." He looked at Alkin. "You still have Back Breaker in spite of everything. Aleksei cannot kill me, for Daina's sake. Will you do it instead, Alkin?"

"As much as I hate doing so, I will," said Alkin. He looked at Daina, regret on his face. "I just hope you're able to look me in the eyes after I do this, Daina."

"Better you than anyone else, Alkin," said Daina. "I won't hold it against you. You'll still be my friend." Daina gave her father one last hug, tears brimming up in her eyes. They whispered a final goodbye to each other as they shared this embrace, the last showing of affection they would ever feel from each other. They eventually released each other and Daina backed away. Vikenti looked Aleksei in the eyes and extended his hand.

"Take care of her for me, Aleksei," he said.

Aleksei took Vikenti's hand carefully and shook it. "I'll protect her from the Goddess Herself if I must," he said.

"I'm going to hold you to that," said Vikenti. They looked each other in the eyes, Vikenti seeing a passion and dedication hidden among those nine red rings. He let go and hobbled his way to Alkin with the aid of his sword, which he had propped up against the wall. "Lead me to wherever you would prefer to get it over with."

Aleksei and Daina watched as the two disappeared around the corner, trying not to think about how only one would be walking back. They looked at each other in contemplation; Daina had moved close to Aleksei and was clinging to him for support, more emotional than physical. Aleksei tried to move their minds off what was about to happen. "You're forgetting something," he said. "We're still missing the fourth ingredient."

"I know," said Daina. She felt her heart start pounding heavier as she remained so close to Aleksei. "My blood. I'm sure there are some vials in these rooms." She let go of Aleksei and moved into the nearest room; it was well-maintained and featured an assortment of weapons on the tops of dressers. Among it all she spotted an empty bottle with a cork stopper sitting on the nightstand. Aleksei followed and stood by her side. "That's covered. We should be fine if we collect it fast enough."

They turned back to each other, Daina looking slightly upward. "Where would you prefer me to cut you?" asked Aleksei. "A cut on the arm, or maybe somewhere else? No matter what I do, I'll have to hurt you."

"I was thinking of something else," she said, slowly moving closer to the kuvi. Both of their hearts were beating faster and faster. "It's all too possible that Abdaas has already started the ritual, even as we stand here. We're running out of time."

The distance closed between them. Aleksei thought back to the kiss on the roof of the building. His *Ateni* picked up similar movement patterns, but he was too stunned to move. His heart felt like it was about to burst from his chest. "You don't mean... that?" he asked, turning red in the face.

"It will speed up the ritual," she said, just as red as he was, wondering how to go about it all in the correct way. She felt lost, drifting, acting on instinct before thought. "And, if anyone was to take it from me, I'd rather it be you. Believe me, I'm so scared right now, and I can't fathom what is coming out of my mouth, but..."

She sighed. She too thought back to the kiss on the roof. She looked away for a few moments, failing to find the right words. She then looked back toward Aleksei and embraced him tightly, again bringing her lips against his. They both relaxed in the other one's grip as the moment seemed to last forever, their affection boiling over and turning into passion.

Alkin and Vikenti slowly made their way to the throne room, encountering no one; everyone else was outside, fighting off the civilians. A servant had placed a shroud over Alkin's father, covering up the horrible sight. They came to a stop several dozen feet in front of the throne. Alkin helped Vikenti stand up on his own by grabbing him a spear to put his weight on. Soon they stood opposite each other, Alkin grabbing Back Breaker and bringing it to his side.

"So, this is how my life ends," said Vikenti. "Brought down by my own blade... It's fitting in an odd way. I can't quite describe it."

"I wish as well that it could be any other way," said Alkin. "But what Daina said could work. I don't know of this Huntmaster the kuvis worship, but if Daina believes Him to be a force for good then we have to trust her, right?"

"You may have your doubts about the plan, but I don't," said Vikenti. "My daughter has proven herself right about so many things, and all this may not have even happened if not for me. Take your swing."

Alkin sighed, working himself up to the task before him. He slowly picked up the massive blade, every fiber of his being telling him not to go through with it. He forced himself to bring the sword back over his shoulder, readying his swing. Vikenti watched and breathed outward, remaining strong. "King Vikenti, may you find your just reward in eternal Paradise," said Alkin, bringing the sword around and cleanly beheading the king.

Alkin somberly walked back to the room where he had left Aleksei and Daina, a bloody sack in one hand. Back Breaker was once again holstered, dripping with the same blood leaking through the sack. The sack bent and contorted freely as there were no bones inside it. In moments he arrived at his bedroom; he had insisted on sleeping in the passageway room in case he ever needed to leave at the drop of a hat. He knocked warily on the door. Why was it shut to begin with?

"Come in," said Daina. Alkin opened the door, revealing Aleksei and Daina standing in each other's grip. Daina clutched a stoppered bottle full of blood. Both of them seemed tired but happy beyond words.

I am never sleeping in that bed again, he thought to himself. He looked at the couple. "I had been wondering about the blood, but even when I pondered it I knew it would come about like this. Now follow me. We have a lot of ground to cover and only so much time before the apocalypse happens."

"Then show us the secret entrance," said Aleksei. Alkin moved around them carefully and made his way over to the back wall. It featured no paintings or decorations of any kind, only a large wardrobe. He fidgeted with the side of the wardrobe for a time before finding a switch hidden in the ornate carvings. He pressed the switch and they heard a loud click as a lock was undone. Alkin pushed the wardrobe and it moved to the side on tracks hidden into the floor, revealing a rather primitive-looking hole in the wall just big enough for a person to walk through while hunched over.

"It's a very long walk, especially given the conditions of the tunnel," said Alkin, "but the building it leads to is right by the bastion. We will reach it faster than we think." Suddenly there was a massive crash, coupled by a shaking as a loud yelling became noticeable. They heard several different voices cry out in pain as more and more frenzied, wrathful voices overpowered them.

"Damn it all," said Alkin. "The mob must have finally broken through." He thought over this development quickly, coming to a decision in almost no time. He handed the sack to Aleksei, who held it carefully. Alkin reached into his clothes and pulled out the preserved eye, which he gave to Daina. "I took it off him. You two travel on ahead. The tunnel's straightforward so you'll have nothing to worry about."

"We can't leave without you, Alkin," said Daina. "We need you!"

"No, you don't," said Alkin, smiling slightly. "Not with Aleksei. He easily trumped me in a fight. I wasn't even a challenge, but I can hold my own against other humans. I'll just stay here, keep them at bay while you two go on. Everyone knows my face so I would only draw attention to you." He pondered this. "Well, it was an honor to know you both. You two live a glorious life in my absence."

Daina gave Alkin a quick hug before breaking away. Alkin and Aleksei shook hands. "Do what you must," said Aleksei. "If only the peasants were smart enough to not attack you."

"Not so much intelligence but force of will," said Alkin. "They're too easily manipulated. But it's too late for that now; go and stop Abdaas before he makes this even worse." Aleksei and Daina nodded, Alkin stepping out of the way to let them enter the tunnel. He waved a final goodbye before moving to the side of the wardrobe. He pushed it back with all his might, effortlessly returning it to its original place.

On the other side of the wardrobe, Aleksei and Daina found themselves in darkness. Aleksei's right claw glowed white before a few bits of fire sprouted on it, creating enough light for him to see by without suffocating them. He grabbed Daina's hand gently with his free claw and led her along through the tight corridor, cautioning her every time the floor got rough and capable of tripping them. The tunnel sloped downward and made slight turns, and overhead they could hear the stomping and trampling of hundreds, if not thousands, of feet. Then they heard something else, a very different rumbling all around them. The corridor only shook slightly, but everywhere they heard shifting and shuffling. It was as if hundreds of things were moving around in the ground surrounding them, making for the surface.

"Daina," said Aleksei, "even if you don't follow Her anymore, you're familiar with the Teachings of the Goddess, correct?"

"I've spent nineteen years learning about the religion," said Daina.

"Is anything special supposed to happen when She wakes up but before she ends the world? Does anything happen prior to Her arrival?"

"It's 'all souls shall rise to the surface and no more shall go on' or something similar," said Daina. "Never really understood the first part. If a soul's under the surface, it's a damned soul about to be consumed by the Goddess... unless there's a colony of people living hundreds of feet below. Even then, I don't think a soul would make such an impact on the world around it. It's an incorporeal entity, I'd imagine."

A horrible thought occurred to Aleksei. "Something tells me this wasn't supposed to happen according to Her teachings," he said.

Alkin stood guard by the wardrobe, watching the closed door opposite him carefully as he heard the peasant army approaching. The civilians slowly went about the extensive palace, slaughtering his faithful subjects, killing the people who had governed over them peacefully for countless generations. He barely even noticed the ground shaking slightly under his feet, pinning the tremors he noticed on the amount of people stomping about. He felt a nervousness grow inside him as the voices came closer. Then outside he heard the screams of death increase exponentially. The triumphant outcries of the peasants and zealots were almost instantly replaced by jarring shrieks of torment and wails of fear. He felt his heart pumping harder as something unknown tore through the commoners with unholy speed, ending each and every last scream as whatever was causing these fatalities completely annihilated the hoard.

Then he heard noises outside of the door. The middle of the door splintered as four sharp, short blades effortlessly pierced through the wood. The claw withdrew and another blow from it obliterated the door, showering Alkin with bits of wood. He looked in the doorway and saw a luminous, blue shape with a red heart and two solid kuvi claws attached to the ends of its arms. Something about it struck Alkin as familiar. Then it hit him.

"Is that you, Wesan?" he asked, readying Back Breaker.

"It hurts, pretty boy," said Wesan, moving into the room. "The humiliation of dying by your hand, the torment I endured by the jaws of your ruling being. I would love to tear you apart right now, but I have someone who would like to see you. He's been broken by the pain, mind you, so he might not be that coherent."

Another kuvi ghost moved into the room, similar in composition but slightly shorter. The claws were a very light gray, and this allowed Alkin to recognize it almost instantly as the kuvi he had killed all those years ago, allowing Tulroy to discover the properties of kuvi relics. "I guess you have both come for your revenge," said Alkin. "Well, I'm not about to run away."

"More flesh!" yelled the nameless kuvi, claws forward. "This hunger, it never ends! It's never sated! It hurts, it hurts so much!" Wesan and the nameless kuvi charged at Alkin, claws outstretched. Alkin could not possibly fight a ghost, but with their claws they could attack him. All the same he readied Back Breaker for a swing and prepared himself for death.

"A fitting death for a warrior," he said as the swing passed through the blue bodies of the kuvis harmlessly and they readied their claws for fatal slices.

CHAPTER 36

There is no tougher survivor than you. You can endure the harshest environments and survive the magics that cut down all the others around you. You are a hunter.
-From the Tomes of the Huntmaster.

Aleksei and Daina finally felt the tunnel gradually slope upward, but it made them feel as nervous as it made them feel relieved. "Huntmaster's mercy, what has been happening above us?" asked Aleksei. "Those were not the screams of humans killing humans. Something far worse did that."

"What could possibly have killed so many humans in such a short time?" asked Daina.

"I don't know for sure, though horrible ideas occur to me," said Aleksei. "I fear I recognize those screams all too well. At least the ones the women were making. I heard them several times when... when I was living in Tantallos as a child."

"So you think it's a group of kuvis?" asked Daina. "Where could so many have appeared from to massacre the entire mob, though?"

"That's the biggest question," said Aleksei. "No amount of kuvis would live so close to one another without running out of prey. Maybe that's why they risked attacking a whole city. Let's hope they're satiated after all those humans. I don't want to fight so many at once."

"I'm not the only one in danger, quill-head," said Daina. "Kuvis can be cannibals."

"Don't worry about me, queen," said Aleksei. "All else fails, run to the bastion while I distract them. You're fast on your feet for a human and I can keep them busy for longer."

"Huntmaster willing it won't come to that," said Daina. "I have no one else now." She wondered if this was how Aleksei had felt for so many years spent alone, surrounded by hostile forces interested solely in killing him. They encountered some wooden floorboards covering the ceiling, which Aleksei tore and broke through with ease. He hoisted himself out of the tunnel and Daina pulled herself out as well, not needing any help from the kuvi. They were in a very small, very cramped building, not even ten feet long from one wall to the other and loaded with brooms, bins and other such supplies; it was a cleaning closet for city staff. There were no windows and only one door. The two of them walked to the door and stopped by it, Daina's hand inches away from the knob. She could not get her hand to move forward.

"Sorry," she said. "Can't help but feel so scared."

"Do it quickly," said Aleksei, "before you have time to think about it."

Daina shut her eyes, grabbed the handle and yanked the door open, nearly hitting Aleksei with it as it swung inward. Aleksei moved to the other side of Daina. She opened her eyes and let out a sigh of relief; the building connected to a stairwell on the edge of the city, well out of the way of the action. Not a single thing of note was in sight.

They slowly walked out of the structure and approached the gateway to the city from the stairwell. All around them they heard screams and shrieks as more and more humans, innocent or not, man or woman, adult or child, met their ends at the hands or claws of this unseen terror. They cautiously moved into the main cavern and Daina barely stopped herself from gasping. Her eyes widened as she stared at the slaughter; the entire mob of peasants and zealots had been torn to pieces. Not a single person still lived. The center of Tulroy surrounding the fountain had become nothing more than a pile of bloody flesh and broken bones, the smell overpowering all of the other aromas that would normally be present. Aleksei felt a hunger growing inside of him as he took in the smell of the meat, but he shook his head rapidly and forcefully. This was in no way the time for such matters.

Then they saw the ones who had massacred the entire populace of the city, moving about among the carcasses, bending down as if feasting on the people they had killed. They were blue and humanoid, with red cores and corporeal claws. "*Mirke dal mi Prosopsei*," whimpered Aleksei. "*Alekis dal kuvi.*"

"In human tongue, please?" asked Daina quietly, unable to look away from the creatures.

"The souls of dead kuvis; kuvi ghosts, basically," he whispered. "But I thought they were just stories meant to scare children."

"Kuvi ghosts?" asked Daina. "But why do they still have their claws, and why are their hearts red?"

"Our claws are identical to those of the Huntmaster's," whispered Aleksei. "He retains his claws in the spiritual realm, so we do as well, no matter if our body's claws have fallen apart. And each red heart is undoubtedly a piece of the Huntmaster. If the stories are correct, these kuvis are completely overcome by their blood-lust and killed all the humans to try and satiate themselves, but in vain."

"They killed all the humans?" asked Daina, readying her dagger, watching a group of blue kuvi ghosts dangerously close to them.

Mirioe saw them, standing at the tunnel entrance, two living creatures waiting to be eaten. Her hunger overpowered all her other desires, but it did not stir her to attack them. It only made her attack humans. One, the taller one, was definitely a kuvi. Huntmaster forgive her if she let herself attack and feed on a kuvi. The other wasn't, but she felt no urge to attack the smaller one. She was definitely a human, but she did not have the internal glow of a human. Humans glowed blue, but this one was glowing red. The Huntmaster was in her heart as well. Like all the other kuvis that noticed the duo, she ignored them. She already had plenty of meat that she passed through her blue, translucent body. It did little, but it helped just enough to make her continue doing it.

The two slowly and carefully walked among the disturbing sights: piles of mutilated bodies, puddles of cooled blood everywhere and kuvi ghosts throughout feasting freely. Each kuvi they came close to looked at them for a time, considered them, then looked away and resumed its attempts to feed itself in vain. Aleksei and Daina walked closely together, an arm around the other while the free hand held the supplies. Even the bloody summoning ingredients did not interest the kuvi ghosts; they were already occupied by the gore freely available on the ground. "How are we still alive?" asked Daina, not bothering with whispering. Ghost or not, any kuvi feasting nearby would be able to hear her.

"The Huntmaster does disapprove of kuvis eating their own kind," said Aleksei.

"How am I still alive, then?" she asked.

"Thank the Huntmaster when you meet Him," he said. Then they arrived outside of the bastion. It was just as imposing close-up as it had been far away. It was a fascinating structure with walls that extended from either side of the building to create a courtyard of sorts. The primary building was a mixture of the main headquarters to the left side and an impressive cathedral to the right. They were connected by a long hallway. Both parts could be accessed by front doors that led into the courtyard.

They moved in, watching warily for anyone remaining. All they found were two kuvi ghosts, blocking their way. However, unlike the other ghosts, these ones approached the two with their claws outstretched. "Ghosts of the kuvis unfortunate enough to have died in this world," said Daina, "I beg of you, please do not give in to your hunger. We are on a journey to the top of this plateau, and we need to get there if we want to save the souls of every kuvi that has been dragged into this world against their will."

"I do not know whether or not these claws will destroy souls, but get any closer to us and I promise you'll find out," growled Aleksei, showcasing his wings and making them glow brightly. One of the kuvis stopped, and the other one did as well once it noticed that its partner was not moving. The first kuvi was slender and feminine in shape, though it was devoid of facial features or any distinctive aspects that would confirm this. Unlike the masculine kuvis, its claws had no arm guards and stopped at the wrists. It looked at the unique wings, then at Aleksei.

"Aleksei," it said. "Is that you?"

Aleksei's eyes widened and he let his wings disintegrate. He stepped forward and contemplated the ghost. Daina moved alongside him. "Felaem?" he asked.

"It is you, Aleksei!" cried out the ghost. It ran forward and brought its incorporeal arms around the living kuvi in an attempt at an embrace. It quickly let go. "It is great to see you, but terrible to see you here. At least I managed to see you as an adult, though. You've changed so much."

"You're the friend who made Aleksei such a great fighter," said Daina. "You're the one who fell victim to Jurek."

Felaem looked at Daina. "I was killed by him, yes," she said. She looked back at Aleksei. "Who is the human with the red heart, Aleksei?"

"She is Daina, former princess and sadly now current queen of Tantallos," said Aleksei. "We are working together to stop the priest Abdaas." He said the next thing quietly. "*Uzas mi misizi.*"

Felaem's eyes would have widened if she had any. She looked at Daina and bowed. "It's a pleasure to meet you," she said. "Aleksei's a good person. I'm Felaem dal Afxanos, and this is Talel dal Spazos. How can we help you two?"

"Why is all this happening?" she asked. "Why is there an army of kuvi ghosts in this city, slaughtering everything in sight?"

"Shortly after the Goddess awakened she expelled us from Her depths," said Felaem. "Nothing short of the Huntmaster's power saved us." She placed a claw over her red heart. "He protected our souls even as the many wicked humans that joined us were completely destroyed."

"I have been condemned to this world for many centuries," said Talel, "and the Goddess was not always like this, so cruel and vengeful. For hundreds of years of my afterlife I spent it in the company of other kuvis, none of us in pain, in the quarters of the Goddess' sleeping chamber. She had told us in our dreams that She would return us all to Proso when She awoke to end Her world. She did not harm any of us, even as She consumed the souls of humans She deemed deserving of Punishment in her sleep."

"The Goddess showed mercy on us?" asked Aleksei, unable to comprehend the thought.

"She was quite merciful and understanding," said Talel. "That is, until something happened. Even I don't know for sure how it happened. Something seeped into the ground, twisting and tainting everything it came into contact with. No kuvi there was susceptible to its corrupting magic, even as the splendor around us was rotted and destroyed. We tried to warn the Goddess of what was happening around Her as She slept, but then the corruption seeped into Her as well."

"What?" asked Daina. "The Decay corrupted the Goddess?"

"We watched in horror as the corruption set into Her core, taking control from its base on the back of Her head," said Talel. "Once it finished She consumed every last kuvi She had been keeping safe, all while still asleep. Ever since then we have been trapped inside Her, in constant torment and subjected to an ever-growing hunger."

"Why She expelled us from Her stomach is something we cannot answer," said Felaem, "though it does not bode well."

Aleksei connected the pieces. "She expelled our indigestible souls to make room for something She'd much rather consume," said Aleksei. "She purged so She could binge."

Daina comprehended what Aleksei was suggesting. "Oh, no," she said. "All these souls, innocent and guilty, deprived of Paradise and placed before Her in the final judgment..." Her eyes widened. "They're all going to be subjected to Punishment!"

"We cannot do anything to stop Her," said Talel. "It has to be you two. Hurry and stop Her from doing such a thing to this world. No soul deserves the Goddess' cruel idea of Punishment." He looked at Daina. "I apologize for insulting your deity."

"She's not mine anymore," said Daina, putting a hand over her heart. "I carry the Huntmaster in me now." The ghosts moved out of the way, allowing Daina and Aleksei to approach the entrance to the bastion's headquarters. A thought occurred to Aleksei, causing him to stop and turn back toward the ghosts.

"I want to thank you so much," said Aleksei. "Especially you, Felaem. You did so much for me. I'm sorry I couldn't protect you."

"I hold nothing against you," said Felaem. "Jurek is a terrifying foe."

"He was, at least," said Aleksei. "I got my revenge against him earlier today. You haven't seen his soul, have you?"

"I have not," said Felaem.

"If you killed him recently it's possible he's either wandering aimlessly around here or his soul got lost on the way to the Goddess' chamber," said Talel. "If it's the second case, he's as good as gone forever."

"Fortunate," said Aleksei. "That's one kuvi I never want to see again, in this world or the next."

"Now go," said Felaem. "Don't let us hold you back. Time is running out."

Aleksei nodded and caught up with Daina, who was standing by the bastion doors. She had tried them already; they were locked and barred from the inside, despite such fortifications being unable to keep out a kuvi ghost. The massive wooden doors were reinforced with metal throughout, the protection disguised with intricate metal designs.

"I don't think they'll let us in, Aleksei," said Daina. "I'd imagine the other door is barred as well. Can you fly up and see if we can enter somewhere else?"

"All they need to know is that we aren't dangerous," said Aleksei. "Let me knock first."

The door exploded inward, turning into a barrage of splintered wood and broken bits of metal, showering every surface in the lobby with the fragments. Daina looked at the completely obliterated door in shock and made a slight clapping motion with her hands. "You're still as strong as ever," she said.

"I've only been involved in two life-threatening situations so far today, Daina," said Aleksei. He did not count his encounter with Tantallos' army nor his flying over the angry mob, just the two fights with Jurek. "Plus, I've had enough time to regain my strength. Huntmaster willing whatever lies inside won't put up much of a fight, though." The two of them walked into the lobby, looking left and right in search of any survivors or kuvi ghosts. They made their way through to the lobby and entered a massive hallway. Not a single dead body could be seen, nor any gore that implied one had been there.

"This is worse than a group of kuvi ghosts," said Daina. "This is so much worse."

"You'd rather see piles of lacerated, dead humans getting fed upon by the spirits of my kind?" asked Aleksei in confusion.

"This has to be a trap of some sort," said Daina. "There's no possible way every zealot in this building went out to lead the mob. They must have left some people behind."

"Are you so certain that they all would not have gone to lead the mob?" asked Aleksei. "Not many things short of a kuvi could take down that door so effortlessly."

"Abdaas has been waiting too long to take such a risk," said Daina.

"There have to be guards watching over the stairs that lead upward, maybe even guards trained to keep kuvis at bay. Though they'll still fall to you."

"At this point I'm willing to believe anything," he said. They both continued walking down the dimly-lit hallway, looking into all the rooms they passed and up each staircase. The rooms were all devoid of life, though they looked like the people inside had fled rapidly. They had not even stopped to push in chairs. All the stairs they found only led up to other levels of the bastion headquarters, not to the top of the plateau. They arrived at the end of the hall, having found nothing of interest.

"We have to be missing something obvious," said Aleksei.

"If only Alkin was still with us," said Daina. "He probably knows where--"

Aleksei shushed Daina quietly and looked around to pinpoint the location of a slight noise he had heard. He walked down the hall toward the room he thought it had come from, careful to make almost no noise with each step. Daina followed along just as quietly. Soon he was right against the slightly ajar door. He gently pushed the door, letting its own motion finish swinging it open. He pondered the furniture in the room; inside was a desk with a chair, a shelf filled with books of various sizes and a massive wooden chest in one corner. He walked over to the chest and lightly knocked against the lid with a claw.

"Go away!" whimpered the frightened person inside. "The demon ghosts are everywhere! This is my hiding spot! Find your own before those demon ghosts get inside the bastion!"

Aleksei felt his quills stand up on end but he stifled his anger; he had bigger issues to deal with. "First of all, we are kuvis, not demons," he said. "Second, I'm not looking to hide like a frightened child and third, I have no interest in hurting you."

"Demon, kuvi, whatever you call yourself, I demand you go away right now!" said the person. "I might be the last person left alive in Tulroy. I had been about to leave the bastion. Everyone else had already left. The doors lock from the inside when you leave. I was preparing to leave for war, only because Abdaas ordered us all to do so. I like the King. I like Alkin. They seem like nice fellows."

"They were indeed nice fellows," said Aleksei. "And now it's likely they are both dead, killed by Abdaas or perhaps the kuvi ghosts. And you're going to be dead as well if you don't leave that chest right now and share what you know."

"I'm dead if I come out of this chest," said the person. "How do I know you're not one of those brutal and cruel kuvis who love torturing their prey physically and mentally before they finally put it out of its misery? How do I know you're not going to disembowel me after you trick me into leaving my protective chest?"

"Because I'm not one of those brutal and cruel kuvis," growled Aleksei. "I'm one of those hot-blooded kuvis who's incredibly short-tempered, and if you don't come out of that damn chest I'm going to set it on fire with you still hiding in it!"

"It won't have to come to that, Aleksei," said Daina, coming forward. "Sir, whoever you are, we just need to find the staircase that goes up to the surface of the plateau. Tell us and we'll leave you in peace so you can hide as long as you want."

"*Miss Pretty Voice*, please tell *Mister Angry* to step away from the chest," said the person. Daina looked at Aleksei, who backed away from chest. Aleksei made sure to stomp loudly. "Good, good. I heard him moving away. Must still be annoyed, given how loud he was. Oh well.

"Now, you want to find Father Abdaas' office. It's up the nearest staircase, then down the hall on the left. Should be at the end. In there you'll find his possessions and a small staircase going up to the surface. Only a few lookout people and scholarly types are allowed up there and only on clear days. He also lets me go up there, but only if I'm accompanying him. He says he set his office up in that room to make sure no uses the dolmens to summon more of your kuvis."

"He's up there right now," said Daina. "But he's not summoning a kuvi; he's summoning a corrupted deity to consume all of our souls. Enjoy hiding."

"I will, I promise you, *Miss Pretty Voice*," said the person. "Hope you get there in one piece; you too, *Mister Angry*. Shouldn't be any hungry ghosts on the way but you never know. Just close the door on the way out, please. Every little bit helps." Aleksei and Daina walked out of the room and quietly shut the door behind them, the person in the chest silent. They ran for the nearest staircase and ascended to the second floor of the bastion. They turned left and walked down the hall, passing by empty rooms. They were just like the other rooms, primarily offices and libraries. Both of them wondered what the highest-ranking members of the Church of the Goddess used the miscellaneous rooms for.

But their thoughts ended as they arrived at the office at the end of the hallway. Abdaas' name was inscribed into a marker on the door, which was adorned with all sorts of intricate carvings. All of them were representative of scenes out of the Teachings of the Goddess. Daina thought back to how the Daina of just a few days ago would have loved to study them. They pulled the door open and saw an office not that different from the others they had passed; a desk, a chair and many shelves of books and scrolls, undoubtedly collections of religious dogma. However, near the desk was an open door, the entryway so small a person would have to stoop to get through it. The doorway led to a larger, less cramped staircase that went up so far they could just barely see its end. They moved into the chamber and stood side by side at the bottom of the stairs. They just had enough room to stand up straight.

"It's quite a walk up," said Daina.

"If only the tunnel was bigger, or at least wider," said Aleksei. "Then I could fly us to the top."

"The time taken will be worse than the exertion from all the steps," said Daina. "I can feel fear growing in me like the worst hunger imaginable." She looked at Aleksei, locking eyes with him. "I'm so scared."

"The Huntmaster will be with us both," said Aleksei. "He's already in our hearts, and soon He'll step out before us. He's a being of destruction; no being of creation can fight Him and expect to win. And, above all else, you have me." He took the ingredients out of one of Daina's hands, moved them to his other claw and held Daina's free hand gently with his remaining claw. "I'm not hurting you, am I?"

"After everything we've been through your hand is the most comforting thing I could hold right now," said Daina. "Thank you for entering my life, quill-head."

"Thank you for saving mine, queen," said Aleksei. They both looked at each other before gazing back up the stairs. They breathed in at the same time and took their first steps up the staircase. They ascended together, their feet in sync. Apprehension and fear continued to grow in both their hearts, resulting in them tightening their grip on the other one's hand. Daina had been correct; even more so than the incredible length of the staircase, the time it was taking them to scale it was far, far worse.

CHAPTER 37

There is no creature or being in existence that can rival Me. As I created this world from a dream, so I can create and destroy anything else, no matter how mighty it claims to be. It will destroy it, and then I shall destroy all those who thought it could even face me.
-From the Teachings of the Goddess.

Abdaas watched with his one eye as more and more of the ingredients sank into the dolmen. He felt the ground shake slightly. He breathed rapidly, not just from the weariness his injuries put him through. Such earthly concerns were beyond him now, especially since his life goal was so close. It had taken seemingly ages for the ingredients to sink in, but already barely anything was left on the surface of the dolmen. Only a few splinters of bone remained; a single mouthful of meat was left; just the end of his own eyeball's nerve remained visible; and the blood was down to the last few drops on the pieces of shattered glass. Abdaas had opted to shatter the vial on the dolmen instead of emptying it to get the blood that had coagulated as well.

He felt his fear that the summoning might not have gone well melt away as the end of the ritual drew closer and closer. Even the shaking ground did not worry him. He looked up in the sky, expecting at any moment for the summoning dolmen's circle of light to form. Once it appeared and became more than just an outline the Goddess would emerge from it, traveling through the fold in the world. He paused in his moment of triumph to glance down, wherein he saw people arriving at the top of the staircase. He snarled as two all-too-familiar faces looked around the top of the plateau.

"I'll confront him," said Daina, handing the ingredients she had been carrying to Aleksei. "Go and get the ritual started. We need all the time we can get. I hope you know how it works, because I sure don't."

"I memorized that book on summoning," said Aleksei. "I'll perform well enough for the ritual to work. I hope you can convince Abdaas."

"If there's any hope of making him stop, it's with me," she said. "He wouldn't listen to you."

"Agreed," he said. He looked to the end of the plateau opposite Abdaas' location and spotted a dolmen of similar size to the one Abdaas was using. "I'll be at the dolmen over there." He pointed to a particularly large one. "Get back to me before She arrives!" He generated his wings and flew toward the dolmen. He let his wings disintegrate and landed feet-first in front of it in less than a minute. He quickly pulled out the ingredients, assembling them on the dolmen as stated in the book. Even as Aleksei worked he felt the ground shaking below him. His intestines twisted themselves up into tight knots as an overwhelming fear he had never felt threatened to overtake him.

Abdaas watched in interest as Daina ran up to him as fast as she could. He did not bother reaching for his weapon; by now his death would not change anything. She came to a stop several feet away from him. "Don't even try to grab the ingredients," said Abdaas. "They are so far sunken in that no force in Paradise or Punishment could remove them. Only I could do such a thing."

"I'm not going to try to take them off," said Daina, "and I'm not going to attack you. That wouldn't solve anything." She glanced at the dolmen and her pale face lost even more of its color. "Especially not by this point. It's almost all gone!"

"Yes," said Abdaas, smiling in satisfaction. "The ritual wouldn't have taken half as long if I had gotten the blood of your maidenhead, but it's of no matter now." He looked toward a red shape in the distance with glowing, graceful wings that also stood by a dolmen. "I see your hell-spawn friend is attempting to summon a creature as well. Unless he violated even more laws of the Goddess and laid with you, I doubt he'll manage to summon anything at all before the Goddess consumes his soul. And yours, too. Don't worry; you'll both be together when you're completely destroyed."

"Not as long as the Huntmaster is protecting my body and soul," said Daina. "The soul of every kuvi the Goddess had consumed has been expelled from Her body. They are running about Tulroy as we speak, killing everyone. Almost no one is still alive."

"It's of no matter," said Abdaas. "Body or no body, they are all about to judged before the Goddess. And it's not like they'll need such collections of matter in Paradise. Even if so many demon souls are roaming about it will be of no consequence. The Goddess will banish them to some barren corner of this world or perhaps eat them again. Whichever option She chooses, it would be a just end."

"The souls are not preparing to be judged," said Daina. "They are preparing to be eaten, regardless of what they have done or not done in their lives." She gestured to the edge of the plateau. "The Decay has done far worse than merely corrupting our landscape and twisting the animals that live throughout our world. The Decay has also corrupted the Goddess Herself!"

"Blasphemy!" yelled Abdaas, deeply insulted by the statement. "The Goddess is a divine creature, pure and incorruptible! Such manifestations of evil would be like throwing sticks at a stone wall!"

"Then it would appear those sticks chipped away enough to cause a collapse!" yelled Daina. "I learned this from the same kuvis She had been keeping in Her depths for the past centuries."

"And you trust the words of some half-crazed, barely-sentient monsters over the unwavering strength of your Goddess?" asked Abdaas, a scowl on his face. He sighed and glowered at Daina. "Then you have truly and completely betrayed the being that created you entirely out of love. May the Goddess have mercy on your soul."

Daina sighed as well. "And to think I used to believe the members of the Church of the Goddess were so wise. I just hope Aleksei finishes the summoning ritual soon so the Huntmaster can save our souls. Even yours."

"He has troubles handling a weak, heretical, spoiled princess without cutting through her pampered flesh," spat Abdaas. "I doubt he managed to place even one ingredient in the proper place. You'd be lucky to summon a demonic slug."

Daina wanted to yell in rage and attack, but it would do her no good. Instead she turned away from Abdaas and ran as fast as she could away from him. All hope vanished for convincing Abdaas to stop; she only prayed she could reach Aleksei in time. Then the final drop of blood sank into the altar.

Elsewhere in the Decay, Kolen crouched by a pile of kindling and logs. He scraped his claw against a piece of flint until it finally sparked, setting the small pile ablaze. He used his alignment to move the fog out of the way and leech even more moisture out of the kindling, allowing the fire to grow without hindrance. He had lost track of the years he had spent out in the Decay. So had Milak, the lesser kuvi near his territory. They had finally come to an understanding concerning borders and hunting; all the better for Kolen. He needed someone to talk to from time to time.

He looked up from his small fire and saw Milak running to him. Kolen sighed, ruffling his dark brown quills with tan ends. Every time Milak ran to meet him was guaranteed to be trouble. He stood up as the bald kuvi stopped in front of him. "What is it?" he asked, folding his arms.

"Just climb up your hill and look into the air," said Milak. "It might be hard to see through this fog, but you won't believe what's happening in the skies."

Kolen sighed, generating his wings and soaring to the top of the hill he lived by. At the top he looked up and indeed saw something moving just above the fog. Intrigued, he jumped up and took off into the air, stopping and hovering just above the fog line. Hundreds, no, thousands of blue shapes moved across the sky.

Each one differed, but they were all definitely humanoid. Men, women, adults, children; the translucent shapes covered the entire spectrum of the human race. But what intrigued Kolen the most were the blue shapes with red cores; he recognized them almost immediately from the stories his elders had shared late at night after all the work was done. The souls of dead kuvis. He landed back on the ground and rushed to Milak. "What could so many ghosts be doing, and where are they going?" asked Kolen.

"Humans often talk about that judgment wherein everyone gets put before the Goddess," said Milak. "Maybe it's that. Perhaps She will listen to us. I have a daughter back in Proso."

"My love was with child when I was taken away," said Kolen, looking downward. The two kuvis looked at each other and nodded. Milak let Kolen reach his claws around Milak's waist, holding the wingless kuvi tight as he took off into the air. They broke through the fog layer and followed the souls to wherever their journey ended. All throughout the dead world many other groups of kuvis had the same idea; even former rivals put their differences aside so every kuvi could ascend to investigate the situation. It may just be the day they had longed for ages to bear witness. They may finally be going back home.

The ground shook so much all three people on the plateau lost their footing. Many of the smaller dolmens moved across the ground as the surface liquefied. The three feared that the city below them would collapse and the entire surface of the plateau would cave in. The souls of the dead rose to the surface, forming an eerie, whimpering lair of overlapping voices covering the ground. More and more kept coming from all around the plateau, ascending alongside the kuvi ghosts who had killed them. They packed themselves onto the plateau, unable to hinder the three living creatures already there. The kuvis who still lived landed on the edges of the plateau, letting go of the flightless kuvis they had been carrying and taking up positions to observe the upcoming events.

Aleksei managed to pull himself up using the dolmen, staring at the shattered bottle of blood before looking for Daina. She got to her feet but found it difficult to walk as the surface kept shaking. She staggered toward Aleksei as fast as she could but it did not take long before she looked behind her and found herself distracted by the astonishing, and incredibly worrying, light show in the air above Abdaas' dolmen. A point of light like an especially bright star appeared, and then another alongside it. More and more points of light came into existence, forming a curve as the individual dots became connected by a bending line just as bright. Soon the curve completely turned back and connected to the original starting point, forming a circle that turned into a solid disk of white in an instant. The circle was colossal, hundreds of feet long.

Then they saw something appear out of the top side of the circle. A head slowly rose out of it, covered in shining white locks intertwined with something green and black that none of them could make out over the intense light of the portal. The being further ascended, floating upward into the air, showing two eyes with vines extending inward to the green irises from the edges. The eyes had no visible pupil; they were the same green as the irises. Along with the eyes came perfect and refined facial features, and then a slender neck.

Soon the entire entity had risen out of the circle and the entire disk vanished into thin air, allowing the entity to descend so it floated about thirty feet above the ground. The being itself acted as a light source, emitting a sickly green glow all throughout its body. It was a titanic woman in what looked to be a suit of light, golden, plated body armor. The armor was the part of her that glowed the least, its spender dull and chipped. All over her grew vines of varying lengths and thicknesses, wrapping around her extensively. They reached from the front of her forehead to the tips of her graceful fingers to each and every toe on her bare feet. No matter what size or location, all the vines connected to a massive outgrowth on the back of her head. It was a pulsating, oozing monstrosity filled to the brim with pus, caught up in dead and withered locks of hair.

Aleksei and Daina looked at the sight in horror, unable to do anything. The decaying Goddess looked down at the two mortals, and then at the mortified Abdaas who stood still, mouth agape. The souls backed away from the Goddess' presence fearfully, packing in tight around each other. They kept low to the ground, several feet below where the Goddess was floating.

The Goddess let out a raspy shriek that one might have confused for a shrill laugh and reached down, grabbing Abdaas in a massive hand. He was not even as wide as one of Her fingers. She raised him to eye level and examined him, Her eyes stuck looking straight ahead by the vines rooted to them. She turned her head and hand to look over the priest. The smaller vines on the tips of Her fingers extended into his robes and fished about, grabbing something and pulling away. They emerged with his kuvi relic. They moved away from Her hand and slackened their grip, letting the relic fall to the ground.

Then Abdaas started screaming in pain as parts of his flesh peeled away from his bones. What little hair he had left withered and his eye sprouted a covering of cataracts. His teeth fell out of his mouth like birds shot out of the sky. His clothes grew moldy and quickly disintegrated, but by the time they had finished falling off him he had been reduced to nothing but a moldy skeleton. As the Goddess let go of his body the bones finally disappeared into the air, becoming dust, only one part of Abdaas still in the Goddess' gigantic hand. Abdaas' soul remained trapped in the Goddess' grip as She brought him to Her mouth. He screamed as loud as he could, begging the Goddess for forgiveness as he was forced inside, shortly before She closed Her mouth on him. In only a few seconds he started his descent into Her depths to experience the most painful thing a human being could ever suffer.

Daina worked hard to compose herself and continue her running back to Aleksei, taking every ounce of her will to move her feet away from the corrupted deity. But she could not move fast enough and the Goddess reached down for her, one of Her thumbs and one of Her fingers trapping the terrified mortal easily. She brought Her hand back upward even as Daina struggled to free herself. But it was all to no avail, and in moments she was before the Goddess' sickly gaze. The Goddess scrutinized Her catch, but Daina knew exactly what was about to happen to her. Her dagger was trapped in her leggings, but mere bronze would have no effect on this foe. The Goddess opened Her mouth and slowly brought Daina closer.

Aleksei broke himself out of his frozen state, generated his wings and took off from the ground at top speed. The kuvis watched in the distance, witnessing a single runt ascending the air at an impressive velocity as the Goddess brought Her second snack closer to Her maw. The Goddess had sensed the foreign presence in Daina's heart; She would not bother with taking away her relic. Aleksei's mind raced before deciding on a way to get the Goddess' attention. Even as he flew closer to the colossal deity he formed and tossed a hail of fireballs, all aimed at the Goddess' face. All of them hit true, one even exploding on the Goddess' eye and burning the vines holding the optical orb in place. The Goddess let out an ear-splitting shriek before retreating Her hand from Her mouth. A vine broke off from Her body and moved to Her hand, wrapping tightly around the struggling Daina and raising her high into the air. The snack could wait until after the foolish kuvi had been dealt with.

More vines broke away from her body, creating a forest of green tentacles coursing with corrupted power. Aleksei flew at top speed, his *Ateni* watching each and every vine carefully as balls of energy formed on their ends. He soared, swooped and dived as the balls of energy changed into beams as sickly and green as the Goddess' body. The energy beams had almost perfect accuracy and if not for his speed he would have been hit countless times. Aleksei moved quickly, disintegrating his wings to avoid a series of beams and reforming them in an instant, deflecting beams with his claws and redirecting them away from the innocents below him. The corrupted energy did not even leave a layer of rust on the metal of his claws. As he came closer small vines swung out to hit him but he generated balls of fire in his hands and collided with them, the explosion severing the vines and coating the tips with flames.

The Goddess let out another shriek as the kuvi continued to elude Her attacks. Every swipe, every swing, every blast... every attack he saw coming. Even Her fake-outs failed to trick him. Not one blast managed to hit the agile kuvi, so the Goddess tried something to guarantee at least one strike. All of her extended vines generated a glowing green ball of energy and fired them simultaneously, filling the sky before Aleksei with an inescapable barrage of corrupted power. Aleksei's eyes widened and he dived downward to escape, but not even he could move fast enough to dodge such a spread. The beams hit him, piercing his wings in countless areas and blasting him over a dozen times. The fire in his claws faded and he went limp as he plummeted to the ground.

The Goddess caught him with Her vines as he fell, bringing his unconscious body closer to Her face. She moved the vine holding Daina so she could see clearly as the Goddess tilted Her head back and moved the vine holding Aleksei over Her jaws. Daina's heart jumped up into her throat, but then came another tremor, quickly escalating into an earthquake equal in force to the one that had heralded the arrival of the Goddess.

CHAPTER 38

I have traveled to countless worlds and brought an end to countless civilizations. I have clashed with innumerable beings as great as Myself and have won every time. You shall carry this tenacity into every battle as well.
-From the Tomes of the Huntmaster.

Aleksei had placed every ingredient in the perfect spot. All that had been left was breaking the bottle of blood upon the dolmen to start the ritual. He had been about to do so when the earthquake caused him to lose his footing. The bottle of blood had gone up a short distance before coming down and shattering on the dolmen, sending the glass everywhere. The blood sank into the dolmen alongside all the other ingredients at a greatly accelerated rate. All that tied into what he had desired to summon, a thought he had emphasized throughout the preparation of the ritual to better target that specific creature. With everything set in motion, the ritual had rapidly proceeded while the Goddess arrived and dealt with Aleksei.

The Goddess watched in interest as a circle of light again formed in the sky, this time vertically and on the opposite side of the plateau. She let the vine holding Aleksei fall to the ground and She lost interest in the defeated kuvi, tossing him in front of the circle of light. The kuvis on the perimeter watched in confusion at her discarding a defeated prey. The circle of light disappeared but not before two massive, black claws glowing with a blood-red outline managed to get through. The closing circle pushed the two hands together, leaving a tear in the fabric of the world. The two claws, identical in almost every way to a pair of kuvi claws, kept the tear open, and the arms the claws were attached to forced it wider.

The kuvis looked in awe, bowing before the sight of their god, kneeling and placing their claws palm-down while lowering their heads to the ground. They raised their heads while still genuflecting, staring into the tear and seeing the visage of their god for the first time in years. It was a flat face like the mouth of a worm, lined with a dozen black eyes that moved independently of each other, flicking this way and that, watching everything at once. Inside the circle of eyes was the god's mouth, equipped with eight fangs parallel to each other, four on the top and four on the bottom. Just past them were two gigantic metal slabs, gnashing up and down like a guillotine.

Beyond the face lay the rest of the god's body, bent forward in the shape of a kuvi's charging stance. Its arms were thick and its claws were just as oversized as any kuvi's. Its legs ended in clawed, massive talons. Its tail extended back as long as its body, covered in long spikes that faced backward. Most notably, the entire body was blanketed in black armor and tentacle-like protrusions ending in smaller kuvi claws, each crack between armor plates glowing with a pulsating red power. Daina stared at this entity with an amount of horror matched only by the being that now held her.

Then came a voice, a voice she did not hear around her but rather in her head. It dominated her thoughts and found its way into every corner of her mind. "*Don't be afraid, Daina of Tantallos,*" said the voice. It was a low, powerful voice, wise and knowledgeable. It was the sort of voice she had imagined only the smartest of scholars, greatest of wizards and wisest of sages would have. "*I am the Huntmaster, the World Guardian of the kuvis. I am Prosopsei.*"

The majority of the Huntmaster's eyes focused on the Goddess as She smirked at Him. The Goddess spoke to Him in a language only something divine could understand; the mortals watching the scene unfold perceived the dialogue as gibberish, growling and mindless screaming. The kuvis on the ground rose from their genuflection, watching the exchange between the two deities and wishing they could understand the conversation. Kolen and Milak moved over to a kuvi ghost watching the scene unfold. The two continued watching, failing to grasp something.

"Greetings," said Kolen. "I'm Kolen dal Richtos, and this is Milak dal Kanos."

"I am Talel dal Spazos," said the ghost. "What is the matter, besides the obvious?"

"Why isn't the Huntmaster stepping through the portal?" asked Milak worriedly. "Or even grabbing the runt on the ground in front of Him? He's beyond powerful. He destroys worlds effortlessly. He could defeat the Goddess in seconds!"

"It's not as simple as that," said Talel. "Earlier tonight I talked to another kuvi who knew more about these matters than I, after I talked to the one who had summoned our god. While the two at the Goddess' mercy made a plan that seemed like it would work, they did not account for variables they could not have possibly known about."

Kolen felt a bad feeling brew inside of him. "What do you mean?" he asked.

Talel looked down, shaking his head. "The Huntmaster could easily kill the Goddess like He has any other being of creation," he said. "As such, the divine beings devised rules to limit the actions a being of destruction could take. Beings of destruction can only enter a world when the end of days has come or when it's been determined the world is dangerous to other worlds. Otherwise they need the permission of the world's being of creation."

"It's the end of days!" said Milak. "Why isn't He coming through?"

"Because the Goddess swore to destroy Her own world when the end of days came," said Talel. "As such, there is no need for a being of destruction and thus the Huntmaster cannot enter the world without violating the laws. Violations result in death, and several beings of destruction would join together to kill our god. He can't even reach in to grab that defeated kuvi; She tossed him there just to taunt Him."

Milak and Kolen stared at each other, deep pits forming in their guts. "We're doomed," said Kolen. "Our god's powerless to save us."

Talel looked up. "Not necessarily," he said. "We're in this world."

It came to Milak. "Kolen, Talel, talk to the other kuvis," he said. "Even if the Huntmaster can't bring Himself fully into our world, He still lies in our hearts. That will be more than enough to bring down this corrupted deity."

"So this is what that tiny little kuvi was summoning all this time," She said, Her voice high-pitched and raspy. "Oh, how humorous. He was so ignorant to think You'd be allowed to challenge Me? Sometimes I have to marvel at the naivete Your followers show. Such blind belief."

"He continues to believe, even in his unconsciousness," He said. "Your corruption has dulled Your senses if You cannot read that from him. She still believes as well."

The Goddess stared at Daina in contempt, unaware of the shuffling about on the perimeter of the plateau between the kuvis. The Huntmaster certainly knew of it, four of his twelve eyes flicking back and forth between various kuvis. He heard every word shared between them and every thought kept in their heads.

The Goddess returned Daina to her place far above Her head and grinned. "Fools love to believe in lost causes," She said, "and I can't think of one more lost than this one. I won't be able to corrupt Your followers, but don't worry. I'll let You remain here so You can watch me consume every last one of them, doomed to eternal pain. I think I'll start with the one human who worships You." She let out her shrill laugh as She started moving Daina closer to Her mouth again. The Huntmaster was not worried. He knew what His followers were about to do. The kuvis let out a collective roar and charged at the Goddess. The kuvis that could fly ripped through the air, carrying lesser kuvis in their arms and letting them drop onto the Goddess' body. The lesser kuvis remaining ran on the ground, throwing each other up to reach the Goddess' feet. The moment they landed they sliced and stabbed at Her, their claws managing to harm the divine being.

The remaining kuvis in the air landed on Her as well and used their alignments to the fullest. Some channeled water into small streams so powerful they could separate metal. Others manipulated the metal plating of Her armor to stab inward, damaging Her. Still others kept to the ground, firing off rocks and earth, and others manipulated Her vines to slow their movement. Those remaining simply burned Her. The Goddess let out another shriek and fought back against the kuvis. Energy blasts, sweeping vines, even swats at them with Her own hands. She used everything She had at Her disposal to knock the kuvis down, firing concentrated beams to make sure they stayed down. It took some time, but She steadily knocked off the hundreds of kuvis covering Her like a swarm of mosquitoes.

The Huntmaster watched it all, then looked to the one kuvi who had not charged forward to join the fray. He lay on the ground before Him, so close the Huntmaster could have picked him up with one of His clawed tentacles if He could step inside the world. But, there remained another possibility. One that He thought the lone kuvi just might be able to do.

Aleksei drifted through vision after vision, each one more horrifying than the last. He saw the same scene play over and over. A flash of a vision of the vine letting Daina go and she dropping into the Goddess' waiting maw. Another flash, the Goddess closing Her jaws and swallowing Daina alive. A flash again, and Daina shrieking in pain as she was messily torn apart in the depths of the corrupted deity. He was powerless to save her, just as powerless as he had been in real life. Now he was unconscious, trapped within his own mind, unable to stand. Even if he could get back up, his wings had been shattered. He could not possibly fight the Goddess and hope to win. Daina was undoubtedly dead by now, stuck in Punishment along with all the other souls gathered on the plateau. He had failed.

He found himself in a black room, a small light shining down from a corner of the ceiling. He huddled in a corner, on his haunches, head in his claws, weeping. But even as he lay there he felt a presence enter the room, something warm and comforting. He held back his tears as he felt a pressure on his back, something rubbing him gently. He looked to the light and saw a tentacle extending from the hole, the claw on it stroking him. "*Mi Prosopsei?*" he asked. "Have You truly arrived?"

The tentacle retracted into the hole and the room faded away, replaced with a flat-topped stone monolith that Aleksei found himself on. He stood up, doing his best to dry his tears with his arms. He looked in the direction the hole had been and saw the Huntmaster standing before him. He performed the kuvi genuflection, standing back up when a claw raised his chin. The monolith was tall enough to place Aleksei at face level with the Huntmaster. He could see the Huntmaster's guillotine teeth gnashing away at nothing, but did not feel worried in the slightest about the god's gaping maw.

"Aleksei dal Kafteros," said the Huntmaster. "It has been so long since you have stood before Me. You were but a child then."

Aleksei nodded lightly. "Thank You so much for tolerating my call for You, *mi Prosopsei*," he said. "We couldn't think of any other possible way to stop the Goddess. I hope You are not angered by our audacity to call upon You."

"A loving father would never stand back and let a monster kill his children," said the Huntmaster. "Which is why I am now here before you. Even as I talk to you in your dreams your brethren attack the Goddess with everything they have. All five alignments, both the additional gifts, and those without any powers, all joining together to fight. Though even now they realize their assault is in vain."

"What?" whimpered Aleksei. "*Mi Prosopsei*, please, I beg of You, please step into the world and save them! Please." He knelt down. "I failed them. I cannot save them."

"Neither can I," said the Huntmaster, "at least directly. Laws older than myself forbid Me from stepping into Her world, so long as She intends to carry out the end of days Herself."

Aleksei looked about ready to fall apart. "Then Daina is truly gone," he said.

"Not yet," said the Huntmaster. "There is still one more option." Two tentacle claws pulled Aleksei to his feet. "I am not allowed to step into Her world, but the laws do allow Me to extend a fraction of My power into Her world. Vastly weaker than My full power, but comparable to the ability of a being of creation in terms of combat. It's to assist the being of creation in the destruction, unless spoken against. The Goddess said She would let Me stay, so I am free to exercise this right. But, I can only do it once."

Aleksei's eyes lit up. "You can save us?" he asked.

"The power will not be enough," said the Huntmaster. "It needs a conduit, a part of Myself it can work through." A lone claw moved forward and an index digit's blade tapped Aleksei's chest. "And I am in all of My followers."

"I'll do whatever it takes to save Daina and the rest," said Aleksei. "Alkin, Vikenti, Felaem, even Wesan and the others. No one deserves this fate."

"I felt you would say that, but I must warn you of something first," said the Huntmaster. "The power you will take into your body is far greater than anything you've ever felt before. It's devastating against foes, but also unstable for the user."

"How so, *mi Prosopsei*?" asked Aleksei.

"You will be, for all intents and purposes, a much weaker being of destruction," said the Huntmaster. "Your size will not be set; you will scale to match your foe's. While you'll be strong enough to stand against the Goddess, you will be subject to the fear all beings of such power have. When a being of either creation or destruction is killed, they are completely destroyed. If you die in this form, your soul will be gone forever."

Aleksei gulped, fear growing in him, but he worked to push it down. "I'm afraid, but it's what I must do," he said. He closed his eyes. "*Mi Prosopsei*, I beg of you, give me the strength to strike Her down!"

"Just remember to, no matter what, keep a part of you alive," said the Huntmaster. "Your past, your beliefs, your name's meaning. The moment you discard everything to win is the moment it all becomes worthless."

The Goddess let out another shrieking laugh as She marveled at Her handiwork. Every last kuvi that had thought to attack Her and interrupt Her meal had been brought down. Most still lived; kuvis are resilient creatures, especially to magic besides their own, but no matter. No creature could retain their sanity when in Her depths. But first, the time had arrived to finally enjoy one of the last remaining humans in the world. She moved Daina to Her front again. Daina stared back at the Goddess both in fear and in sadness. She did not scream for help; no help would come. Her arms were trapped under the vine. She could possibly move an arm out from under the vine but the Goddess would surely notice her grabbing her dagger. She looked at the Goddess, and then at Aleksei. She let her head fall forward; he had killed himself trying to protect her. She felt the guilt grow in her even as the Goddess' jaws came closer and closer.

The Goddess stopped as a third earthquake shook the plateau, the few kuvis able to stand falling to the ground again. The Goddess snarled; was another being coming to interrupt Her meal? This one She would not be so merciful with, oh no. She would kill this one. The corruption gave Her power like no other being of creation had. She looked down at the place where the earthquake had originated. Aleksei pulled himself to his feet, standing up straight, defiant of the Goddess. She smirked at the gesture; how cute, seeing one of the smallest adult kuvis she had ever encountered returning for a second round of pain. Aleksei's eyes glowed brightly as a massive snarl formed on his face.

Then a beam of red energy shot from the Huntmaster's tear, striking Aleksei in the back. Aleksei let out a scream as intense pain nearly overcame him, overloading his nerves. The Goddess watched in both confusion and interest as more of the Huntmaster's energy flowed into the small kuvi. Then came the change. Aleksei continued howling from the pain as the metal on his claws extended upward, sewing itself into his skin as a series of metallic plates. The prososium armor reached his shoulders and continued both upward and downward, coating all of his body in a protective layer unmatched by anything created by mortals. His flesh became flexible, versatile, and incomprehensibly durable. The armor traveled up his neck, covering his face and even layering his eyelids just enough so he could still open and close them. Every space between the plates glowed red, the same red as the Huntmaster.

The pain ended and Aleksei saw the ground fall away from him even as he still stood on it. He grew in size, shooting up hundreds of feet. The Goddess watched, fascinated by the entire process. Aleksei continued growing, souls and kuvis moving out of his way as he finally stopped at a height comparable to the Goddess' colossal size. He even felt his mind expanding, taking in information he had never known before because his mortal mind could not comprehend it. Namely the language of the gods.

"Welcome back, little kuvi," hissed the Goddess, dangling Daina in front of Her. "I see the Huntmaster discovered another way to get under my skin. You're certainly more intimidating than you were when any one of my toes was bigger than you, but it's of no matter. I'm going to enjoy killing you, but not before I let you watch Me eat her." The Goddess moved Daina behind Her to ensure she stayed out of Aleksei's reach. The Goddess watched the kuvi carefully, waiting for a response. Aleksei stared back, a new-found contempt in his eyes. He did not see a deity; he saw a woman due to be his thirty-ninth victim.

"Do you have anything to say, little kuvi?" the Goddess asked mockingly.

Aleksei readied his charging stance. What he said next, he said with no malice or anger, nothing but stating what he perceived as fact. "I am going to kill you," he said.

The Goddess let out a laugh and spread out Her glowing vines, making Herself look as big as possible while she balled her fists. Two golden semicircles formed around the knuckles, extensions coming out of the center and ending in large blocks of energy. A pair of hammers, suitable for denting plate armor. She and Aleksei both let out roars as they charged at each other.

Aleksei knew the Goddess' tricks, and even now he reevaluated Her tactics when facing a creature of similar size. Largely the same tactics as when She attacked a smaller creature. She relied on Her vines' energy beams to create a kill zone so large no creature could hope to dodge it. He did not know what to think of the hammers, but his claws would endure them. Nothing could destroy them. He did not have much time. Every second hurt him, the Huntmaster's energy coursing through him rapidly. Mortal bodies were not designed to hold so much power for any length of time; he had precious minutes to kill the Goddess or he would succumb to the ever-growing pain and be left wide open. That or the energy would tear him apart. Or he would revert back to his mortal form. Whatever happened, it would be his end.

His claws glowed white-hot as he readied his fire. The Goddess faked to the left, floating along the plateau as Her vines fired their beams. Aleksei stood his ground and held up his claws, deflecting most of them back at the Goddess. The beams hit Her dead-on but did little damage. The dozens of beams Aleksei had not deflected hit him all over his armored body, making him stumble back slightly. Even though his prososium armor absorbed most of the magical energy safely, all too many had hit the spaces in between plates. Had he simply been a larger version of his normal self he would have died. He had no idea how to comprehend the sensations. It was beyond any sort of torment a mortal could feel without collapsing or dying. He let out a roar in pain but quickly worked to compose himself as he saw Daina watching in awe from her perch. He had to win. To save her. His life didn't matter. His soul didn't matter.

Flames coated his arms, burning blue with intensity significantly greater than anything he had ever generated before. He could effortlessly melt or burn anything imaginable save for that which covered him. He pointed his claws at the Goddess and unleashed a river of blue fire, blocked by the Goddess' vines forming a protective barrier in front of Her. Daina's vine stayed far out of danger. The Goddess pulled her vines back even as they burned away rapidly. She shrieked as one vine snapped and fell to the ground, blackened by the fire. Another fell, and then another. Aleksei readied for another assault of flames.

He dodged to the left as the rest of her vines shot forward like spears, attempting to skewer him by getting underneath his plated armor. The attack completely missed him and allowed him to emit more blue fire onto the vines. The Goddess pulled Her vines back quickly and slammed them against the ground, trying to kill the flames. Instead, the vines cracked and fell off. The Goddess let out a roar. "I look forward to tearing your skin off plate by plate!" She yelled as She pointed a hammer at the ground away from the plateau. Out in the Decay the monsters all watched in confusion as the water rose out of the bogs and ponds, collecting in a massive, amorphous ball of fetid liquid. The water compressed itself as much as it could and then fired off as a small, concentrated blast powerful enough to tear apart metal.

Aleksei heard it coming well before he saw it and readied a claw to block the blast. It hit with an intensity he had not fathomed, knocking him off his feet and onto his back, scattering souls and soaking every part of him. He pulled himself back up before the Goddess could move in and strike, but the damage had been done. The water could not have harmed Aleksei, not with the metal covering him, but it had not been meant to. The Goddess had lost Her ranged power, but now Aleksei had as well.

Aleksei shook off his claws and started heating them up again before charging at the Goddess, watching Her carefully. She let out a laugh and floated to the left, dodging Aleksei's stab. He turned back and instead saw himself looking at three Goddesses. He saw through it easily; it was an illusion. Only one was real. If he attacked one of the illusions the actual Goddess would slam Her hammers across his head. He instead made a massive horizontal swipe, sending his claw through all three and hitting the real Goddess on the far left. The blade tore through Her golden armor like paper and the force sent Her to the ground. He was about to rush over and stab Her through the back when he saw Daina, hanging hundreds of feet in the air in the clutches of the vine. No. He had to save her. Even as chances of him surviving when he reverted waned.

Daina watched it all unfold, her heart beating rapidly as Aleksei fought with the Goddess. He countered each trick of the Goddess' with his own power, but each time a killing blow presented itself he held back. The Goddess followed these missed opportunities with a punishing attack of Her own, Aleksei managing to keep standing after each one. *It's me*, she thought guiltily. *He's not finishing Her off because it would kill me.* No. She could not let him do that. He did not have to risk everything for her. She did not deserve it. All throughout their time together he had saved her, the helpless human. She had almost never been in a place to contribute meaningfully. It could have been anyone else besides her that he had been so devoted to. That had to end.

She looked down at the back of the Goddess' head. The core of the infestation lay in plain sight, pulsating, brimming with pus. The skin was so thin she could see the yellow-and-green bile just past it. It looked fit to burst, so close to doing so it would only take... it would only take the slightest prick. She reached into her leggings with her hand, carefully grabbing her dagger by the handle. She slowly removed it from her pocket, holding her breath as the tip left it in the hope she avoided accidentally dropping the dagger. She let out her breath when she did not drop it, the dagger firmly in her grip.

She wiggled her arm, moving it up out of the vine's bonds. Her dagger cut against her slightly, but it was of no matter. All that was important was that Aleksei did not die. She managed to get her hand out from underneath the vine, which tightened to ensure she did not slip out of its grasp. She moved her fingers so she was holding the dagger by the blade. Aleksei charged at the Goddess again, trapping the shafts of Her hammers in between the blades of his claws. He doubted he would survive after he reverted back; the punishment he had taken would have killed the normal him several times over. He pushed on the Goddess as She held Her ground, pushing right back at him. Aleksei glanced at Daina, for the first time noticing what she was doing. He kept his position, controlling the Goddess' weapons so She did not move out of the way.

She took aim, breathing outward. *Huntmaster, help me*, she begged as she threw the dagger with all her might.

The dagger landed on the edge of the core, piercing the skin and providing an area to relieve the pressure. The filth shot out of the Goddess' head, causing Her to break away from Aleksei and scream in horror. Daina shrieked from the pain as the vine tightened on her, barely managing to survive the punishment.

Aleksei watched carefully as the Goddess stumbled, working hard to keep Her balance. Her head went forward, Her white hair flowing over it as She shook slightly. Her hammers disintegrated as Her fists relaxed. She slowly rose Her head; the irises were now gold and She had pupils as black as any human's. Tears flowed from Her eyes freely.

"Take her," the Goddess begged in a much more beautiful voice, moving Her vine forward to drop Daina into the palm of Aleksei's claw. Daina landed roughly, staring up at the giant kuvi's face. Aleksei stared back, but only for a moment before turning around and placing her right in front of the dolmen the Huntmaster's tear had formed over. He turned back to the Goddess, who looked around at the Decay. "The world has paid the price for My rest. But at least My people are safe." She looked directly at Aleksei. "Kill Me," She pleaded, Her fingers starting to ball up again and the hammers reforming. "The Decay is taking Me again! Kill me, before... Gah!" She screamed, Her voice shifting back into the raspy voice of the infestation controlling Her. Her eyes reverted to their pure-green color and She readied Her hammers. New vines rapidly sprouted from her back, extending to full length in seconds. "This ends now!"

Aleksei charged forward quickly and swung his claws as hard as he could. The Goddess attempted to parry his blows with Her hammers but the force of his strikes and his anti-magical nature ripped through the energy constructs. She backed away in horror, raising Her arms as Aleksei swung again. The blow cut through Her arms effortlessly, leaving Her with two stumps shooting out golden ichor past the elbows. She backed away, crying from the intense pain. She slowly sank down from Her hovering until Her feet touched the ground again. She looked at Aleksei, begging with Her eyes, the conniving deity attempting to appeal to some sort of pity in the kuvi's heart.

"Please," She begged. "Please, show Me mercy."

Aleksei snarled, but kept himself under control. He so longed to kill Her tortuously, to make Her pay for everything She had done and had tried to do to those he loved. But it had not been the Goddess; it had been the corruption. The corruption deserved such contempt, not the host. The host simply deserved a quick death. The Goddess steadily rose back into the air, vines sprouting out of the stumps of Her arms as more vines pointed forward from Her back, readying all of Her corrupted energy for a final attack. Aleksei saw every vine charge up, only seconds remaining before they would all fire on him at once.

He moved one hand into a claw position and brought it behind him, the red lines between his armor plates pulsing rapidly. His readied claw, then his entire arm, turned white as he moved all of his own power to that single claw. A glowing ball of world-destroying fire hotter than any star in the sky, the product of utmost lucidity, formed in the center, reaching from his thumb to his other digits before he brought it forward and slammed it directly into the Goddess' face before She could attack. Everyone on the plateau averted their gaze as Aleksei's last attack landed, exploding and emitting a light so brilliant anyone who would have looked upon it would have been blinded. The blast burned everything past it into nothingness for countless miles, an inferno so concentrated and controlled it had not even touched those behind Aleksei.

Aleksei watched Her decapitated, smoldering body slowly fall to the ground on its back, leaking ichor. He stumbled back, the punishment he had taken over the course of the battle catching up to him at full force. He shrank back to normal size, even as the Goddess' corpse finished its collapse. He stood on the ground, the metallic armor moving off his body and disappearing until the only metal parts of his body were his claws. As he finished reverting back, the Huntmaster's power diminished, becoming dormant within his heart. With not even an ounce of strength left in him, Aleksei collapsed to the ground. Daina ran to him and brought her ear to his chest, growing increasingly worried as she failed to hear his heartbeat. She moved him onto his back and made sure he was flat, frantically searching for any sign he was still alive. He could not be dead. He had to survive. He was a kuvi. They always survive. Don't they?

Everyone else on the plateau, whether living, dead or immortal, looked on in amazement as the corpse of the Goddess faded away. Flecks of Her broke away from the main body, floating off into the air, reducing themselves into smaller and smaller pieces until they finally disintegrated. Layer by layer She went, every part of Her form taken back by Her dead world. Even the ichor on Aleksei's claw broke away, leaving nothing behind on the blades. In moments the Goddess' corpse had faded away into nothingness; She was gone forever.

CHAPTER 39

Remember, beyond all else, that I love you and that I'll always be there to look after you.
-From the Tomes of the Huntmaster.

Aleksei drifted through more visions, but they contained nothing. The dreams were not bad, nor were they good. They were blank, barely there. Eventually he left them behind, slowly opening his eyes and finding himself on his back in a strange new place. The sky was bright and something soft and long brushed up all over him. He pulled himself to his feet and examined the things touching him. It was a long series of small bladed plants covering an entire valley. Grass.

"Aleksei!" cried a voice. He looked to the left and saw Daina kneeling down and wrapping her arms around him, hugging him tightly. "Words cannot describe this. They simply cannot."

Aleksei returned the hug to the best of his ability; he still felt weak. "I'm sorry. I'm not feeling as strong as I usually am."

"It's all right, quill-head," she said. "It's all right."

She let go of Aleksei and helped pull him to his feet. He managed to keep his balance on his own, allowing him to better look at his surroundings. The green valley was massive, spreading in each direction for miles. On one side of the valley was a sizable lake and on the other was a path up the hills. Forests surrounded the valley on all sides, even past the lake. But even more amazing than this sight were the creatures moving about. Dozens of different birds flew through the air and all sorts of animals moved among their feet. By the lake they could see large creatures bending their necks down to the ground and feeding on the grass. The creatures walked on four hoofed legs and had massive outgrowths of keratin growing on the top of their heads. "What place is this?" he asked.

"Welcome to Paradise," she said. "You're not dead. Neither of us are. The Huntmaster moved us here so we would be much safer while he ferried the souls between this place, the old world and Proso. He brought you back to life by restarting your heart and keeping you strong."

"I wish He was here," he said. "I have so much to thank him for."

"And I you," said a deep, wizened voice. They both turned and saw the last thing they had expected to see; a human, at least to an extent. Its face was soft and its eyes were human, but its irises were red. It had human hair as red as Aleksei's quills. And while it did not have kuvi claws it wore a pair of smaller blade-like claws on each hand. Similar, but different.

"*Mi Prosopsei*?" asked Aleksei in confusion.

"I chose a less intimidating and much smaller form," said the Huntmaster. "This is but one of many forms I could manifest in, though it's not My true form. I have finished moving the living and the dead to their proper places, save for you two. It has been a long time, but a battle with a deity is not something a mortal comes back from quickly. You took so much punishment you died, but not so much that I couldn't save you."

"Thank You so much for helping us, *mi Prosopsei*," said Aleksei. "I fear I have no way to repay You for what You have done for us."

"Parents raise their children out of love, not out of expecting a reward," said the Huntmaster. "And I only gave you the power to succeed. The effort was all yours, Aleksei."

"But what separated me from all the other kuvis You could have given your power to?" asked Aleksei.

The Huntmaster tilted his head some before righting it. "Why do you say that?" he asked. "I gave My power to you as you were the best kuvi for it, the only one I would trust with the power. You may be smaller but you're more durable than most kuvis and could have endured it for much longer than them."

Aleksei bowed. "Thank You, *mi Prosopsei*," he said.

"You've done well," said the Huntmaster. "Both of you. And I'm sure you have several questions for me."

"This world is Paradise, right?" asked Daina. "But I've never seen such brilliance in my life."

Aleksei almost nodded but stopped himself; he did not wish to insult his god. "It's fine, Aleksei," said the Huntmaster. "Proso is not as lush as the Goddess' world once was. Proso was made without removing the tainted elements, while Her world was pure. I did not create Proso, so you are not insulting Me."

"What could possibly have destroyed such brilliance?" asked Aleksei. "*Mi Prosopsei*, do You know where the Decay came from?"

"I think the only one who could say for certain is now dead," said the Huntmaster. "But the borders of Her world ran alongside those of countless others, Proso included. Once humans figured out how to summon creatures with blood magic, they discovered these different worlds by bringing creatures over from them. mire beasts were not indigenous creatures, for example. But more so than any other world they robbed from Proso, My children stolen away right from the arms of their parents."

Aleksei looked down at the ground. The Huntmaster reached out and raised Aleksei's head by the chin. "Don't feel so sorrowful, Aleksei," said the Huntmaster. "Your mother still lives and so does Pisti. Time in Proso is much slower than in this world; barely a year has passed for your mother now." Aleksei felt a great weight lift from his heart, a weight that had been on it since the moment he had arrived in Tantallos. "With so many worlds bordering My own I could not tell which one was stealing My children," said the Huntmaster. "Most worlds are closed from gods like Myself so I could not search them, and many beings of creation like the Goddess lie in wait of the end of days, not talking to other deities. It wasn't until your ritual trying to pull Me into your world that I could confirm the location of My children.

"But according to the children who have been here the longest it had not been bad at first," He said. "Unlike those of the Decay, the humans welcomed the kuvis and treated them kindly. They let them live off among themselves, cloistered and hidden away in the wilderness so they could hunt and harm no one."

"But then the Decay arrived?" asked Daina.

"No one there could say for certain how it happened," said the Huntmaster, "but all it took was one botched summoning that, instead of connecting to Proso, connected to some discarded world left behind by an unskilled god of creation, a place so corrupted and twisted not even kuvis could thrive there. Even in that short time the taint had been pulled in, where it festered like a disease until it corrupted everything on and below the world.

"And if the Goddess' infestation was a sign, the corruption most likely took the form of a plant. The plant spread throughout the world too rapidly to be contained. Cities fell, forests and valleys like these withered away, and the lakes became foul and fetid. Harmless animals were destroyed or twisted into half-crazed monsters by consuming the plant. Perhaps then people blamed My children for their own mistake, giving them the epithet of demon like the monsters from their religion.

"But now that world, and everything in it, is gone," said the Huntmaster. "I moved all the survivors to this world, even a man hiding in a chest. All that remains is a dead place; nothing mortal or immortal will ever set foot upon its blighted soil ever gain."

Aleksei and Daina contemplated this, standing close to each other. Their possessions, their homes, their whole world, gone. Destroyed by a single mistake made countless decades ago. They both only had one thing left that was important to them.

"The other mortals, be them kuvi or human, have made their decisions concerning where they want to go," said the Huntmaster. "I intend to return to Proso and would be willing to take passengers on My back. But I understand your emotions toward each other complicate matters."

"Take Aleksei back to his world," said Daina. "Let him be with his mother so he can be happy again."

"I don't want to leave you, Daina," said Aleksei. "But I can't take you with me; you would not survive in Proso. Not even I could protect you."

"I don't want you to be alone among humans," said Daina. "Be among your own kind and be happy."

"I don't care if I'm the only person with claws instead of hands in this realm," said Aleksei. "Just make sure people don't look into my eyes and everything will be fine."

"Please, Aleksei," begged Daina. "It's what would be best for you."

"Please, Daina," begged Aleksei. "I love you too much to be without you."

Both of them sighed and looked each other in the eyes. They wrapped their arms each other tightly, holding this embrace like it may be their last. For all they knew it was.

"I won't force either of you to do anything," said the Huntmaster, "but I can present you with a third option."

They broke off from each other and faced the Huntmaster as He backed up and placed a hand on the ground. He brought up the hand, a red line of energy trailing behind it as it moved. He moved His hand in an arch over Himself and brought it back down on the ground again before backing away and moving in front of it. The arch then filled in, making a red gateway.

"This is a summoning gate of My own design," said the Huntmaster. "Unlike the summoning gates of your world, this one goes the other way. It leads to another world, a world I know little about, where you could both survive. I cannot tell you precisely what awaits you, but you two would be together."

Two smiles grew on their faces. They faced the Huntmaster and genuflected, Daina imitating Aleksei's posture to the best of her ability. "Thank You so much, *mi Prosopsei*," said Daina.

"I shall praise Your name for as long as I live," said Aleksei.

"Thank you," said the Huntmaster. "I may not always be as close as I am now, but you two will still always have that piece of me in your hearts. And you, Daina, will have something else of mine." He reached into His pocket and unearthed a small, black dagger. He handed it by the hilt to Daina, whose eyes widened. It was identical to her old bronze blade. "It's the least I can do, after you've lost everything. It's made of prososium as well. Only you or a kuvi could lift it. Perhaps you'll need it in this new world."

"I'm grateful," she said.

"A good father makes sure His daughter knows how to protect herself," said the Huntmaster. Daina nodded and pocketed the dagger. "And remember; even in the great unknown I shall look after you. I love you both.

My presence shall be ever greater in your hearts, and at the worst moments it may surface again."

"I could become like a god again while in this world?" asked Aleksei.

"Hopefully you never have to find out," said the Huntmaster. They gave their thanks to the Huntmaster one last time before turning back to face the portal.

CHAPTER 40

Never fear the unknown; instead make it known so you know it is not worth fearing.
-From the Tomes of the Huntmaster.

Aleksei and Daina stood side by side, contemplating the portal as it glowed and shimmered. They could see nothing of the world that lay beyond it, but this did not make them afraid. Daina's hand found Aleksei's claw and they held each other gently as they walked toward the portal. Their steps synced with each other as they reached the threshold. The sounds of the world around them faded away, leaving nothing but the slight crackling and humming of the portal.

They both took a deep breath and stepped in, entering another world entirely...

THE END

Justin K. Arthur

About the Author

Justin K. Arthur lives in the St. Louis area and has been writing for most of his life. He is currently attending the University of Missouri-St. Louis and hopes to turn writing into more than just a hobby.

© Justin K. Arthur

www.ingramcontent.com/pod-product-compliance
Lightning Source LLC
Chambersburg PA
CBHW060402260626
47160CB00006B/2405